Echoes in Obsidian

Cover illustration by Kazzi Allen @Kazzi Allen Art on Instagram

ISBN 979-8-9986301-0-1 (paperback edition)
ISBN 979-8-9986301-1-8 (ebook)

1 2 3 4 5 6 7 8 9 10

https://daniellekucky.wixsite.com/daniellekucky

ECHOES IN OBSIDIAN

PLAYLIST

The Blasting Company – Prelude

Sleep Token – Give

Ghost – Mary on a Cross

Heart – Magic Man

Austin Giorgio – Dangerous Hands

Florence + the Machine – Which Witch

Hozier - Francesca

Stardew Valley – Fall (Ghost Synth)

Kate Bush – Running Up That Hill (A Deal With God)

Echo & the Bunnymen – The Killing Moon

Girl in Red – We Fell in Love in October

Hozier – NFWMB

Bring Me The Horizon – Follow You

Sleep Token – The Night Does Not Belong To God

The Witcher 3: Wild Hunt – Child of Elder Blood

TRIGGER WARNINGS

Body horror
Blood & Gore & Violence
Extreme Pining
FMMC with high anxiety
Negative Self Talk
Drug Use
Breath play

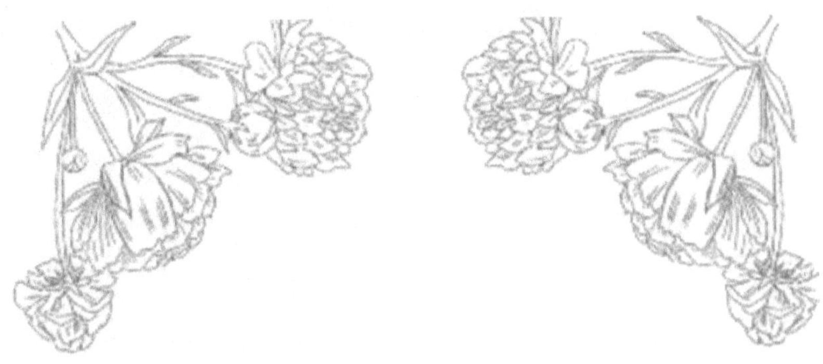

To everyone who likes their bad-boy's a little bratty
and who like to be choked consensually.
Enjoy, Kitten.

Contents

PROLOGUE

This was *not* how her night was supposed to go.

The weird beast screamed a piercing otherworldly yowl that sliced through the night. Its foxlike head thrashed, trying to remove the glowing blade from its eye. Razor-sharp teeth snapped and snarled as it flailed. Claws reached for the other blade in its shoulder, unable to reach the spot despite the beast being nearly eight feet tall.

Amity watched in horror, her body shaking uncontrollably. Her breath leaving her in short, hot puffs of smoke in the freezing air. She didn't even feel him shaking her until rough, ringed hands grabbed her face, forcing her to look into those beautiful blue *glowing* eyes.

"Move, Amity!"

He pulled her back through the mouth of the alley and down the abandoned, unlit city streets. Amity's back hit the icy brick wall, scratching her skin through her shirt.

The man towered over her, one hand gripping his bleeding side and while the other leaned above her to support his weight. She glanced down at the fresh blood seeping out onto the dark pavement. It was almost ridiculous to think how only a few days ago she smacked into him for the first time, spilling coffee all over his clean white shirt, which miraculously ended with him asking her out on a first date.

"I told you to stay inside tonight. Why didn't you listen?" Those glowing eyes bore into her, illuminating his gorgeous, scuffed-up face. Even with blood staining the edge of his mouth, Luka was still the most gorgeous man she'd ever seen.

"I . . ." she began in a shaky voice. She took in a breath, giving her brain the time it needed to cut through her paralyzing anxiety. "How the hell was I supposed to know there was some kind of m-monster. Just what the fuck was that thing?!"

"Why couldn't you just stay," he muttered through gritted teeth, pressing harder into the wall. Did he even hear her? She glanced at his now-bloodstained white shirt.

Fuck, that looks like it really hurts!

Her eyes widened, piecing back together the events, as the initial shock faded, from the moment she first stumbled down the dark alleyway to now.

"You were asking it for something," she said. He took in a sharp breath. "You were asking if it had a message for you. What was it?"

Luka was silent. His breathing grew heavier.

Brown eyes narrowed on him.

"What the hell do you need from some weird fox monster?" she demanded, pushing her shock. "Answer me—hey!"

Quickly she grabbed his limp body as it fell, pulling it toward her. She struggled beneath his tall stature, adjusting his weight over her shoulders. He groaned loudly.

This was not how her night was supposed to go.

She was *supposed* to be at home with her cat. Curled up in a ball of blankets with a hot cup of autumn tea and her smutty book. Amity sneaked a glance at him.

His body was hot against her, consuming her in a fiery heat against the chill of the night, and in the sweet smell she had been craving since she first ran into him. Seasalt and sandalwood. She felt her cheeks flush.

"What the fuck did I get myself into?"

ECHOES IN OBSIDIAN

CHAPTER ONE

Four days earlier.

A high-pitched yowl tore Amity out of her nightmare, sending her into a half-dazed panic. Her body propelled upright, sending her layered blankets in disarray along with the book that was covering her face as she slept across the room. Her hand went to her racing heart, trying to force it to slow down as she tried to find the source of the sound.

Golden cat eyes stared at her through a mound of black fur.

"Freaya, it's not breakfast time yet." The words fell out of her mouth in a long exhale. Remnants of a nightmare evaporated. Disappearing from her brain's reach.

Another one of her cat's yowls rang through the apartment in response, followed by several *dings* from her phone charging on the nightstand.

Amity yawned loudly and reached for it. Her eyes widened as she read the texts from her coworker.

She jumped out of bed, scattering its many decorative pillows onto the floor.

"I forgot I was opening today!"

Frantically she tore off her pajamas, grabbed a pair of semi-clean-looking jeans out of the hamper and a dark shirt out of her dresser, and dressed. It wasn't until her shirt was over her bonnet before she realized she forgot her bra. The most important thing!

By the time Amity was able to properly dress herself, fifteen minutes had gone by.

An aggressive meow came from the kitchen.

"Fuck fuck fuck!" she muttered, finishing off her mascara and throwing her bonnet onto the floor of the bathroom, her hair tumbling down in a cascade of long frizzy curls.

Quickly she refilled Freaya's food and water bowls, much to her pet's foul attitude.

Her stomach growled loudly when she opened her fridge. Amity was immediately disappointed but not at all surprised to find nothing to eat. Pulling on her shoes, she made a mental note to eat at the coffee shop . . . for the fifth time this week.

"Goodbye, Freaya, I love you, watch the house!" Just before she was about to close the door Amity turned on her heel remembering her phone, wallet, and keys, but most importantly her book.

"Ah!"

She ran back into her room in tiptoed sprints. Once her discarded book was in her hands, she grabbed her other essentials, shoved what she could into her pockets, and ran out the door. Amity didn't even realize she forgot her jacket until the brisk mid-October wind nearly sent her flying through downtown Hartford.

"This is ridiculous, Connecticut has cold autumns but this is insane!"

Amity tried desperately to retie her hair up in a bun as she power walked down the dim, foggy street, becoming more frustrated with each failed attempt. She tried shoving her book under her arm, in her shirt, her already-tight waistband of her pants. She finally clutched the worn paperback between her legs, stopping the brief few seconds to tie her hair up.

The streetlights flickered above her a few times before turning off completely, adding to her frustration.

"Great, now it's cold, dark, *and* foggy! Perfect combo for a single millennial woman walking alone." If she had the time, she would be a little freaked out by all that, but she didn't have time.

Her fingers scrambled but finally she was able to throw her hair into a messy bun. Smiling at the brief success she picked up her speed. She was almost there! Just around the corner and—BAM!

She smacked face first into a wall, or at least it *felt* like a wall, and something splashed onto her. *Is that coffee?*

"What the hell?" came a gruff voice.

Amity wiped the still-warm liquid splashed on her face and on—her eyes widened—the most pristine white T-shirt she had ever seen. Or at least it would be if it wasn't splashed with black coffee.

"Oh my god, I am so sorry!"

She scrambled to pick up the discarded cup and her book that flew out of her hand upon impact.

"I'm so so sorry! I was running late and I wasn't look-ing and I really have to go." Frantic fingers pushed the half-empty cup back into his hands and straightened his jacket. She was so frazzled she barely caught a glance of his face. Only the briefest glimpse at his blueish-green eyes.

"I'll make you a new one I promise. Come to Halley's right down this street."

"Wait a minute—"

"I'm really sorry. I'm super fucking late. I'll make it up to you! Promise."

She yelled, running farther down the street and fighting against the whipping wind. If he called out to her again, she didn't hear him.

Amity flung the door open, drawing the attention of the long line huddled inside of her parents' coffee and book-shop.

"Sammy! I'm here!" she wheezed, clutching onto the doorframe like her life depended on its support. *I really need to get in shape.* Running was *not* her strong suit. Cardio was her enemy.

Sammy, a full woman in her forties with short vibrant pink hair and reading glasses hanging slightly crooked on her nose, peered around the line from behind the counter.

"Jesus, kid, what the hell happened to you?"

Amity practically flung herself onto the end of the countertop as she tried to catch her breath. She patted her face dry in the back wall mirror. Sammy was right, she looked like hell.

"I'm so sorry, Sammy, I was reading and I must've fallen asleep and didn't hear my alarm—"

"Tell me all about it later, kid, right now we have customers."

She pulled her apron over her head and retied her windblown hair.

Great start to the day, Amity. Just fucking great.

The sun slowly crept in through the shop's windows as the line dwindled from an overwhelmingly long to somewhat manageable occupancy. Despite the literal run-in she had this morning due to her oversleeping, the fact she'd gotten an already-angry finance bro's coffee order wrong, the seemingly endless businessmen and women who all had 8:00 a.m. meetings, and the swarm of yogi's before their seven o'clock class, everything was pretty smooth. Everything except her hair.

She narrowed her eyes at her reflection on the back wall mirror. The messy bun she had thrown it into was quickly unraveling. Loose dark curls were sticking out in all directions, making her look like some witch that crawled out of someone's nightmares.

I bet you're getting a big laugh at this, huh?

If her hair could talk back she imagined it would say yes with a wide, amused smile.

Why won't you ever do as you're told? It's like you have a mind of your own!

Amity tucked a frustratingly frizzy curl behind her ear before finishing off the cappuccino she was working on.

She sighed haughtily before placing it on the pickup counter. *Stupid hair.*

She turned and stole a quick bite from the muffin she had hid on the back counter beside her book. Her glorious, wonderful, filthy book.

A romance novel incorporating the Norse gods. As she stole another bite, a blush crept onto her cheeks remembering the part she was at before she passed out the night before. She imagined the God of Mischief's voice dark and husky as he whispered terrible sweet things into the heroine's ear. Her cheeks darkened. *The things that man has said!* Amity could never imagine a man saying those kinds of things to *her*! They were too bold, too dirty, and just absolutely fucking *irresistible*.

Her lips pressed together dejectedly. She'd had a few relationships in the past but none of them ever lasted more than a few months. Never long enough to try out anything even remotely close to the things mentioned in her books, like light choking or playing around with being dominant or submissive. Not even something as simple as dirty talk! She'd always wanted to try those things but, in the end, decided that only a month of dating was too soon to ask for those things if she ever calmed her nerves and knocked up the courage to ask for them. *They probably would've laughed and made fun of me even if I did ask for those things.*

She bit into her lip, shaking away the thoughts and fresh embarrassment and focused back on her book. Much like the heroine of the story who had a new necklace made out of the god's fingerprints, this book had her by the throat.

She only had a few hundred pages left; if she really sat down, she could have it done in a day or two. Maybe.

A brisk tap on the shoulder dragged her out of her thoughts.

"Amity, I need to pee like a racehorse, take over the last few customers for me?"

"On it." But if she were being honest, she'd rather be cozied up in one of those old leather chairs.

How Amity managed to help the rest of the line without Sammy was a miracle beyond her understanding. Besides one of her regulars, a well-dressed redhead, she didn't remember anyone else. Luckily their order tickets printed out automatically, otherwise she would've forgotten those too. No, her mind was occupied by the worn pages that sat beside her, just begging to be opened. To be read. To take every ounce of her attention.

A smile came to her face as she hoped for the time when her shift was over and she could curl up in bed with those pages. Maybe she would even use her favorite toy as she read . . .

A low voice pulled her out of her thoughts.

"Ah! I'm sorry, what was that?" She practically shouted, finally noticing the new person in line.

"I said we just keep running into each other don't we?"

His voice traveled across her skin, leaving small bumps in its wake. Amity's eyes widened as they collided with cyan. The eyes of a god.

She gaped at him.

"What?" she asked, slightly tilting her head to the side. Completely stunted by the mysterious bad boy.

Was it possible for someone's brain to just stop working? Cause that's what just happened.

"You don't remember me?"

Something flashed across those beautiful eyes, but it was too quick to catch.

Besides, who could forget a face like that? Those cheekbones, that sharp jaw, those perfect lips, that cool nose ring. That face was handsome and screamed "mischief". He opened his leather jacket, revealing his white T-shirt. A once crisp white that was now stained with dark coffee . . . thanks to *her*.

Oh fuck! I smacked face first into the hottest man I've ever seen and doused him in his own coffee.

"It's you!" She smiled nervously. Her voice came out a little too loudly and in a high pitch.

And now I'm yelling. Great. Job. Amity. If he wasn't pissed off before, he sure as hell will be now.

The man laughed, running a tattooed hand over the top and longer half of his dark hair that was pulled back into a braid. Her curiosity peaked. Was it a vine? A snake? Amity made a mental note to get a better look at it soon.

"So you *do* remember me." He smirked.

That laugh seemed to melt her nerves.

"Yes! I am so sorry about this morning! What can I get for you? Black coffee right? I think that's what you had." Relief rushed through her, making her words tumble into something that sounded like one continuous thought rather than complete sentences.

He turned his head slightly, biting his bottom lip to stifle another laugh, giving her a perfect view of his undercut that began at the top of his ears.

"Yes, a black coffee would be nice."

Amity smiled up at him and rang up his order before immediately canceling it.

"I'll grab that for you right away."

Her face fell when she turned and caught her reflection in the mirror.

Right. I look like some witch that crawled out of someone's nightmares.

Quickly she tied her hair back, taming some of her frazzled curls.

"What do I owe you?" he asked, following her down the counter as she made his coffee.

"Oh no, please. After crashing into you this morning, it's the least I can do." She smiled; feeling his eyes on her. Her smile widened as she remembered how great her ass looked in her jeans. *Maybe that will distract him from the fact I look like hell,* she thought hopefully.

"Here you are." She smiled, sliding the coffee across the counter. His eyes glinted with mischief as they slowly tracked from the coffee cup to her open gray henley and then up to her big brown eyes.

"Tell you what," he began. He plucked the pen out of its holder and grabbed a spare napkin.

Her eyes widened, *Is he doing what I think he's doing?!*

"I'll pay for the coffee if you go on a date with me tonight."

He held the napkin out to her with a playful smirk. She glanced at the napkin and then back up to his piercing cyan eyes. The corner of her lips tilted into a small smile trying desperately to keep her excitement under control.

Holy shit he is! He's giving me his number!

She wanted to squeal; she was so excited! No one had ever been this forward in asking her out. At least no one she was remotely interested in. She tracked a silver chain necklace that slipped beneath his shirt.

Okay, calm down. You got this. Just be cool!

"And if I have a boyfriend?" she asked playfully.

He hummed, amused by the game. "You don't."

"And if I already have plans?"

"I'll pick you up *here* at seven. You're not closing tonight, right?"

"Not tonight."

She took the napkin from his tattooed hand, sneaking a better look. A reptilian tail in black was wrapped around his wrist and flicked out on the back of his hand. She unknowingly bit her lip imagining the tattoo coiled up his arm. Wrapping around his forearm, bicep, and all the way up to his chest—

"Until then, Amity."

He flashed a charming smile at her, left a five-dollar bill on the counter, and then sauntered out the door. Amity tracked his way out, smiling as she realized her ass wasn't the only one that looked great in jeans. She could bounce a coin off those cheeks! She sighed deeply as the door closed with a creak, leaving her alone with daydreams of her new date.

Maybe she will finally get lucky with someone tonight. It had been so long she didn't want to think about it. She groaned.

"Nope. Let's not count. Counting hurts my brain."

She inhaled deeply, and underneath the thick, fresh smell of coffee beans, she smelled something else. Something woodsy.

Sammy rushed through the bathroom doors, adjusting her glasses.

"Sorry, I really had to—wow!" She straightened her glasses and glanced around the shop. A few customers had already set up their laptops in the big comfy chairs, but other than that, Halley's was empty. "You really cleaned out that line."

"Yeah." Amity finished off the rest of her breakfast with flushed cheeks, replaying the interaction in her head.

He was so smooth! And I was so smooth! How the hell was I that smooth?

Sammy poured herself a fresh cup of coffee.

"Oh!" She picked up a small tag off the counter. "You forgot your name tag."

"Hm?! Oh! Thanks, Sammy."

She collected her name tag and the napkin the mysterious bad-boy had left on the counter. Without another word, she plopped down on the small stool in the corner with her book in hand and her name tag fastened to her apron. Now that the morning rush was over, she would have plenty of time to read before the lunch rush.

Just as she opened her book, more than eager to get back to her God of Mischief, something dawned on her.

If he didn't learn my name from my name tag . . . She pondered it for a moment. *When did I tell him my name?*

She curiously pulled out the crumpled napkin from her pocket. His handwriting surprised her. Each letter was neatly penned with sweeps and curves, like some kind of fantasy elven script. Her smile widened as she practiced the sound of his name on her lips.

"*Luka.*"

CHAPTER TWO

Amity was never more thankful that Sammy offered to close that night. They'd arranged it so normally she would open and Amity would get to sleep in and walk in at noon. With the shop open from 8:00 a.m. to 8:00 p.m., it was easy to rearrange and swap hours based on their plans and schedules . . . *A little less easier now that Mom is out of commission thanks to the accident.*

Amity threw two outfit choices onto her bed, which was covered in layers of blankets and pillows. One thing she loved more than anything was being snuggled into a nice cozy ball under all those blankets and enraptured in a good book. She smiled, remembering when the weather first changed to a crisp 50 degrees at the start of October, a.k.a. the best month ever.

She had already decorated her apartment with pumpkin spice candles, white glass jacko'lanterns, and as many cinnamon brooms as she could afford. Or at least more than she had already decorating her walls. Those would stay up year round; everything else would unfortunately have to be taken down for Christmas decor at the absolute latest possible date. She inhaled again with a soft humm. The sweet scent would automatically fill anyone who visited her domain with a sense of whimsy.

"That is if anyone ever came."

Freaya, in all her glory, pressed against her leg as she passed. The black cat stretched lazily before sprawling on the floor in front of her feet. Amity scooped her up with ease.

"Yes, darling, I did mean that as a double meaning."

It had been a year since her last serious relationship . . . or was it just a fling? She couldn't remember. Either way, every time she tried to bring someone home or tried to define their relationship, they always came up with the most random excuses, or at least the *men* would come up with the most random excuses.

"I'm just not ready for a relationship"

"You're amazing. It's not you, it's me"

"I'm actually in a relationship, but it's open and I didn't want to say anything so I lied."

Blah blah BLAH!

The liars were the worst. She hated them.

She kissed Freaya's soft head and continued to stare at their reflection in the tall mirror leaning in the corner of her room.

"Not this time. This time he approached me!" Freaya squirmed in her arms. "I know, I know. We're not going to put all our eggs in one basket. No matter how hot he is." *And fuck is he hot!*

She looked back at the small box on her nightstand where her favorite toy was.

She sighed and shoved her face into Freaya's soft belly.

"Goddamnit! There isn't any time for that." Freaya swatted her head and leaped out of her owner's arms.

"Rude." Amity sighed and looked back at herself in the mirror. Her makeup was fixed with a simple wing with some orange eye shadow. Hair was freshly washed and styled, at least partly styled. Her hair wasn't completely dry, so it hit her bare skin in long damp ringlets. She was still wearing her jeans from this morning, high-waisted and washed-out black . . . *Is it wrong to wear the same jeans I wore all day to my date?* She adjusted the tight waistband around her round stomach, then rocked on her tiptoes trying to remember the height difference between them. Luka looked to be at least six foot two, maybe a little higher. It was hard to tell from where she stood at only five foot two. *It's just the first date, so I shouldn't dress too fancy. And I did do my makeup a bit more than usual, just a light contour and some concealer—*

Her phone quickly brought her out of her thoughts. Her brown eyes widened.

"Mom! Hey! Are you okay?" Amity panicked, thinking of the worst-case scenario. Her mother laughed on the other line.

"Oh, honey, I'm fine, your father has got me well taken care of."

"That's good, I'm glad to hear that." She sighed with relief. Her eyes widened as she saw the time: 6:35 p.m. She was running out of time fast, and she was still only half dressed. She quickly flipped the phone on speaker and put it onto the bed.

"Yes, but the doctor said I should stay off my feet for at least the end of October, so I'm afraid you might have to keep working long hours with Sammy."

Amity sprayed a perfume cloud into the air and walked through it, letting it coat her in a fresh sweet scent.

"That's fine."

As long as her mother was okay, that was the main thing that mattered. A few longer shifts with Sammy wouldn't kill her. Hearing about the horrible car accident her mother was in did send her into a full-blown panic attack last week.

"Amity? Why do you sound so far away?"

"I have you on speaker, Mom!" Amity called from the closet.

"Oh, that's fine, honey. Anyways, are you sure you're okay working more hours? I know things have been a little slow for you since you lost your job in the pandemic but—"

"It was an admin job, Mom. It wasn't that hard." That was true, the administrative job she had for a small tech company a few years ago wasn't exactly challenging or thrilling, but it offered a sense of stability and routine after fine arts school. Now, working at her parents' coffee and bookshop was routine.

"But don't you want to do something else?"

"I . . ." She paused. Did she *want* to do something else?

Her arms hugged around the curves of her stomach as she thought about it. She did want to do something else; she could feel it scratching the inside of her brain. What was it she wanted to do? Something daring, maybe a little dangerous? A searing pain shot through her, cutting her focus.

"Ow!"

"Are you okay? I know that things have been slow, there's no rush! You could try selling art again, or who knows, maybe you'll take over the shop once your father and I retire."

She quickly threaded a belt through her jeans then picked up the shirts sprawled on her bed before tossing them to the side. No one really showed much interest in the art she made when she was trying to sell it. Which of course felt like a sword to her confidence and made her stop commissions altogether. Taking over the shop didn't sound like the worst idea in the world. The coffee shop was consistent; it gave her a sense of routine. But was that what she really wanted?

"What's all that noise?"

Amity groaned. "I'm getting changed."

"Oh! Are you going out with your friend Rex tonight?"

". . . I have a date, Mom."

Her mother exhaled excitedly on the line. "Oh! That's wonderful, honey! It's been so long! Who is he or . . . she?

Anyone I know?" Amity facepalmed before grabbing her jean jacket from the front closet.

"It's just some guy from the coffee shop, Mom."

The most gorgeous guy I've ever seen in my life.

"Oh! Babe, did you hear that? Amity has a date!"

And now I regret saying anything.

"Motherfucker," Amity grumbled. Shirt. She still needed a shirt.

"That's great, honey!" her father called.

"Yeah, thanks, Dad." Black turtleneck. *That will work. Black goes with everything.*

"I just hope you're not wearing *all black* again, honey. You always wear black."

Amity stopped putting on her turtleneck halfway for a moment.

"I'm not!"

"What's his name again?" her mother asked.

Amity pulled her hair from the neck of her shirt and tied her amethyst pendant around her neck.

"Luka. His name is Luka." Amity adjusted her hair slightly and threw on her jacket. She quickly grabbed her phone, noticing the time. Her eyes widened. 6:50 p.m. Shit.

"Luka . . . Hey, babe, don't we know a Luka?" her mother called to her father.

"Okay, Mom, I love you, gotta go, *bye!*" She rushed, quickly hanging up the phone and shoving it into her pocket.

She ran quickly into the kitchen and filled Freaya's food bowl. Rummaging through the cabinets for a quick piece of chocolate, she found nothing except that strange cabinet filled with herbs. Amity was moving so fast she almost knocked over her replica dagger from her favorite film series off the wall. Running back to the mirror in her room, double-checking her outfit before scrambling for her phone and keys. She paused just as she was about to open the door to go. Her eyes fell on the far side of her apartment where a small jar filled with water, rosemary, sage, and clear quartz sat in the corner. She could feel her pulse spike.

Amity didn't remember putting the jar there. And she certainly didn't remember filling it with herbs and crystals. This jar was an enigma. More than once she thought about moving it, but she always had this gnawing feeling that if she did, something horrible would happen. Brown eyes stared at it for a moment more. She had the same feeling about the cabinet of herbs. Never remembering where they came from but knowing they were too important to move or dispose of. Her breath caught in her throat before she shook the thoughts and strange panic away.

Nope, we're not spiraling right before a date.

"I'll be back late tonight, Freaya!"

Quickly she walked around the few blocks it took her to reach the shop, catching every red light and slow walker in her path. She was just about to turn the corner when she stopped herself and backed around the corner again until she was out of sight of the shop entrance and the tall bad boy guarding it.

Doublechecking her reflection in the window of the neighboring shop. Her curly brown hair was still damp from when she restyled it earlier, but it should quickly dry with that soft wind blowing through the city. Nervous fingers straightened her plain black belt with the silver buckle and adjusted her pants. Her black turtleneck had a low neck, peeking just above the folded collar of her light-wash jean jacket. Her mom would be proud since technically she wasn't wearing *all black*.

Slowly she took in a deep breath, calming herself. A crisp breeze blew past, sending the sweet scent of sandalwood and seasalt her way. Her eyes widened, remembering where this smell came from, or rather *who* it came from. She inhaled again, letting the smell completely fill her. She could get hooked on that smell—imagined herself buried in it.

"Woah! One step at a time," she reminded herself. *After all, this is only the first date.* Amity smiled at her reflection and quickly rounded the corner, slamming her face into something hard and warm. Something that smelled like sandalwood.

"At least let me treat you to dinner before you have your dessert." Luka's chest rumbled when he laughed, sending her hair slightly askew. She jerked her head back.

"I'm sorry, I didn't do that on purpose!" Amity yelled with a flushed face. She tucked a loose curl behind her ear, accidentally getting her moonstone bracelet caught in it.

Her wrist was in his grasp in a second, gently holding it as if it would crumble in his grip. She stood perfectly still watching him untangle her hair with his other hand. His face was dangerously close to hers, his blue eyes fixated on her bracelet. The smell of sandalwood was stronger now.

Amity drew her eyes over his every detail. His hair was freshly washed and thrown back into a loose bun. He was still wearing his black leather jacket with a new white henley underneath. The pendant she caught a glimpse of earlier was a small black horn . . . a tooth? Something about it seemed oddly familiar. He was also wearing some thick bands on his fingers. Plain, unlike hers that had small stones in them. She noticed the small stud in his nose.

His lips curled up into a smirk when he noticed her staring.

"Sure you didn't," he teased.

A chill wind blew past, making her wrap her jacket tighter around herself.

"So," he began, taking a step back, "I was originally thinking coffee, but seeing as you work in a coffee shop . . . maybe Italian?" She laughed warmly; if he was trying to make a joke, it was a bad one but the attempt was there.

Brown eyes looked up at him with a curious glint. If she was being honest, she expected him to take her to a brewery or out for drinks. An Italian restaurant seemed *fancy*. Maybe under that bad boy exterior he was a bit of a gentleman?

"Italian sounds great." She smiled.

They walked for about ten minutes in the crisp weather, their boots crunching on the many fallen leaves under the faint orange glow of the streetlamps. Unfortunately they missed sunset, but the encroaching darkness didn't stop the crowded streets or their idle chattering the entire way, or rather *she* was chatting and he was just listening except to nod or agree with her about fall being the best season to ever season. She talked about the leaves, the smells, apple picking, pumpkin picking, and Halloween.

Everything about autumn was just so comforting and, well, cozy! Somehow that led to a conversation about her favorite film series—comparing the books versus the films, her favorite parts in the films, characters' backstories that span hundreds of years prior to the starting of the first film. She knew she was going on one of her tangents that her friend Rex specifically warned her to stop doing on first dates.

"Guys are dumb and scare easily. You've got a vast imagination and are interested in a lot of things, which is great! I know you get excited when you meet someone new, but try to get them to talk about themselves sometimes."

Amity cut herself off mid-sentence and stopped on the broken cobblestone street. Luka stopped beside her and patiently waited for her to continue. When she didn't say anything more, he spoke up.

"What's wrong?"

His words jolted her out of her thoughts.

"Oh, it's nothing. I didn't mean to talk your ear off . . . sorry," she said with a small smile. He tucked a loose curl behind her ear, blue eyes gazing into hers with a feeling of understanding.

"Don't apologize. I could listen to you talk all night." He smiled down at her, then laughed at her flushed face. His rough hand tousled her hair gently before walking on.

Amity stood there in a daze. A weird feeling of déjà vu came over her as she caught up to his wide stride. A faint pain hit the back of her skull as she tried to figure it out. Something else dawned on her, something that didn't seem like a big deal at first but in hindsight should've raised a flag of caution.

"Hey, I've been meaning to ask. I wasn't wearing my name tag this morning. How did you know my name?"

He slowed his gait just enough for her to catch up.

"Hm? Oh, I heard someone say it when you gave them their coffee," he said with a shrug. "Why?"

"Oh! No reason, I was just curious."

That checks out. She mentally lowered the flag of caution. A lot of people who come into Halley's in the morning are frequent customers and usually call her by her name.

He led her into the farther, more crowded parts of the city to a small family-owned Italian restaurant, one that smelled of fresh basil and warm bread tempting any passer-by to stop in and have a taste. If he tried to hold the door open for her, she didn't notice. After all, he is taller than her. She thought she heard him snicker behind her as she charged toward the hostess stand.

Two hostesses waited with a smile, smiles that grew brighter when Luka approached.

"Hi there, reservation under Luka." He smiled. *That damn smile. Did he have any idea what those ladies were thinking because of that smile?*

One of them eagerly nodded and quickly led them to a table by the windows. Amity quickly put her jacket on the back of her chair and made an excuse to go to the bathroom. If Luka was about to pull out her chair for her, she didn't notice.

Amity stared at her reflection, trying to find some minute detail to fix. Finding none, she sighed heavily.

"Why am I so nervous?" She lightly touched the spot on her head where Luka messed with her hair. Her cheeks heated and she giggled. *He may look lean but he is all muscle,* she thought sweetly. *Okay! Let's get back out there and do this! And hopefully him. He did say he was my Dessert.* She winked at her reflection and strode out of the bathroom proudly. This date was going to go perfectly like pumpkin spice and autumn!

The restaurant was gorgeous. Shelves of curing limoncello lined the walls as she passed and made her way back to her seat. The sun was completely set, leaving the dim lights above to light the restaurant. Luka was sitting at the table with his cheek in his palm, staring idly out the window, lazily running his tattooed hand over the candle flame. He looked stunning like one of her book boyfriends. She swallowed hard.

One step at a time, she reminded herself.

He smiled mischievously at her, like he knew some dark secret behind those cyan eyes.

One. Step. At. A. Time!

Amity looked hesitantly at the dishes listed and then their price tags. Her eyes widened. She refocused on the cheaper options on the menu, noting they were all appetizers. *If only I didn't spend all my spare money on books and candles . . . Stupid perfect candles with their perfect vanilla pumpkin scents—*

"You're looking very scrupulous over there." She peered at him over the top of the menu.

"Hm? Oh! It's nothing, I'm not really that hungry, so I'll just eat the appetizers." As if to spite her, her stomach growled very loudly. Luka burst out laughing.

The waiter came around with their appetizers and swiftly placed them on the table.

"Are you ready to order, or would you like a few minutes?" he asked, placing two taster glasses of red wine in front of her. She was about to ask for a few more minutes when Luka quickly responded.

"I'll have the butternut squash Sacchetti and she'll have the pumpkin cavatelli. Then a bottle of whichever she prefers." He finished handing the waiter the menu, then gestured to the two small glasses of wine in front of her.

Amity was momentarily stunned by the way he listed the dishes. "But—"

"Amity. It's fine." He smiled coolly.

She quickly shut her gaping mouth and sipped each glass of wine. The first glass made her wince because it was so dry, which earned a snicker from Luka. The second was a little sweeter.

"This one, please." The waiter nodded with a smile and turned to go. When he was finally out of earshot, Amity turned her surprised eyes on the glass in front of her.

"That's going to be so expensive."

"Maybe."

"Maybe? It is! Luka, I can't let you pay for all this."

He shrugged his shoulders nonchalantly and took her small plate from in front of her.

"It's too much—at least let me—"

"*Amity.*" His voice was deeper when he said her name.

She sighed in defeat. Why was she trying to fight him on this? Anyone else would jump at the chance of being pampered with Italian food. Her lips went into a pout.

"You don't like that I'm paying on our date?" he asked, puzzled with a hint of teasing.

"It's not that . . . I'm not really comfortable with people paying for me"—Luka patiently listened as he placed a full plate in front of her. He had placed the caprese salad on top of the sliced garlic bread. It looked delicious—"Thank you. Even when it's just between friends and they offer to buy me coffee or something. I'm not really sure why—" She took a bite of the delicacy. "This is really good!"

He smiled at her enthusiasm before taking a bite from his own plate.

"Hmm."

"You don't like it?"

"It's not that, I can make it better." He smirked.

"Confident aren't we? What are you a professional chef or something?" she teased.

He laughed, "No, I'm not that fancy. My family is originally from Italy. My nana taught me everything she knows about cooking and baking bread."

"You're from Italy?"

"Sort of, my family originally immigrated over to Wethersfield, Connecticut, in the sixteenth century, then back to Italy and then back to the US at the start of the nineteenth century."

"Wow! That's a lot. My family also came over around that time, the nineteenth century, right through Ellis Island. Why did they move back before?" She stared at him with wide, curious eyes.

He paused for a moment to add more caprese to a slice of garlic bread. "I'm not sure."

He went quiet for a moment, lost in his own train of thought. Amity watched him, silently getting lost in her own thoughts. His phone rang, jolting them back to reality. Luka looked at the phone screen before grunting, then put it on silent.

"So how long have—"

The phone vibrated loudly on the table. He checked the caller ID and immediately hit ignore.

"It's my mom and dad's. She usually works the longer shift, but she was in a car accident—"

His phone vibrated again.

"I'm sorry to hear that," he said, checking his phone quickly before turning it back over.

She was sure he meant to sound sincere, but his annoyance with his phone added a bite to it. Amity smiled awkwardly, feeling the tension radiate off of him.

"It's okay, it's not your fault—"

His phone vibrated again. Amity chugged her water, remembering that she was very thirsty.

"You can get that if you need to."

"No. It's fine," he said, his patience clearly running thin. Steadily he refilled her water, which she quickly thanked him for.

Silently she could feel herself sink with unease into her seat, grateful for the distracting view of his tattoo. It was definitely a snake's tail that flicked on the back of his hand and wrapped around a small branch with tiny flower buds on it. It coiled around his wrist and disappeared up his sleeve. She was mesmerized by it. The realism of the ink made it look like it could slide off his skin. He caught her eyes on it.

"It's a—"s

His phone buzzed. He took a deep breath in through his nose and gently set the glass water pitcher down. Slowly he flipped the phone in his hand and checked the message preview on his lock screen. His eyes went wide.

Luka shot out of the chair, nearly knocking it over. Amity recoiled back in surprise.

"What's wrong?"

A few people turned to look.

Luka didn't speak, only grabbed his coat and thrust it on. He checked his phone again, reading the message more thoroughly. He ran a hand through his hair roughly.

"I have to go. Emergency. Don't wait up for me." Amity's mouth hung open, unsure of what to make of this.

"Oh. That's ok—"

"I'll call you later." He turned and stormed out.

Amity blinked once. Twice. Then a third time.

Did he just run out on me? She bit off half a slice of garlic bread, chewing slowly.

No! He said it was an emergency! She chugged her water and accidentally slammed the glass onto the table with a bang. Her mind raced.

Was it something I said? Was it because I made a fuss about him paying? He barely talked throughout our walk here and then through appetizers . . . Wait. Appetizers.

"Oh no."

"Hello, miss, here we are." The waiter smiled at her and gently placed their food on the table.

Oh. No.

That fucker left me with the bill!

She fumed as the realization dawned on her while simultaneously attempting to keep a "nice smile" on for the waiter. *Think of something!* She scrambled for an excuse. The waiter smiled at her but glanced at the empty seat across from her. He definitely saw Luka—that bastard—run out. The waiter took the wine bottle off the serving tray and was about to open it, but Amity held up her hands.

"He—um . . . had to go. An emergency." Embarrassment filled her. *I swear the next time I see that smug-faced blue-eyed prick . . .*

"I can just pay now and take everything home."

"Oh, no, miss. He's already paid."

Amity was dumbstruck. "Huh?"

The waiter smiled, taking back the food tray.

"Yes, he paid before leaving. I'll take these in the back to wrap up. Would you like the appetizers as well?"

She ran a hand through her hair, unsure of how to absorb this. But she was sure of one thing. She was going to take this delicious food and sweet wine home. And she was going to have every last bite.

"I'll take all of it."

CHAPTER THREE

It took him an hour. A fucking hour to drive into the middle of Connecticut's Farmington Woods, where his mother anxiously awaited him. He finally spotted her tall stature leaning against the front door of a cabin at the end of a long gravel driveway.

She watched in anticipation as he pulled his black SUV into a dirt lot off the driveway and then made his way over to her.

She had called him twice on the drive over, asking where he was. When he said where he was on the highway, he could hear her say she was fine, but Luka knew she wasn't. He knew they were short on time.

She held his warm cheek in a frigid hand; she must have been waiting outside for a while, or at least that's what he would think if this was any *normal* situation. Luka knew better.

"I haven't performed this kind of exorcism in a while," he said, unable to meet her blue-eyed gaze.

"I know, but I wouldn't have asked you to come unless I absolutely needed you." She clutched her cornicello close before kissing it quickly. He knew what she couldn't say.

Demons were known to torment people with their own fears, feeding off them like leeches, growing stronger the more their victims were provoked. Something he had unfortunately had firsthand experience with.

His mother was the most gifted sorceress he knew of. She even used to teach at Mene's Academy of the Arcane, one of the most prestigious schools on the East Coast. A place she had been very *adamant* in keeping him as a professor.

Luka pushed his dark hair out of his eyes and tied the top back into a braid, like he always did. She needed him to be alert. The demon could use his mother's relationship with her friend against them. *That* was why he was here. To make sure that never happened.

Of course there's nothing to stop it from trying to mess with us as well.

She led him into her friend's cabin without another word. It was rustic and cozy, filled with all kinds of crocheted blankets and soft furnishings. An old wooden easel was propped in the corner of the kitchen with a half-finished landscape painted on it.

He smiled. *Amity would like this place.* He quickly shook away the thought, reminding himself to focus and *not* think about the woman he just stranded in an Italian restaurant.

His mother placed her tea onto a woven coaster on the table and handed him a large jar of seasalt. Seasalt they had blessed under last year's supermoon.

She really isn't taking any chances.

She picked up the silver sickle beside the rickety table leg. A gift from Nana. Handcrafted with a wrapped leather handle and ancient runes. Infused with magic and bathed monthly with the full moon's light.

His mother's long cardigan whipped behind her as she approached the door to her friend's bedroom. She inhaled deeply, centering herself, preparing herself. He did the same.

Magic pulsed behind their eyes, illuminating their cyan color.

With a steady hand, she turned the old knob and shoved the door open.

The temperature plummeted, hitting the exposed skin of his undercut like a thousand sharp needles.

A woman was sprawled on top of the bed, the covers in disarray beneath her. She had been fighting for a while. Probably before his mother called him for help. Despite her matted hair that stuck with sweat to her body and the animalistic sounds that escaped her throat, Luka recognized her. She was Rosa. His mother's old friend who ran a crystal shop alongside her.

Rosa pulled and chafed her wrists and ankles against her restraints. Luka tensed at the thought of his mother tying up her friend like that and the struggle she must've endured before he got there. Bloody green eyes flicked from him and then his mother. A wiry grin spread across her face.

"How *sweet* . . . the witchling's spawn." The demon's voice was raw and shallow, like the sound someone made when they were struggling to breathe.

"The salt," his mother instructed.

Without a word, Luka slowly circled the bed, dropping a line of salt in his path.

"Poor little witch boy. How many demons have you exorcised this week? Six? Twelve?"

Those slitted eyes tracked him with every step, waiting for any flinch, any reaction to its words.

Luka exhaled, the hot air leaving his body in a trail of smoke.

"He's been waiting to play with you again." Burning cyan eyes met green. His focus dropped.

The demon smiled wide with Rosa's lips, pulling at the seams of her mouth. Its chest rumbled with strangled laughter. A sound that was both Rosa and not.

His mother held up her sickle before her and began to chant. The runes burned brightly on the blade. Almost as bright as her eyes.

The demon pulled harder against the restraints. Her wrists began to bleed.

Luka took a breath, recentering his focus on the task at hand. He'd fucked up. If his mother hadn't interrupted . . . Luka shook away the thought. This demon could hold a clue for him. He couldn't look desperate for it.

Luka held his hands before him and started to chant with his mother. If this demon did have a clue, he would wring it out of it.

He threw salt onto the bedsheets, the creature immediately jerked away as it sizzled and spit onto its sweating skin. Something stirred under Rosa's shirt—no, not her shirt, under her *skin*. It poked and prodded as if ready to burst out of her chest.

They chanted louder, feeding as much energy into their words as possible. It screamed, sounding more human than before.

Almost there.

Luka's eyes glowed brighter as he watched whatever demon this was swelling inside Rosa's throat, ready to burst out.

One green slitted eye bore into him.

"Witching hour," it seethed.

Luka's eyes widened. It did have a message for him. After almost a fucking year! At long last. He found his first clue!

The demon struck at his brief reaction. It shot out of Rosa's throat. A wet, feral heap of scales. Its snakelike body struck at him only to fall back inside the salt barrier with a horrid hiss. The scales that made contact began to fester and crack. It recoiled, ready to strike again. His mother was faster. Her curved sickle removed the serpent's head from the rest of its body before it could strike the barrier again, an inch from Luka's nose. The headless body twitched and writhed on the floor, coiling and thrashing in a silent scream.

She looked at her son with cold eyes. He finally pulled his gaze away and back to the writhing headless creature.

"I'll draw her a salt bath later for her physical wounds. Psychological wounds will take longer." She sighed. "For now I want her to rest until that miasma is gone."

Luka only nodded, watching the creature's body corrode and sizzle until it was nothing more than a wisp of black smoke. She studied her son, knowing full well that, although he was quiet, his thoughts were racing. Her soft lips pressed his forehead in a warm kiss.

"I'll clean up here. Go wait outside."

"I hope this didn't ruin your date. It's been a while since you've gone out with a girl." She sat on the porch beside her son and sipped her tea quietly.

Luka snickered. Knowing Amity, she was probably watching her favorite fantasy show, yelling at her TV, and stuffing her face with all that leftover food. At least that's what she would do a year ago. He groaned, running his hands through his hair. *She's gonna be so fucking pissed . . . not that I can blame her.* A small laugh escaped him. *Fate threw us together again only for me to piss her off.*

His stomach grumbled loudly, reminding him of just how little he had eaten that day.

His mother laughed beside him. "Sleep home tonight. I'll make you food."

He gave her a small smile and rubbed his tired eyes. It wasn't a surprise the demon knew they were mother and son; their resemblance was uncanny.

"I'll just get something on the way home."

Her blue eyes went icy as she studied him.

"What?"

"You're not eating enough. You need to eat."

"I *am* eating."

Though, he had been doing more work than eating as of late. Six demons slain, seven including the one this morning, and one exorcized within a week, and only *this* one had a clue.

The witching hour.

She rustled his hair with a jeweled hand.

"Your nana would beat you if she saw you lie like that." His mother snickered.

He laughed softly and stifled a yawn. Her smile quickly faded.

"Is it about her?" she asked, concern lacing her voice.

Luka's eyes narrowed defensively.

"No," he answered curtly, trying to end *that* conversation before it even began.

"Luka . . . you can't keep blaming yourself for what happened."

Her son stood abruptly. He was exhausted and starving, it was a long drive back to Hartford and he was *not* in the mood for the same argument.

"I have the time. I just need a location and a date."

He zipped up his jacket. Even without the demonic presence plummeting the temperature, it was colder out in the woods than it was in the city. Rising he brushed off the dirt on his pants then started walking to his SUV.

"Luka!" she warned.

"I'm not stopping until I find him. Not until I fix her." *Not after the Norns pulled us together again.*

His mother pinched the bridge of her nose, knowing she was getting nowhere.

"Drive safe. I love you."

He stopped short of opening the door and turned back with a small smile.

"Love you too."

CHAPTER FOUR

Amity woke up from her couch that morning with her hair in complete disarray from not being properly put into a bonnet the night before. Dressed in an old shirt and baggy pants she didn't remember putting on. A brief moment of frustration hit her after she rubbed her tired eyes.

At least I remembered to take off my makeup.

Freaya peered down at her from her spot on the armrest of the coach. Not good. Now that Freaya knew she was awake, there was no stopping her. Amity groaned, and as if on cue, Freaya started meowing. And meowing. And *meowing.*

Amity rolled off the couch and grabbed her phone from the coffee table. The first thing that appeared after she unlocked it were her texts to Luka.

Oct. 10, 9:00 pm

Hey, I hope everything's okay <3

Oct. 10, 9:30 pm

Thank you for dinner by the way, that was really sweet of you! :)

It was now the twelfth. And she was still glaring at those messages. Messages that were still waiting on a response. The least he could do was let her know he was *alive*. But no, he left her with no answer the entire night after their date and then all of yesterday!

She wanted to throw her phone across the counter at the skinny brunet who was casually reading a book he just purchased. But she wouldn't. He was a paying customer. And he was *not* Luka.

She inhaled deeply. *Maybe he's just not interested. He faked an emergency and ran out. That's it . . . and then he felt guilty for lying so he paid for everything before he left. Fucking asshole!*

Amity grabbed her phone and quickly typed out a message before tossing it onto the counter. Luckily it didn't break. Aggressively she sipped her iced white lavender latte before abruptly stopping to grip her head when the brain freeze hit. Despite her aggravation, and the now-searing pain, it was still her favorite drink. One day she was experimenting with flavors and BAM! Perfection in a cup.

Tired fingers massaged her temples as she scanned the cafe. It was relatively steady that morning with about ten people sitting among the scattered worn leather couches and chairs either reading, idly chatting, or simply sipping their coffee.

She picked up her phone again to check the time. 1:30 p.m.. A rumbling erupted from her stomach, reminding her she hadn't eaten lunch yet. A grimace dressed her face then she reluctantly double-checked the message she'd hastily sent.

Oct. 12, 1:27 pm

I ate all the food.

"Great job, Amity. Because *that* will get you a second date, if he was even interested at all," she scolded herself.

The door creaked open and closed with a soft *click*. Amity refocused her attention, putting on her customer service face. She would have to think about whether or not he deserved that text some other time. Right now she had a job to do.

"Welcome!"

"I'm surprised more students don't come here for their breaks," a cool voice answered.

Amity's smile grew wider and the customer service façade fell away as her best friend, Rex, approached the counter.

Unlike Amity, Rex was tall and lean and covered in piercings—a septum, an eyebrow, and a few gauges. Their long black coat flowed behind them as they approached the counter.

"Probably because the schools are too far away . . . Speaking *of*." Amity elongated the word. Rex ran a hand through their freshly shaved head with a sheepish smile.

"Aw come on, I just came by to see my best friend." Rex beamed, peering at the sweets in the display case on the countertop. Amity laughed. She couldn't blame her friend; she also had a sweet tooth. The fresh scones they got in this morning were to die for! Blueberry-lemon-coconut and *perfect*.

"How's your mom?" Rex finally asked.

"Better. She got out of the hospital last week, just needs to rest her knee now. I keep telling her I'll visit but she keeps saying she's fine," Amity said, giving in to the temptation of the scone.

Rex unloaded their jacket and flopped onto the barstool next to the pastry display, eyeing one of the tarts.

"Same old Barbara." Rex laughed, placing a small bag on top of their jacket.

"Come on, Rex, you could've just texted me. Why'd you drive all the way to the other side of town on your day off?" she asked, taking a large bite of her scone.

Rex worked at the University of Hartford's Art School as a teaching assistant after they and Amity graduated with fine arts degrees. They were also simultaneously building their art career by working on commissions and displaying their work at local shops. Her mother even held a small gallery at the bookshop for them. It was a great success, even if their creations were a little . . . odd.

"Alright, you caught me. I came for the coffee"—Amity stopped midway from placing a pumpkin tart in front of her friend and narrowed her eyes. She knew her friend like the back of her hand. There was another reason they came to visit—"*and* to bring you this!"

Rex held out the small paper bag with a smile. Amity's eyes lit up. She traded the pastry for the bag and carefully unwrapped the wad of old newspaper inside. Whatever this was, it was heavy and felt breakable.

The newspaper revealed a ceramic pumpkin-shaped jar, bone white with a beautiful gold stem. Amity removed the stemmed lid and peered inside. It was painted gold. Absolutely stunning!

"Oh! I love this, thank you so much!"

"I thought you could use another jar; you know, for all those herbs in your cabinets." Rex smiled, taking another bite from their tart.

Herbs . . . Amity thought about that for a moment. Back to her full cabinet in the kitchen. There was quite the stash. Everything from mugwort to lavender. Something about those herbs seemed so familiar to her, like they were for some purpose but she couldn't remember what that was. She couldn't even remember buying any of it. She brushed some loose crumbs off of her still-unfinished book that lay next to the checkout tablet, trying to taper down the creepy sensation it gave her.

"Hey, how long have I had those?"

There was a moment of silence as Rex swallowed their mouthful savoring every last bit. They looked at her strangely through bat-winged glasses.

"What are you talking about? You've always kept stock of those." Amity's eyebrows furrowed. She picked up the worn book and flipped through it idly—like giving her jittering fingers something to fiddle with would help her solve this strange anomaly. Okay a little more than strange. In fact it was starting to get really *creepy*.

"I don't remember buying them. And I don't remember putting the jar there."

"Jar? That thing's been there for a year. I thought you made it last Halloween?"

"Halloween . . ."

She fell quiet, trying to think, trying to chase that feeling that something very important happened that day but a sharp pain in her head stopped her thought process in its tracks.

"Are you feeling okay? You've been acting strange for the past year. I didn't want to say anything before but you're starting to worry me," Rex explained, concern lacing their voice, just as the door creaked open letting in a chill breeze and a sweet scent of sandalwood.

"I guess I haven't been feeling like myself," she admitted quietly.

Amity tugged the sleeves of her white henley down to her fingertips and turned to greet the new customer.

"Hi there—" Amity immediately cut herself short when she locked with blue eyes.

The door closed with a soft *click*. A light blush dusted across her cheeks in either aggravation or by the way that turtleneck was a little too tight around his chest—she wasn't sure. Or was it that his hair was tied back in a cute, messy man bun?

Rex looked over from where they sat with a curious glance. They smirked back at Amity who immediately looked away in embarrassment.

"He's totally your type!" they whispered.

"We went out the other night but he left halfway through and never texted back!" she very quickly explained in a hushed voice.

Rex's eyes widened with interest. "Really?!"

"Shh!"

Luka's jacket clinked softly against his belt buckle as he walked. Not walked—*sauntered*. This man "sauntered" over to her, never taking his eyes off of her. Amity secretly hoped her plum lipstick was still intact. She tucked a curl behind her hair nervously, also hoping her simple smoky wings she spent way too much time on were also in one piece. Her hair, however, was *perfect*. For once, it did exactly what it was supposed to.

Rex quickly pulled out their phone pretending to scroll through something but obviously watching their friend.

"What can I get for you?" she asked without looking into those beautiful blue eyes. Those eyes were dangerous, almost making her forget he left her without a response for almost two days.

He hummed softly, studying her makeup like it was a nice surprise.

"I think. I'll take. A black coffee."

Her eyes narrowed at him in annoyance as her friend burst out in laughter. Was he trying to annoy her? That smirk of his said he not only was but that he enjoyed it. She nodded and rang up his coffee order.

Black jacket, black turtleneck, black jeans. Really living up to that bad boy title, she thought irritably, both toward him and herself for liking the bad boy vibe.

She also noticed his nose piercing—a simple black hoop—as well as the small earring that dangled from his left earlobe. Her eyes went to his tooth—a black stone reflecting the warm light—then to his black leather jacket. It was old and worn in, creating lines in the material where his arms bent. It looked comfortable.

He leaned against the countertop. "Look—"

"I'll be right back with your coffee," she quickly said, abruptly turning away from him.

"Look, sorry I haven't been in touch. Things have been a little . . . *hectic.*"

Amity could hear him tap away on the tablet as he paid for his order but she didn't turn to acknowledge him.

She opened her mouth to speak but choked on the words. For a moment she set the coffee cup down.

Breathe. Tell him how you really feel.

"If . . . if you wanted to just leave you could've said so instead of being a total . . . jerk." She could hear him try to stifle a laugh. He knew what she meant to say but hearing his cute laugh just made her more irritated.

She placed his coffee a little more aggressively than intended on the counter and slid the to-go cup toward him. When she finally looked up, his phone was inches away from her nose. Luka's mischievous smirk was wiped from his face as his phone Illuminated the message thread from his mother days ago.

Oct. 10, 8:01 pm

> *Pick up.*

Oct. 10, 8:02 pm

> *LUKA!*

Oct. 10, 8:03 pm

> *SOS*

He watched her read the messages carefully.

"Believe me now?"

Amity turned her face away in embarrassment. *Can't be completely mad at him if it was actually an emergency.* A pout formed on her lips.

"Y— . . . Yes."

Those beautiful cyan blue eyes stared at her for a moment too long before he nodded.

"Next time we'll do something better. In the meantime," he put his phone away and shuffled something in his pocket, "why don't you cool off with a new read? You're almost done with that one right?"

He gestured to her book on the counter, the one she *still* had yet to finish.

She sneered. *Did he just tell me to cool off?!*

As she was about to clap-back at him when he slid something towards her. Those beautiful eyes held her stare for a moment, the color almost glowing in the shop's light. Rough fingers squeezed her hand lightly.

"I'll call you. Bye, *kitten*," he finally said before turning and leaving.

"K-kitten?!" she stuttered, momentarily stunned by the small affection and the new pet name.

"Call me? I'll call you!" she yelled after him. Amity exchanged a quick heated look with Rex. "I mean, you better call! And don't think I'll be free when you do. . . ass."

Luka looked back at her as he reached for the door. A wide smirk spread across his lips. He winked. Then left.

Rex leaned back against the counter, raking her gaze over him as he walked out and past the shops windows. "And what a nice, plump ass he has. Just look at it *bounce*. I bet he wears tight jeans on purpose."

Amity flushed. She was clenching whatever he slipped into her hand. Her eyes widened and her mouth hung open when she realized what it was. It was a small card wrapped in brown paper with an elegant script on it.

I'll make it up to you, promise.

She carefully unwrapped the paper revealing a bookstore gift card.

He bought her a gift card. To a bookstore. So she could buy books.

Not just to any bookstore either, it was the really fancy one downtown! The one that had every new spicy release waiting in their shop window just begging her to buy it!

Her eyes were sparkling, but she quickly remembered that this was an apology gift and no matter how happy she was, she was still *slightly, maybe, kind of, sort of* mad at him still.

Is it possible to want to kiss someone's face off and punch them until they collapse at the same time? . . . Yes.

CHAPTER FIVE

Amity leaned her head back against the recliner's headrest, letting the worn-in leather soothe her growing headache. She had a horrible nightmare that kept repeating all night. When her alarm finally sprang her out of bed, it took her a solid fifteen minutes to calm her nerves and steady her breathing.

She took a deep breath preparing for a sneeze. When it never came she laid the new paperback on top of her face. It was one she bought from the bookstore downtown last night on her way home. A book about the Norse gods. One she couldn't put down last night. She groaned against the pages. Her irritating headache was gnawing at her, keeping her from focusing on the words typed on the pages. Keeping her from the magical world she wanted to dive headfirst into.

Halleys was a homely size with small leather couches and chairs on either side of the deep-red runner that ran from the front door to the register. It also helped protect the old wooden floor from being run into the ground. The couches and chairs were divided into little nooks of their own with small coffee tables. Amity had made it a point to test every piece of furniture before her mother made the final purchase.

Maybe running this place wouldn't be the worst thing in the world . . . she reluctantly pondered.

Along the walls were tall bookshelves with the latest bestsellers. They were also displayed in the windows so passersby would be enticed. Sometimes they had books with sprayed edges and special covers. Those were highly coveted by customers and especially Amity.

The white marble bar top separated her and Sammy from the rest of the store. It held the tablet where they would ring up the orders, the sweets display, the pickup window at the far end that they used during busy hours, then the high barstools at the opposite end. On the back counter was where all the coffeemakers and teakettles nestled. Amity put those kettles to good use this morning. She had made herself a nice cup of autumn-harvest tea—a special blend of cloves, cinnamon, blood orange, chamomile, and ginger. In other words, perfection. She would be making more for herself soon.

Luckily the shop was empty, letting her take a well-deserved rest. The longer hours were starting to take their toll, cutting into her sleep—well, her reading time, which then cut into her sleep—which in turn ramped up her anxiety. She snuggled deeper into the soft chair. *No one's going to walk in; I can just rest my eyes for a second.*

Someone lifted the book gently off her face, slowly sliding their thumb against her forehead as they did so.

At first she thought she imagined the light touch. She didn't hear any footsteps approaching and she especially didn't hear the creaky door open and close. *Maybe Sammy came in early for her closing shift.*

Amity opened her eyes, but when she saw who it was, her pulse raced and her body stiffened.

There he was—a black leather jacket, an unbuttoned white henley revealing his black-tooth necklace and a faint glimpse of a tattoo, and hair tied back in a cute man bun. The one who *technically* bought her that book.

Luka placed her worn bookmark—one of the shop's business cards—between the pages he'd parted, keeping her place, then flipped farther into the book. He scanned the page before a wide smile spread across his lips. His eyes sparkled with amusement.

"Well, well," he mused.

Amity's eyes went wide. She forgot this book was . . . *spicy.* Actually, she didn't forget. It was one of the reasons why she bought it. Gorgeous Norse gods, action-packed journeys, life-altering sex scenes; she ate these stories up like candy. She just didn't expect to be *sharing* it with someone else.

Amity watched his cyan eyes read farther down the page then flick back to her. He leaned one hand onto the back of her chair, right next to her head. She swallowed hard.

"Glad to see you liked my gift but . . . I didn't know you were into these kinds of books." He leered.

Her eyes narrowed. *Yet you got me a gift card to the spicy bookstore?*

"Give. It. Back."

He leaned forward slightly.

"Not a chance, *kitten*."

Her eyes narrowed on him once again, but he continued reading.

"Isn't it a little early to give me a nickname? You're not even my boyfriend yet."

"That can be arranged," he said, peering at her behind the erotica. She felt her face flush. Something about a man hovering over her and reading her erotic books was, well, so fucking hot.

Breathe, she reminded herself. *Slow down.*

A long breath left her. "Take me on a *real* date first and I'll think about it."

"A second date," he corrected.

"Regardless . . . I was promised 'dessert.' "

Luka watched her silently, then closed the book with a slap. His tattooed hand sunk into the chair on the other side of her head. He remained hovering over her, closely. A fact she was *fully* aware of. He had never been *this* close before. Some of his dark hair fell forward out of his bun, barely scraping the tip of her nose. Her mind raced.

Is he going to kiss me? No one's around. He could kiss me. No, he should kiss me. Does he taste like sandalwood too? Or seasalt?

"You work tonight?"

She shook her head stiffly, no.

He studied her for a moment; she was wearing red lipstick today. A bold choice to match an even bolder decision she'd purchased for the first time last week. A decision that she was also wearing under her clothes. He glanced out the window out of the corner of his eye. Something caught his attention, but Amity didn't look to see what it was. If she did, she would have seen two men staring at her through the window with judging eyes. He straightened himself but didn't remove his hands.

"Good. Stay off the streets." His voice was a cold warning.

She gave him a curious look as he slowly raked his gaze over her. Her square-cut top at this angle gave him a perfect little peek at her bright-red bra. He smirked.

"I bet you'll be otherwise *preoccupied.*"

She quirked her head to the side. His smirk kicked up on his lips.

"Reading about the God of Mischief's 'throbbing member.' "

He laughed, placing the book onto her flushed face. She scrambled to catch it before it fell. In her struggle he bent low, bringing his mouth to the shell of her ear, and ran his hands up her arms slowly. His touch was rough and hot, like fire caressing her skin through her shirt. Luka's voice became a low rumble.

"Maybe I'll even show you all those *naughty* positions. Hear you gasp for air as I taste you. Stretch you with my fingers and then with my—"

She swatted him with the book, colliding it with his shoulder. He laughed darkly and rubbed the spot. Her face was bright red.

"Easy, *kitten*. You'll have to beg me for it."

She went to swat at him again only to be momentarily paused by her phone beeping. Her short break was over, along with whatever peace she managed to obtain.

Luka turned on his heel and strode out the door. Amity cursed under her breath as she watched him leave. She swore there was a pep in his step.

When the door finally clicked closed, she hid her face in her hands, embarrassment burning through her.

This confirms it. He *did* like getting a rise out of her, and today he damn well succeeded. She adjusted her pants and straightened her apron, praying he was unaware of just how much he succeeded. She stood abruptly and fanned herself with her new book. Thank fuck no one else was in the shop! She was too hot and too bothered to deal with anyone at the moment.

Lightly she touched her forehead, quickly looked around the shop to double-check if it was empty, then opened her book to where her bookmark marked her place. She breathed deeply, trying to calm her racing heart.

Seasalt and sandalwood.

Amity had been sitting in the far corner of her living room, diagonal from her door, staring at the small jar of water, rosemary, sage, and clear quartz for an hour.

Freaya rubbed against her back again, like she had done so many times that night. *Her pet* trying to calm her racing mind no doubt. If Amity was any kind of aura, it was one of anxiety, frustration, and jitters.

It had started when she finally got home and properly put away the jar Rex had gifted her on her kitchen counter-top. Then she went through the kitchen cabinet, the one filled with herbs, and paced around her apartment trying to figure out how and when she bought them, but just like this morning, she could think of nothing. Even though the answer seemed to be within her grasp, it was also the furthest from her reach, leaving her with nothing but a headache.

The same feeling filled her when she looked at this jar. Again, she studied it carefully. Everything was in a tall mason jar, sealed with black wax. Amity quirked her head to the side and mindlessly pet Freaya as the void made a nest in her lap. Soft fur against shaking hands wasn't a cure, but it was tampering down that spooky feeling this jar sent her body into.

"Just where the fuck did you come from?"

Amity had thought about moving the jar for a while, and a half hour ago she finally tried, even though that gnawing feeling at the back of her skull said she shouldn't.

When she did try to move it—"try" being the correct word considering it seemed glued to the ground—it wouldn't budge. She finally gave up for fear of shattering the jar all over the floor and slicing her hands open.

The good news was this jar was just that, a jar. There wasn't any small camera inside of it for a stalker to spy on her. Nor was it giving off any kind of electricity or ticking noises indicating a transmission or bomb. It was just a jar, with crystals and herbs, sealed with black wax.

Her phone dinged loudly from its place on the couch. She stood on shaky legs and rubbed her ass as she hobbled over to it. Sitting on hardwood was *not* the best idea she'd had all night. Just like how she couldn't stop thinking about a certain someone every time she opened her book.

Her phone lit up with a text from her brother, Alex.

It was a ticket to see an EDM DJ downtown.

Oct. 14, 6:45 pm

My girlfriend's friend is DJing tonight at The Burrow. We have an extra ticket. Come with us

Amity groaned audibly. EDM was not her first choice of music. It was nice at times but it was already dark out. She just wanted to curl up in bed with her book and her favorite toy. Her phone dinged again.

Oct. 14, 6:45 pm

When was the last time you went outside?

She narrowed her eyes at the screen. Just as she was about to type out her answer a new message appeared.

Oct. 14, 6:45 pm

Walking to and from work doesn't count

Her tongue clicked audibly and laughed. He knew her too well.

Oct. 14, 6:46 pm

You're coming

Amity sighed. Her brother was right, although she'd never admit that to him. And despite how he literally had to drag her out of her comfort zone sometimes, she really did appreciate how close they were and that he cared that she interacted with other people on occasion. She typed out her reply.

Oct. 14, 6:46 pm

Fine. Be there soon.

Freaya yawned loudly in the corner then shook out her black fur. Amity narrowed her eyes on her. *I bet she'll be so happy to have the place to herself.*

Freaya glanced at her briefly then nonchalantly scratched behind her ears.

Amity quickly touched up her makeup and sprayed some perfume on her neck before leaving. Normally it would be overshadowed by the smell of coffee beans, but she feared it would be overtaken by the smell of sweaty people. She waved goodbye to Freaya, promising she would be back later that night, and then walked straight to the venue.

Yes it was cold and yes she *should've* worn a jacket, but the venue was a fifteen-minute walk. If she wore a jacket she would be all sweaty when she got there. It made enough sense. Plus she was wearing jeans, so her keys clipped onto her belt; her wallet and phone fit in her pockets. There was no need for a jacket.

With a shiver, Amity groaned at the outdoor entrance to The Burrow. She had been here several times before, but just thinking about everyone crammed into the underground club made her a little queasy. Then there was what Luka told her earlier.

She tapped her cheeks, refocusing her attention.

We're going to have a great time, she reassured herself. She always had fun whenever Alex dragged her out of her introvert cave, a.k.a. her apartment, something that had been happening more frequently since she started working at their parents' cafe.

Amity pulled out her phone and showed the bouncer her ticket, who quickly scanned it from the stack of pumpkins they'd been sitting on and opened the door to the descending staircase.

The dimly lit stairs were a lawsuit waiting to happen. Luckily Amity was wearing her boots so she would be sure-footed. She gripped the railing tighter the deeper she went. The noise from the crowd got louder as she reached the bottom, consuming her in rowdy conversation and cheers under jacko'lantern and ghost-string lights.

She immediately saw her older brother Alex at the bar because he was the *only one* who was hyper focused on the entrance. After pushing through a few people Alex pulled her into a tight hug.

"I haven't seen you in forever," she said as he kissed her forehead.

"I know, things have been busy." He took his jacket off the chair beside him for her to sit.

Anyone could tell they were siblings. They were in fact so similar that people could mistake them for twins. They had the same dark hair and eyes, the same straight nose. The only thing they didn't share was a personality. Growing up, Alex was the bolder of the two while Amity trailed behind him and his best friend . . . Bruce? Adam? Luke? Whatever his name was, she never remembered it.

"Where's Krystal?"

Alex grabbed the bartender's attention, who nodded from the far side of the bar.

"She went to the bathroom. She hasn't been feeling all that great but really wanted to come anyway."

Amity narrowed her eyes at him.

"So you invited me even though you're not staying?"

He shrugged, "A change of pace is good once in a while. If I *hadn't* told you to come, you would've sat home alone with your cat and spent the whole night reading some fantasy book." He was shouting over the music, narrowing his eyes on her. Alex really did know her too well.

"I like my fantasy books. And my cat, thank you very much," she yelled, raising her voice to meet his volume and punching his arm lightly before ordering her drink.

"You need to be with someone other than your cat!"

"She's the only one that understands me!"

"She's a cat!"

To anyone else listening they might think her and her brother were screaming at each other, but this was how it always was between them. There was a normal talking level and then there was "family level." Shouting was just normal family level, Especially when her entire family got together, all thirty-three of them.

A moment passed between them before they burst out laughing. He tapped his against hers and drank. She did the same. For tonight she would have a cranberry vodka, not too strong but just strong enough. She had to walk home later but, most importantly, Amity was a lightweight.

Alex ran a hand through his freshly cut hair.

"I saw some shady guy in the shop with you earlier."

"You were spying on me?"

"I was stopping by to *check* on you. There are real creeps out there this time of year."

"He's not like that." Amity wanted to smack herself in the face for saying something so predictable. She didn't really know Luka all that well, and despite his forwardness, he seemed better than most guys she dated . . . so far. Unfortunately for her the words left her mouth before she realized it.

"Rex said you've only been on *one* date."

She took an aggravated sip of her drink.

"Rex talks too much." Her eyes narrowed, they were both close friends with Rex, but did they really need to tell her nosey brother everything that happened in her life? This wasn't anything too crazy but still!

"Amity—"

"Okay, yes! *Officially* we've only been on one date. Why do you care anyway? You never show this much interest in my love life." It was a legitimate question. Not that Amity had many boyfriends in the past. She would secretly listen in when her brothers and his friends talked about girls they liked, and what she heard was not good, so naturally she just stayed away. Granted, her brother grew out of his pathetic misogyny but that didn't mean the men she finally did date did.

Her few relationships with "real men" were less than . . . no, they were just less—*never* enough but somehow she was "too much." Which only made her more anxious when dating. But who needs real men when elven princes and fae lords in her books were already perfect. Which is why it's been a very, *very* long time since her last relationship with a man.

"He—" Alex cut himself short before he even started. With a frustrated grunt he took a long sip of his beer. "I don't like him."

"You saw him through a *window*," she deadpanned.

"I just . . . just stay away from him okay?" He ruffled her hair aggressively. She quickly shoved him off, almost knocking him off the stool.

"Alex! You know how long it takes for me to do my hair!" she yelled, trying to fix it in the dirty mirror across the bar. He reached for her again only to be shoved away.

"Alex! She's not a kid anymore, loosen up a bit would you?" Alex immediately stood, giving Krystal his seat. More people had crowded the place and there clearly wasn't enough space for everyone. Amity internally cringed; soon she'd be smashed between people.

"I'm sorry about him, Amity. He's an ass." Krystal jabbed him playfully in the side.

"It's fine, don't apologize for him." She laughed and Krystal smiled at her before gathering her straight dark hair back into a bun.

Krystal and Alex started talking about her DJ friend, occasionally asking for Amity's input on EDM genres, which she would chime in for. She liked a few bands that used a lot of synth-pop sounds but those weren't the same thing.

When they weren't looking, Amity fixed her shirt in the mirror, pulling it up just enough so it wasn't too low but then scoffing when it rode up on her stomach. Her high-waisted jeans covered a lot of her stomach but it still peeked out under the bottom of her top. She glanced over at Krystal. Gorgeously toned Krystal, but to be fair she worked incredibly hard to look like that. She once told Amity her workout schedule and afterward Amity felt dizzy. Then she was explaining her yoga studio she started with her friends and that made Amity's head spin even more. This woman was a powerhouse!

Just gotta work your way up there. You'll get there. Just takes time, she reassured herself. *Just takes a little agency.*

Her brother messed with her hair again, earning a scolding from Krystal.

"Wake up, nerd, the show's about to start."

CHAPTER SIX

Luckily they stayed on the outskirts of the crowd. Actually, they didn't even move too far from their spot. Alex tried pushing through the crowd when Krystal's friend started performing only to make it a few feet away. So they stayed, which was perfect for the girls.

Despite Krystal's stomach and Amity's lack of interest in EDM, they were having a good time. Her friend had some fun Halloween-themed remixes blaring from the speakers that had everyone going nuts over. Amity cheered loudly with the rest of the crowd several times. Some people even showed up in costumes, sort of. It was more small wings attached to a backpack or bright glow-in-the-dark paint, and glitter. Lots and *lots* of glitter.

Alex smiled smugly as he messed with her hair again. She tried to swat him away, but he was considerably taller than her. Just about as tall as Luka.

"Thank you!" Amity shouted over the reveling crowd.

The crowd started to get a little rowdy the more the DJ played. People began shoving and pushing each other closer to the stage. It seemed the rowdier they got, the more Amity's energy shrank. Krystal's was falling fast too. She was leaning on Alex's arm, looking very under the weather.

He leaned over to her and asked her something Amity couldn't hear over the noise. Krystal shook her head no. He wrapped an arm around her and put the back of his hand to her forehead. He spoke again with a look of determination on his face. Amity knew that look all too well. It was the same one he would give her when she was being stubborn. After a moment, Krystal finally nodded and Alex helped her with her coat.

"We're going to head out."

"Okay." Amity glanced around the room quickly. It had become stuffy and hot with all the people, not to mention the fog machine in the corner making it harder to breathe. She nodded; her social battery had fallen to a critical low for the night anyway. "I'll come with you."

They inhaled the cool air outside like it was the first breath they'd ever taken. Amity shook out her shirt; she was just as she feared, sweaty. Alex wrapped an arm around Krystal's shivering body.

"Where the hell's your coat, Amity?" he scolded.

"I left it. I didn't want to be all sweaty when I got home."

He looked at her for a minute.

"You know I can drive you home."

"It's not that far . . ."

"You have your mace?" he asked, looking down at her keychain hanging from her belt. She nodded. He sighed in defeat.

"Just text me when you get home. And stay in the damn streetlights." He pulled her in for a quick hug and kissed the top of her head. She hugged him back.

"Yeah, yeah, I know. Feel better, Krystal."

Krystal waved a shaky hand and nodded, looking pale. *Good thing we left when we did.*

"I mean it, Amity. Love you."

"Love you too."

Amity stretched her arms high above her head, hearing a satisfying crack. The cold air pricked her stomach as her shirt rode up, sending a shiver up her spine. "Well at least it's not *bone-chilling* cold."

A stiff wind blew past, almost in mockery. It sent fallen leaves cascading in all directions, one smacking her in the face. She hugged herself tightly.

"No need for a jacket, huh?" she scolded herself. Kicking the pile of leaves on the cobblestone sidewalk, aggressively sending them flying.

Other than her, the streets were deserted. She glanced at her phone to check the time, 10:00 p.m. So the streets being near deserted were not completely unheard of at 10:00 p.m. on a Saturday night, especially since The Burrow wasn't in the heart of the city. She made her steps lighter as she walked. Not an easy task in her boots, but she made do.

The sound of the crunching leaves beneath her feet and her keys jingling at her side filled her ears. Unease slithered up her spine, making her shiver for a completely different reason. Her heart beat faster. She stopped suddenly and checked behind her. Then across the street.

No one.

Just empty streets. She unhooked her keys from her belt and held her mace in her hand. Just in case.

Amity had never had to use it on someone before, but there was always a first time for everything.

The fact that I have to carry it at all is fucking ridiculous! I shouldn't have to be scared of running into psycho creeps when I walk home. I shouldn't have to be scared to walk home at all!

She took a deep breath; she could worry about the fucked-up society she lived in later. Right now she needed to get home to her cat and the mischievous god in her book. She'd stopped right at the good part.

Amity started walking again, keeping a mental note to stay focused. Luckily there were plenty of streetlights downtown, but a few of them seemed to be out. She jumped a little when a dog barked ahead of her. Its owner tugged it along hurriedly and passed by without a word.

"What's his rush?" she mumbled. Then she *felt it.*

The temperature was colder the farther she traveled. The air felt like ice in her lungs.

What the hell? It wasn't this cold before . . .

She hugged herself tighter and rubbed her arms. Good thing she had thick hair to protect her neck from freezing. Her feet grew heavier as she continued down the cobblestone path, making her steps slower, her stride smaller.

Something stopped her dead in her tracks.

Amity's eyes went wide as she checked her surroundings. The man walking his dog was long gone. The streets were empty. Fear crawled up her skin and choked her from taking a full breath. A strange sound rang through the night. A constricted scream.

What the fuck was that?

Did she imagine it? That horrible sound. *Maybe it was a fox?* She took in a reassuring breath before reason sunk in. *It's not a damn fox—I live in fucking Hartford, not Woodbury!*

She heard it again. *That does sound like a fox! But it's .. . wrong.*

It sounded like a low groan. Something between a fox and a human.

She shuffled her feet in place; she dared not move from under the streetlamp. The next one she'd have to pass under was broken, and across from it was the mouth of an alleyway. As if she wasn't already spooked enough.

Luka's voice came back to her. A cryptic warning. She brushed his words off.

A low fog tumbled out of the mouth of the alleyway, sending a few leaves scattering toward her. Another sound reached her. Not that horrible animalistic one. It was a person. A person's scream.

Amity clutched her mace tighter. Was it a gang fight? She had never seen any in person before, but they were all over the news. She shook away the thought. *No, what made that sound before wasn't natural.*

She wasn't far from her apartment, only a few more minutes. If she ran she could—

"Just stay down!" a man shouted inside the alleyway.

Amity began to shake. Her mind ran to the worst possible scenario. Was someone in trouble? Were they hurt? Was she, whoever she was, walking home alone too . . . ?

Amity's feet felt like they were glued to the cobblestones but she forced them to move. She couldn't just stand there and listen to—

She stopped that thought from entering her brain. *Nothing is certain. Maybe it was some alley cats. Yeah. That's it. Cats. Freaya makes weird noises all the time! That's gotta be it! Someone's yelling at their deranged cat and there is no woman in danger from walking home alone late at night.* Her next step was sure. Though the cold air still stung, her breaths were deeper.

Before she could register how far she walked, she was standing in the mouth of the alleyway, in the midst of the fog. She could faintly see a dim green light lighting the back. Small flashes of blue flickered brightly at the other side. Amity strained her eyes to see farther as she carefully made her way down the dark narrow way toward the green light at the end. That horrible animalistic sound cried out, echoing toward her.

Amity held her mace in front of her. *Just a cat,* she reassured herself. Though that comforting thought was quickly dissipating.

She made it halfway down the alleyway when other sounds were clear as day. Grunting. Slashing. Something pawed at the asphalt, and whatever it was, it sounded *big*.

It was a fight!

"Tell me where he is!" the man demanded.

That horrible animalistic voice answered him, "Closer than you think."

What the fuck was going on?!

Amity was about to turn and run the other way when something was thrown into the dark alleyway. She screamed as it hit the wall just above her with a loud crack and then tumbled in front of her feet with a loud groan.

Not some*thing*—some*one*!

The man she heard shouting now lay with his face in the dirty ground.

"Fucking hell!" he cursed gruffly, pushing himself onto his hands and knees.

He gripped his side in pain and took note of the fresh cut. A necklace swung quietly, glowing faintly with blue light, as he examined the fresh blood on his hand. She saw his body tense under his worn leather jacket when he noticed her shoes a few feet from his face. Slowly his eyes traveled up her body until cyan met brown.

His eyes widened in panic, then narrowed in anger. Amity said nothing. Her body was frozen, her heart hammering inside her chest as Luka rose to his feet, towering over her.

"Where the fuck is your jacket?"

Something stalked behind him. Its body massive and unnatural. A giant fox, at least eight feet tall. It had large unnatural eyes, enormous paws, and sharp claws that clicked on the ground as it walked. Its fur emitted an ominous green glow.

Amity instinctively recoiled from it. Just as Luka was about to turn around, it sent a sharp claw into his leg.

He breifly screamed in pain before quickly turning. Pulled something from his jacket then threw it toward the weird beast. Luka spoke quickly, a language of deformed words and mumbles Amity was too paralyzed to follow. Two knives struck the beast. One in the eye and the other in the shoulder. They glowed blue against its green fur.

The beast shrunk away, screaming and shaking its massive body like the knives were burning through its flesh. It turned to flee.

Amity felt Luka tugging her. Yelling at her.

"Move, Amity!"

CHAPTER SEVEN

She hobbled down the street as best she could with Luka's arm slung across her shoulders. The height difference made walking extremely difficult. If she wasn't just scared half to death she would've laughed at how ridiculous they looked.

Luka grunted with each step. Clutching his side where blood was staining his white henley. Amity glanced over, wincing.

Fuck, that looks like it hurts.

After they ran away from that "creature," he went into a scolding mode, reprimanding her for not listening to him earlier. Just as she was yelling back at him, the guy *collapsed*. Any sensible person would've left him there, gone to the cops and—

And say what? "Hey, Mr. Policeman, this guy I went on a date with was fighting some weird monster in an alleyway." Like that would fucking work, dumbass!

Her eyes traveled to his tooth—now its normal black. Not to mention the strange feeling that overcame her. The one that forced her to lift him over her shoulders and drag him down the sidewalk. The one that screamed she *couldn't* leave him. His shirt was fully unbuttoned, revealing a tiny peek of his tattoo and stealing her attention. Luka smirked at her. Her face flushed in embarrassment; he caught her.

"You have a lot of explaining to do!" she yelled, tugging him along.

"Take it easy," he half groaned and half laughed in disbelief.

"This isn't fucking funny, Luka! What the fuck was that thing?!"

"You're cute when you curse."

Her face flushed deeper.

"Luka!"

He stopped suddenly, putting more of his weight onto her. Panic rushed through her.

"Hey!"

"No hospital," he said gruffly.

"What? Of course you're going to the hospital."

"Amity." He leaned upon her more. He could easily crush her if he wanted to. "No hospital," he said in her ear.

A high-pitched noise escaped her, and she quickly set him straight again.

"Fine! Just—don't you dare pass out on me!"

She looked around for a sense of direction. Luckily no one else was around to see them or her red face. They must have walked farther than she thought; her apartment building was across the street.

Carefully Amity led him in and onto the elevator, leaning him against the wall and nearly breaking her finger from how hard she pushed the button. Her apartment was old, so luckily there were only four floors.

"You have a lot of explaining to do," she scolded.

With a heavy hand he wiped his sweaty hair back and out of his eyes with a smirk. Cyan eyes looked at her with a mischievous glint.

"Scold me more."

"Stop doing that, I'm serious!"

Was it the loss of blood making him like this? She huffed, slinging him back over her shoulder and shuffling him out of the elevator. His smile fell as she struggled to her door at the end of the hall.

She fumbled for her keys. She glanced up at him when she noticed she wasn't carrying his weight on her shoulders anymore. He was leaning above her with one arm above his head on the doorframe. The other was around her back, gripping the other. She was caged in. She took in a shaky breath. Sandalwood and seasalt. She was now covered in it.

Amity fumbled with the lock and carefully pushed the door open.

"Freaya, I'm home!" she greeted, making sure the black void wasn't trying to run out after she opened the door. Luckily she didn't. Luka trailed in after her, then quickly removed his shoes, placing them as best he could onto the tray on the floor next to Amity's. She hurried back from the bathroom with a worried expression, holding a first aid kit.

"It's all I have."

Luka ran a hand through his hair and shrugged off his jacket. He hobbled, tossing his jacket onto the back of the couch on the way to the kitchen.

"Where are you going? Sit down already. You're going to . . ." she yelled, trailing after him. He was already going through her cabinets.

Luka hung her teakettle over the faucet, letting it fill as he opened her "herb cabinet" on the other side of the counter. She watched him, dumbfounded. He wasn't "rummaging." He never picked the wrong cabinet. He *knew* where everything was. Her pulse spiked.

"Wha-what are you doing?"

Several bags were pulled out of the cabinet and spread over the small countertop. Gently, he took a pinch of each herb and sprinkled them into the kettle. He mumbled something softly under his breath and placed it onto the stove.

"Y-you need to sit down."

He lit the kettle on a high heat.

"Luka!"

Again, he mumbled softly to himself, completely dismissing her. A creepy chill slithered up her spine.

"What was that weird green fox thing!?"

He ignored her and leaned back onto the counter.

Amity could feel her blood beginning to boil along with the water. She quickly shoved the first aid kit back into the bathroom cabinet. By the time she made it back Luka had removed the teakettle from the stove and poured himself a mug of whatever it was he made. He took a long sip, downing half the mug in one go. Luka winced and took in a deep breath before finishing the rest. Amity watched him, confused. She called his name again, but he didn't hear her. Something snapped back into place. Luka gripped his side in pain, groaning loudly. Quickly he ripped a paper towel off the rack and dipped it into the kettle. Shoved the bottom half of his shirt up and into his mouth revealing his bloody cut them, with another grunt, he pressed the wet cloth to his wound.

"Don't, it'll get infected!"

She was by his side in an instant, ripping his hand away. Her jaw dropped. The wound wasn't bleeding anymore. Amity watched in silent horror as Luka's skin stitched itself back together.

She hesitantly reached for it only to be stopped by his shirt falling back down. She stood frozen.

Did that really just happen?

He studied her silently.

"Amity . . ."

She slowly dragged her eyes up to his. He went to reach for her but she jumped back from his reach. She grabbed the closest thing she could see and pointed it at him.

His mouth hung open in disbelief, then he ran a hand through his messy hair. She watched a long exhale work through him.

"Really, Amity? Really!"

She squared her feet and held the dagger higher. It was just a replica, so it wasn't that sharp, but he didn't need to know that. Nor was she about to tell him that. She also wasn't about to admit she had absolutely no idea how to use it and this was all bravado.

"Tell me what the fuck is going on," she demanded.

Luka retied the top half of his hair back, taking in a deep breath.

"Put the knife down."

"This isn't a *knife*, it's an elven dagger, you cocky bastard!" She jabbed it toward him, prodding the air, but he didn't seem to notice.

" 'Cocky bastard'?" He repeated the phrase with wide eyes, then burst out laughing. Amity flushed with embarrassment.

"Shut up!"

Freaya rubbed up against her leg. The poor baby must've been woken up from her nap by all the racket. She walked into the kitchen and stretched lazily between them before making her way over to Luka. Her eyes sparkled and her tail stood straight up. He watched her with a small smile as she rubbed against his leg, then circle and continue to mark him with her scent. She meowed loudly at him, demanding affection. Amity's eyes flashed between them in shock.

"Sh-she *never* does that."

He moved to bend low and scratch her head but thought twice about it. He slowly ran his gaze from the dagger to Amity's. He held up his hands and took a small, cautious step toward her. Seconds ticked by that seemed like minutes. His voice was low and calm. Cyan eyes fixated on her own.

"Take a seat. You can hold onto the replica if it makes you feel better, but I swear if you try to stab me, I'll take it out of your hand faster than you can blink."

Amity shifted her stance wider and jabbed the dagger between them with shaky hands.

"Oh yeah? How—"

She didn't blink. She didn't even *move*. She only saw Luka move his hand, or at least it *looked* like his hand. Everything happened so fast. Before she could process it, her dagger was in his hand. There was no cocky smirk on his lips. No mischievous glint in his eyes.

"*Sit.*"

He held the dagger toward her. For a moment she thought he would use it on her, but his eyes and tone weren't threatening. Still, her body stiffened. He turned the dagger so the handle faced her.

"*Please, Amity.*"

Her attention flicked between him and the dagger a few times before hesitantly taking it.

She took a step back, giving him a wide berth. Luka took cautious steps toward her and waited a second too long when he was close. In that moment she had a strange thought, that he would bend down and kiss her temple, but he walked past her and took a seat on the far end of the couch. Freaya followed him, making a warm nest in his lap.

Amity looked at her cat, dumbfounded.

What the fuck is going on?

She gripped the dagger tighter. Luka watched her silently from the couch, gently scratching the top of Freaya's head, as her confusion and anxiety morphed into frustration.

"She's only acting like that because you're pretty. Don't think she won't claw your eyes out." Luka smirked and leaned his chin onto his tattooed hand, a tattoo she had *still* not seen in its entirety.

"You think I'm pretty?"

She glared at him. At this rate she really would want to stab him. He held up his hands innocently, then gestured to the other end of the couch. She walked over to it, never taking her eyes off of him. She did not sit. He didn't seem to mind.

They stared at each other for a moment before Amity placed the dagger on the small coffee table in front of her, far out of his reach. Those cyan eyes watched her carefully take in a deep breath.

"What was that *thing* outside?" He gazed at her as if tracing every tiny detail—her disheveled curls, faded-red lips, her square black shirt that was just a little too low. She inhaled deeply, then exhaled with a defeated sigh.

"A demon."

Her eyes went wide and a laugh crawled out of her throat. Quickly she covered her mouth to suppress it but failed miserably.

"A demon." She repeated the word over and over until the absurdity of her situation faded into a strange acceptance.

She threw herself down onto the other side of the couch and hugged her knees close to her chest.

"Of course . . . Of course the first guy I date in months would be fighting some weird demon fox thing!"

She laughed again, gripping her hair, giving her fingers something to do as they shook. Luka carefully lifted Freaya from his lap, rose from the couch, and placed her into Amity's arms. The void was reluctant to leave her warm spot, but that didn't matter now. Amity hugged her close to her chest, slowly rocking back and forth.

Her acceptance developed into a strange curiosity, something that should have struck her as ridiculously odd. That weird feeling of déjà vu also came back stirring in the back of her mind, out of sight. Out of reach.

"A demon, like a Christian demon? Like Japanese yokai? Like in anime? Are those demons real? Does this make you an exorcist or something? How long have you been fighting demons? How long have they existed? You were saying something to it. It was speaking! Why are you just sitting there!?" Amity's questions poured out of her faster than she could process her words. Luka was silent the entire time, listening and watching as she ranted, never once lifting her eyes from Freaya.

"You're taking this much better than expected."

She finally looked up at him. One of his knees was propped up on the couch, the other leg hung off the side. He was lounging! As if she wasn't having a mental breakdown five seconds ago. And not only that: Her eyes briefly traveled across his shirt. He was more toned than she originally thought, and his shirt was bunched behind him making it look tighter than it actually was.

"How *exactly* did you think I would take this?"

His gaze slid away.

"I'm not sure," he whispered.

Amity stopped petting Freaya, who immediately took the opportunity to leap far from the couch. Luka sounded . . . remorseful. She quirked her head slightly to the side.

"Are you looking for someone?"

His gaze shot to hers.

"No," he growled.

Her gaze narrowed on him.

"You said, 'Where is *he*?' Who is *he*?" Luka rose from the couch and went to grab his jacket. She snatched it quickly, tugging it back out of his reach.

"Are you some kind of demon slayer or something?"

"Amity. Let. Go."

"Why? You haven't told me a thing!" she pressed.

He leaned over her, his patience visibly running thin.

"Because," he pressed closer to her, his voice low and serious, "I need to kill that thing before someone gets hurt."

His face was inches from hers. Amity swallowed hard; this was the first time she had seen him like this. He was intimidating and yet . . . Her gaze flicked down to his lips and then back up to his eyes. He was too close to miss the gesture. Something about him—this tension— seemed *familiar*.

Luka slipped the jacket out of her grip and shrugged it over his shoulders. Amity's heart was racing as Luka calmly made his way over to his shoes and slipped them back on. She grabbed him by his jacket just before he could turn the doorknob.

"I'm coming with you!"

The words left her mouth before she knew it.

What the hell am I thinking?! Why did I say that?!

"Absolutely not."

Again. That strange feeling of nostalgia. Did she have a conversation with him like this before? No! *That's not possible.* She must've been comparing this to one of the many arguments she'd had with Alex. *Yeah that's it. That's why this is familiar,* she resolved. And yet . . . she was curious.

"That thing—"

"*Demon,*" he corrected.

She pulled his hand from the doorknob and slipped in between him and the door with arms outstretched. He towered over her, but it didn't matter. She wasn't going to let him leave.

How's that for fucking "agency."

"Whatever! It saw me *too,* and it gave me this creepy look," which was a lie. "I won't be able to sleep at night until it's sent back, wherever it came from . . . and I-I wanna see how it's done."

There was a moment of silence between them. When she looked up at him he was looking at her with that same look as before. She didn't mistake it. It *was* remorse.

Luka bent down to meet her gaze on equal level. Rough fingers brushed her cheek gently and smoothly glided below her chin. The corners of his mouth tilted up into a small smile.

"No," he ordered, his lips so close to hers she could almost touch them.

She blinked, and he bent further down and slung her over his shoulder as if he benched twice her body weight.

"Whoa, Luka! What are you doing?"

He ignored her and marched right to her room. Without a word, he tossed her onto her bed.

"You're staying right there, kitten," he said.

Then he left.

Amity sat on her mattress with her mouth hung open as she heard her door close and his footsteps fade down the hall.

Did he just . . . ?

She felt heat pool in the bottom of her stomach. Her face flushed a dark red.

"Fuck."

CHAPTER EIGHT

Amity slunk against the brick wall as carefully as she could. She gripped her arms tightly, shivering against the breeze. The night had gotten much colder now that it was later, and she ran after him so quickly that she forgot to grab a jacket.

Amity rubbed her arms, scolding herself for the tenth time that night. She should've remembered that the closer she got to the demon the more the temperature plummeted.

Stupid.

What was she—crazy?! Why did she have to follow him out into the cold? Amity narrowed her eyes trying to remember. No, not "have," *want.* Why did she *want* to follow him? She racked her brain for answers but had nothing except a sting from thinking too hard. Just a feeling in her gut? Something about prowling the streets after dark. Talk of demons and whatever Luka made in that kettle with the herbs. A potion? What he made—what it *did* was *definitely* magical. In fact, it was *miraculous*.

Something about him was miraculous, but more importantly, something about him was familiar. She could *feel* it.

Amity had tracked him about a block away from where she saw him fight the demon . . . *battle* the demon? Cautiously she shook her head. Fight, battle, it didn't matter. *Same thing.* She peeked back out onto the lit street from her hiding place in an alleyway entrance. His footsteps were so light that she thought more than once she'd lost him. Her heart raced in her chest.

There he was. Under a broken streetlamp he stood as silent as a shadow, a hot breath leaving him in a thick roar of smoke. His tooth glowed a faint blue against his shirt. He pressed it to his lips in a quick kiss.

Amity silently cursed the streetlight for being out. The shadows hid him too well, and she wanted to see his face. Luka turned in her direction.

Quickly she threw herself back into the mouth of the alleyway. The hammering of her heart made it difficult to slow her breathing, but she tried. She wrung her cold hands together. His footsteps were audible, softly tapping the cobblestone with each step he took. They grew louder as he approached.

He stopped a few feet from where she hid and scuffed his boot into the ground impatiently.

"I know you're there, kitten. I can hear your heartbeat." His voice was a low purr.

"N-no you can't—I mean . . . Fuck!"

She didn't hear him take another step. His hand was in her hair, gripping at the roots and guiding her out of her hiding place.

"I told you to *stay*." He growled in her ear, sending shivers up her spine and her skin to warm.

"You're not the boss of me," she countered, shoving his hand away.

That mischievous glint returned to his eyes.

"Maybe I should change your nickname to brat. You're certainly acting like one."

He stepped toward her, effectively backing her into the brick wall.

"No, I'm not," she pouted, turning her face away.

She refocused her attention on his necklace, hiding her face as small wind blew her curls astray. She reached for it, then thought twice about it and hugged her arms. A sigh escaped his lips.

"Is this why you left our date? To kill demons?"

He watched her closely for a moment, only answering when she glanced up at him. Even if it was just for a moment.

"Yes."

Determined brown eyes met cyan.

"Then the least you can do is prove it to me."

She could see the wheels of his mind turning the longer he gazed, wrestling with his choices. Whatever his answer was she would follow him regardless, and that filled her with a strange excitement.

He let out a frustrated sigh and nodded.

"Alright, let's go."

She tried to brush past him but was stopped by a cold hand wrapped around her throat. Rough, padded fingertips pressed harder against her smooth skin and guided her back into place until her back was pressed flush against the wall. His grip tightened briefly but never in an oppressive way, never uncomfortable. Still she took in a shaky breath surprised by the sudden action, but at the same time thrilled by it.

"I need you to stay in the shadows," he said, staring at his hand on her throat.

She nodded.

Her pulse thrummed against his thumb.

"I need you to be quiet."

Again, she nodded. His grip was light now, barely holding her. He swiped his thumb against her pulse.

"And whatever happens. I need you to do *exactly* as I say."

She raised an eyebrow.

"Yeah, I get it already. You don't have to . . ."

He lifted his eyes to hers. That rough hand rose to cup her cheek.

"Amity. Promise me."

There was no playfulness in his voice. No mischievous glint in his eyes. He was pleading. Those eyes were desperate and filled with remorse.

Her skin warmed at his touch.

Amity brought her shaky hands to his face, gently bringing his forehead down to hers. Something about this gesture was sacred to her. Like something she had only planned to do with someone she loved for a long time. Whoever that person might be. He breathed her in and she warmed his lungs.

"I promise."

Luka nodded against her, took one more long inhale, then pulled away. Amity immediately missed his warmth, until he wrapped her in it. He pulled his jacket tightly around her and rubbed her arms beneath it. Amity quickly embraced the heat, letting it engulf her and her senses. It wasn't his naked body, but it was the next best thing. Her face flushed at the sudden thought.

She walked beside him as they made their way down the dark path.

Once they reached the mouth of the alley, Luka pulled a few throwing knives from his back pocket. They glowed a faint blue, like his tooth. Amity adjusted the jacket and zipped it up tightly. It was big on her, but it was his and it was warm.

He caught her curious gaze.

"I blessed them with a protection charm," he explained briefly.

She nodded, understanding. She fiddled with the breast pocket of the jacket, pulling out a small black bag that smelled of seasalt and sandalwood.

He smiled down at her and plucked it from her hand, gently tucking it back into the pocket.

"A charm bag. For protection."

She nodded nervously.

"Remember—"

"Stay in the shadows . . ."

". . . *and* Out. Of. Sight."

Air filled her lungs, regaining some of Amity's composure then she followed him to the mouth of the alleyway.

"How are you sure it's still here?" she asked as they descended further into the darkness.

"Because I trapped it here."

Ah, that weird thing he mumbled when he threw those knives, she remembered.

A faint green glow was cast at the end of the narrow path. Luka prowled toward it, as if it was his light to claim. Amity pressed herself against the wall behind a large dumpster halfway down the corridor. She didn't dare move further, not this time.

Silently she watched as Luka slipped into the light and around the corner. The creature growled at him, the horrible sound ringing through the air. Amity buried her face deeper into the collar of his jacket so only her eyes were visible, the same way a child would when they thought they saw something in the shadows of their bedroom. *I guess that doesn't seem so ridiculous now.* When she was younger, she claimed she saw many things go bump in the night, though no one believed her.

Although she couldn't see the creature, she could hear its claws rap on the asphalt as it dodged and danced in the narrow space. Luka was too quiet to hear, but every few moments she heard an audible breath quickly followed by an unearthly screech.

Something massive and heavy fell to the ground. The soft green light began to pulse strongly. She heard another loud *thud*, which she assumed was Luka's foot slamming into the creature's head. It whimpered.

"You have a message for me." Luka's voice was a low rumble that rang through the night. The creature huffed and snapped its jaws. Something cracked, followed by another loud *thud*. It cried out again.

"Tell. Me."

Amity gripped the jacket tighter around herself. She was glad she couldn't see him because from the sound of his voice, he was very, *very* angry.

"Riv . . . Riverside Park," the creature whimpered.

Something was cut open, then it fizzled. The soft green glow was gone.

Amity was about to move from her hiding place but stopped herself.

Silence. A long excruciating silence engulfed the night. Her pulse raced in anticipation. Was the air warming up, or was that her nerves?

Soft footsteps filled the narrow alley, each slow haunting step more painful to listen to than the last, until she saw the familiar frame of a man.

Luka stopped in front of her. Cyan eyes that once burned bright were now a faint glow. They inspected her carefully. Amity stood frozen, unsure of what he would do next. Something deep in her gut told her no matter what this man would never hurt her. Even when he grabbed her before, it wasn't rough or aggressive. He had never hurt her.

But he was a man, and most men, Amity had discovered, were liars.

Cautiously she reached out to him and tapped his tooth lightly. It wasn't glowing anymore. Neither were his eyes.

"Your eyes. They were glowing like your necklace."

He placed a cold hand on her shoulder and lightly squeezed.

"It happens sometimes."

She nodded. Without another word, he rested his hand on the small of her back and she let him guide her back to the mouth of the alley where it was freshly lit from the streetlights.

"You stayed," he said, almost too low for her to hear.

"I promised."

His hand fisted into the back of his jacket. The jacket that now smelled like them.

CHAPTER NINE

Amity ran the warm towel across her freshly washed face. She had wiped off her makeup already and applied a tinted chapstick as well as changed out of her tight high-waisted jeans and into some extremely comfortable pajama pants. Adjusting her boobs so her red bra was no longer showing she then looked herself over in the mirror for the twelfth time before nodding to her reflection.

"I'm surprised you didn't drink this already," he said smoothly when she emerged from the bathroom.

He handed her one of her stemless wine glasses filled halfway with the sweet wine he bought for her on their first date. She took it gladly; after everything that happened tonight she needed a drink.

"Congratulations on surviving your first demon." He smiled and held up his glass.

A laugh left her as she gently tapped her glass with his. They both drank. He was right, the wine was sweet. Holding the glass in both hands she tapped it nervously.

"You stayed . . ." she began.

He watched her expectantly waiting for her to continue. She took another sip feeling the liquid warm her lungs and her courage. Her nervous smile tugged into a smug smirk.

"You were so eager to get rid of me earlier, now you want to stick close?"

A playful smirk spread across his lips, and he let out a low laugh.

"Don't act so cocky, creatures who pass through realms tend to leave part of their essence in the air, and especially *on* the things they interact with. It attracts others," he explained, making his way over to the couch where his jacket was slung over the back.

For a moment Amity thought he would grab it and make up some excuse to leave. Not Luka. This man lounged on one end of her couch with his legs spread exactly as before. His eyes focused on her mischievously.

"Besides, you like it when I'm close."

Amity turned her flushed face away trying to hide her smile, which failed miserably. She sat on the other end, facing him and leaning back on the soft mound of blankets.

Silently he watched her, taking a long sip from his glass. "Your tooth."

"Cornicello," he corrected sweetly.

Amity knew she must've heard that word before, but the way he said that word made heat pool in the pit of her stomach.

"Cor-ni-cello?" she pronounced carefully.

He nodded.

"It's an Italian horn."

She thought about that for a moment, that familiar nostalgia hitting her again.

"I'm sure if I listened to my Zia more I would know more about it. I never paid any attention to her religious talk." She sighed.

A small laugh escaped his lips as Luka twirled it with his tattooed hand

"It's just a protection charm. Nothing too special but . . ." Amity watched his fingers curiously as they moved the charm effortlessly between them. "It was a gift."

Her gaze turned. It was a gift. A *gift from a woman?* Amity knew it for certain, and although it seemed ridiculous to be jealous about that, she was.

"Do you miss her?" she asked, sinking into the cushions and stifling a yawn. Was she getting tired? What time was it anyway?

"Sometimes. Why, are you jealous?"

"No!"

A smile pulled his lips as he watched her finish off her wine with a frustrated huff.

"Uh-huh, *sure*, you can't hide from me, kitten. It's written all over your face."

Amity attempted to respond to the nickname but was too flustered. Whatever she was trying to say came out in an inaudible jumble of sounds. Luka tried holding in his laugh but failed. It burst out of him so hard his head threw back. Amity kicked him angrily, or tried to. He caught her foot and pressed the center of it lightly. Before she knew it she was laughing along with him. Amity wiped the tears from her eyes when her laughter receded to faint giggles. After everything that happened tonight, all the fear and suspense, it was nice to laugh together.

This was nice.

Luka smiled at her from the other end of the couch and gently placed her foot on his leg. She watched his hand, silently curious of what would happen next. Brown eyes traveled from his hand to his waist, then to his shirt, his once crisp white henley now torn open in a few places and stained with dirt and blood from the wound that had magically stitched itself closed.

Amity stood from her place on the couch and stretched her arms high above her head, her shirt riding up in the process.

"Come on, I'll get you a shirt to sleep in." She motioned for him to follow her into her bedroom.

"Now you're trying to get my clothes off? At least take me to dinner first, kitten," he teased.

He couldn't see her bright flush as she rummaged through her dresser tucked away in her closet. Was it the nickname? Her exes never got too creative when they gave her one. Mostly sticking to baby or hun. Both boring and generic. Maybe it *was* the nickname? Maybe it was the way it naturally rolled off his tongue and sent a thrill right to her—

Amity huffed out a hot breath and stood abruptly. She pulled out an oversized men's shirt she had bought on her last snowboarding trip to Colorado. Ones she often wore it to sleep.

She turned quickly to face him. "Then don't take it . . ."

He stood just in front of her bed. He was shirtless. And he was *glorious*.

"You like what you see?"

Amity was carefully raking her gaze over him. To say he was toned was an understatement. He was made of lean muscle.

How the fuck does this guy exercise?!

There wasn't an ounce of fat on him. His chest was defined and plump.

I can describe a guy's boobs as plump right?

Can I call them boobs? They're made up of the same stuff; I don't see why I can't. Right? His chesticles?

Amity shook her head. No matter how she described them, it didn't matter. They looked like the softest pillows in the world, and she wanted to bury her face in them.

On his left pec was the head of a giant black serpent. Or was it a dragon? Its jaw was opened slightly and coiled back like it was ready to strike. Its body went to his left arm and wrapped around until the tip of its tail reached the back of his hand. There were flowers wrapped in its coils, some in full bloom and others in small, budded stems like the one on the back of his hand. The farther they went up his arm the larger they became.

"Your tattoo, I thought it was a snake, it's a dragon?"

"Close . . . It's the Midgard Serpent. You can get a closer look if you want, don't be shy, I don't bite—"

Before he could finish speaking she was already running her fingers along the creature's head. The new shirt was discarded without a second thought. Luka flinched under her featherlight touch. He watched her fingers glide across the creature's head and to his shoulder.

"Did it hurt?" she asked softly, lost in wonderment.

"In some areas," he admitted, feeling his skin catch fire with each pass of her fingertips.

"What kind of flowers are these?" she asked, stopping at one in full bloom on his bicep.

It was wrapped in the serpent's thick body. Wide eyes admired the effortless shading and white highlights with curiosity.

"Peonies . . . They're my favorite flower, so . . ."

Amity lifted his arm above her head, inspecting it further with bright curiosity.

"Wow! It really just wraps around like that! This is beautiful . . ."

She looked up to meet his eyes, surprised to find they weren't where she was looking at all. They were fixated on *her*.

"I–I also have a tattoo!" she said nervously.

Feeling that warm heat pooling in her stomach again. She dropped his arm and turned away. Fidgeting fingers gripped the sides of her shirt. He hummed curiously.

"Don't laugh! I know it's a little cliché but I really like it." With shaky hands, she removed her shirt, discarding it onto the floor beside his. Gently she gathered her hair over one shoulder so he could see her tattoo fully.

Luka was silent as he gazed at her back. She had the moon phases running up her spine. Black ink with white highlights just like his. There was no finite outline to them. The circles were merely implied when the shadows did not take up their entirety.

He reached out, resting the tips of his fingers on the new moon at the base of her spine. A nervous shiver ran through her when his rough fingertips made contact. Patiently, he waited a few moments for her to adjust then lightly ran his fingers up the curve of her spine. Lukas touch was light and gentle, but to Amity it ignited her skin like fire. He stopped at the band of her bra, even though the phases rose past it.

"Ah, sorry, is it in the way?"

"No." He gathered her hair in his hands, twirling it gently. "Do you always wear bright-colored underwear?" She jumped at the question and held her hips in her hands.

"No . . . this is new. I wanted to branch out of my comfort zone."

Hesitantly she turned to face him, but she didn't look up to meet his gaze.

He waited patiently, taking in the sight of her. Her full breasts. The vicious red of her bra that had a cute red-laced trim around the cups and band. Her cute stomach. Her strong shoulders. The small freckles on her collarbone. Brown eyes finally looked up at him.

He wasn't the first man she'd had shirtless in her room, nor was he the first man to see her half naked. Far from it. But it had been so long. Despite the desperate need to pounce on top of him, a strange nervousness came over her, like this moment was something she'd wanted for far longer than she had known him. But that didn't make sense.

Luka wrapped his hand gently around her neck and lifted her chin with his thumb until their eyes met.

"I'm glad you did. And I hope you realize just how breath-taking you are."

Brown eyes widened at the sincerity in his voice. It glided over her skin in a warm caress. She stared into his blue eyes, getting lost in their cyan color. His attention flicked to her lips and then back up to her eyes, silently asking for permission. Begging for it.

Gently she pushed herself onto her tiptoes, and he leaned down to meet her.

His lips were softer than she imagined and tasted sweet from the wine. It was a chaste kiss like one she would read about in her books, at least the tame ones. It felt long overdue and full of unspoken words. But that wasn't possible, was it? Amity let the thought die before it could fully take form. He gently pulled away and parted from her with wide eyes, like he couldn't believe they had kissed. Or at least that's what she hoped it was. Amity was about to rock back onto her heels when she was pulled back up for another kiss.

These kisses were bolder, each one leaving her more breathless than the last. She writhed in his grip, wanting to wrap her arms around his neck and pull him closer, but he was holding her tightly by the shoulders, hovering over her like he was desperately trying to keep from losing control. Amity lost her footing, nearly falling, but a strong arm wrapped around her. He kissed her deeper, following the arch her body made.

"Hold onto me," he moaned against her lips.

She wrapped her arms around his neck tightly, gasping when rough hands gripped her ass and hoisted her up like she weighed nothing at all. Instinctively her legs locked around his hips and gripped him tightly. Her pelvis pressed against his, forcing a moan out of him. The sweet sound vibrated against her lips.

Luka carried her until her back pushed into the wall. Strong hips rolled against hers. Now it was her turn to moan. He was rock hard, his erection straining against his pants and grinding against her center.

One of his hands slowly glided to her cheek, leaving every spot it touched hot and wanting in its wake. He pulled away from her for a moment to catch his breath.

"Is this okay?" he asked.

She adjusted her legs around him, causing him to swear. "Yes."

Amity kissed him long and hard, sliding her tongue over his bottom lip before pulling it between her teeth. She bit down gently and a shaky moan left him.

"My kitten likes to bite."

She nipped his lip playfully again.

"Yes—"

He claimed her mouth again, sliding his warm tongue over hers. Amity felt an ache deep inside her as he explored thoroughly.

Luka's pelvis ground against her again and she moaned loudly into their kiss. She gripped onto him tighter.

Strong hands lifted her again and placed her in his lap. Thighs tightened around his instinctively. Luka kissed her sweetly before pressing his lips then the corner of her mouth and trailing kisses across her jaw.

"Is this alright?" he purred against her neck.

With one hand he palmed her ass, massaging the flesh there. With his other, he slid it up her arm, which was gripping his bicep in anticipation, up the other side of her neck, tangling in her hair. His grip was gentle as he pulled her head toward her shoulder, giving him more access.

"Yes."

Quickly Luka kissed her neck before continuing his way down to her collarbone. Her thighs tightened around him. His tongue traced back up her neck. Smooth velvet against her thrumming pulse. He kissed the tender skin, sucking lightly, then dragging it between his teeth in a teasingly addictive bite. She tried to speak but the words were lost in a moan.

"Use your words, kitten," he said, nipping her collarbone.

He paused for a moment, letting her catch her breath. She was a panting mess. She took a deep breath trying to clear her mind of the thick fog it had become. Her fingers gripped around his bicep tighter and tangled her other hand through his hair. He pressed into the touch.

"I appreciate you asking for consent. Like I really, *really* appreciate it! You're just so—like seriously some guys are just . . . and you are so—*fuck*." He had nipped her again teasingly, trying to bring her back on track. She took in a shaky breath. "I am the type of person who—where it's a yes until I say no, so . . . you don't have to ask for consent for everything because I will let you know. Does that make sense?" Amity threw her head back in embarrassment, hoping her way of explaining her type of consent made sense. Not like she could think straight anyway.

Light chills ran through her at the new touch of the tip of his nose along her collarbone.

Fuck, I could Die. Consent checks, pet names, the way his tongue feels. Where has this man been my whole life?!

"Yes, perfect sense." Without warning, he glided his warm tongue from her collarbone to her earlobe, then playfully nipped it. Amity pressed her lips together tightly, trying to suppress the sounds that escaped her. Her thighs tightened around him. "Thank you, kitten."

His undercut was sharp against her fingers when she pulled him back to her for a aggressive kiss. Each time their lips parted, they met again with more desperation than the last until they were a swirling mess of tangled tongues, clashing teeth, and shallow breaths.

Amity pushed him roughly onto his back and he rushed her down to meet him in a kiss. Rough fingertips cupped her cheeks gently and pulled away, breaking their kiss. He glanced down at her breasts, lingering on them for so long that Amity almost came out of her lavender haze. Those cyan eyes lifted back up to hers, silently asking for permission. She nodded breathlessly and kissed him again and again. Luka palmed her breasts outside of her bra, gently exploring until he found the stiff peaks of her nipples. He teased them through the fabric. She let out a satisfied sound and reached between them, fumbling for the belt buckle.

"Amity, wait—"

His words were cut off by another sweet kiss. One he almost gave in to it. *Almost.* He grabbed her hands and effortlessly flipped her onto her back. She was partially stunned by the sudden shift. It gave her brain enough time to register that they had moved to her bed. When did they move?

CHAPTER TEN

Luka took a moment to catch his breath. She had successfully undone his belt; if he waited any longer, his pants would unzip themselves. He was already reaching his limit.

"It's late, I should go," he finally managed.

A mix of emotions flashed in her eyes. Confusion. Anger. Fear. And one he knew all too well and hoped he would never see in her eyes. *Abandonment.*

He leaned back, taking his weight off her. She pulled herself up. They were eye level.

"You want to go?" she asked softly.

Luka nodded, then immediately shook his head no. Leaving was the last thing he wanted to do. He noticed he was still holding her wrists in his hands. She quirked her head to the side in that cute curious way that reminded him of a cat. He released her.

"Then stay."

The hopeful tone of her voice shot through him. He finally looked up at her, into her beautiful brown eyes. He needed to stop now. This was wrong and he knew it.

"I can't," he said with a shaky breath. He scrambled his brain to find an excuse. "We've been drinking, it's not right."

She took his cheeks in her hands pulling him closer to her.

"We had one glass, Luka."

The way she said his name. *Fuck* it did things to him. He had waited so long for this. Years. To feel her. To touch her. To give himself completely to her. But he could wait a little longer. He *had* to.

Amity kissed him softly.

"It's alright," she whispered.

No, it wasn't. Nothing about this was okay.

He let her kiss him again, pull him back on top of her. Amity lips were gentle and sweet. She smelled of spring flowers from her perfume and cinnamon from the many cinnamon brooms she decorated her walls with.

Luka kissed her desperately.

I need to stop. I have to stop. Cyan eyes glowed slightly. His heart was racing. He pulled back just enough to whisper a command.

"*Sleep.*"

Amity's arms untangled from him, falling beside her onto the soft blanket. Luka waited only a moment before sitting back. Rough hands ran through his hair in frustration and buried his head in his hands. Fresh hot tears stung his cheeks.

"I'm sorry."

He repeated it over and over until his heartbeat steadied. Amity lay unconscious on her bed with a peaceful expression on her face.

Luka watched her silently, for how long he didn't remember. A soft meow brought him out of his rampant thoughts. Freaya jumped onto the bed and rubbed against his back. He smiled down at her and gently scratched the inside of her left ear, just how she always liked it.

"That was close, Freaya, too close."

Luka went back into the living room. Silently he cleaned the now-empty wine glasses then recorked the bottle and put it in the kitchen. He smiled at the ward jar in the corner of the apartment, happy it was still there. Slowly he went around and turned off each and every light. He pulled a pair of old oversized pajama pants from her dresser and changed into them. Luka didn't bother with the shirt she pulled for him earlier.

After turning off her bedroom light, he carefully tucked her into bed. Hesitant hands pulled her close to him, wrapping his arms around her torso. She felt like fire in his arms. He sighed deeply taking in the sweet perfume she rarely wore. Gently he pressed his lips to the top of her head.

"I'm sorry, but I can't. Not until I fix everything. Not until I find him."

CHAPTER ELEVEN

Sandalwood, seasalt, and the sweet flowery scent of her perfume filled her senses, waking her up from a well-rested and euphoric sleep. Amity nuzzled her head against her pillow. It vibrated underneath her. Eyebrows furrowed together despite her closed eyes. She clutched the bedsheet and pulled it closer to her face. Her hand grazed the mattress lightly. Her warm *breathing* mattress.

Amity stretched her legs only to have one of them caught. No, not caught. *Entwined.* Entwined in someone else's strong legs. Amity nuzzled into the warm chest she was using for a pillow. She felt the shoulder beneath her move as the hand attached to it flexed and tightened around her. Yawning into the blankets she nuzzled deeper until the covers were over her nose. Opening her eyes was a reluctant struggle. She didn't want to wake up yet. If this was a dream, Amity wanted to stay here for as long as possible. Forever if she had the option.

A tattooed hand gently tucked her hair behind her ear.

"It's alright, I have you. Go back to sleep."

Luka's voice was deeper in the morning, and she felt it rumble through his chest when he spoke. Tired fingers unclenched the bedsheets and traveled to hold his side as a rough padded thumb traced idle circles on her hip beneath the covers.

"You stayed," she finally mumbled.

"I did," he hummed, and then kissed the top of her head.

"I'm sorry I fell asleep," she said, looking up at him apologetically.

The last thing she remembered was kissing until her lips were swollen. They were about to take off the rest of their clothes and then she passed out. She must have been exhausted. His muscles tensed around her.

"You have nothing to apologize for," he said, kissing her forehead again. "Sleep. I want to stay like this a little longer," he cooed, wrapping his arms tighter around her. Luka was like a furnace, engulfing her in his body heat. She wanted nothing more than to give in to it. To stay with him just like this. Holding each other in a serene bliss.

"How long were you up?"

He adjusted himself beneath her so they were eye level. Gently she brushed his hair back out of his face. Instinctively he leaned into her touch with a content smile gracing his lips.

"Not long," he admitted.

He pressed his forehead to hers gingerly. Amity's cheeks heated at the gesture.

He's so cuddly in the morning . . . Adorable! She rubbed his chest lightly.

"Your *favorite* spot," Luka teased.

Teasingly she pinched his nipple causing him to grip her tightly. She shrieked as he pulled her even tighter, holding her flush against his chest that rumbled with warm laughter. He pecked her lips quickly.

"You don't have work today, right?" Luka asked, running his fingers up and down her spine.

She wiggled one of her arms free and curiously tapped his nose ring.

"No, shop's closed on Sundays."

He caught her finger lightly before she could poke him again while his other hand settled on the small of her back.

"Then go back to sleep, kitten."

Amity smiled down at him, then leaned down and gently pressed her lips to his. Those lips were addictive and sweet. Each time she pulled away she immediately went back for more. Never satisfied.

"That's not sleeping." He smirked between kisses.

She hummed in agreement, letting him guide her back down onto the mattress. It shifted beneath his weight as he leaned over her. Rough fingers trailed up the sides of her body sending a delightful shudder through her. Amity reached up and gently cupped his cheeks in her hands. Those cyan eyes closed and he took in a deep breath, leaning into her touch with a deep humm of approval, enjoying the moment to its fullest. Amity licked her lips in anticipation when his gaze fell on her.

"Amity, I have something to tell you—"

Someone knocked at the front door. Luka froze. Brown, tired eyes narrowed at the horrid interruption.

She glanced out the window trying to find an indication of time. The sun was high in the sky, which considering it was late October gave no real indication. It could be 10:00 a.m., 7:00 a.m., or even noon. Exactly what time was it? Brown eyes narrowed on the front door, which she could barely see from her bedroom.

"I'm not expecting anyone," she groaned.

Luka followed her gaze with a narrow stare. Whoever it was, they were persistent and knocked again.

With a heavy sigh, he reluctantly rose from the bed.

"I'll go," he reassured.

Luka scanned the floor for his discarded jeans from the night before and shrugged them on. Then a shirt. It was a deep blue and said Breckenridge in bright colors across the front. Amity sat up at the edge of the bed, intent to go with him. Cyan eyes glanced down at her chest, where her fiery red bra covered her breasts, and then back up to her flushed face. She covered herself in embarrassment and tossed a small pillow at him. He laughed, catching it with one hand and tossing it to the floor where her shirt lay in a puddle. Luka crawled over the bed to where she bit her lip in anticipation. He kissed her hungrily, and just as he slid his tongue across her bottom lip ready to explore her mouth once more, the knocking persisted. Louder than before.

Luka sighed in annoyance and turned to go but not before playfully nipping her bottom lip.

He trudged over to the door ready to immediately turn whoever it was away, nearly tripping over Freaya who started demanding food the second she saw him. He picked her up gently and kissed her head. The black void struggled in his grip, wanting food more than cuddles.

Amity stretched out her arms high above her head hearing a satisfied crack. She fell back onto her bed with a wide smile. An excited heat pumped in her veins. She clutched one of the pillows in her arms and rolled to the edge of the bed, burying her face into it, feeling her cheeks flush. She inhaled deeply, smelling only him. Only Luka. Once more she stretched out her legs with a soft humm, then leaped off the bed.

Amity went to the mirror in the corner of her room and fixed her hair. Her reflection beamed back. Flushed cheeks, messed-up hair, no makeup, and the goofiest grin she had ever worn. She threw on a loose crew neck from her closet and let it hang off one shoulder. She peered closer into the mirror, pulling her hair to one side. An unstoppably silly grin spread across her lips with a little giggle. He marked her, faintly, but they were there. Little bites along her neck and collarbone. Amity exhaled audibly. Why did that make her so happy? Fuck it, it didn't matter. She was happy and that's all that mattered.

God, she wanted to run around her apartment and shout at the top of her lungs. Silently she planned out the rest of the day in her head. They would order food and stay in bed for the next hour or so. They would finish what they started last night, then he would ask to borrow her shower. I have a better idea, she would say. Then they would shower together and repeat everything all over again. Her eyes drifted closed imagining it. Imagining *afterward*. Where he would hold her in his strong arms and they would fall asleep together, just like last night. And if she could walk by the end of the day, maybe they could go for a nice autumn walk.

Amity exhaled a soft humm letting herself get lost in the fantasy. Wrangled her hair into a braid then let it hang off of her covered shoulder. *Let him see his marks and want to make more.* She giggled with giddy excitement, only to have it cut short by someone yelling in her living room.

"What the fuck are you doing here?"

Amity's eyes went wide. She knew that voice. *No no no! Why is he here?!*

She ran to her living room nearly tripping over her own feet. Luka was holding a struggling Freaya in his arms. His eyes met hers and, gosh, what did he say to him? Luka looked like he was dealt a heavy blow. Those cyan held that same remorse they had last night when she asked to go with him and then again when he asked her to stay out of sight.

She narrowed her eyes on the man in front of him. Alex briefly glanced at her but then refocused on Luka. Her brother's brown eyes narrowed on him like he held some personal grudge and was at the end of his rope.

Alex was really angry. That alone scared her. One time he and his friend brought her to a college party and she watched him beat the shit out of someone. She had to pry him off of the poor kid before he did permanent damage. Amity swallowed hard.

"Hey, what's u—"

"I've been calling you *nonstop*," he demanded, refocusing his attention on her.

"My phone was on silent, or it's dead somewhere." Honestly she didn't know which. Between everything that happened last night, the whereabouts of her phone was the least of her worries. "I just forgot to text you, I'm sorry," she quickly added.

Freaya squirmed again in Luka's strong arms, releasing a struggled yowl.

"What the hell is *he* doing here?"

Alex's tone was accusing. Amity took in a deep breath and marched toward him, her anger bubbling to a low simmer. The last thing she wanted to do was get angry in front of Luka; she hadn't even asked him to be her boyfriend yet. Well he kind of did already, in a way? Freaya tried swatting as Amity got between the two men. In any other situation she would look ridiculous. Standing on her flat feet she only came up to their chests, but she spent her whole life talking back to Alex. She stood her ground.

"I *invited* him here. This is *my* apartment. *You* don't get to barge in here and—wait." She looked between them, remembering the way Alex looked the other night. He was about to say something about Luka, about why he didn't want her hanging around him, but then cut himself off. She stepped back from them. "Do you two know each other?"

"No," Luka quickly said, placing Freaya down on the ground before she'd swipe his eye.

Something inside her chest tightened. Did he just *lie* to her?

"Cut the shit, Luka. I told you to stay away from her."

"I didn't bring her along last night, she found me."

"Last night? What happened last night?"

Alex was speaking to *her*. His voice a low growl. Brown eyes slid down to her neck where the marks she was so proud of a few minutes ago were visible. She wished she had kept her hair down.

"I—"

Freaya called from the kitchen, demanding her breakfast.

"Nothing happened." Luka cut her off, shifting slightly in front of her.

That just made Alex's temper rise. He ran his hands through his hair, exasperated.

"This is all your fault. Why can't you just leave her alone?" he shouted.

Luka's body tensed in front of her. That knot in her chest hardened. *What the hell is going on?*

"I followed him. It's my fault!"

She motioned to step forward, but Luka held up a hand stopping her. Alex didn't miss the gesture. His eyes widened like he'd seen a ghost or a demon. But Amity didn't mention the demons. He grabbed Luka by the collar and shook him.

"Alex!"

"Are you insane? After what happened last time? You're the reason why her memory was wiped!"

Amity's head slowly tilted to the side. *What did he just say?* That pit inside her chest felt heavier like it hardened into stone. The air around her chilled.

"What?"

"He didn't tell you yet? Of course not, why would he?"

Luka shoved him off, forcing him to stumble back a few feet. He looked at Amity, his wide eyes meeting hers.

"It's not like that."

He was talking to her, but all Amity could focus on was that heavy feeling in her chest. *He lied.* The warm happiness she coveted was now gone. Iced over. Frozen solid. Not just Luka. *Alex* lied. That felt like a stab in the gut. What was he talking about, "memory wipe"?

"It's *exactly* like that!" Alex shouted.

"It was an *accident!*" he pleaded, refocusing on her brother.

"What the hell are you two talking about?!" she shouted. They didn't hear her.

"An 'accident'?" Alex exhaled a frustrated breath. He ran his hands through his hair, gripping it at the roots. "How many times are you going to say that? You told me she had a year. Time's almost up and what do you have to show for it?"

"I almost found him!" Luka's voice cracked.

Fuck, it actually *cracked.* Amity hugged her arms close, giving her fingers something to touch. She needed something to ground herself. Nothing they were saying was making any sense.

"Alex!"

"Almost isn't good enough Luka!"

Freaya cried out again from the kitchen. Amity gripped the center of her crew neck. The stone in her chest was heavier. It was getting hard to focus. She tried to slow her breathing down. When she finally spoke, it was almost a whisper.

"A *year*? *Memory wipe*? What are you both talking about?"

"This dumbass brought you on one of his *jobs* and . . ." Alex went silent as he finally looked her over.

Amity's eyes were wide. Her face was flushed and her breathing was fast, too fast; though she was doing her best to keep it steady. She was holding onto her shirt like it was a goddamn lifeline. He fucked up. Quickly he glanced at Luka. Them cleared his throat making sure his voice was level when he spoke.

"Nothing. It's nothing."

"It's not nothing!" she breathed. He wasn't going to backpedal out of this!

Silence hung heavily between them. It became so thick she could choke on it. Luka took a small step toward her.

"It's nothing." Luka repeated.

His voice was soft, like it had been when he said he wanted to stay in bed longer. Amity wished she was back in bed with him now. How did everything turn upside down? He reached for her.

"Amity—"

"What. Happened?"

Luka's hand fell limply by his side. He hung his head low. Alex's brows creased and he fixed his stare on the knot she had bundled the front of her shirt into. He swallowed hard.

"Luka took you on a job last year and . . ." He exchanged a glance with Luka. Brown eyes met cyan.

"And?"

"I . . ." Luka inhaled deeply. "It didn't go as planned. Your memory was fractured. It wasn't a punishment for you. Godsdamn demon." His voice was shaky as he spoke.

Amity quirked her head just a bit. This wasn't making any sense. *Wasn't a punishment for me? What did that even mean?* Her eyebrows furrowed in confusion.

Luka leaned into the back end of the couch, letting out a frustrated sigh. He was about to continue again, or start over, but Alex spoke first.

"The demon, it fractured your memories." Amity's eyes flashed between them. Her memories were . . . *fractured?*

"I don't understand," she said, gripping her shirt tighter.

If she was being honest and wasn't in the middle of a panic attack, what her brother said made perfect sense, in a world where demons existed and fucked-with-people kind of way. A way she was just now aware of . . .

Wait. She looked back at her brother, confused. "How do you know about demons?" He exchanged another glance with Luka.

Something wasn't adding up. Amity's thoughts became clouded and fragmented. How did her brother know about demons? *Did* he and Luka know each other? They must judging from how they were acting, especially now. Why was he so mad about him being here? Why did he tell him to stay away from her? And her memories . . . ?

Amity dove deep into her mind trying to find the source of something missing but found nothing. Nothing—except . . . She glanced at the jar in the corner of her apartment. The one sealed with wax.

"I don't have any missing memories! Just that stupid jar and those herbs," she insisted.

"Herbs? That's—" Alex began but was cut short.

"Me, Amity. *I'm* the fractured part of your memories."

Everything seemed to stop. Did she hear him correctly? That stone in her chest felt like it weighed a hundred pounds.

Freaya called angrily from the kitchen, and Alex silently muttered a curse and went to feed her.

Amity could feel her jaw hang slack. "What are you . . . ?"

Luka turned to face her. Gently he untangled her clenched hands from her sweatshirt, leaving massive wrinkles behind. The sadness in his voice was indistinguishable. "Your memories of me were taken," he said.

Her grip tightened on his hands unintentionally. Her mind raced. What he said was ridiculous, wasn't it? A laugh burst from her, but it was hollow. She glared at their hands. Then furiously shook her head.

"No. No! Because we just met. We just met a week ago!"

"We've known each other for a very long time, Amity. We all have."

She pulled her hands out of his grasp. Hesitantly Alex stepped out of the kitchen.

"Alex, this is some sick joke, right? Like the ones you and your dumb friend used to play on me?"

The words left her mouth before she could properly think them through. She knew they sounded stupid. Knew they were wrong. She was wrong and had to face the truth of it.

"Do you remember that dumb friend's name?" he asked.

Amity froze. No. She didn't know the friend's name. Her brother's best friend. She racked her brain for answers. She saw him. He was tall with brown hair dyed blond on the top. They played volleyball at school together. She would watch them practice in the backyard. She pressed her palms to her temples, trying to see his face. She couldn't. Every time she tried, there was a black smear over it like someone had thrown paint across the picture. A piercing pain shot through her head.

Luka gently took her hands away from her face.

"Don't do that. You're going to hurt yourself."

She finally looked up at him. Really looked at him. He looked hollow, like he hadn't slept in days. He didn't look like that this this morning: He was smiling. He was laughing and teasing her. He was holding her close in a tight embrace. He was full of fire, and now . . . God, he looked like he was *broken*.

And why wouldn't he look like that? He'd just been caught in a lie. Amity's wide eyes narrowed on him.

That's right. He *lied*.

He knew who she was the moment she ran into him that morning. He knew who she was when he asked her on that date. He wasn't being cheeky; he *knew* she didn't have a boyfriend. He knew she didn't usually go out after work.

Rage bubbled deep inside her. Luka watched carefully, his eyes growing wide. He knew what was coming.

Just what the hell were we? Friends? Lovers? Were we a couple? Did he think he could just manipulate me into a relationship because I was now a blank slate for him?!

She ripped her hands out of his grasp.

"Freaya knows you. You knew where all the herbs were."

"Amity—"

"You knew I didn't have a boyfriend when you asked me out. You weren't being cheeky! You knew everything about me—my schedule, the shows I watched, that I didn't go out after work—"

"Yes, but I didn't . . ." Luka tried to interject further but she was in a rage and there was no stopping her. Her face was heated with anger. Tears pricked her eyes.

"Was this your chance? Did you think you had a better shot at manipulating me into a relationship because I was now this blank slate for you?!"

"You were never that to me . . ."

Amity couldn't hear him over her own anger.

"What was your plan anyway? Were you just going to trick me into a relationship and let my other memories disappear forever?"

She was charging toward him, forcing him back until he hit the door with a loud *thud!* When did she start walking?

"Did you even care?"

"Amity, that's enough."

She turned on her brother.

"I don't want to hear another word out of you! You've been keeping this from me for a fucking year. A year, Alex. You're my brother. You're supposed to protect me from guys like him." Tears stung her cheeks.

"Alex had nothing to do with this, I asked him to—"

"And you." She jabbed Luka so hard in the chest she nearly broke her finger. "How can I believe anything you say, anything you've *said* . . . ? Did you even try to get them back at all?"

"Amity."

Her brother's voice pulled her back, but it was too late. She had crossed a line. She could see it in Luka's face. Those beautiful cyan eyes were devastated; worse, they were heartbroken. And she was sobbing. She hid her face in her oversized sleeves shamefully.

"Just get out. *Both* of you."

CHAPTER TWELVE

Amity let her arm hang over the edge of the tub, beckoning Freaya forward, but the little void was persistent in her sitting position by the bathroom door. Sitting, staring, and standing guard. Her usual routine whenever Amity bathed.

"I bet you were a creepy pervert in a past life. Why else would you be staring at me?" Amity mocked.

She had been soaking long past the point her fingers pruned, but she refused to leave. Too tired to wash her hair, it was thrown into a haphazard bun. A heavy sigh left her lips again like it did before for the thousandth time that day. How long had she been in the tub soaking? An hour? Two? Thirty minutes? It didn't matter; she needed to actually wash her body and get out soon before she passed out.

Originally she decided to bathe to clear her mind. To calm her nerves.

To. Stop. Fucking. Crying.

Turning over in the warm water and slowly sank down into its heat. Resting her chin in her hands just above the water and slowly rocked her stomach against the tub's smooth bottom.

As if to spite her further, Freaya jumped onto the toilet lid, quirking her furry head slightly to the side. Amity sighed audibly, sinking her head deeper into the water until it barely touched her nose.

Why had she been crying so much? That bothered her like a thorn in her side. Was it that he lied to her?

Sure, that pissed her off, *monumentally* pissed her off, but that couldn't be all. Amity rose from the tub suddenly and with consequence. Head spinning, she caught herself on the tiled wall at the back wall of the shower. *Steady*, she told herself.

Was it because something had been taken from her? Her memories . . .

Amity searched her mind again, like she had been trying to do all morning. She couldn't see anything, but she *felt*. She could feel *things. Emotions. Anger. Joy. Rejection. Love*. They surrounded someone. Swirling among them like shadows.

They stood in a vast space on top of frozen water. A soft blue glow shining at their center where their heart should be. It was a man, tall and lean, but he wasn't all there. Looking like he was made of a dozen different brush strokes of molten black paint. He turned to her as if sensing her presence.

Then something screeched, like metal on top of glass. It screamed and pounded in her head. She cried out, jerking back and accidentally banging her hand against the tiled wall.

Amity heaved until her breath steadied. Leaning her head against the cool tile gave a small sense of relief from the throbbing pain.

A horrible feeling of helplessness slithered up her spine. Was it the fact she couldn't remember him?

Yes. That was a big part of it. A frustrated breathy groan rumbled through her. That wasn't *all* of it.

Something was taken from her. *Stolen.* That was what angered her the most. Her mind had been *violated.* Something Luka and Alex both knew and decided to keep from her.

Wet feet nearly slid when she stepped out of the tub. The soft towel gave a small sense of comfort around her when she quickly dried herself. It wasn't enough.

Freaya diligently stayed, making sure all the water had properly drained from the tub. Amity smiled down at her and scratched the back of her ears.

"Good girl."

Leaving the towel to dry on the rack in the bathroom Amity went to her room and slipped back into the clothes she had been wearing that morning. The thick cotton of the crew neck grounded her, holding her in a safe embrace.

Something bunched beneath her feet, drawing her attention. Her eyes widened at the red stain of blood in the once crisp and now-slashed shirt. Gently she neatly folded it, brought the soft fabric close to her chest, and inhaled. Seasalt and sandalwood . . . Did she still love that smell? A part of her wanted to throw the now-torn shirt in the garbage, along with everything else that scent touched. But that was ridiculous. She knew that. Not to mention extremely unsustainable.

She smelled the shirt again and cursed at the memory it brought back. Of his arms around her. Of him saying he just wanted to stay in bed longer *with her*. Warmth spread across her skin.

"Goddamnit."

Before placing the shirt gently onto her messy bed, she dragged off the fluffiest blanket and wrapped it around her shivering frame. Whether she liked the smell of him or not, it was everywhere now. Her hair. Her clothes. Her mattress. Her kitchen. Her couch. *All over her couch.* She buried her face into her oversized sleeves.

She planned to take a very large edible and become a potato on her couch for the rest of the day. Despite it only being early in the afternoon, she was utterly exhausted.

Amity just wanted to turn her brain off and forget she still loved the smell of sandalwood. Forget how angry she was at her fucking brother. But especially forget that horribly hollowing feeling that a demon violated her own mind. Something so sacred and treasured. Something that was hers alone.

A shaky breath filled her lungs and left her ragged.

Her gaze shot to the small box on her bedside table. The one that held her favorite toy. She groaned again, knowing exactly how this night would end.

She would indulge . . . in more ways than one.

She would take a small piece of her cute little chocolate edible bar from its shelf in the freezer, grab a bag of popcorn and a large glass of water, throw herself onto the couch, put on her favorite show, and let her mind be lulled into a serene, laxed state. Completely avoiding today.

And despite how much she hated how she loved how he smelled, she would wrap herself in that sweet scent and send herself over that beautiful edge.

All. Night. Long.

Amity opened the shop the next morning with sluggish movements. Something that customers *loved* beyond all belief. Just kidding. They absolutely loathed it. She threw her hair back into a ponytail and continued making coffee while casually sipping some of her own. The lavender scent hit her strongly, followed by the sweet taste of vanilla, then the bitterness of the extra cooled espresso shots she added. Luckily her father had offered to help her this morning. He calmly pushed his mop of brown hair back under his worn cap then plugged in the next customer's order. He was the level-headed parent, and definitely the reason the shop had stayed open for so long. Especially when the pandemic had closed down so many small businesses.

She was grateful for that at least. Despite the very pleasant quality time she had with her favorite toy last night, *she* woke up furious. Furious at the fact she had thought of *him* while using it. And it felt fucking *incredible*.

Not to mention Alex had yet to apologize for keeping that fact a demon stole her memories a secret. Even if those memories were just of Luka.

The ice scooper went into the bin aggressively. A little *too* aggressively. Amity was pretty sure she scared the poor girl on the other side of the counter. Once the caffeine hit her system, vanquishing the lag left over from the drugs last night, she picked up the pace, moving quickly, grabbing each new cup her father had passed her. The line, which started out the door, to her surprise, was now manageable.

Amity placed a few fresh lidded to-go cups on the counter, calling out the names of each customer as she did. Then went back to her father and the next empty cup waiting for her. There were about five people left in line, or at least that's what it looked like from her quick glance at the back wall mirror.

Out of the corner of her eye she watched her father smile at someone. He must've known them. Amity wasn't paying attention. She needed something to do. To distract herself from what happened yesterday, last night, the night *before* that. The fact that Luka could walk in that door any second while she was looking like a raging, crazy cat lady.

Luka. She narrowed her eyes on the next cup, even though it did nothing to deserve her wrath. What was he thinking trying to date her when she couldn't remember who he was? That was total manipulation! And Luka was a fucking rat bastard for it.

She paused for a moment as she pumped the vanilla into the warm coffee cup in her hand. Was he really trying to manipulate her?

Yes, because all men are bastards.

Was he though? Did Luka give her any indication that he was like everyone else? Now that she thought about it, he never acted like that asshole bad boy type that he looked like.

Except for that time that he left me at dinner . . . Her eyes narrowed as she called out the coffee owner's name. *Which he paid for and then explained for.*

Amity sighed, picking up the next cup. How could she know for certain though? She literally didn't remember him! Which apparently was also his fault. *He also never tried to explain any of this before—*

Her hands stilled. The other day when she woke up wrapped in his arms, he was trying to tell her something.

She shook her head, sending a few loose curls tumbling on either side of her face. Practiced fingers poured the dark roast into the large cup. *Whatever, I'm still mad!*

Making her way over to the pickup counter, she quickly wiped the sweat off her forehead. Brown eyes widened when she glanced down at the name written on the cup. *Oh fuck.*

Those stupidly beautiful cyan eyes locked with hers, almost making her drop the scalding hot liquid all over herself. Almost. Amity swallowed hard, unsure of what to do or say. She still held the cup in her hand, unaware that it was beginning to shake a bit.

Rough hands reached out, taking the hot cup from her and then placing it delicately on the counter. His eyes never left hers. For the briefest of moments, it was like she saw him for the first time. The curve of his jaw. The small dangling earring. His nose ring; he still wore the small black hoop. The fresh dark circles under his eyes.

"Is there something on my face?" he asked.

His voice was calm. Laced in that small gravel that it had the other morning when he was in her bed. She blinked the memory away, forcing it back into some dark corner of her mind.

"What?"

"Or do you see something you like?" His lips curved into a small smirk, testing the waters of her mood.

Wrong. That was the wrong thing to fucking say. Her previous anger filled her. She took in a deep breath through her nose, her nostrils flaring.

Amity stomped off and swiped up the next customer's cup. Her father gave her a strange look, and then he glanced at Luka in a familiar way, one she couldn't even remotely process right now. She heard Luka curse under his breath.

"I came here to talk to you," he began from the other side of the counter. Amity turned her back to him, pouring another steaming cup of dark roast for some other guy who was probably a dirty bastard.

"You haven't answered any of my calls." Amity put the fresh cup on the counter and called out the man's name. It was an older gentleman who smiled kindly at her, making her feel bad for judging him. Luka mirrored her movements. "Or my texts."

Amity took the next cup from beside her father and read the name scribbled on the back like it was the most interesting thing in the world.

It was true, she hadn't answered anything from him. She turned off her phone as soon as he and Alex left her apartment and she didn't turn it back on until this morning. It chimed over a dozen times! All with texts from him. She then put it on silent and kept it on the back counter of the shop, not wanting to look at it.

"Amity—"

"I want to remind you that as a manager I am under obligation to be nice to you in order to coerce you into buying more." She spoke slowly in a low voice trying very, *very* hard to rein in her temper.

The last thing she wanted to do was explain anything to her father of all people, who, despite continuing to work, could hear every word they were saying. Speaking of, she glanced at her father. There were only a few more people left in line.

Damnit! She was grateful the rush would be over soon, but that meant Luka would have the perfect chance to drag her into a conversation or drag her *away* to have a conversation. She didn't want that.

Abruptly she turned to the ice machine, taking out her frustration as she dug longer than necessary into the frozen cubes. As she reached for the caramel syrup, she caught sight of her reflection, leaving her momentarily stunned. She *did* look like some raging crazy lady. Cheeks flushed in embarrassment, and she quickly set the cup to the side. Skilled fingers wrangled and retied her hair into a ponytail. It wasn't much but it would have to do. *And of course he sees me like this!*

She wanted to scream.

Luka's mouth hung open like her words stung him. An audible breath filled his lungs.

"I will buy this whole damn store if you just listen to me—"

"However, that does *not* mean that I have to be nice to you."

Amity turned, quickly finished the drink she was making, then called out the person's name. It was another regular, a sweet girl who stopped in after her early-morning yoga classes, who slowly looked Luka over before taking her drink. He didn't notice. Amity did, and that only made her more pissed off.

The regular walked off, and before Amity could turn away again, Luka leaned over the counter, rough fingers wrapped around her wrist.

"Kitten."

Her cheeks flushed at the nickname, the one she hated. The one she liked only when it passed his lips. The one that she hated how much she enjoyed hearing pass his lips.

"Don't call me that. Take your dark roast and get out."

A new wave of embarrassment crashed over her. Flustered in front of all these people, looking like a mess. Angry with him for so many reasons that she couldn't even think of all of them. He was still holding her hand.

Their eyes found each other. Fuck, the way he was looking at her. He looked desperate. His voice was softer now.

"Please, Amity."

She took her hand back, almost dragging him along with it. Her teeth ground together behind her lip. *Don't you fucking cry. Not now. Not here. You've cried enough!*

Yeah, like that was any help.

She marched off to the end of the counter where there was a small gap for people to walk through. Then stormed straight into the bathroom.

By the time she came back, Luka was long gone, the shop was empty, and her father was glaring at her from behind his paper. She grabbed a clean rag from under the counter and the cleaning solution and sprayed the rag a few times, enjoying the sweet scent for a few moments.

Her father peeked up from his paper. He was casually leaning against the counter, wearing his usual paint-stained jeans and a long sleeve from his favorite eco-friendly adventure company. His cap was also from the same company, *obviously*. It seemed to be the only brand he owned. Amity recalled that Rex had described him as . . . "crunchy" when they first met him. Perfect description really.

He liked painting in the mountains, loved hiking, and spent the majority of his life in the Colorado mountains as a ski bum where he met her mother at a Phish concert. So yeah. *Crunchy* was the perfect description for him. *Granola* crunchy.

"Sorry, I had to pee."

A basic excuse but a fair one.

"What are you fighting about now?" her father asked in a lax tone, as if this was some mundane question he'd grown tired of asking.

Amity quirked her head when she met his gaze in the mirror. Was he talking about Luka?

"I swear you kids just love to argue."

Amity's eyes widened. He *was* talking about Luka!

Her father laughed when he saw her mouth hang open in surprise.

A feeling of triumph came over her. This was her chance to know more about Luka. Her father was a total chatterbox, if she just let him ramble like usual . . . She went to clean the counter, making sure she was actively listening but trying not to make it too obvious. Like when she had asked Rex directly about the herbs in her cabinet, who had immediately given her a questionable look.

"You know," her father began, elongating the word as long as he could, "I always thought you two kids would end up getting together." He went back to his article. Amity's ears perked up.

Her father had said "end up getting together," which meant they weren't a couple before, at least as far as her father knew. That meant Luka was close enough to her so that her father knew him, and judging by the way Alex was acting around him the other day, her brother knew him as well. Was Luka a family friend then? Did she grow up with him?

"Why would you think that?" she said, trying very hard not to sound like she needed to know the answer. Luckily her father didn't notice the shift in her voice.

He lifted a shoulder in a shrug, then flipped a page. "Well, when you were little, you were always following him and your brother around like a little kitten."

Amity's eyes went wide. So Alex did know him! Not just know him, by the sound of it they were childhood friends. She quickly sipped her drink, a drink she should be replacing with tea because her nerves were now too jittery by the new discovery. And that wasn't even the *biggest* discovery.

I followed him around like a kitten?! Amity closed her eyes in embarrassment. *God, was that where he came up with that nickname?* If that was the case, it meant he was paying attention to her, noticing her. Just when did he start doing that?

Her father continued when she didn't respond.

"Your mother and I actually had a bet going when you were teenagers, guess I lost." Amity's head whipped in his direction.

"You lost?"

She nearly choked on her coffee. With the way her mother constantly questioned her about her love life, she was shocked her father was more interested than *her.*

"You're surprised?"

"I just figured that since Mom is so *invested—*"

"I'm *invested,*" he insisted, folding up his paper roughly.

Amity looked at him blandly. He narrowed his eyes at her before running his hands through his hair, a nervous trait he passed onto his son.

"And besides, I didn't lose."

Amity's hand froze mid-swipe across the pickup area's countertop. Her father smiled at her flushed cheeks.

" 'I would buy this whole store if you'd just listen to me,' I believe is what he said." Her father teased.

Amity's cheeks heated in embarrassment. She turned away, causing her father to laugh again.

"Oh, I can't *wait* to tell your mother."

She slurped loudly and tossed the now-empty latte into the trash with more force than necessary. Her fingers thrummed on the now-clean counter, trying to come up with something to say but finding nothing believable.

"She'll be so excited, she'll get off your back about taking over the shop."

He said with a knowing look, like he was aware just as much as she was that this shop, this life, wasn't what she really wanted. Maybe what she *did* want was tied into her fractured memory somehow?

Her father grabbed one of the empty trays in the corner, making his way past her to pick up any abandoned cups or trash in the cafe.

"She means well. You've just been off your game the past year or so. *She* thinks it's a lack of agency, I think you just need time. There's nothing wrong with not wanting what your parents set out for you."

A shaky breath filled her. Her father could be so sincere at times. But her mother—Amity had to fight the impulse to burst out laughing at the word agency.

If her mother only knew what agency Amity took a few nights ago.

CHAPTER THIRTEEN

It had been three days since he last saw her. Three whole days.

No texts.

No calls.

Nothing.

Luka slowed his jog and came to a stop. Throwing his head back, he let out a tired sigh. Hot breath drifted into the cold morning air like dragon smoke. This morning had been particularly cold. He had left his apartment wearing his running pants along with a compression shirt and a light jacket. It was barely enough.

He leaned against the railing that lined the riverside and wiped the fresh sweat from his brow. Despite knowing full well he would've heard any incoming messages through his earbuds, he opened his phone to check. First he went to his call log.

No new calls.

Inhaling sharply, he opened his texts.

Oct. 15, 10:30 am

> *I know you're still there, pickup.*

Oct. 15, 10:35 am

> *Let me explain.*

Oct. 15, 10:40 am

> *Please, Amity!*

Oct. 16, 7:45 am

> *Are you busy during your lunch hour? I want to talk to you about yesterday, if that's okay.*

Oct. 16, 9:00 am

> *Please get some sleep tonight . . .*

Those last two were sent the sixteenth.

It was now the nineteenth.

No texts.

No calls.

Nothing.

Luka gritted his teeth, turned off his punk music, and carefully put his earbuds back into their case before shoving it back into his pocket. He reread the last message he'd sent her.

Get some sleep? Get some sleep?! He wanted to dive head-first into the river. *What the hell was I thinking?!*

He leaned harder onto the railing. He needed to apologize. What happened wasn't his fault; he knew that, but *she* didn't! She thought he was a manipulative scumbag. He exhaled a ragged breath and pressed his sweaty forehead to the chilled metal of the railing

He opened his text messages and typed fast, immediately erasing them after he typed.

I miss you.|

I was wrong.|

I lied but not in the way you think I did.|

I'm a terrible fucking asshole and I deserve to have my balls cut off and fed to the ducks.|

He looked up from his phone at the little family of so-called ducks. They idly quacked as they drifted past.

Maybe that last one was a bit excessive. Regardless, he did need to apologize. With a heavy sigh, he shoved his phone back into his pocket, rested his head in folded arms that were starting to numb from the cold railing, and stared into the river.

Its sides had already iced over, but the center flowed smoothly. His eyes drifted to a close listening to the churning of the water, tuning out the sounds of other joggers and happy couples in the park as they passed by.

Since their "argument," Luka had done nothing but prowl the streets. In fact, last night was the first time he got a decent night's sleep. He rubbed his eyes against his jacket sleeve. Last night was lucky. Last night he finally got the last piece he'd been searching for. It would be easier if he left his clues like a normal person instead of giving them to random demons. But that *thing* was anything but *normal*. It was a demon, and the worst sort.

Now all Luka had to do was prepare for the battle ahead. His gaze shifted from the river to the sky. It was painstakingly clear, even though he distinctly remembered the forecast saying it was going to be cloudy. Maybe that's why the park was bustling?

A small voice in the back of his mind resurfaced. Whispering in a horrid voice. Almost like a screech but dampened. He hated that voice.

What if I get her memories back?

What if she still hates you? it whispered.

Then it would've still been worth it.

Are you sure? it sneered.

Luka rubbed his temples in aggravation. He couldn't think like that. Not when he was so close. But the voice was right. What if she still hated him by then?

He would have to apologize, and *soon*. But how?

"How the hell am I gonna fix this?" he muttered to himself.

"You can start by getting some fucking sleep!"

Luka turned from the river and looked at his old friend with wide eyes.

"Alex?"

A chill breeze blew past as Alex made his way across the road, almost getting knocked over by two rollerbladers. He was wearing a thick jacket and a black face mask. Very carefully carrying two steaming cups of coffee. Luka leaned back onto the railing and stretched out his calves. Alex watched him, uncomfortably shifting from one foot to the next. An awkward silence passed with another chill breeze. Alex shivered, nearly dropping the coffee in his hands. Luka straightened to his full height but didn't move. Alex narrowed his eyes, and if his mouth wasn't covered, Luka would have confirmation of a frown.

"Where's your jacket? Never mind, will you just take this. I know you haven't slept," he said, shoving a coffee toward him. Luka took it only so it wouldn't spill.

Alex immediately shoved his free hand back into his pocket.

"What's this for?" Luka asked, silently reading the label.

Hot chocolate coffee. *What the hell was that?* A part of him wanted to throw the coffee into the river or back at his face. One would lead to littering, the other would lead to dragging his ass to the closest hospital. Amity would probably hate him more too. His eyes narrowed on Alex.

"You know I only drink—"

"You liked it when *she* made it for you," Alex recalled, glancing back out to the river.

He lowered his mask and took a sip of his drink. The same drink he got for Luka. An audible breath left the witch, and he leaned back onto the freezing railing.

"That's completely different."

Alex smiled out of sight, knowing that if Luka saw it, he would jog away. He bridged the distance between them, leaning against the railing and facing the river.

Amity had made these drinks for them a few winters back. She was so proud of her accomplishment, even if it was just a chocolate mocha. She was practically beaming when Luka tasted it and said it was the best thing he'd had all season.

"Look . . ." Alex began.

He turned, placed his coffee on the railing and ran a hand through his hair. Luka held his own cup a little tighter, letting the heat warm his freezing fingers. Now that he was standing still, the cold was creeping into him faster. He glanced over his shoulder, waiting for Alex to continue.

Heavy boots scuffed the pavement as Alex shuffled from one foot to the next.

"I was an asshole, okay. She should've never found out that way."

A moment passed. And then another. He turned toward Alex.

"Wow." He elongated the word. "That looked like it hurt."

"Shut"—he was interrupted by a sneeze. A *painful*-looking sneeze. Poor guy had his head between his hands. He ran his fingers through his hair and glared at Luka, who was trying very, *very* hard not to laugh—"up."

The laugh burst free in an instant.

Luka leaned an elbow onto the railing, looking his friend over. Was "friend" even the right word now? Sure they had known each other since they were ten—they went to high school together, were on the volleyball team, followed each other to college, and all with Amity trailing behind them—but that all changed when . . . Luka shook the thought away. He stopped laughing.

Alex heaved a heavy sigh. "Look, I know coffee isn't going to magically fix everything. I wish it could."

Luka wished he could smile at that. Alex knew full well that Luka could spell a coffee to make someone feel a certain way, something he had never done before, save for the occasional prank here and there. But he couldn't bring himself to smile. He waited for Alex to continue.

"I said some things. Horrible things. And not just on Sunday." He ran a frustrated hand through his hair, and Luka felt a knot form in his chest. "I . . ." He drew in a cold breath. "I should never have said those things. And hearing Amity say them to you made me realize how awful that was of me. I know that's not an excuse but . . ." He took another sip from his drink.

Another chill wind blew by, sending shivers down Luka's spine. Alex shuddered in his coat. Luka swallowed hard; all he could do was stare.

"God, how did you even meet anyway?"

Luka blinked until he came out of his daze; the knot in his chest loosened a bit. The corners of his mouth tilted up as he remember the fated encounter.

"She ran into me, *literally*."

"Fuck, even without knowing you, she still found you."

It was Alex's turn to laugh. If his sister was anything, it was persistent. Luka cracked a smile. A small moment passed after the masked former-friend's laugh faded. He looked at his old friend and toyed with the fresh cup in his hands. A smile clearly visable beneath his mask. "She still likes you."

"Not anymore," he bit out, too quickly for his own good. Alex smirked.

"Oh she *definitely* does. She would've never let you do that in the shop before."

"So that was *you* snooping on us? Bastard." Luka clicked his tongue.

Alex lifted a shoulder nonchalantly and took another sip of his coffee.

"There are real creeps out there, and when my sister starts hanging out with some pretty bad boy with a nose ring, I definitely have to do a thorough investigation."

Luka stared at him for a moment before fully relaxing against the railing. The corners of his mouth tilted up. It wasn't a full smile, but it was a familiar look to Alex. Something that wasn't entirely happy but slightly amused.

"I'm a *very* pretty bad boy."

Luka all but purred the word pretty. A jab to Alex's ego.

Back in high school, Alex was the one who was popular with the girls, but Luka? Luka peaked in college. Everywhere they went, Alex caught men and women staring at Luka, following him, watching him as he read in the library, which he did often. Alex never knew anyone who liked to read as much as he did; well, except for Amity. Oh! And then when he started reading romance novels in the school library, novels he discovered when he swiped them from Amity's bookshelf when she wasn't looking, it was over. Alex had to fight people off just to see his friend.

He huffed out a breath before sneezing loudly again. Luka burst out laughing, nearly spilling his coffee. This caused Alex to start yelling, only to be sent into another sneezing fit that only made his friend laugh harder. It didn't take long until Alex was laughing too. By the time they both calmed down, they had fresh tears stinging their eyes.

Luka held the cup in both hands, then pressed one palm to his cheek. Alex was right, he should've worn a thicker coat. He was almost frozen. *Almost.*

"Why are you out here if you're sick, and on the other side of the river?" He wiped away the last tears before the bitter cold made them sting.

Alex hesitated for a moment then tossed his now-empty coffee cup into a nearby trash bin. With eyes focused on the river, he pulled his mask back up. "Krystal is sick with a cold, and I . . ." He ran a frustrated hand through his hair before throwing up his fur-lined hood. "And I needed to see you."

Luka felt that knot in his chest again, but it wasn't heavy. It felt warm. He waited expectantly for his friend to continue. Alex's eyes stared out into the river, and Luka saw the faint amber in them. He looked at his friend. Truly looked. He knew he and Amity shared similar features. Their straight noses, dark brown eyes, and equally dark curly hair—Amity's being curlier, of course. They were so alike and especially in their profiles. He could see traces of her. Maybe that made Alex a little pretty too.

"You can fix this right?" Alex turned his full attention from the river to his friend. His tone was deeper now, serious. In all the years Luka knew him, he had only heard him speak this way a few times before.

Luka faced him and nodded curtly. "I have everything I need now. I'm going to fix this." His cyan eyes gave a faint glow as he spoke sending a chill up his spine.

"When?"

"Halloween."

"Fuck, that's soon!"

Luka nodded curtly. It was close. Too close.

A silence grew between them, filled with the idle chatter of people passing by and of the small family of ducks in the river, quacking and fluffing out their feathers. Alex glanced at his friend.

"Luka?"

"Hmm?" He muttered, lifting the cup to his lips.

"I'm sorry. This was *never* your fault."

Luka hesitated, stopping just before the rim of the cup touched his lips. That warm feeling in his chest burned and grew heavy again. He felt hot tears prick and sting his eyes. He gritted his teeth trying to bite them back, but it was no good. They ran down his cheeks, leaving an icy pain in their wake. He chugged his coffee, draining the now-tolerable, tempered liquid. It wasn't as good as when Amity made it.

Luka looked himself over in the nearby shop window for the twelfth time. The sun had set a few hours ago, creating lovely, vibrant shades of warm oranges, reds, and pinks before drifting to cooler tones of blues and purples until it faded into a beautiful, dark night sky. Luka took several pictures of it before making his way over to the shop. He wanted to show them to Amity later. Fidgeting fingers fiddled with his cornicello. *Maybe not tonight though . . .*

When they were kids they would often watch the sunset together. Luka inhaled a cold breath of air.

"I'm sorry. This was never your fault."

That. That stung. Even he wasn't completely sure why. But it sent him into a crying fit when he made it back to his apartment. He cried so much, he ended up falling asleep on his couch. It was a very well-deserved and long-overdue nap.

Luka gently tugged on his hair tie holding the top half of his hair in a braid.

It wasn't his fault. He knew that. But it still . . .

He swiped a stray tear under his eye.

Get it together, Luka, he ordered his reflection.

He straightened his leather jacket over his black compression shirt, adjusted his belt that looped through his dark wash jeans, and fixed his black hoop in his nose. He winced as the cold metal brushed his skin, making him regret that he didn't switch it out for a stud. With a huff he adjusted the triangle stud in his ear.

Enough! You look fine!

A small laugh escaped him. That's exactly what Alex would say if he were here.

With a curt nod to his reflection, he rounded the corner toward the shop. Opening the door a little rougher than intended and drawing the attention of people reading in their chairs and scattered about the shop. Amity sat on a stool behind the counter, a sketchpad balanced on her lap as she swiped the eraser of her pencil across the page.

When she finally acknowledged him, her gaze didn't travel higher than his waist. She tossed her sketchpad onto the counter next to an old hat, the same one her father wore a few days ago.

He must be helping out more now . . .

"Hi, what can I get for you?" she asked mechanically; not even bothering to look up at him. Cyan eyes looked her over for a moment.

The bags under her eyes were finally gone and her eyes were no longer puffy. *Good, that's good.* However, the fact that Luka knew he had caused both felt like a punch in the gut. *And by punch I mean stabbed with a serrated knife.* The fact she didn't realize who was standing in front of her also hurt. Alex said before she'd been working eight-to-ten-hour shifts. *They must be getting to her.*

His eyes narrowed before slightly widening. He was going to apologize to her but first he had to get her to *look* at him. The corner of his mouth tilted into a smirk. If there was one thing Luka knew how to do, it was how to get her attention.

"That's all I get? For your favorite customer?" He spread his hand on the counter revealing the end of a snake's tail entwined in tiny flower buds.

The corner of her mouth kicked up, but it was nothing close to a smile.

"Or not—"

"Sorry. What can I get for you?" Her voice was a little strange. Like she couldn't decide if she was amused or angry. *Another good sign . . . maybe?* It was better than her being dismissive and storming off like last time.

He pursed his lips in fake annoyance as she moved to the pay tablet still hadn't looked at him.

"Get me my regular."

Her brows furrowed. *Okay maybe that was a little too aggressive.*

". . . Okay."

". . . and a white chocolate lavender latte."

Her eyes narrowed on the screen. She knew that wasn't his regular coffee order.

"Okay—"

"Iced."

"Right!" Her eyes narrowed at the screen as she typed in the order for the third time. His smirk grew.

". . . with almond milk." With flushed cheeks she aggressively she tallied his order again. He leaned his cheek into his palm, his eyes sparkling up at her—*just one more push.*

"Aren't you curious who it's for? It's for someone special."

"I couldn't care less who you're flirting with!"

She turned the tablet toward him and slammed her hand onto the counter, brown eyes searing into his blue ones.

He paused for a moment, noting how close their faces were to each other. She had leaned over the counter a considerable distance in her rage, causing her fresh curls to tumble over her shoulders. His smirk kicked up again. Cyan eyes darkened triumphantly. She finally looked at him.

"There you are," he breathed.

That smirk spread into a smile as he took in a familiar scent. Amity was wearing her perfume again. A moment passed between them as he watched her cheeks flush deeper for another reason. If he just leaned in. Lifted his head to hers. He could kiss her. He *wanted* to kiss her.

As if the feeling of her soft lips against his was something he needed to survive. He could still remember what she tasted like. Sweet wine. He imagined she would taste a little differently now, but just as sweet. Maybe even sweeter. He pulled his bottom lip between his teeth, immediately catching her attention. Luka could think of somewhere else that was even sweeter. Someplace aching, warm, and wet. Amity jerked away and faced the back counter.

A shaky breath left him—so *close*.

Silently she prepared his order. In an attempt to suppress his impatient hand from reaching for her, he ran a it through his hair, watching her carefully. Amity was flushed, at one point she even dropped one of the plastic cups and had to get a new one.

Luka swaggered over to her when she set the drinks at the other end of the counter. He swiped up his drink and took a long sip, then exhaled, sweaty. Cyan eyes never left her stare—or was it a glare? She seemed to momentarily forget he ordered a very feminine drink, but now that look was all over her face. He hoped that glare was out of jealousy. *Fucking adorable.*

"I'll see you around, kitten."

Brown eyes rolled with a frustrated He turned to leave with that sly smirk. The fact she let him call her that was another good sign. Amity mumbled something under her breath as she watched him go. He only made it a few steps.

"Hey!"

He stopped, turning gingerly on his heel, a look of faint ignorance on his face.

"You forgot this." She strained over the counter, standing on her tiptoes, holding the latte out for him to take. Slowly he walked back over to her. He wrapped his rough fingers around hers, noting the smoothness of her skin. Cyan eyes watched as her faced flushed deeper and creep across her face as he placed her hand and the latte back onto the counter. Brown eyes traveled down to his cornicello and lingered on his chest. She inhaled sharply.

Luka leaned in closer until she had no choice but to lean back onto her heels.

His eyes bore into her. A consuming, endless cyan, glinting with mischief and especially trouble. The kind of trouble that would definitely make her parents have to close down the shop while this place was deep cleaned. The way she was looking at him now made him want to do all kinds of things with her in every space of this damn shop.

"I told you." His fingers traveled up the back of her hand and toyed with her spare hair tie. "It's for someone special."

Luka removed his hand from hers, too quickly, and immediately missed the warmth of her skin.

With wide eyes and a flushed face, she watched him. He smiled softly at her again, watching the realization dawn on her. Just before he turned to go, she spoke up softly.

"I want to apologize . . . for before." She managed, fiddling with the straw of her coffee nervously.

His eyes widened hopefully. "You have nothing to apologize for."

"I do and I will. I was too angry to listen to you when you were here last. So . . . sorry." That stubbornness returned to her voice, causing his smile to widen. Perhaps her need to apologize had something to do with those people-pleasing tendencies a customer service job gave her? Regardless, her stubbornness made him feel nostalgic. She was more sure of herself before the *incident* of her memory loss. "This, of course, does not mean that you don't also have a lot of explaining to do, Luka."

He bit back a laugh of relief, thankful she was going to hear him out.

"Yes, I do. That's why I'm here." He glanced around hesitantly at the shop's patrons scattered about in their own huddles. There were too many of them. And this conversation was something private. "Though, I think it's better if I do privately."

"Are you . . . working tonight?" The fact that she was also referring to demon slaying as something simple like "work" was amusing considering it was how *he* referred to it. Luka immediately regretted what he had to say next.

"Yes." That brightness faded from her eyes. "But . . . I can stop by when I'm finished." She beamed up at him, then he saw that question burn behind her stare. She was obviously debating on asking it, which was fair. It wasn't like Luka knew when he would be done either, but the fact that he knew Amity would be waiting on him would make him "work" faster. "I'll let you know when I'm done. Promise. Your place?"

She nodded, then took another long sip from *her* coffee. Luka's gaze didn't faulter.

"Perfect."

CHAPTER FOURTEEN

Luka was practically skipping down the street with joy.

She wanted to see him!

He was going to see *her*!

They would have a very serious conversation that would probably end in tears, but who fucking cares!

He inhaled the night air with a wide smile. Still smelling her perfume. Sweet and flowery. An impatient thumb swiped his thumb across his lips. *I can't wait to taste her again. And again. And again*—he felt his body warm beneath his jacket and tried to hide a smile as it spread wider across his lips. Luka swore he could feel her writhing against him again. Feel her swollen lips on his. Hear those little moans she made when he kissed up her neck and whispered in her ear. The way her thighs clenched around him.

Luka ran a hand over his braid and quickly averted his gaze as a couple passed by, knowing full well he looked ridiculous. Secretly he loved it. He wanted to do so much more, *see* so much more. Make up for all the wasted time he let slip through his fingers if he would've just knocked up the courage to tell her how he felt. *Fuck,* he just wanted to feel her wrapped around him as she slept. Clinging onto him like a koala. *Fucking adorable.*

Hmmm, should I buy her flowers? he pondered. Luka's smile faded a bit as that unwanted conversation loomed over him like a dark cloud. That stubborn knot formed in his chest again as a cold wind blew past. *I should buy her more than just fucking flowers.*

He drank the last of his coffee and then tossed it into a nearby trash can. Another chill ran through him.

"Everything's going to be fine," he mumbled to himself. The knot tightened. Growing heavier with a foreboding weight. "Everything is going to be fine."

A smooth practiced breath that left his lungs like fire. Luka zipped up his jacket.

When did it get so cold . . . ?

Cyan eyes widened in alert. He pulled out his cornicello, which hummed in response, glowing a faint blue. Luka felt himself lock up as he heard a voice he knew all too well. One that haunted him. Latching onto his innards like a viper. Twisting. Biting. Venomous.

The voice was a wet screech to his ears.

Yes . . . everything will be alright, witchling.

CHAPTER FIFTEEN

The door to Halley's closed with the loudest creak imaginable, something that sent a chill up Amity's spine. She never liked closing the shop by herself and then walking home alone. Something that was becoming more frequent with her longer shifts. A sigh left her lungs. Her feet were also killing her. They tapped against the ground impatiently as she double-checked the lock.

Curtains shut, lights off, security camera on, and finally the door is locked. Safe and secure, the opposite of how she felt. Inhaling a steady breath to relax herself, Amity tried desperately not to remember the last time Luka "worked," and she went outside.

"Everything is going to be fine—" Someone's hand landed on her shoulder.

"Hey—"

She shrieked, turning sharply and smacking whoever it was in the face with her book and sketchpad.

"Amity, it's me! It's Alex!" The masked man shouted with his hands up as she continued to beat him.

She paused, her book hanging just above his hooded head. Then it came down hard on his shoulder.

"Stop!"

"What the hell are you trying to do? Give me a heart attack?" That heart was hammering inside her chest.

"I had to see you."

He flung his hood back out of his face and abruptly turned, a fit of coughs rushing out of him.

"At eight thirty at night?" He continued to cough under his mask. "So not only are you stupid but you're contagious?" She smacked his arm again, lighter this time.

"I came to walk you home. Didn't you get my text?"

Amity pulled out her phone to see this so-called text. Her phone was with her the whole time; there was no way she could've missed—

The new text from Alex lit up on her screen, mocking her.

"I guess I missed it. You better not get me sick," she mumbled, turning her face away.

"I won't." He straightened, clearing his throat. "Come on, I gotta talk to you."

The heels of her boots tapped on the cobblestone as she rocked back and forth. The weighted feeling had returned to her chest, pressing down like a stone. He had *a lot* to apologize for.

"You're not coming in, I can't get sick." *Plus Luka is coming over*, but she decided not to add that last part.

He shivered beneath his jacket. "That's fine."

Their boots hit the pavement in sluggish steps, crunching over leaves as they went a full block without speaking.

"So . . . I'm sorry."

She stopped, anger heating her skin and raising her pulse. *Sorry? That's it?!*

"You need to do a lot better than fucking 'sorry,' Alex."

Amity got a better look at him under the streetlight when he stopped beside her. Despite only seeing half of his face, she could tell from those puffy glazed-over eyes that he was in no shape to go outside. The fact that he looked like such a mess made a part of her happy. As if his current state could make up for the part he played. Despite that, this was still her brother and relishing in his demise made her feel horrible. However, because he was still out here trying to apologize, despite feeling like shit, made her happy.

"I know I—"

"What happened?" she demanded.

Amity could see the mask extend and close again with his jaw. With a shaky hand, he guided her to the edge of the sidewalk under the shadow of one of the buildings.

"I don't know all the details," he began slowly, like his foggy sick brain was trying to catch up with his mouth. Now she really wished he wasn't sick. She waited in anticipation.

"Luka called me over to your apartment after it happened. He said it was supposed to be an easy job, that you were supposed to wait in the car. Leave it to you not to listen—" He caught her piercing glare. "Anyway, something went wrong. Something about you not remembering who he was. He had to knock you out just to get you back home." Alex paused, rolling into a sneezing fit before continuing. "I-I can't remember everything he said. I was too angry. I said some pretty horrible things to him and told him to leave you alone for good."

"And instead of telling me that a demon violated my mind you decided to keep it from me?" That stone inside her chest lightened as her brain caught up with her.

His head leaned back against the building.

"I thought it was better! Better than you remembering and being traumatized. I just—I don't know. You were the one he talked to about this crap. I can't help with this magic shit."

The utter helplessness in his voice was unmistakable. Amity watched him silently, her mouth hanging slack. He was right.

If Alex had told her the truth that night she either (1) would've been emotionally devastated by the news and felt utterly helpless—Alex also didn't know any magic and nei-ther did she, so attempting to get her memories back from a demon was hopeless; or (2) she wouldn't have believed him—Alex was never interested in magic and demonology, so hearing him say "Hey, you went demon hunting with my friend and had your memories stolen" was unbelievable.

Brown eyes glanced up at her brother, then widened. "Are you crying?"

Alex immediately hid his head in his hands, then rubbed his tears up through his hair.

"No!"

She wrapped her arms around his thick coat, holding him close, now thankful he was sick. He was usually never this vulnerable.

After making sure Alex got back to his car okay, Amity got home and only did one thing. Clean.

The garbage and recycling were taken out. The floors and couch were vacuumed. Freaya's litter box even got cleaned!

Then she folded all the soft blankets littering her bed and couch, laying a few decoratively over the ends, then put the rest away in the large wicker basket in the corner by the television.

The kitchen was next on Amity's cleaning spree, but her stomach put an end to that. It growled so loudly it forced her to stop and remember she hadn't eaten since lunch. She glanced at her phone screen, 10:00 p.m.

"What?!" How did she go so long without eating? Amity raced to her refrigerator. Empty. The freezer was next to check, opening with a blast of cold air. There was nothing but vanilla mochi. Her stomach growled loudly.

"I can't have mochi for dinner," she whined.

Freaya approached the kitchen silently then sat on the white tile, silently watching her mother as she closed the freezer then leaned her head against the door in utter defeat.

Amity's mind scrambled trying to think of any place that might be open this late.

"I guess I could just make waffles again."

She sighed heavily. Freaya sat quietly licking her paws. Judging.

Amity pushed away from the door, her narrow eyes locked with Freaya's. They stared at each other—glaring at each other—until Amity had to blink.

"Fine!" she yelled, throwing her hands up. "I'll be back soon."

Amity marched back down the empty main street with a wide smile on her face. Under one arm she clutched her fast-food bag, while holding onto the freshly-grilled cheeseburger and with the other clutching a large soda.

She took a long satisfying sip before taking a large bite out of the cheeseburger.

"Yup. This was just what I needed." She smiled, stopping briefly under a streetlight to take another bite of the grilled delight.

Amity rounded the corner, making sure to keep in the lights; it was now almost 11:00 p.m. She wasn't too far from Halley's now, which means she was close to her apartment.

I'm gonna cuddle up with my book and Freaya and go to sleep—

Her heavy boots stopped short, remembering her long-forgotten plans for the evening. Did her late-night run to satisfy her hunger take over her whole brain?

Luka. Luka was supposed to come over. She set her soda down on a nearby bench and wrapped the remainder of her burger. *Fuck! How did I forget Luka was supposed to come over? Stupid!*

Amity shoved a handful of fries into her mouth, stuffed the food back in the crumpled bag then fumbled for her phone. She let out a frustrated cold breath and shook out her aching arm.

"Cause you were too busy stuffing your face dumbass."

Did he call? I already missed that text from Alex tonight. Don't tell me I missed a text from Luka!

With a huff she fumbled for her phone. It was freezing, blinking a few times back to life when she unlocked it with a thumbprint, revealing a missed call from none other than the magic man himself. Quickly she called him before her phone could blink to a black screen again.

It rang a few times before it went to voicemail.

Crap! I hope he didn't show up while I was out. Quickly she shoved her phone back into her pocket and rubbed her shivering hands together.

"When did it get so damn cold?" Amity fluffed her coat before zipping it all the way up to her neck, then picked up her things, the liquid stinging her palm as it sloshed inside the cup. Just as she turned on her heel, the streetlight she was under flickered. Brown eyes glared up at it in confusion as it blinked once, then twice, until finally it died out.

"Great," she huffed, causing another thick cloud to leave her mouth. Pulling the straw between her teeth, she turned on her heel to continue walking.

A small sound made her stop short the straw fell out of her lips. Save for the faint glimmer of the streetlights a few blocks down, the street was dark. The streetlight above her head beyond any hope of resuscitating. Heart hamming in her chest, she slowly turned her head down the mouth of the alleyway beside her. Her whole body went rigid as the faint outline of someone made its way toward her through a low swirling fog. They were grunting and muttering under their breath, something too low for her to understand.

Amity's hands began to shake, her breath turning into frantic pants.

No. Don't panic. She tried to calm herself. Trying to make as little noise as possible, she put down her bag of food and soda onto the bench, which had turned so cold it hurt to let go of.

The person drew closer, close enough for her to realize it was a man. He was limping on one leg, dragging the other behind him through the dead leaves that littered the ground. Coupled with his moaning, it was the only sound filling the emptiness. He was clutching his side in pain, visibly wincing with each step.

Amity slowly removed her keys from her pocket which, to spite her, made a loud *clunk* as they crashed together. The man raised his head to hers.

Damnit!

Amity glanced around. She was alone. She willed herself to take longer breaths as her heart continued to race. Hammering faster inside her chest.

She could make a run for it, double back, and then take a different route to her apartment. Amity might not be a great runner but she would still be faster than someone who was limping. Heavy boots squared beneath her, ready to run.

"Amity?"

Brown eyes went wide as they turned back to the man. He was much closer, approximately twenty feet away. *How did he cover that distance so fast? Fuck that, how does he know my name?!*

"Amity!" he whimpered, falling to his knees. His voice was clearer now, recognizable.

"Luka!?"

Her boots hit the pavement hard, propelling her towards him. She caught his limp frame before his face collided with cobblestone. Gently she brushed the loose hair from his braid, now sticky with sweat and blood, out of his eyes. To say he looked like a mess was an understatement. His jacket was gone, and he was clutching his side with a bloody hand. Luka grunted loudly as he leaned back onto his heels. Dark hair was matted with blood. It was running down his face and into his eyes. Amity's heart raced faster.

"What happened? How did you—Where?"

So many questions. All of them half formed when they tumbled past her lips. The side of his mouth kicked up in a halfhearted attempt at a smile.

"It's a long story," he bit out with one eye swollen shut.

She gently went to wipe his face, but he caught her wrist in his free hand. His touch was frigid. He was breathing heavily. He was losing too much blood.

"It's fine."

"Nothing about this is fine! I'm calling an ambulance."

She fumbled for her phone with her free hand, her stiff fingers pressing the on button so many times she thought it might crack the screen. It remained blank.

Fuck!

The grip around her wrist tightened, making her wince.

"Amity," Luka growled.

The last time he made that noise she felt her entire body instantly heat, like she had jumped headfirst into a hot spring, but now . . . A chill slithered up her spine, making it tense and stiffen.

Luka closed his eyes and inhaled deeply, then released a slow hot breath.

"So sweet," he hummed, opening heavily lidded eyes. Eyes that were glowing green.

The hair at the nape of her neck stood on its ends. She gently tried to pull her wrist from his grasp. His grip tightened, latching onto her so strongly she cried out.

"Amity." Green eyes met hers, staring at her feverishly. It made her entire body shake.

His voice was deeper now, *hungry*. His lips peeled back into a smile too wide for his face, pulling hard at the seams like it would tear any second. His teeth grew right before her eyes, becoming sharper with each new heavy breath he took. Amity's eyes widened as she tugged harder against his grip. He was too strong.

What the fuck is going on? What is this thing?!

Amity tried pulling free from his grip again and again, a futile effort that had him latch on tighter. Another piercing cry escaped her when she could feel her *bones* rub together. A scream tore through her throat, her body twisting to punch him with her free hand.

The thing laughed in her face, and it's smile contorting with amusement. Like the thought of her fighting back was *cute*. She kicked out, aiming to shove her heavy boot in its face.

A brief moment of relief filled her when her boot collided with something hard, but that relief quickly vanished. Her foot hadn't made contact with his face. A bloody hand held it in suspension. That amused smile peeked out from behind her boot.

Its eyes gleamed at her. Like it was happy she was trying to fight back. It inhaled another deep breath, releasing it with a satisfied humm.

Amity's body began to quake. Was it *smelling* her?

Its smile turned wolfish.

"Let me have a bite," it growled.

Amity tried to scramble back, tugging her foot and failing miserably. It was strong! Stronger than anyone she knew. She kicked and twisted and punched. Anything to try to get away from this *thing*. She wished she had run. She wished she had stayed inside. She wished she had eaten stupid waffles for dinner. She wished she had apologized to Luka.

Stupid! Stupid! Stupid!

Now she was going to be eaten by something wearing his face.

Amity was so frantic, writhing and lashing out, she didn't see the shadow looming over whatever held her.

A bloody hand gripped its braid.

"Touching her was the last mistake you'll ever make!" a voice roared.

The thing's head was fiercely yanked back by its hair just as hot blood splashed against her cheeks, then *burned*. In a panic she wiped the hot blood away. The grip on her leg loosened, giving her enough leeway to pull free. Frantic fingers dug into the cobblestone as she quickly crawled away. Turning she saw a thick blade glowing a bright blue, protruding out of Luka's—no, that *thing*'s chest.

Amity drew in a shaky breath as her eyes traveled up its body. Luka towered over it, his eyes glowing bright blue, murderous as they glared down at the monster—no, the *demon*. It cried out and screeched. Its face started to twist unnaturally, filling the night with the sounds of bones breaking and rearranging.

"*Silence*," Luka ordered.

The air around him pulsed with something Amity could only describe as power. Pure power.

The demon's screeching ceased. It writhed in Luka's grasp. Its face now distorted between Luka's and half feral wolf. Amity felt her stomach churn at the sight of it. With clawed fingers, it reached for him, but it wasn't fast enough.

Luka lifted it with ease, pulling out his blade with a ragged twist before slamming the demon down onto the cobblestones. They cracked under the force.

Amity was frozen with horror as Luka thrust the the long blade into the demon's chest.

"*Stay.*" The air pulsed again, sending Amity's hair flying back out of her face. Luka pulled something from his jacket. The slim throwing daggers she had seen him use before. He whispered something to the glowing blade. It *hummed* in response. Then it *grew.* It grew longer and thicker until it was the length of his arm. The demon stared at him horrified, writhing against the blade in its chest, unable to speak, unable to get free.

Luka's eyes glowed brighter. The demon raised its hands to him, trying to block the inevitable. It was no use.

In one swift motion, Luka struck. Amity blinked once and the demon's arms were cut clean off at the elbows. They flew across the street, landing by some trash can.

Luka perched on top of it, hovering his sword just above the demon's head.

"You have a message for me. *Speak it.*"

The demon's lips peeled back and coughed up the mass of blood that had been forming in its mouth when it was magically sealed shut.

"They said bring the girl."

Luka's blade came down between its eyes. It *twitched* beneath him, and Amity felt her stomach churn again. She was going to be sick.

Once the body stopped writhing and twitching, it started to fizz. Its flesh melted as if it was acidic, creating a horrible smell. Amity covered her mouth and slammed her eyes closed, trying to hold in the contents of her stomach. She ran for the garbage can.

Her stomach heaved as she shoved her head over the garbage can's opening. When it was finally emptied, she went to pull her hair back only to touch the gentle hands that were already there, holding her curls back out of her face. She knew who it was even if he said nothing. Luka. That's right, the demon was dead now. Only her and Luka filled the dark streets. Her head turned away in embarrassment. She didn't want him to see her like this. Shaky, pale, and scared out of her fucking mind.

The soft press of a rough hand ran up and down her back reassuringly. Moments passed in silence as the air warmed around them. Light illuminated them as the streetlamp slowly flickered back to life. His warm hand pressed into her back firmly.

"Amity."

She didn't look at him, she *refused.*

"Catch me."

Wait, what?

He fell hard against her, pressing his weight into her. She had barely enough time to turn and catch him.

"Hey! Hey! Luka?!"

"I guess . . . I went a little overboard," he mumbled into the crook of her neck.

"A *little*?"

She pulled back his jacket. A little was the *biggest* understatement of the year.

His compression shirt was in tatters, and if he wasn't bleeding, Amity would be happy to see the exposed skin. That shirt made him look—

This wasn't the time!

"Don't you fucking pass out on me. You hear me?"

Luka made a small sound that was half a laugh and half a groan.

". . . Yes, kitten."

Amity's cheeks flushed. Now was definitely not the time for pet names!

I'm starting to think you enjoy getting beat up.

"Shut up and tell me where to go," she ordered, adjusting him so he was leaning on her side. Her heart was ramping back up to a quick pace.

He laughed lightly before viciously coughing up a storm.

". . . Your place," he finally managed.

With a huff, she turned him back in the direction of her apartment. Grunting with each laboring step, Luka was heavy and the height difference wasn't doing her any favors.

"You . . ." She huffed out a frustrated breath before giving into a smile. "You could've just said your place or at least a damn hospital. Not to mention you're totally wrecked . . . *again*," she lectured, hobbling with him down the street.

Luka shook his head.

"Can't go home . . . I promised."

Amity stumbled a bit. A light blush dusted her cheeks.

"Well . . . don't think you're sleeping in my bed. You're sleeping on the couch, and I don't care if it is too small. And you still have a lot of explaining to do!"

She tried to get a better look at his wounds, but from this angle it was near impossible. Silently Amity hoped that whatever mixture or potion he made last time would work. *But his wounds weren't as bad as—*She shook the thought away. What she needed to do was get him home. Luka leaned heavier on her shoulder and her heart skipped. She needed to keep him talking.

"We need to stop meeting like this."

A laugh grunted out of him.

"I don't know, I kind of like this . . . You taking off my clothes . . . cleaning my wounds." His voice was rougher when he spoke.

That blush spread all the way to her neck where his voice tickled her skin. She let out a shaky breath.

"Honestly I don't know whether to kiss you or punch you."

He nudged her neck, sending a shiver across her skin.

"You can do anything you want to me . . . I'll let you." She stopped walking and straightened underneath him. He struggled to place a heavy hand across her chest and onto her other shoulder, then dragged it across her collarbone. Those rough bloodstained fingertips grazed up her neck and then traced her jawline. He turned her chin toward him and lightly brushed the tip of his nose against hers.

"And I'll enjoy every second of it."

Yeah, says the demon slayer I found half dead in an alley-way.

He leaned his forehead to hers sweetly. Cyan eyes half closed, at least one of them was. The other was fully shut, probably because of the blood streaming down his forehead from somewhere in his hair. She tilted her chin up and—his head fell forward, his body falling heavier on top of her.

"Hey! Hey, hey, hey! Don't you fucking dare! You hear me?!"

She braced her feet, successfully catching him before he fully crushed her into the street.

"We are almost home, just stay awake. You listening?!" She took a heavy step forward. "I have you, just stay with me."

He smiled against her.

"Freaya, I'm home!" Amity announced, kicking her door shut behind them. She brought him over to the couch and, as delicately as she could manage, laid him down. His limp body hit the cushions hard, forcing a groan out of him. Amity ran into the bathroom for the first aid kit.

"You have work tomorrow?"

"No, I don't!" she called from the other room.

Quickly she grabbed a soft dark towel and ran it under hot water, wrung it out roughly in the sink then fetched the first aid kit, and made her way back to him.

He closed his eyes and leaned his head back. "Tomorrow's Friday."

"Yeah well lucky for you my father gave me the day off, said I wasn't getting enough sleep. You want to tell him why?"

Without hesitations she touched the warm cloth to his forehead and carefully cleaned it. Luckily this blood wasn't his; well, not all of it anyway.

Luka winced faintly trying to force his body to stay still. "I didn't think so."

Amity removed his shirt carefully. The corner of his mouth kicked up.

"Taking advantage of a defenseless man. I'm impressed."

"I suppose I should be grateful you can still flirt."

Shaky hands placed the damp cloth onto the open wound just below his navel. Although his shirt was slashed, the scratches that did it were only that, a scratches. But this one. This was deep. Amity's eyes narrowed on it.

She swallowed hard as she reached for the rubbing-alcohol wipes. Luka watched her carefully.

"This is going to sting like a bitch."

Luka straightened on the couch, repositioning himself so that Amity was between his legs. Her cheeks flushed. She tore open the alcohol wipes.

"I'll enjoy anything you do to me, kitten."

His voice was slow and deep. Amity could watch it vibrate through him. Her gaze lingered on his Adam's apple as he swallowed hard. A few stray hairs had slipped out of place and over his eyes; without thinking, she reached up and tucked a them behind his ear. He leaned into the touch. Amity watched him silently, studying him, worry blooming in her chest. He was struggling to keep his eyes open and was still breathing heavily.

"This is going to hurt. *Badly*."

Luka eyes squeezed shut, and she tracked a few breaths rising his chest before his chin dipped into a nod.

Brown eyes traveled down to his lips, but Amity caught herself just as she started to lean in. Her fingers entwined in his hand that rested on his thigh. She inhaled deeply and he followed suite, inhaling with her, then she pressed the cloth to his open wound.

Luka's gritted his teeth trying to bite back the scream. He did not squeeze her hand. So she squeezed his until he had no other choice. Swiping the wound thoroughly was painful to do but Amity would rather have him be in brief pain from sanitizing the wound then from it festering with infection later. Once the gash was cleaned she finally spoke.

"That thing you did with the herbs, will that fix—" She stopped herself before finishing that sentence.

Luka brushed his thumb over her fingers.

"Yes, but it'll take a lot more energy to heal this. I'll probably pass out right after." He inhaled deeply, leaning his head further into the cushion, heavy eyelids closed.

"Don't pass out now!"

CHAPTER SIXTEEN

Amity tapped the edges of the mug nervously as she pressed her back against the wall, just outside the bathroom door. The bathroom door which was *conveniently* propped open. Bright light seeped through the small gap, along with the sound of rushing water. Every so often she could hear the occasional hiss of pain. She tried telling him that taking a bath would be easier, but he insisted. Now he was in her bathroom. Naked in her shower. And she was standing just outside the door like some pervert.

An audible sigh left her. Tired eyes fell back down to the steaming tea in her hands. Before Luka showered, he had shown her the correct herbs to boil like he'd made for his "potion." However, she was too focused on his skilled fingers to pay attention to which herbs he actually picked.

That and—she shuddered—that disfigured wolfish grin kept crawling back into her thoughts sending her pulse racing.

Don't think about it! Now is not the time to have a fucking breakdown.

Soft black fur rubbed against her leg with a small meow before walking through the bathroom door. Freaya jumped up and sat idly on the old sweatpants Amity had set on the toilet lid. Golden eyes stared at the shower with wide curiosity.

A small laugh bubbled up her throat and she aggressively wiped a stray tear from her cheek.

"How many different types of demons are there?" Amity asked through the door.

"Hundred. Thousands."

She listened to the running water silently, actively trying to stop imagining what it looked like running down his body. Down his tattoo, through his hair, between the muscles of his abdomen, and down to his navel where his scar was—He needed to clean that again, ASAP.

"And the demon you've been searching for?" she pressed.

The water stopped, filling her apartment with the last patters of water droplets and finally Luka's sigh. She shifted uncomfortably on her sore feet before taking in a deep breath. Her fingers tightened around the mug; luckily it was still hot.

"You asked the last one where some other one was and it said Riverside Park, then this one says to bring me to meet someone?"

Though why she needed to be there was a mystery.

The shower curtain opened roughly, and Freaya meowed with delight. *Damn cat.* Amity pursed her lips as jealousy rose in her. A wonderful image formed in her mind . . . Steam wrapping around his body. Small water droplets trickled over his skin. Dark wet hair sticking to his cheeks as he looked at her with those beautiful cyan eyes. If she looked down, she was sure to see his massive—

Stop getting distracted!

She shook her head aggressively, willing the images out of her mind.

"What's going on, Luka?"

On the other side of the door, Freaya meowed again in a demanding tone. A towel was pulled from the rack and shuffled around. *He must be drying off . . .*

"I'm handling it, you don't have to get involved."

Amity's irritation grew. She wished she had finished her damn cheeseburger before throwing it up. She was embarrassed she had thrown up in front of her crush. She was horrified that that demon looked like him and said something that would've been sexy under entirely different circumstances. She was mad that she was patching up Luka *again.* This man who was being secretive with her *again* when he was supposed to be *explaining everything.* Most importantly she was mad that this man was naked in her bathroom with her cat and not *her.*

Shifting the mug to one hand, Amity gripped the doorknob. With a harsh shove, she slammed the door the rest of the way open.

"*Apparently* I already am!" She stopped and took in the sight of him.

Curled within his tattooed arm was none other than Freaya, who purred happily as he kissed her head. Amity swallowed hard as her cheeks flushed a deep crimson. What was it about half-naked men holding cats that made them look hotter? He looked up at her through wet hair; he must not have dried it yet. She followed a small waterdrop as it fell from his dark locks, around the curve of his cheek, down his jaw, and landing softly on his collarbone. It made its way quickly past, between his chest—absolutely her favorite place—down his stomach, and catching in his belly button. Amity could watch water drip off of him for hours and never be tired of it.

He reached up to brush his hair out of his eyes, wincing badly, so badly that Freaya scrambled and jumped from his grasp. His wound was bleeding again. Blood trickled down his navel along the line that cut its way down to his—

Fuck, this was Not. The. Time!

It was only then when her brain registered he'd changed into her pants, which hung distractingly low.

Without spilling a drop, she thrust the mug into his hands. "Drink!" The corner of his mouth kicked up, confirming he had been watching her while she was watching him. She gestured to the deep gash. "Get some sleep, we can talk tomorrow once you're better."

That burning curiosity and need to know what he had to say had to unfortunately wait. Amity handed him the damp towel he had neatly put back, which he tiredly took then lazily dried his hair as he followed her out to the living room. She stopped short, almost making him drop the mug.

"No. I'll sleep out here. You can have the bed."

Fidgeting fingers fiddled with the hem of her shirt. Her cheeks were lighter in color now, but she could still feel the heat of them. Tired eyes narrowed on her.

"But you said—"

"Luka, take it, please."

The towel dropped from his hair onto his shoulder. Silently he watched her until she glanced up at him.

"What?"

He took her hand in his and brushed his thumb over the back of her fingers; her heart warmed at the gesture.

"Stay with me tonight."

". . . I'm still mad at you. Fuck, I don't even know *why* I'm mad at you." *Not true, I know exactly why.*

Gently he pulled her closer to him and put his chin on top of her head. Her eyes drifted down to the bleeding gash in his side. "Tomorrow. I'll play with you tomorrow, kitten."

"You mean you'll *explain everything* tomorrow." She glared up at him but let a tiny laugh escape past her lips.

His chest vibrated with a loud humm, as if he was thinking it over. Amity pinched him playfully in response. A warm chuckle left him, then his torso stiffened. A sharp hiss of pain slipped through clenched teeth.

"I'm serious, Luka!" She stepped back and glared up at him. "You're not leaving until you explain yourself. Drink!" she ordered, lifting his hand holding the mug and pressing it toward his lips.

With a light chuckle, he lifted the mug the rest of the way that was beyond her reach and did as she asked. Brown eyes watched him work through the entire drink before the corner of her mouth turned up into a small smile. Quickly she took the mug out of his hand when it parted from his mouth, half afraid he would drop it. He did say he might pass out.

Luka bent forward, wrapping his arm around her, burying a groan in her hair as the potion did its work. He leaned into her, his body growing limp. Wet lips pressed a long kiss onto her forehead, followed by the touch of a heavy sigh.

"Tomorrow. I promise."

Amity stretched her feet out lazily under the warm covers, humming softly into her pillow as her joints popped. She snuggled deeper into her cocoon, not wanting to wake up.

With eyes still closed, a happy reminder filled her. She had the day off. She could stay in bed all day if she wanted to. A sleepy smile spread across her lips.

Wait . . . bed?

One tired brown eye peeked open. Amity was definitely in bed, Freaya's golden eyes were silently watching her from her perch on the pillow next to her head.

"You were definitely a pervert in a past life," she mumbled.

Freaya tilted her head in response before yawning incredibly loudly in that way that cats do, where their jaw gapes and their eyes go wide and wild.

Amity grumbled trying to remember *how* she got into bed.

She distinctly remembered putting Luka to sleep in her bed after bandaging his side after double-checking that his wound had started healing. Freaya had immediately jumped in with him and snuggled by his side.

Amity glanced at Freaya who was idly cleaning her paws.

Then she had sneaked into the living room and fellen asleep on the couch.

A loud sigh left her. It's not that she didn't want to sleep with him. She did. She really, *really* did. But it wasn't the best idea. If this potion didn't work as fast as the last one, which she suspected from his lack of energy, it wouldn't; then his wound would take longer to heal. Amity didn't want to slow the healing process further by clinging to him all night.

She stretched her arms high above her head with a satisfied moan.

"Did he carry me back to bed?" A smug smile spread across her lips. *That's so fucking cute!*

Amity sat up in bed so fast that Freaya jumped back. She glanced at the other side of the bed. Her smile faded when Luka wasn't there.

"Luka!" She called, waiting for a response that never came.

Confusion filled her as she glanced around.

"Did he?" Anger flashed.

"Oh. Fuck. No."

Amity jumped out of bed, sending her covers scattering and Freaya running across the apartment. She sprinted to the living room. Empty. The bathroom. Empty. The kitchen. Empty. He was nowhere to be found, but every room she checked was strangely clean, like super clean, not that she stopped long enough to notice. Her glare fell to the door. Anger rose higher. She went back into her bedroom, marching toward her nightstand where her phone lay peacefully on top of it. Peacefully next to *his* phone.

Amity swiped it up in a tight grip then marched back to the front door.

"If he thinks he can just walk in here after he gets the shit kicked out of him and *then* leave without saying a word, he's gotta another—"

She thrust the door open, ready to throw the innocent phone into the hallway, but she came face-to-face with someone's chest. A low laugh rumbled through it.

"Good morning, kitten," Luka said with an amusing tone.

Amity stepped back, quickly hiding his phone behind her back. Luka sauntered into her apartment with a small bag and a coffee tray with two cups in one hand. In his other hand were her keys, which he put back into his pocket.

"I wasn't gone too long, did you miss me?"

Amity didn't answer; she stared at him with wide eyes, then glanced down at the items he brought.

"You bought breakfast for me?"

Such a simple thing, yet it warmed her heart.

"No, this is all for me."

Brown eyes narrowed on him, knowing full well he was joking but still that feeling in her chest vanished.

"Asshole," she grumbled, slapping his free arm lightly.

Luka's smirk kicked up and he laughed loudly on his way over to the couch. She trailed behind him, grabbing a warm blanket out of the basket and wrapping herself in it after placing his phone *gently* on the coffee table. Luka sat in the center of the couch gesturing for her to sit beside him. She did, but not before swiping up her coffee. Her favorite coffee. She leaned her back against the pillow-covered armrest and shuffled her cold toes under his leg. Damn he was warm!

Luka shuffled off his jacket and laid it on the back end of the couch. With a smile, he took her feet in his hands, wrapped them inside the blanket, and draped her legs over his lap. Her cheeks heated at the gesture.

"Your feet are freezing." He murmured quietly rubbing them

He held them firmly when she tried jerking them away. Defeated she sipped her coffee quietly and watched him. That warm feeling filling her again.

This was nice. Them sitting on the couch. Relaxing. It felt cozy . . . couply. *Is couply even a word?* Her feet were warming up fast.

Luka tugged at the collar of her old shirt, which she assumed he must've gotten when she fell asleep. His smirk was gone now.

"You moved me last night," she finally said, pulling the straw of her lavender iced latte between her teeth.

He nodded silently, no quick snide remark, just a small nod. He held her feet with one hand and started running the other along the plush blanket covering her shins, then up to her knees, before finally resting on her thigh. Her cheeks flushed red. She watched him with anticipation, but he didn't look her way, not once. His eyes were focused on the small paper bag he put on the coffee table. She was about to say something cute and flirty, but he spoke first.

"It's been a year. I've been trying to figure out a way to say this for an entire year."

Amity's smile dropped at his serious tone. Her fingers fiddled with the straw of her coffee. After a moment of silence Luka's eyes slid to her fingers. Gently he took the coffee cup out of her hands and placed it back on the coffee table. His large hand wrapped around her hand, effortlessly enclosing it and ceasing her fidgeting.

"Would it be okay if I showed you?"

A hint of a smile appeared on his lips when her head slightly tilted to the side. Those cyan eyes finally met hers.

"I can use a memory projection spell. That way you can see my memory of what happened."

Brown eyes blinked at him.

"Right, because that's a completely uncomplicated and entirely normal thing to say," she deadpanned.

He chuckled and stood, gently laying her legs back down onto the couch.

"Demon hunting, healing potions, levitating throwing knives, that weird speaking commands thing, now this? You're the real thing then, a full-fledged witch?" Luka nodded with a small smile, no doubt picking up on her rising nerves. "This is still a lot to process for me." He motioned for her to lie down on the couch, which she did. Damn, the fact that he was *this* handsome and *this* close to her was still hard to process!

"Are you comfortable?"

Big brown eyes blinked at him again. Did her brain even process that she did exactly what he said without question?

"You're just going right for it, huh? No foreplay?" she teased, trying to hide her nervousness.

The corner of his mouth tilted up just for a moment as he tried very hard and failed to hide a smirk. She folded her hands over her covered stomach and took in a deep breath.

He watched her for a moment before nodding.

"You'll be hungry afterward and you might be a little tired, but that's normal. Just relax for me."

Amity nodded stiffly, keeping her eyes on the ceiling.

He sighed softly and rough hands folded over hers, giving them a reassuring squeeze. The couch shifted when he gently leaned over her and placed a slow kiss on her lips. Amity felt her body immediately relax at the touch. He pulled away just enough so the tip of his nose touched hers. A reassuring and now recurring gesture.

Her eyes narrowed on him suspiciously when the warmth of him left.

"Is kissing me the only way to do this?"

"No. I just wanted to give you something sweet before something bitter."

Her cheeks flushed deeper and her heart swelled. Luka pressed his forehead gently against hers.

"Ready?"

She nodded and followed his lead as he inhaled deeply. When their breath released, their eyes were wide and glowing bright blue.

Everything around her faded into nothing. Her apartment, the couch she was lying on, the blanket that covered her, Luka.

Amity was in an empty void of darkness. A panic quickly rose in her as she pushed herself off the floor. Black and covered in a thin layer of water, tauntingly splashing about, as she scrambled. She gripped her shirt tightly, feeling a painful jolt run through her. She turned so many times, she felt dizzy. Amity screamed. Her eyes widened, fear slipping through her veins. Lightly she touched her lips. There was no sound.

She kicked the water under her feet. Nothing. Not even a water droplet. It remained still beneath her. The only thing she heard was her pulse pounding in her ears. She tried to scream again. Felt it move from the pits of her stomach and out her throat, but there was still no sound.

"*Breathe, Amity . . .*"

She knew that voice. She spun around, but he was nowhere to be found. It came from nowhere and yet surrounded her. Amity cried out his name in a silent scream.

"I need you to breathe, Amity . . . just breathe."

She hugged herself tight, running her hands up and down her sides. She willed herself to slow her breathing, swallowing her panic.

"Breathe in. One. Two. Three. Four."

"Breathe out. One. Two. Three. Four."

Slowly her heartbeat steadied. It wasn't until it was stable for a few breaths in a row when she heard his voice again.

"You might feel a little dizzy."

A harsh wind blew against her, then around her. Her arms flew up, protecting her eyes from her thrashing hair. It howled and groaned until the whipping wind subsided into a small breeze barely above a whisper.

Amity peeked out from the protection of her arms. The dark void was gone, replaced by the early-morning sun shining down on Halley's. She was across the street. A feeling of nostalgia swelled inside her.

It was autumn, late October if she had to guess. A few people wearing light coats had walked out of the storefront; one of them was in a thick scarf. All of them carried steaming coffee. One of them had a jacko'lantern sugar cookie.

Yeah, definitely late October.

She felt her breath hitch as she saw Luka swagger out the front door. His hair was shorter than when she saw him this morning. More tiny pieces had fallen out of his topknot.

Amity was about to run across the street toward him, but something stopped her—no, *someone*. A young woman was holding the door open for him, then quickly closed it behind her. She turned her straight nose in the air. She was saying something to him, but Amity couldn't make it out from where she was. She saw Luka say something back, which quickly made the woman spin, her curls sent scattering.

Amity's eyes widened as she watched as her other self tried to push her hair out of the way so she could yell at Luka.

"This is so trippy." Her voice returned, not that she or anyone else around her noticed.

She—the other Amity—made her way down the street with Luka—the other Luka. He appeared to be laughing about something. Amity felt her cheeks heat up in response. Something about that smile felt different. Like there wasn't anything holding it back. Free.

"*Follow them . . .*" Luka instructed.

Amity nodded and followed them down the street, focusing a little too hard on her hair. Well, her otherself's hair. Amity's eyes narrowed. *Is that really what it looks like from the back?*

Her foot caught on one of the broken cobblestones, sending her legs tangling. She reached for the lamppost to catch her fall but twisted and landed flat on her ass.

Amity looked at her hand strangely. She definitely grabbed it just now. Confusion blossomed as she rubbed her ass, noting no soreness. *That was a nasty fall.*

Her eyes narrowed on the lamppost, and she slowly grabbed at it. As her hand closed, the metal fizzed and glitched around her fingers. Like when you're playing a video game and a deer miraculously walks right through a tree in the forest.

She paused, her mouth hanging agape in amazement. A wide smile spread across her lips as she passed a hand through the lamppost, then grew wider as her arm passed through. Her foot. Her leg. Her whole body!

An excitement bubbled through her as she ran into the middle of the street. She spread her arms wide as a woman drove her car right through her. Amity let out a triumphant laugh as she watched the image slip over, around, and through her.

She turned, watching the car continue on before skipping over to the other side of the street with excited laughter.

That was amazing!

A low laugh accompanied her own. Even though she couldn't see his face, she knew what it looked like; his eyes would be narrowed on her and his mouth would be in a tight smile trying to suppress a laugh that he knew was inappropriate because he was also angry with her for her lack of—

"*Focus, kitten . . .*" he reminded her.

A smirk kicked up on her lips as she caught up to her other self.

Don't tell me what to do.

Amity kept a reasonable distance. Even though she was certain they couldn't see her, it still felt weird to walk next to herself. She focused on the other Luka.

"Let me come with you," her other self begged.

Luka replied with a quick no.

"Come on! I wanna watch you work!"

"No."

Oh, yeah this is definitely familiar. Amity scratched the back of her head in embarrassment.

"I'm the one setting all this up in case you've forgotten," her other self said. "The least you could do is show me your side of it."

I'm sorry, WHAT!? I was helping him with this? How? When? WHY?! Amity's eyes darted between the two in front of her as if it would answer her reeling questions. *We are definitely going to have a very long talk about that little detail!*

He glared at her.

"Amity. Drop it."

Oof, his voice has that deep edge to it, not good.

Her cheeks flushed remembering that time he used this voice on her when she followed him back to the alleyway. When he held her by the throat. How she didn't *entirely* hate it.

"Come on!" The other Amity planted her feet, nearly causing Amity to crash into her—well, crash through her. "Then we're through."

"What?"

She lifted her chin stubbornly.

"You heard me."

Luka stopped and turned to her.

Wow, he really does tower over me.

He ran his hand through his hair and spoke in that voice that carried an edge. A voice that should scare her if it weren't so fucking hot.

"Kitten, it can get dangerous."

Did he just call me kitten? Wait, are we dating? Were . . . were we dating? Oh fuck, are we dating right now?

"So you expect me to let you go alone?"

He sighed and pinched the bridge of his nose. This was clearly not the first or even the tenth time they've had this argument. The other Amity pressed on.

"It's a lesser demon. One quick job. Then we can get icecream and laugh it all off."

Their eyes were locked as a long pause passed between them. Luka looked away and back down the path they had come. Amity felt her breath hitch; he was looking directly at her. Eyes were wide with remorse. A horrible knot grew in her chest.

"Fine . . ."

She—the other Amity—hugged him tightly.

"You need to do everything I say."

She huffed, pulling away from him almost as quickly as she latched on.

He was faster, knuckles already under her chin, tilting it up. Making her look at him.

Amity's eyes narrowed on her other self-memory self? Whatever. Jealousy bloomed.

Was it possible to be jealous of yourself? There have been many stranger things to think about. It must be possible. Besides, her eyes went back to him, she knows him. She knows him better than I do, longer than I have—

"I mean it, Amity. Do exactly as I say."

Now would be the time, right? Now's the opportune moment.

Amity's eyes widened; those weren't her thoughts. That smooth voice was coming from everywhere just like it had done before. When she first arrived. When she was told to follow them. The one who just kissed her real self.

She watched her other self's cheeks flush. Brown eyes were wide.

Now.

Her other self shoved against him hard.

"I get it! You can stop teasing me already!"

Amity's mouth hung open as she watched them continue down the cobblestone street.

Three realizations dawned on her at the same time: (1) She was hearing Luka's thoughts just then; (2) he was going to kiss her for the first time, which meant they were *not* dating yet or even intimate, but more importantly *she* just ruined her first kiss with Luka!!!—and (3) something very bad was about to happen to her.

CHAPTER
SEVENTEEN

The wind rose behind her, sending her curls over her shoulder and toward her other self. It picked up fast, quickly turning into another strong gust, taking her surroundings with it. Amity shut her eyes and covered her face.

Was that it? Was that all of it?

When she uncovered her face, it was nighttime and she was standing at some abandoned industrial warehouse.

What the hell is this place?

Although she knew it would pass right through her like the car did, Amity still jumped back out of reflex when a black SUV pulled to a stop beside her.

She waited by the trunk of the car as the low rumble of the engine came to an abrupt stop.

Luka got out first followed by her hesitant other self. She took one step away from the car as Luka made his way to her. A half smile appeared on Amity's lips as her other self fiddled with her necklace nervously. A black cornicello, matching Luka's.

That was cute, but this wasn't the time to think about that now.

Amity rubbed her arm, sensing the tension in the air.

I really need to work on my poker face. Amity observed her other self whose face had grown significantly paler since she last saw it.

Silently she watched her other self take in a deep breath and with a determined gaze stride forward toward the warehouse. She didn't get far.

Luka caught her hand, stopping her mid-stride.

"Remember, do *exactly* as I say."

"I know . . ."

He was still holding her hand in his. Her other self didn't jerk away. A few moments of silence passed before brown eyes looked from her hand in his, then back up to cyan. Her eyes narrowed her eyes at him suspiciously.

Cyan eyes narrowed right back at her.

"I need you to stay here."

"I can do this!"

She tried to rip her hand from his grasp, but he pulled her back toward him, causing her to stumble. He turned her so she fell back against the car door.

"I know you, you can." He cupped her cheek with his tattooed hand.

Amity held her face in her hands. Her mouth hung open.

Is he gonna do it?! Oh my god oh my god oh my god oh my god oh my god! Is it wrong to freak out over someone kissing your past self??? I feel like I should have popcorn for this!

He leaned in close. She—both Amitys—watched him with wide eyes.

Now would be another opportune moment. But I can't risk it. I have to stay focused. I can't focus with her so close.

What?

Her other self watched him with curious eyes, looking at him like he was some magical being. *Well, he was—is—that magic man.*

He gently ran the tip of his nose against hers, tracing the length of it. A perfect triangle. Her eyes fluttered closed at the gesture. That wonderful flush quickly spread across her face.

Good. Her color is returning. That's good. But this. This is torture. And I have only myself to blame.

That thought was so quiet Amity barely heard it.

He swiped his thumb across her cheek.

"Remember?"

". . . Yes."

Those lips that she loved to kiss ghosted over her other self's. He mumbled something low and incoherent.

Amity watched with anticipation as her other self leaned toward him. Cyan eyes widened, and he pulled back. Those lips kissed her forehead instead, lingering a moment longer than they should have.

Huh?

"Good girl. Now stay."

He quickly jumped back, watching her eyes flutter back open as her expression changed from flushed to confused and then finally, as she tried to step toward him, to shock and anger.

"Luka?"

What?

He turned and left her there. She shouted after him. One angry insult after another, but he didn't turn back. That spell wouldn't last long.

What the fuck was that?!

Amity watched her other self try to pull her feet free from their spot. They were locked in.

"Did you just use a fucking spell lock on me, or whatever it's really called?! Did you spell me in place?!" Amity yelled towards the sky.

"Amity, *focus* . . ."

Focus? Focus? How could she focus as her other self was trying to pull her feet free from where they were standing? How she yelled after Luka, who didn't even look back!

"Don't tell me what to do!" she shouted towards the sky.

With a burst of angry energy, she took off after the other Luka towards the warehouse, leaving her other self to struggle alone.

The gravel made no sounds as she ran across the uneven ground. Finally she found him sneaking around the side of what appeared to be an abandoned warehouse. He was trying to peek in through one of the windows with a serious look on his face.

Low moans and small incoherent phrases echoed inside the building. Amity tried to jump up to get a peek, quickly realizing it was in vain. She wasn't just short but also a terrible jumper. Not like she ever needed that skill before.

Luka turned to her, and although she knew he couldn't see her, a fact she had to keep reminding herself of, Amity still felt her body stiffen under his intense glowing gaze.

The light glow from his cornicello quickly intensified. It shone brighter than Amity had ever seen it. He clutched it close to his chest, then kissed it.

I need to make this quick.

Luka's thoughts were louder this time. Amity no longer questioned them. He silently made his way back to the front towards the opening, crouching out of sight. One by one he pulled out his knives and counted. Six. Amity stood behind him, silently watching.

This wasn't her memory, but she could still feel the tenseness in the air. She watched Luka's back slowly rise and fall with each inhale. That weight in her stomach from before intensified. It grew heavier. Thicker. Darker.

Her arms instinctively wrapped tightly around herself and took a timid step back. She could easily peek into the warehouse or stand in front of the opening to see what was inside, but she didn't dare. It didn't matter that whatever was inside couldn't see her.

Luka whipped around the corner so fast she blinked and missed it. Amity darted after him and froze at the sight before her.

There was a small group of kids lying on the floor, no older than sixteen. All lying in a heap on top of each other, all except one. They were sitting straight up with their mouth hanging open and with eyes wide. Wide and glowing bright green. Their short hair stood on end and swayed slowly as some kind of fog seeped out of their mouth and into the air.

It was vivid and bright, morphing in and out of all different colors and shapes. There were images of flowers and small animals, bunnies and deer frolicking and jumping through a meadow, bees buzzing warmly inside flowers before moving onto the next.

A horrible sound escaped the teenager's throat; it gurgled and bubbled until it transformed in a horrified scream. Tears streamed down their face.

The miasma changed rapidly. Its once warm colors shifted in on themselves until there was a disgusting hue of green, then brown, and finally gray and black. The once perfect bright meadow had turned to ash. The flowers wilted and withered into nothing, taking the buzzing bees with them. The animals' flesh melted from their bones before collapsing to the earth, and then finally their bones evaporated into the air.

Amity was going to be sick.

Luka stood strong and swiped his hand across his chest, releasing a bright blue light that sliced the air, heading straight for the teenagers.

It was going to kill them.

"Luka, stop!" she screamed.

He didn't listen. He couldn't hear her.

"Luka!"

Amity ran over to him and tried to shake him out of his spell, not stopping to think if that would work or not. Unfortunately, like the car and the lamppost, he fizzled right through her. Amity's attention whipped to the teens. The spell passed over the ones on the heap. It went straight for the one sitting. Frantically she covered her eyes, not wanting to see the damage. When she had the courage to uncover them, the teenager lay on the ground with the others. The miasma was sliced from their body, floating into the air. Her mouth hung open as it turned on itself, changing to pitch black. Rolling over and over until it formed an orb of shimmery blackness. Then something *moved* inside of it. Then it started to *thrash*. It was so powerful it shook the warehouse.

Luka inhaled deeply, "Wake up and get out!" he commanded.

One by one the teenagers started to stir; once the screaming started, they quickly ran for the entrance. They scrambled past Luka, giving him a wide berth, tears streaming down their faces. None of them dared to look back at the thrashing orb. Luka didn't take his eyes off of it.

It stopped thrashing around and slowly turned over, revealing a long white slit, which opened into a green snakelike eye. Amity felt her knees shake under her.

She took in a deep breath, forcing her lungs to fill completely.

"It's alright. It can't hurt me. This isn't even my memory, this is your memory, and you fought hundreds of demons, right? How bad can this one be . . ."

Her reassurances faded as she saw the look on Luka's face.

His body was tense and his shoulders began to shake. Sweat started to drip down his forehead past those wide cyan eyes she loved. He was *terrified*.

The eye narrowed on him.

"Well, well, well," it began, in a strange, smooth voice, as if there were another speaking at the same time in a calming hiss.

The orb turned quickly, spinning until its shape reformed into something more human, but not completely. It stood on two terrestrial-type legs that were sharply clawed and had a long snakelike tail swirling with delight. Horns stood on each shoulder and cascaded down its spine. Its face was partly covered by a diamond-shaped mask of layered dark green wood, revealing a wide smile with sharp teeth. It also revealed the creature's signature one eye. It flashed in the direction of the car and then back to Luka. It pointed one clawed hand at him. Midnight skin sparkled in a mesmerizing way, like a glittering galaxy.

"If it isn't the witch boy. Come to play with me again?"

Luka viciously tried to shake off his nerves. It helped a little but not by much. She could tell.

Again?

What does it mean by "again"?

"... Dramaur." His jaw locked, as if saying the name held a sharp sting.

Amity watched him silently. A small shift in his stance caught her eye, and then she noticed his hands. They were clutched as his sides so tightly that a small trickle of blood seeped between his knuckles.

Dramaur flashed another sharp smile, scenting the blood. The fact that Amity understood the reason behind it made her skin crawl.

"Feeding off some kids' bad trips? Doesn't seem like something you would do."

"I'd hardly call those brats children. Considering what they were doing before I slipped into their lucid dreams." It inhaled deeply as if remembering the taste. "I don't usually like sweets, but something about their shyness, their innocence, was just so." It brought one of its clawed fingers to its mouth. A forked tongue darted out, circled then sucked on it. "Delicious."

Luka swiped his hand across his body. The six small knives glowed brightly and rose into the air around him. He lifted his bleeding hand in front of him. Amity marveled as she watched the blood reform into a sword.

He wasn't digging his nails into his palms out of fear, he was using his blood as a weapon! That thought made her gape in awe, but also question the masochism of the act.

That spell won't hold at this rate.

Amity stepped back behind him. Far back. Not even stopping to think about *which* spell he was thinking about. She glanced hesitantly at Dramaur, whose tail thrashed about, slapping the floor softly. That horrid eye fell on her again—but that wasn't right, it was looking at the entrance.

"Oh," it mused, "the witchling *does* want to play."

Its front fangs elongated. Its jaw unlatched and separated. Amity's body shivered at the sounds its bones made. Drawing back on its haunches it launched itself toward him.

The demon collided with him roughly, sliding him backward. Sharp claws gripped Luka's blood blade tightly before it quickly jumped back with a *hiss*. It narrowed its one eye toward its claws, which fizzed, as if burned by acid.

That eye widened in amusement, "Oh that is clever."

Luka smirked, and launched himself toward it. That wicked sharp smile spread, and a horrid laugh bubbled out of Dramaur's throat.

It turned and lashed its tail out toward him, aiming for his legs. Luka jumped high into the air, easily avoiding. He aimed his blood blade at that snakelike eye.

One clawed hand swiped and sent him down hard onto the cold concrete. He skidded across the floor.

Dramaur watched him with anticipation as Luka quickly rose to his feet with obvious struggle. There were slashes across his arm where he tried to block the blow.

Dramaur's claws began to sizzle. It flicked the blood off with one quick motion of its hand, then observed the damage as if it had chipped a nail.

"I see you've been practicing your purification rituals. Blessing one's blood is a taxing business. Seems a little dark for a sweet kid like you!" Its eye narrowed in annoyance.

Blessing his blood? Is that why it burned? How does that even work? Again she was both bewildered and horrified. She mentally noted that these emotions seemed to be a common theme of this . . . dream trip? Memory share? Amity had already forgotten what Luka called this process.

Luka darted toward it, sending two blades flying toward its eye. Dramaur easily sent them flying, swatting them away as if they were nothing more than gnats. They clattered to the floor noisily as Luka struck, slashing the blade across Dramaur's chest. Each stroke was blocked by beautiful galaxy-skinned arms.

The demon let out a frustrated breath, feeling the sting of each slice. Its tail snaked around Luka's leg, throwing him off balance and pulling him to the ground. Luka barely had enough time to block his head from shattering on the concrete before he was flung farther into the warehouse. Two daggers went flying, cutting through the air with extreme speed. One was thrown aside, but the other . . . The other slipped inside that snakelike eye before Luka hit the ground.

Dramaur howled with pain and gripped at the dagger tightly. It made a horrible slick squishy sound as the demon pulled it out.

Amity quickly covered her mouth; she was definitely going to throw up!

Luka got back up on his feet, gripping his side. Did he fall hard? Amity didn't see but from the way he was standing, he must've. He wiped the blood dripping from his mouth with a small satisfied smile. A laugh bubbled up his throat.

"Stop fucking laughing, you idiot! You're a fucking mess!" Amity yelled from the entrance, knowing full well he couldn't hear her.

Dramaur tossed the bloody knife away, flinching as two of the forgotten blades struck its back, landing between a few spikes.

Amity's stomach reeled again. She collapsed on the hard ground.

That beautiful galaxy color whirled underneath its skin, churning until there were no more glittering stars. Becoming a deep-sea green. Its eye was oozing blood and some other liquid, one Amity didn't even want to begin to think about, and was very slowly fusing back together.

Her stomach heaved, and she finally threw up.

"Now this is starting to get fun." Its sharp smile returned.

That one eye was glowing a bright green, the way Luka's did blue, illuminating the entire eyeball. It took one step toward Luka, then froze.

Luka's eyes were wide, that satisfied smile was wiped clean from his face as he stared past the demon.

Dramaur's head turned slowly to look over its shoulder. Its eye narrowed in confusion for a moment, then widened with realization. The reptilian tail flicked back and forth with delight.

Amity wiped her mouth with the back of her hand and lifted her head. They were staring right at her.

"Now. Isn't. This. Interesting," it mused, its smile growing too wide for its face. Its jaw reattached itself and the tips of its smile were hidden behind the mask.

Amity fell back on her ass, her body paralyzed by fear. She couldn't move. She couldn't think. She couldn't *breathe.*

"But that's not possible! You can't see me!"

The demon's body shifted toward her as Luka made his way around the other side.

"I can see you, *witchling.*"

Amity gaped at it. *What the fuck is going on?!*

Light footsteps behind her caught her attention. It was *her.* Her other self stepped through the entrance of the warehouse, clutching small stones in her hands. Her cornicello glowed a bright light blue like Luka's.

Dramaur's attention flicked between her and Luka, who had now made his way back to her. He stood in front of her and called back the other knives to him. They sliced through the air and hovered around him, sharp tips pointed toward the demon.

"I told you to stay." He scolded, plucking of the knives out of the air and handing it to her. Hilt first.

"Yeah, well, your spell wore off."

"Plan's changed." His eyes narrowed on his opponent.

Biggest understatement of the fucking century!

"A lesser demon wouldn't have caused you to use something as dangerous as blood manipulation." She threw away the stones and held the knife as if she knew how to do more than stick her opponent with the pointy end.

Blood manipulation? Was that what it was called? When he used his blood to make that sword?

Amity turned her attention back to the demon who was looking at them all too happily. Her stomach turned again. She braced herself for something terrible.

Dramaur laughed in amusement and then clapped its hands together. The sound echoed in the space, raising the hairs on the back of her neck.

"Let's play a *new* game of witching. You stole my fun for the night, so I'll *take* something of yours."

Luka squared his stance in front of her. It was no good. Dramaur struck fast, charging through Amity as if she was nothing but smoke and flinging Luka to the side as if he was nothing more than a rag doll, sending him crashing into the ground.

The other Amity struck the dagger into its neck.

Only making its smile widen.

With one hand, it lightly tapped her forehead and then pulled back. Her eyes glowed brightly, and her head was thrown back. A bright blue light, almost white, seeped out of her forehead like smoke following the demon's claws. It flowed into her cornicello.

Dramaur plucked it from her chest with a sharp claw.

Amity watched horrified as her other self's body went limp and collapsed onto the cold ground.

"Amity!"

It jumped back, floating into the air as it marveled at its prize. Luka ran toward her other self, clutching her limp body tightly. His eyes glowed brightly, so bright it hurt to look at them.

"What did you do?" Luka's voice was deeper and raw, like some cornered wild animal.

The pooled blood at the corner of his mouth and from the wound on his arm began to hover over him, morphing into a large ball before forming into sharp spears. They started to slowly grow in size. The veins of his neck and face jutted out starkly. His skin was paling by the second.

"What the fuck did you do!?"

The demon's skin once again churned until it reverted back to that beautiful midnight color, but there were no glittering stars. Its one eye shone down at him with delight.

"You have one year. One year to find me. I'll leave clues with some lesser demons. Find me, and I'll give this back."

Then it vanished.

Everything went quiet.

Luka's blood dripped from where it hovered above them, pooling onto the concrete as Amity watched her other self open her eyes.

"Who are you?"

CHAPTER EIGHTEEN

Amity shook her head furiously. Her mind was racing. The memory of her life with Luka hadn't returned, but now she at least knew how she lost her memory of him. She still had so many unanswered questions. And Dramaur. Her stomach turned. When she closed her eyes she could still see that midnight skin. That smooth voice that echoed with another's whisper. Someone was calling her, but she couldn't make out the words.

Everything had swept away from her in large gales leaving only darkness in their wake. She could feel that snakelike eye on her even in the blackness.

The voice grew louder over and over again—it called. She recognized that voice. His voice.

Brown eyes flashed open. She took in a large breath, too large; sending her into a coughing fit as her body propelled upright. He caught her by the shoulders.

"Amity, it's alright! You're alright. Just breathe." Luka's voice was in a panic.

He wiped her forehead; which was drenched with sweat. When? For how long? It didn't matter. She was hyperventilating. There was no space to think. To *breathe*.

Warm hands cradled her cheeks. He pressed his forehead to hers.

"It's alright, I've got you. Breathe with me," he whispered. His voice was soft. No trace of panic. He inhaled deeply. Held. Then exhaled.

With each breath she tried to mimic him, until they started to breathe as one. A smile warmed his features. He traced the shape of her nose with his.

"That's it. Good girl."

A giggle escaped her, then grew into a deep laugh. He started to laugh too, but it quickly faded when he realized the reason *why* she was laughing. Yes, calling her a "good girl" was strange, and she probably started laughing because of it, but this deeper laugh wasn't humorous. Amity was in shock.

Gently he guided her to her feet, but it was no use. She fell against him, her knees weakly crumbling beneath her weight. It was to be expected. Memory projection was taxing, especially if the people involved weren't properly trained or prepared. At least that's how Luka explained it.

Luka brought her to the bathroom as her laughter faded. Sitting her down on the edge of the tub, then silently filled it. Amity kept her attention on the floor, as she grew unbearably quiet. Just the thought of lifting her head exhausted her. Luka went back into her apartment, returning quickly. Silent as a ghost, she watched his feet as they stirred. Luka sprinkled some things inside the tub as it filled. Checking the water periodically before finally stopping it when it was full and the temperature was just right. She watched him walk out, then stop just at the doorframe. He faced the hall.

"I won't look, unless you want me to."

Amity lifted her heavy head and stared at his back for a long moment. That wasn't a cheeky comment.

Luckily she wasn't wearing much, but her arms felt heavy as she undressed, her clothes sticking to her skin with all the sweat, making the surprisingly difficult task harder.

Slowly she descended into the tub. The warm water engulfed her, flowing over her skin with a vibrancy she desperately needed. Amity slipped her body under the water until her head the last to descend. Then with eyes closed she adjusted her body so her knees were bent out of the water then let herself fully slip under the surface, remaining there for a few moments before bursting free.

Luka turned toward her, made his way over to the edge of the tub then sat on the floor with his back against it. He kept his promise. He didn't look at her once.

Amity pulled her knees into her chest, hugging them tightly. Her feet scuffed the bottom of the tub, feeling a roughness under her toes. Salt . . . Luka had scattered the bottom with seasalt. A warm feeling blossomed in her chest.

That wasn't all he did. Floating on the water's surface were small buds of lavender.

That feeling traveled down to her navel, blossoming with a warm, familiar heat he frequently sparked inside her.

Freaya strolled into the bathroom and made herself comfortable in his lap. She meowed and purred, begging to be pet. Luka obediently obliged with a small smile. It wasn't long before Freaya's purrs filled the quiet space.

Amity fiddled with a small lavender bud on top of her knee. Her mind had been reeling when she was in his memories. For every answer she received, she gained a dozen questions. She should be interrogating him. Figuring out exactly who that thing, who the demon Dramaur, was. What happened to those kids afterward? How does blessing one's blood work? What happened to *her* afterward? *I guess I have a vague idea, based on what Alex said last night.*

She pulled her hair over one shoulder, letting the steam of the bath rise against her back. Amity should be interrogating him, but now there was nothing but a vast emptiness.

"You . . ." His hand stopped for a moment, and she watched him take in a shaky breath. "You hate me."

He didn't state it as a question. He said it as if it was something he knew for a fact. Amity waited patiently for him to continue. Luka slumped forward slightly and took in another breath.

"You can hate me, that's fine. I . . . I failed." That voice she loved wavered slightly. "I deserve it." Unsteady fingers continued petting Freaya, to stop her glaring at him. "I should've stayed away, I . . ." He gritted his teeth and took in another shaky breath, "I should've let you live a life without me in it." Amity shifted in the tub, letting her legs rest on the floor. Anxious fingers began fiddling with the lavender buds, piling them on top of her nearly dry hands and knees. If what she hypothesized earlier about her desires being tied to her memories, how would she have lived her life without them? She didn't have a strong desire to take over the shop, but would she have ended up doing that anyway? She didn't want to think on it. "I did try . . . I stayed away for so long but then you ran into me and I-I couldn't." He gritted his teeth once again. "I'm a selfish bastard, and you deserve to know what was taken from you. I won't stop looking for that demon until they give you your memories back. They made my biggest fear come true. You shouldn't have to suffer as well."

His elbow rested on the tub beside her, but he still didn't look her way. Maybe he felt grateful for that? Amity didn't know for sure. Damp fingertips traced his tattoo that vanished under his rolled-up sleeve. She reached out, wrapped the soft fabric between her fingers and held onto it lightly.

For a moment he watched her them out of the corner of his eye, still not looking at her. After a while his rough fingers enclosed around hers in a tense hold. She swallowed hard as a flush spread across her skin.

"Luka, look at me."

He turned and he did. He looked with those beautiful forlorn eyes traveling slowly up her body. Starting with her fingers entwined with his. Up her sore arm. Then back to her knees where she had stacked the lavender buds. Up her dark hair. Then finally to her eyes. Amity's pale cheeks flushed deeper, and her heart hammered against her chest. Instinctively she squeezed his hand tighter and took a breath, refocusing her thoughts.

"This is not your fault," she said. Cyan eyes widened on her. "Thank you for not giving up."

He turned her hand over in his and kissed the inside of her palm. She could feel his lips shake against her skin.

Amity shifted onto her knees, wincing at the slightly painful position, as he placed her palm against his cheek. The warm water rushed over her when she sat up and turned his face toward her.

"I'm glad I found you again." She finished. Gently pressing her forehead to his,. Luka smiled, blinking back a few tears. He met her eyes once again, and his smile grew.

"I'm so happy you found me."

Affectionately he traced the outline of her nose with his, causing her heart to melt at the tender gesture. Heat rushed through her body, like his touch sent tiny warm waves through her, lulling her into a state of comfort. Like snuggling under a cozy blanket on a crisp fall day. A deep breath filled her lungs; brown eyes drifted to a close.

"Seasalt and sandalwood," she mused.

"What?"

"You smell like seasalt and sandalwood, from the charm bag you carry around."

A light chuckle passed his lips. "Yes, kitten."

Amity opened her eyes, expecting his to be closed, but they weren't. Those cyan eyes were watching her in awe.

"I like . . . it." Her cheeks heated in embarrassment. She pulled back, shifting her arm over her chest while he still held the other.

"I like . . ." He trailed off, tracking her movements. How the water swayed against her thighs, how she held her chest a little too tightly, barely covering any of it.

Luka glanced up at her quickly, a small smirk on his face. Amity ripped her hand out of his grasp and splashed him roughly with water.

"Pervert!"

He quickly covered his face with a wide smile as Freaya went running out of the bathroom.

Amity turned her back to him, crossing her arms even tighter over her chest. Luka's laughter softly faded as he sat back down, his back to hers.

She waited until the blush receded from her cheeks, then pumped some soap into her hands.

Lathered it between her fingers, trying to keep her mind from wandering to a situation where she would very much like this bath to go. How it could easily turn into a shower. How Luka could easily take off his clothes; well, partly her clothes. A smirk crept onto her lips at the thought he was wearing her clothes. She liked that very much even though she couldn't pinpoint the exact reasons why. The soap formed large bubbles in her hands before she realized it. She shook her thoughts away trying to clear her head. The heat of the water combined with his presence was making this very simple task extremely difficult.

Amity glided the soap up her sore arms, carefully rubbing it against her tender skin. As she brought warm water up to her shoulder to wash the suds, she imagined Luka's hand instead of hers—pumping more soap into her hands, then gently gliding the cool liquid up her other arm. Up to her shoulder. Her collarbone. Then to her chest. Her thighs pressed together.

Amity could see him in her shower. Sweating in the steaming water. His hair sticking to his face as he kissed up her shoulder, up her neck, and to her swollen lips. One of his hands palming her breast as the other held her up against the wall. Her legs wrapped tightly around him as he thrust deep inside her at a tantalizingly slow pace. She felt another rush of heat in her lower belly. It churned and swirled in a demanding way as she continued to imagine Luka thrusting inside her. A shaky *audible* breath escaped her.

"Now who's the pervert?" Luka's low voice echoed off the tile walls as he pressed the back off his head to hers.

Amity froze. She glanced down at her hand palming her left breast while the other had slipped under the water between her thighs. She wrapped her legs closer to her chest, keeping her hands within sight.

"Tell me, *kitten*, what were you thinking about just now?"

"Nothing!"

She could practically hear him smile wider. He shuffled to a stand but she didn't turn to look.

"Since you're feeling *so much better*, I'll head home." Amity refused turn around; she only gripped her knees tighter. "I put your food in the fridge for you. Call me if anything comes up. Spend the rest of the day resting."

For a moment she thought she heard him walk out.

"Wait!" She turned quickly, covering her chest with one hand.

Luka wasn't leaving. He didn't even make it out of the bathroom. All he did was stand. Patiently he waited for her to continue. She took in a deep breath, unable to find the right words.

The corner of his mouth tipped up into a small smile. Without a word, he slid one of the towels off the wall rack and held it in between their faces.

Amity blinked a few times before she was able to process what he was doing. Was he going to dry her off? Her cheeks heated at the thought. Slowly she rose on shaky from the tub, allowing a few moments for the water to drip off of her naked body before timidly stepping onto the plush bath mat. Carefully she stepped toward him. A part of her wanted to take the towel from his hands and pull him into a kiss. A kiss that would quickly become something more. Or even just have him dry her off—watch him slowly run the towel up her legs, her arms, her chest—only to have that quickly become something more too.

She did neither.

Amity stepped in front of him, then turned and wrapped the towel around herself, like she would do with a blanket.

Rough fingertips went to her temple, then gently gathered her hair up. Luka was tying it into a loose bun when she finally spoke.

"I stabbed a demon," she said quietly.

In all honesty that very thought terrified her, a distinct contrast to the way Luka's talented fingers felt.

"You did."

Skilled fingers wrapped an elastic around her messy bun, then ran down the curve of her neck before resting on her shoulders. He rubbed them softly through the towel.

Her eyes narrowed. "It called me 'witchling.'"

"It did." His hands moved to her arms, massaging the sore muscles.

"Did I know magic?" she asked, turning toward him with sparkling brown eyes.

Luka tucked a loose curl behind her ear, fingers stilling at the curve of her jaw.

"I was teaching you. You had more skill with herbal remedies."

She thought about that for a moment before tilting her chin up to meet his gaze.

"Hence the cabinet full of herbs."

He nodded and started sweeping his thumb just below her ear, lost in thought.

"Dramaur," she said, and his thumb froze in place, "they have my memories."

Luka nodded stiffly.

"I want them back."

He nodded again.

"I will get them back, I promise."

His thumb made another sweep as Amity felt a spark ignite within her.

"We."

It froze just at the curve of her jaw. Amity turned into the touch, facing him.

"What?" Cyan eyes widened. Staring at her as if she said something insane.

"*We* will get them back." She repeated with confidence. "That's what the other one said. It said that they—which I'm guessing is Dramaur—"

"Stop saying its name."

Luka seethed. His eyes started to glow faintly.

Amity took a breath and held the towel a little tighter. She didn't expect that reaction.

"It said to take me with you—"

"No."

"That's what it said!"

"I said no, Amity!"

"They're my memories!"

"Enough, Amity!"

"And why did they take them anyway? I doubt it was because you ruined their 'fun.' It knows you, doesn't it?"

"I said *enough!*"

Luka grabbed her tightly by the shoulders, too tightly. She winced. Instantly he adjusted his grip and gently rubbed the now even throbbing spots.

"I'm sorry, I . . ." He sucked in a breath. Rough padded fingers grazed up her neck. Gently holding her face in his hands. Luka's voice was a little shaky when he finally spoke. "I'm going to fix this."

"Just like last night? The time before, when I dragged your ass back to my apartment?"

Determined brown eyes stared at him. Cyan eyes narrowed on her.

Stubborn bastard.

His hands fell from her face, and she immediately missed their touch.

Luka turned and started walking out into the living room, put her keys onto the couch then slung his jacket on.

Was he just going to leave? Just like that? In the middle of an argument? Amity ran out of the bathroom, gripping her towel tightly around herself.

"Luka!"

"You need to eat, then I want you to rest for the rest of the day."

"Luka—!"

He closed the door roughly behind him.

CHAPTER NINETEEN

Fuck.

Luka pinched the bridge of his nose as he leaned against the hood of his car. It took him a while to remember exactly where he parked, wandering the side streets next to Halley's for at least fifteen minutes.

A groan escaped him, wishing his jacket was just a little longer; he already got one jogger to snicker at him; he didn't want anyone else to notice.

Now here he was. With a ticketed car. A hard-on. And *extremely* agitated.

He ripped the ticket out from under his windshield wiper, and with a low grumble the paper evaporated in his hand.

Normally he wouldn't do this kind of thing, but today was an exception. Today his patience was too short. And it was—All. Her. Fault.

The fucking nerve of her. Teasing him like that. Luka slammed the door to his apartment and locked it with too much force.

Luka shucked off his shoes and threw his jacket onto the coat rack before storming off to his room. Falling back onto his bed with his hands in his hair. *Fuck!* He could smell her all over him—see her in the bathtub when he closed his eyes. The steam surrounding her flush body. Her wet hair hanging over one shoulder, dark, almost black against her skin. Her flush, soft, skin. And the way she was looking at him.

Luka groaned feeling shifting against the uncomfortable tightness of his pants. He let out a shaky breath and moved to the head of the bed, tearing off his pants. Impatient fingers grabbed a small jar on the bedside table, quickly unscrewed the lid, then tossed it somewhere onto the bed.

Cheeks, still chilled from the October air, flushed a deep crimson, and heavy eyelids fell to a close.

Those beautiful big brown eyes. Her red flushed cheeks. The way she held her legs to her chest.

Luka shucked off his briefs, throwing them across the room. He reached into the jar, taking a small amount of its contents between his fingers. He watched as the small white mounds began to melt away in his touch. Coconut oil. His eyes closed lazily as he inhaled a shaky breath. A smile spread on his lips as the oil warmed in his hand. Smooth as silk. Slippery. Warm. Wet.

He imagined his fingers inside her. She would be soaked. Hot.

"I bet she feels even better than this."

He leaned back onto the mattress, remembering her in front of him. How he managed not to pounce on her was a fucking miracle.

No.

No it wasn't.

It was *right*.

Luka gritted his teeth.

He wouldn't do that. He wouldn't go that far with her. Not until she was ready. Not until she remembered him. Until he fixed everything . . .

He shook the thought away with an angry growl. *Not now, don't think about it now.* He recalled her in the bath again. The smile quickly returned.

Her breasts, peppered with lavender buds, pushed tightly against her knees. Heaving with each breath she took. If she lifted her shoulders just a little bit, they would burst free.

He moaned softly as he wrapped his oiled hand around his cock and began stroking himself from base to tip.

"Everything's going to be fine."

CHAPTER TWENTY

Despite the remainder of Amity's day not going the way she planned—sexless—she did as he said. A quick trip to the grocery store a few blocks away and then straight back to her apartment. Where she curled up on her couch and remained there until it was time to crawl into bed and sleep. Her sheets welcomed her with the smell of sandalwood and seasalt. Amity closed her eyes, letting the scent fill her, warm her, and lull her to sleep. *Pretty bastard.*

Amity topped off the large mug of hot mocha coffee with coconut whipped cream. Then she lightly tapped the jar of hazelnut spice over it, giving it a nice dusting. Carefully she brought it over to the bar top side of the counter where Alex sat with his hands in his hair. He had decided to work from Halley's today, something about letting Krystal rest in peace. Her cold was still raging.

"Shouldn't you be there?" Amity asked, placing the steaming mug in front of him. The corner of his mouth tipped up as he thanked her.

"She kicked me out." He exaggerated, running his hands through his hair with a sigh. "I'll work half a day here and then go back." Alex worked in the IT department for a start-up tech company, completely remote. Despite his busy schedule and current frustration, he really liked it.

The keyboard of his computer clicked quickly as he finished typing out a work ticket. Then he closed his laptop with a heavy sigh, pushed it to the side, and pulled his mug in front of him.

Alex took a long sip from his hot coffee, then lightly tugged at the collar of his black turtleneck, avoiding her eyes. "About the other night—"

"When you scared me half to death?"

"I texted you first." He sniffled, trying to hold off a sneeze.

"You mean last week?" she said. Brown eyes glanced up at her, confused. Alex's brain definitely wasn't free of the fog of his cold. "Yeah, I'm still mad at you about that."

"Yeah, well, I apologized. Whatever, then . . . sorry about that." He sneezed loudly inside his sweater.

"Wow." Amity elongated the word in a monotone voice as long as possible. "That looked like it physically hurt."

"Hey—!"

She put her finger to her lips, silencing him; the shop wasn't busy, but it wasn't empty either. Frustrated fingers ran through his hair again.

"I'm sorry, okay? I shouldn't have . . . well."

"Banged on my door at the crack of dawn? Went psycho on a guy I was trying to sleep with? Dropped a monumental, life-changing bomb on me, making me go into a panicked life crisis? Ruined my good morning by interrupting me having—"

"Stop talking! I don't ever want to think about that. *Ever.*"

The corner of her mouth kicked up into a smirk as she went back and poured herself some tea. She tapped her phone screen lightly as it charged beside him on the counter. With a huff, he shrugged off his jacket that he had slung over his shoulders like a blanket.

"I take it he told you everything?" he asked.

Amity nodded.

"Did you apologize?" she asked.

Alex nodded.

"Like *actually* apologize, or did you give a half-assed apology like the one you gave just now?"

He took his coffee a little too roughly, spilling some on the saucer it was on.

"I *apologized*."

"Mhm," she hummed. Something popped into her head. "So did you do that too? Hunt demons? Are you some kind of witch too?"

Alex almost spit out his coffee. "Hell no!"

"But you knew about it? About Luka?" His sister prodded, knowing she was right.

Alex took another sip, then licked the excess whipped cream off of his lips. "Yeah I knew. Kind of hard to hide it when you're a kid, I guess. But I never learned or anything. You were the one he was teaching, you two became closer than we ever were. Spoiled brat." He mumbled that last insult, but it was still loud enough for her to catch it.

A small smile crept on her lips, but it didn't stay long. Brown eyes swept attention over the soft couches; apparently word had gotten out that their cafe was a nice study place. A few students were by the window having a small conversation before they started looking at the biography section. Most of which was composed of band biographies and memoirs. *They must be on a date*, she thought warmly.

On the other side of the shop was a man she had seen a few times before. Clean-cut with dark curly red hair trimmed short at the sides. He took one last sip from his coffee before bringing the empty mug to the dish station in the corner of the room, just beside the counter. Green eyes smiled at her as he made his way over.

Amity smiled politely at him; she couldn't remember his name for the life of her, but he always took home some type of dessert before he left. Probably why he was making his way over to her now.

Amity guessed he must have been some type of businessman from the way he dressed, or maybe even a lawyer? He wore a white button-up shirt with a black tie, black slacks, and a black peacoat. *Very fancy.*

The man placed his briefcase on the counter beside him as he pulled out his wallet.

"Hi, Amity," he greeted with a smile.

"Hi—" She cut herself off, giving a sheepish smile.

"It's alright," he smiled. "It's Rune."

"*Rune.*" Her eyes widened curiously. "I like it."

His eyes practically sparkled hearing that. Alex side-eyed him from his spot. He took an obnoxious sip from his mug.

"What can I get for you today?" she asked, sending a sneaky but brief glare at her brother. Rune didn't seem to notice.

"I think I'll have something sweet today," he began, looking over the dessert display. There were still a few blueberry scones left as well as some pumpkin tarts and a few lemon cakes. "How about one of those lemon cakes, please."

"Good choice." She rang up his order and turned the tablet around for payment. She pulled a small bag from under the counter and placed the dessert inside, careful not to break it.

"Here you are," she said with a smile, handing him his treat.

"Thank you!" put the treat inside his briefcase. "I was wondering . . ." he began, catching her attention just as she was tying her hair up into a ponytail. Amity brushed off some flower that had gotten on her black turtleneck when she got the desert, and waited for him to continue. "Would you like to get coffee sometime? My treat of course."

Amity's cheeks flushed. Did he just ask her out?! Before she could open her mouth to speak, Alex spoke up first.

"She works in a coffee shop. She doesn't want to go to one."

Brown eyes glared at him as Rune tried to laugh off his words as some kind of joke.

"That is a little redundant now that I think about it. We don't have to get coffee if you don't want to, we can always get lunch or—"

"She's spoken for," Alex cut in with a sharp tone.

"Alex!"

Brown eyes glared right back at her, taking another sip from his mug. Rune pulled his bottom lip between his teeth watching them silently.

Amity rubbed her forehead irritably and heaved a sigh. She put that polite customer service smile back on her face and turned back to him.

"Please excuse *him*," she said. Rune's eyes lit up as Amity collected herself. "Thank you, Rune, I'd love to but I'm already seeing someone."

A smirk crept on his lips. "Seeing or dating?"

Amity froze. Were they a couple? It's not like they had any time to talk about that. He did ask her kind of, sort of, not really? Were they? Did she even know? No!

"*Dating*."

Rune glanced over at Alex out of the corner of his eye. For a moment his smirk kicked up.

"It's alright, no harm done," he smiled. He pulled a bill out of his wallet and placed it on the counter.

"Until next time, Amity. Please, keep the change." Rune flashed a vibrant smile, one that made the many freckles on his cheeks rise, then turned on his heel. He held the door open for Rex as they strode in wearing a heavy winter coat. They leaned against the counter, tracking Rune as he walked by the windows with hungry eyes.

They whistled. "Who's the *fox*?"

"Close your mouth, Rex, you're salivating," Alex scoffed, shuffling his coat over his shoulders with a shiver. "And who the hell says fox."

Rex ignored him and threw their coat on the empty seat beside him. Like their friends, they were also in a turtle-neck. The weather had taken a turn for the worst that morning, bringing in a light snowfall and very, *very* cold winds.

"I see Amity's collecting all the studs." They smiled at her, causing her to flush. She hid her face in her hands and turned away.

"He's just a regular," Amity mumbled under her breath, ringing up Rune's order then depositing the change-at least ten dollars-in the tip jar. Rune always over-tipped when she worked. "What brings you to this side of town?"

she asked, changing the subject. Grabbing a small plate, and a pumpkin tart on it.

Rex tracked the plate as Amity made her way over to them.

"Thank you, ma'am!" Rex handed Amity their card, who rang up the total. "I was just in the neighborhood." Amity gave them a look of disbelief. "*Fine*. I haven't heard from you in a while and I wanted an update on that guy. What's his name? Luka! The guy with the nice ass."

Amity almost dropped Rex's coffee to the floor. Her eyes went wide as they darted from Rex to Alex.

"Oh, I told him al—"

"I know you told him!"

With a smug smile on his face, Alex went to back behind the counter to refill his coffee.

"Alex said apparently they're old friends."

"Very old friends," he tagged on. Amity glared at him.

"So have you seen him since—I mean, I haven't heard anything about him from *you*." Rex took a satisfying bite of their tart.

"She has." Her brother answered.

That smug prick leaned against the counter sipping his coffee right next to her. She wanted nothing more than to knock it out of his stupid hands.

"Can you *stop*! God why are you even here? Go home already!" Amity huffed. Frustratingly retying her hair. Ignoring the patrons that turned her way. "Can we please talk about this later when *he's* not here?" she yelled in the loudest whisper she could muster, flipping him off from behind the counter so the patrons wouldn't see.

Rex laughed from their spot, amused by the conversation.

"After-work drinks?"

After a quick stop to feed the demanding black void known as Freaya, Amity met Rex at a small bar downtown. One known for their cheap, strong drinks and hipster atmosphere.

They were all decked out for Halloween. White fake cobwebs hung across the wooden ceiling beams as well as a few skeletons leaning across the industrial-style bar.

Amity slid off her jacket, which she *did* remember this time, and slung it on the back of her bar chair.

Rex arrived about ten minutes later and plopped down right next to her.

"Who're you texting?" they asked with a smirk.

Amity took another long sip from her cranberry vodka and flipped her phone over. She had been contemplating calling and texting Luka. She wrote out at least a dozen messages.

Let's talk this through like normal adults.|

The fuck did you run out on me for, asshole?|

She immediately deleted them as soon as they were written. The fact was she wanted to see him. *Needed* to see him. But she wasn't about to start an argument over text. Even though he did walk out on her. Amity thought about calling him immediately after he left, but she was so tired she passed out on the couch as soon as she got back from the store. That damn couch that had his smell all over it. Her bed was even worse!

She patted her cheeks trying to hide her blush. "No one," she finally answered.

"Uh-huh." They knew exactly who Amity was texting—or rather *trying* to text.

After a few more drinks and a basket of fries later, Amity brought Rex up to speed . . . well, kind of.

Amity slammed her hand down onto the bar top.

"I just don't see the problem! Why is he acting like this?!" she raged, shoving a handful of fries into her mouth.

Rex couldn't help but snicker at that.

"Well let's think about this again," they said, trying to calm their friend's growing frustration knowing full well Amity could get a little . . . unpredictable when she drank. Luckily, despite the bar being close to full, no one tried to talk to her. That would probably just make it worse considering she was already agitated.

"'Kay," she sighed, elongating the word and leaning her chin in her palms in a loud pout.

"You said he took his last girlfriend rock climbing, right?" they asked, taking another sip of their drink.

Amity closed her eyes trying to think, before finally remembering she had covertly replaced "demon slaying" with "rock climbing."

"Yeah!"

"And then she got hurt?"

"Right!" Amity shot her head up, almost falling out of her seat. "But those were completely different circumstances, it's not like I was actually gonna climb, I was just gonna watch." Amity lied.

Rex leaned into their palm and laughed. "You? You really were just gonna watch him climb a rock?"

Amity shrugged her shoulders and ate two more fries before responding. "Yeah . . . maybe."

"Uh-huh, that's what I thought. It just sounds like he's a little traumatized," they said, sliding the basket of fries their way and taking some.

"But it wasn't his fault! I told him so!"

"That's not how it works, Amity, you know that."

". . . I guess." It took her a while to get over a guy she once dated who was two-timing her. She drank the last of her second drink and ordered a soda.

Rex watched her for a moment before scanning over the crowded room, their eyes landing on some familiar faces.

"That's something he needs to work through. Until then he's just being stubborn, which is stupid, and all men are . . ." They paused, looking back to their friend expectantly.

Amity smiled wide with a giggle and lifted her glass.

"All men are stupid."

Rex smiled and clinked their glass to hers. They laughed warmly.

"But on a serious note, I'm glad you found someone you like. It's been a while." Amity's cheeks flushed. "*And,*" Rex began, their eyes sliding back to the familiar faces across the way, "something tells me he'll apologize soon."

Alex had been staring over at the bar top of the small hole-in-the-wall bar that Luka dragged him too. They had come here often before their fallout, and the whole place was decked out for Halloween. Cobwebs hung from the wooden beams on the ceiling and a few skeletons sat on the bar top. That's where Luka thought he was looking the whole time he groaned on and on about his most recent fight with a certain curly-haired brat. *That's definitely her new nickname now!*

"She's just so stubborn!" he exclaimed, shoving a fry into his mouth and glaring at his phone.

Alex turned his attention back to his friend, took a sip of beer, and stole a fry. "Absolutely, she's always been like that." He took another greedily.

These fries were good. Real good. Sweetened with something neither of them could define. Cinnamon maybe? It didn't matter; they were too good.

Luka shoved another fry into his mouth and swallowed hard, "I mean, why can't she just let me do this? This one thing?"

Alex took another long sip of his beer. "Did you tell her that?"

Luka chewed on another fry, averting his gaze at all costs. "I said I would take care of it . . ."

Alex stared at him through narrowed eyes.

"What?"

"Well she's involved now, it's not like how it was before."

Luka grunted, taking another long swig of his beer. He reached for another fry only to have Alex pull the basket farther away at the last second.

"And these are her memories. If your roles were reversed, would you trust that she would 'handle it'?"

"So you're saying she doesn't trust me?"

Alex glanced back at the bar top, sorting out his thoughts. "Well, 'trust' maybe isn't the right word . . . Maybe she just doesn't feel comfortable with it, you know?"

Luka put down his drink.

"No, I don't know."

"Well, if you were in her shoes, would you be okay with someone else fighting a demon to win back *your* memories?"

"I—" He bit back his response. ". . . It's too dangerous."

"Uh-huh, and would that stop you?"

Luka snatched the fries back out of his friend's hand and looked away. No. *Absolutely not. That wouldn't stop me no matter what.*

A smirk kicked up on Alex's face as he watched his friend munch his frustration away.

"She's not the only one who's stubborn." He finished off the last of his beer, then turned his attention back to the bar top. "And it's not like I'm exactly *happy* about her going with you either." Despite Alex mumbling that last part under his breath, Luka heard every word.

He swallowed the last of his fries before following his gaze to the bar top. There she was, sitting tall with her hair a perfect mass of dark curls, her rosy cheeks, and a wide smile. A wide smile directed—not at *him*—at some tall blond that looked way too happy to be standing next to her. Rex rolled their eyes and met Luka's across the room. Their eyes widened, darting between Luka and the stranger next to Amity.

You've got to be kidding me.

Luka stood from his spot and carried both their now-empty glassesp. Alex begrudgingly trailed behind him, then went straight for his sister while Luka brought the glasses to the drop-off station at the end of the bar.

Alex leaned upon the back of Rex's chair. "Well, well, well, fancy running into you two here."

"Pretty sure you just followed us here."

"Me? Never!" he said, taking a few fries from the basket between them. The man turned his attention to Alex, stepping behind his sister.

He was tall with messy blond hair and dark eyes. Not her type. But cute. Luka paused, placing the glasses on the bar mat. *What was her type?*

Now that he thought about it, he'd only heard of a few of her boyfriends but he'd never seen any of them. He looked himself over in the bar's mirror and rebraided the top half of his hair back.

I'm her type, duh! He glanced back at the blond who had now placed his hand on the back of her chair. Luka's eyes narrowed. Between everything else going on with her, their argument the other day, the fact a certain *someone* had been hanging around Halley's, and now this new guy, his frustration was reaching its peak.

Don't make a scene, he warned himself, brushing off his jacket and adjusting his nose piercing; he went for a black stud today. Just before turning, he overheard Alex and Amity again.

"Your boyfriend's here," he heard Alex say slyly.

The guy behind her tensed and removed his hand from her chair, but she tilted her head in that cute little way with her cheek in her palm.

"I don't have a boyfriend."

Luka's eyes widened.

Not cute, not cute. Not. At. All.

He quickly checked his reflection again. *Fuck it.*

CHAPTER TWENTY ONE

Amity's face brightened at the sight of the tall brunet walking her way. "Luka!"

The corner of his mouth tilted up into a smirk and his blue eyes shone brightly. "We just keep running into each other."

"We sure do," she murmured happily.

Luka stopped just between her brother and the newcomer. Amity didn't really remember his name. Derek? Chris? Something like that. He was grabbing a round for his friends at a table in the back. Maybe?

Whatever. That didn't matter. What *did* matter was that Luka was too far away from her. And in tight jeans too, the ones that made his ass look like she could bounce quarters off of it! She let her eyes travel down to his waist and then back up to his chest.

"What are you doing?" Alex asked, giving her an accusing look.

"Nothing!" she exclaimed, turning back to her drink.

"Uh-huh, *sure.*" They all laughed, and Amity's cheeks flushed.

That was sloppy. Stupid tasty alcohol and stupid tasty drinks!

"Looks like someone's a little *tipsy,*" Luka teased, swiping her drink out of her grasp. She watched him dumbfounded as he took a long sip.

"You!—You won't even like it." She went to grab his arm, but even with her elevated on the barstool, he still avoided her easily.

"Hmm? How do you know that?" Tauntingly he took a long sip from her drink.

"You don't like sweets—"

"Oh look, here they are! You want to help me out with these?" The blond asked with a wink, holding a few freshly poured beers in his hands. Amity looked at him, unimpressed.

"Yeah, man, I said I would," she deadpanned, a fact she "miraculously" remembered. His name apparently wasn't as important. Alex and Rex laughed, then went into their own conversation.

"You're so cute," he laughed.

She looked between the two men with a confused expression, choosing to ignore the warning bell going off in her head.

The man stepped back so she could maneuver out of her chair, a maneuver that she was having difficulty with. Luka gripped her by the shoulders and put her back into her seat.

"You stay right there. I'll go."

If Amity was just a little bit more sober, she would've noticed that tight smile across his face. Luka placed a tightly fisted hand on the bar top and leaned down close to her ear. "I'll take you home, kitten."

"It's fine, man, she's got it. Come on—"

Luka cut him off. "I said I'll help." His voice was curt, as if his patience was on a short fuse.

"Dude, she's *fine*. Back *off*."

"She is not fine. And if you were paying attention, you would—"

"Enough, Luka, I said I would help, so I will."

"See, she's fine. Why don't you go and bother someone else and leave us alone."

"Hey."

"I said I would help. Take it or make two trips."

"What is your fucking problem. Just leave her alone."

"Hey."

"Amity, get your coat. Now."

"You want me to spell it out for you? Get lost. She's not interested in some punk who looks like they can't pass a background check."

"Oy!" Amity turned quickly in her seat, grabbed the man's shirt, and thrust her fist into his lower abdomen. "Don't *ever* talk to my boyfriend like that."

The blonde keeled over, coughing and spilling the two beers in his hands all over him. Before she could register what she did, Luka pulled her off the stool and was running out the door, one hand carrying her coat and the other entwined with hers.

They ran a few blocks before pulling her onto a side street and then the mouth of an alleyway. She was panting by the time they stopped. *Stupid fucking cardio!*

The hot air looked like smoke in the frigid night air. Thank fuck she remembered her coat because the temperature dropped even lower after the sun had set.

Amity leaned on her knees, becoming more conscious with each breath. Luka wrapped her coat around her shoulders. *Did I just???*

Luka leaned back against the brick wall laughing.

"I can't believe you just punched that guy."

Amity straightened, the realization hitting her that she did punch someone. That's assault! She just assaulted someone! Her eyes grew wide with panic.

"I—You! You *let* me! Why didn't you stop me? I stopped you!? Oh fuck, I just assaulted someone! I'm going to jail."

She held her face in her hands trying to slow her breathing. Luka watched with an all too amused face. Stomping up to him, she jabbed his chest with her finger. Her eyes narrowed.

"Why didn't you stop me?"

Luka's laughter faded and his tone leveled and a serious stare met her own. Rough fingers wrapped around her own.

Sounds of the night traffic drifted through the alleyway and beyond, but there was nothing else. No chill wind. No people. Just them. Just him staring into her eyes with his own. Those beautiful eyes that she was all too easily and all too willing to get lost in. That smirk had vanished from his face.

"Because you're a better person than I am."

Fuck . . . All she wanted to do was wrap her arms around him and kiss him until she forced herself to stop, or until he did. Which, judging by how he was looking at her right now, she didn't think he would. Or was that just the alcohol giving her the extra bravado? *Who cares?* Unfortunately for Amity, she remembered the last saw him and how he stormed out of her apartment. *Fuck that's right,* she thought bitterly. *We're still fighting.*

Amity pulled her hand out of his grasp and turned determined brown eyes upward.

"I'm coming with you."

It was a *statement.* Not a question.

Luka forced out an agitated sigh, obviously not wanting to even start—*continue*—their conversation . . . *fight?*

"Amity . . ."

"I am."

"You want to do this now?"

She nodded curtly. "Yes."

Cyan eyes narrowed on her for a moment. *Stubborn.* He tried to step around her, but she shoved him back against the wall. Something he wasn't expecting judging by his shocked expression. Nor did it look like he expected her to cage him in.

A small laugh escaped him before he quickly covered his mouth. This obviously wasn't the time for him to laugh, but deep down she couldn't blame him. She knew how ridiculous she looked right now. Her arms were at his biceps' level, and she was so close she had to turn her chin up to look into his eyes.

He quickly regained his composure. "No."

She pushed him against the wall again, a little too roughly.

He gritted his teeth and held her back by her shoulders, forcing her to step back.

"Don't push me," he growled.

Brown eyes narrowed on him.

"Stop being so stubborn!" Amity pushed him again, a little lighter than before.

Luka grabbed her by the arms tightly. "Don't get physical," he warned.

"You had no problem being physical with me."

Shit. The words left her mouth before she even registered what she was saying. *Stupid alcohol. This was not where I wanted this conversation to go!*

His hand went to her throat. Rough fingers wrapped around the smooth skin, holding it, letting her feel the weight of its presence. That smirk spread across his lips, a contrast to bite off his next words.

"I don't exactly remember you 'hating' it, *kitten*." Luka applied the slightest amount of pressure.

A bright flush spread across her cheeks—and it wasn't from the cold. "You should've asked first!" she stuttered.

He hummed, amused by her embarrassment and obvious arousal. His grip loosened.

"I should've. I'm sorry."

Rough fingers released her throat, and she immediately missed their heat. His hand traveled down her jacket sleeve and to her hand, the one she had punched that guy with, holding and turning it between his fingers, examining it thoroughly. She had somehow cut them on something, probably on the guy's belt or something sharp judging by the bleeding scrape. Gently he kissed the back, then blew on her knuckles.

The heat of his breath spread over her knuckles and over her palm. The dried blood disappeared. Her skin healed before her eyes. Amity's awestruck gaze turned to him. This wasn't the first time she had seen him do this type of healing magic, but she could never get used to it. It was like witnessing a miracle. In a way, magic itself *was* a miracle. Especially without a potion.

Brown eyes watched him, following the sharp curve of his jaw up to his cheek bones. His straight nose. The faint lines on his forehead. His dark hair that he braided back, reminding her of some Viking show. She couldn't remember the name. Maybe they watched it together?

"I'm sorry I pushed you . . . twice," Amity finally said.

"Three times," he corrected, a small smile making the faintest appearance on his lips. Soft lips kissed the back of her hand once more before letting it hang between them. Her heart skipped at the gesture.

"Three times," Amity repeated, glancing away. "They already took my memories of you. What more could they take—" She cut herself off.

That was stupid. No, that was *the stupidest thing* she could've said. She silently cursed herself. Once again her mouth was too fast for her brain.

You.

That word hung in the space between them like a bog. Thick. Uncomfortable. *Suffocating.* She swallowed hard, narrowing her eyes on some random piece of trash on the ground.

Luka was quiet and still for a very long time, so long Amity contemplated running off.

His hand squeezed around hers ever so slightly. The other lifted and curled around her ear, then followed down the curve of her jaw. The rough pad of his thumb lifted her face to his, carefully bringing her to face him. She didn't look at him, at first, knowing exactly what he would say. She didn't want to hear it. Not that. After a very long battle, brown eyes met cyan.

Those cyan eyes silently studied her face as if it was the last time he would ever see it.

"You. They could take you."

She felt tears swell. A few slid down her cheeks, cutting her skin like glass, the weight of what she asked finally sinking in. He kissed her forehead with a warm exhale, then delicately traced her nose with his own. Both frozen.

Amity's heart pounded inside her chest. She loved that. That small intimate gesture. Silently she wished for more. More small moments like this. As many as she wanted. A thousand a day. She would never be satisfied. Never get enough of him.

She loved it.

"And I will *never* let that happen. Not ever."

CHAPTER TWENTY TWO

Amity rocked back onto her heels behind the counter, then stretched her arms high above her head. The rush had just ended, leaving her exhausted. Not the morning rush, not the afternoon rush, just rush. The morning and afternoon seemed to blur together in one giant mass of people. Some wanted the latest read, which her father had just put out front before he opened with her. He originally didn't want to sell the new supposedly "spicy" book; something about it not being the "right vibe" with Halley's. And despite her father's accurate use of the word vibe, Amity still insisted and persisted—and absolutely not for the reason that she wanted a copy for herself. This book had gained a lot of popularity online for being spicy—no, "spicy" wasn't quite right. It was *filthy*. Downright *dirty*. "Ravishing," some even described it.

Amity sighed heavily and threw her hair into a hair tie, turning it into a giant pom-pom of curls on her head. No matter how badly she wanted to read it today, she didn't have the time to pick it up. It was just too busy, even with her father working with her earlier. She glanced at the clock. 2:45 p.m.

He said he would be back around 5:00 p.m. and close by himself, which was good news for her. Amity smiled blissfully. Just a few more hours and she can change into some comfy clothes, curl up next to Freaya, and read that wonderfully delicious, ravishing book—

Her face dropped. "Fuck, that's right," she grumbled.

Today Luka was coming over after her shift, something she would normally be ecstatic about. The thought of him in her apartment again was definitely as equally delicious as that new book was promised to be. Those cyan eyes staring into her with the promise of leaving her sweaty and whimpering beneath him was absolutely *ravishing*.

Her cheeks flushed at the thought, and she leaned against the countertop harder.

Unfortunately, that was also something she wouldn't have *time* for.

She took a napkin between her hands as her mind slipped. Last Friday night, after she assaulted someone, Luka brought her back to her apartment. The corner of her mouth tilted up into a small smile as she remembered him holding her hand the entire way. That was adorable.

Something she would definitely demand more often. It was when they got back to her apartment that was the problem.

Freaya, the traitor, had gone right over to him, rubbing up against his leg as if she owned him. It wasn't until she heard Amity filling her food bowl that she noticed Amity was even there!

Damn cat. I'm only your mother and give you everything you want but it's Fine. Try to steal my man. I'm FINE!

She'd made her way back over to Luka and was surprised he hadn't moved from her doormat. He didn't even take off his jacket or his shoes, which was . . . weird. Especially considering the first time he was there, or at least that she was aware of it, when he walked right in as if he lived there too. So, yeah, *weird.*

Amity had snaked her arms under his jacket and wrapped them around his waist. He returned the gesture, but something was just . . . off. She couldn't pinpoint it, but something was definitely off. He had that guilty, slightly pained look on his face. The one he would so obviously try to mask with a blank stare. But she knew him better . . . or at least better than she did when she first met him, for the second time. Amity obviously didn't know him as much as she did before her memories were wiped.

Obviously.

Her eyes narrowed. That bothered her—there was a side to him she and only she used to know but now didn't. Agitated fingers rubbed her temples briefly before assuming their assault on the innocent napkin. Thinking about her past memories and comparing them to her most recent ones was getting confusing and making her head hurt.

Last night she had asked him to stay. She kissed him. He kissed her.

Amity began to unintentionally tear the napkin.

He'd kissed her like he was holding himself back. Why? She knew everything that happened between them, as far as the demon Dramaur was concerned. A shiver slithered up her spine, giving birth to a realization that Dramaur was still alive.

Well, of course he's alive. Stupid. A sigh escaped her. *Maybe "alive" wasn't the right word then. Maybe "present"?*

Sure he had a meeting scheduled with Luka, but who's to say he would abide by it? What if he showed up sooner, or any other demon for that matter like the fox or that horrifying shifter?

Amity shook her head so hard her curls almost tumbled out of their hold. *Don't even start thinking about that now! You'll never get any sleep if you do.*

She refocused, scrambling to remember what had her so fixated before. Brown eyes widened. Luka.

Of course. Why was he still acting like that?

Last night when he stood in her doorway, he let her take off his jacket. He kissed her harder. *Hungrier.* Needier. *Is that even a word? Whatever!* Strong arms wrapped tighter around her waist as hers snaked around his neck. She pulled his bottom lip between her teeth, and he let out the sweetest little sound. Something like a whimper. *So fucking cute.* Amity wanted to hear him whimper like that all night long. Hear herself whimper for him all night long. Last night was the night they were gonna have so much amazing, mind-blowing sex that they would be turned into puddles. Unable to walk. Unable to even *move*. They would cuddle each other until they passed out from exhaustion. Covered in bruises and sweat and *themselves*. Or at least that was the *plan.*

He'd pulled away just as she slipped her hands under his shirt.

"I have to go."

"You can stay, you can *always* stay."

He had pressed his forehead to hers and took her hands in his own, despite his obvious half-hard cock she could feel through his pants pressing against her stomach, and said, "Not tonight. Not yet."

She didn't question him. Didn't fight him.

If someone wants to stop, You. Fucking. Stop.

She knew that better than anyone from past unfortunate partners who tried crossing boundaries she hadn't properly set.

Was it the fight?

No, they resolved it.

Was he waiting for her to ask him out?

Possibly?

After he'd left last night, she ran over those and millions of other possibilities as she tried to get some sleep, which of course the overthinking and overanalyzing was *not* helping.

Whatever. They would have sex tonight.

Mind-blowing. Multiple-orgasmic. Steamy. Sex.

Amity sighed heavily; the napkin she had been fiddling with was now nothing more than small torn-up scraps on the counter. Luka was coming over for an entirely different reason.

He texted her that morning, saying her training would start today after work, whatever "training" meant.

A strong breeze blew past the shop's windows, catching her attention. Leaves of all shades and colors whipped by. A woman shivered and wrapped her scarf tighter around herself. Her boyfriend pulled her into his oversized jacket. Amity swiped her thumb nervously. The thrill of starting her demon-fighting training was equally thrilling as it was terrifying.

"I guess I'll find out soon enough."

Amity furiously tied her matted hair back in a high pony-tail.

"Are you fucking serious?!"

Luka watched her silently with his arms crossed over his chest. He had just successfully proven just how much of an incompetent fighter she was by throwing her down onto her ass five times. Although she knew she had little to no hand-to-hand combat experience, at least that she could remember, she obviously still wanted to prove him wrong. Whether that was through pure spite was something she wouldn't admit. She was actually surprised that she managed to block a few hits, even though she had no idea how. Maybe he'd trained with her in the past? Or maybe she just watched too many shonen anime. She grunted furiously rubbing her sore arm where he'd pushed her down.

Amity didn't land a single blow, and he wasn't smirking about it either; he was looking at her like she was a disappointment. Honestly, she didn't know which was worse.

"Yes, Halloween. Midnight."

Yeah, because him repeating it again made it sound so much better . . . especially in that disappointing tone.

She stared up at him as he went back to where his coat lay in a pile next to hers on the grass.

He had shown up at her apartment a few hours ago and told her to dress for yoga . . . outdoor yoga. So now here she was kneeling in the grass in her leggings and turtleneck in the dark park.

Luka said it would be ideal for a training spot. Not a lot of people came to the park at night, but just in case, Luka set up a ward—an invisible shield meant to keep people or things that would do you harm out. This one he said was more of a "privacy screen." The way he said it with that tiniest smirk, like he said something clever but didn't fully commit to it . . .

Amity put her head in between her knees, feeling her pulse skyrocket.

With heavy boots cutting into the hard ground, he made his way back to her and slipped something into her hand, something cold and flat. She didn't even notice.

"How are you so calm about this?! That's a week away!"

Luka picked a leaf out of her hair and tossed it aside, something that would have been adorable and made her heart skip if it was under entirely different circumstances. Despite that, her cheeks flushed deeper.

"I'm not."

He rose to his feet, extending his hand. A nervous laugh burst through her, but she took it, accepting his help to stand.

"He says calmly."

That signature smirk appeared on his lips. Amity glanced at her other hand, the one she just registered was holding one of his knives.

Knives? He was going to have her train with *knives?!* Luka casually walked back to his starting place a couple yards away.

"Now, try to cut me," he instructed.

She blinked.

"Because that's a totally normal thing to say, Mr. Don't Get Physical With Me."

His eyes narrowed on her, unimpressed. This was serious and she knew it. It was no time for stupid quips.

"I—are you sure?"

Apprehensively, she looked back down at her blade that shone in the dim streetlamp light.

"Amity, it's alright. Just stab me."

She looked at him for a moment and blinked one too many times. He burst into laughter, which she immediately joined, filling the tense, dark air between them with warm laughter, her nerves fading into obscurity.

"You! You did that on purpose!" she wheezed, clutching her side.

"I did."

A rare smile graced his lips. One of the largest smiles she ever saw him wear.

Once their laughter faded she rose and squared her feet.

"I guess I did stab a demon. Stabbing you should be easier," she teased.

In the dim light she could've sworn his eyes sparkled with delight.

"Then come and do it," he smirked.

Luckily for Amity, and most importantly her conscience, she did *not* stab him, but she came very close to it.

She charged forward and swiped across his stomach with only the slightest bit of hesitation. He jumped back, easily dodging her. Lunging, she tried to grab his leg with her free hand only to be dragged to the ground when he pulled it back. Her face crashed into the hard ground.

Amity pushed herself up onto her knees with a huff and wiped the dirt from her face. Luka smirked down at her. Not the *worst* view she'd seen.

"That was good. Using everything you have at your disposal instead of focusing only on the knife in your hand is smart. However, you're not skilled enough for that. Focus on the basics I showed you earlier. You'll get to switching hands, weapons, and multitasking soon." Again he offered his hand, which she took without hesitation. "It just takes time."

Once Amity was back on her feet, he flipped the blade in his hand, handle first, then held it out for her to take. When did he even get it? Amity's eye narrowed on it, reluctantly taking it back.

"Time which we don't have," she said through gritted teeth, nerves and agitation settling back in.

A chill wind blew past as he studied her. She was sweating, breathing in unsteady pants. Her hair was a mess, filled with dirt and crushed leaves from her most recent fall, and it wasn't just her hair. Dirt, leaves, and torn-up grass stained her clothes, and no matter how hard she tried, she couldn't stop shivering.

"It's late."

Her head shot up. "I'm not done!"

Cyan glared back at her. "You have to open tomorrow. You need sleep."

"I can do it. We don't have time to—"

"Amity." His eyes flashed brighter, making her bite back whatever she was about to say. Her head fell, avoiding his gaze.

"I want you well rested."

Amity nodded, refusing to look at him.

After an excruciatingly long pause, she felt his hand wrap around the back of her head and pull her into his chest. Her favorite place.

She inhaled deeply, feeling her nerves taper down a bit.

How can his chest be both soft and firm at the same time?! That was both annoying and amazing. But despite how *amazing* he felt, she was still frustrated.

Frustrated with not learning these . . . "skills" fast enough, even though apparently people train for years like this and then become masters.

Frustrated that she might have already learned these skills and was now *struggling*.

Frustrated with Luka for giving her such a disapproving look. And also for him feeling so soft yet firm. *And* for smelling so nice. *And* for being a personal heater in this cold weather.

Warm lips kissed the top of her head sweetly. "You're doing very well."

Unintentionally she snuggled deeper into his chest causing an amused humm to vibrate through him. Rough fingers gently gripped the base of her hair and tilted her head back until her brown eyes met his glowing ones. Her cheeks flushed, causing his smirk to tilt higher.

"Did I unlock something?" he mused.

Amity's eyes went wide. "What?"

The grip on the back of her head tightened slightly while his tattooed hand tucked some loose hair behind her ear then slowly traced her jawline.

Very. Slowly.

Amity could feel the heat pooling inside her. Her mouth hung open slightly, waiting.

"Since you've been doing such a *good job* for me. One more round. If you can manage to cut me this time"—His thumb stopped just below her bottom lip. It moved up over the plump curve, then, at a tantalizing slow pace, he dragged it down. His pupils dilated—"I'll give you a reward."

She instinctively leaned into his touch, but right before she could wrap her lips around it, his thumb was taken back. Luka kissed his thumb teasingly, watching her as she stared, ravenous, at his lips.

"Would my kitten like that?"

Amity felt a heavy breath leave her. Her thighs pressed together in anticipation. She didn't say anything. All she could manage was a nod.

"Good girl. That's my kitten."

Amity's eyes fluttered shut as she pressed up to her tiptoes. A cold wind blew past.

When her eyes opened, Luka was a good distance away with a wide smirk. Frantically, she shook away the embarrassment.

Amity squared her feet, just like he showed her, and prepared to charge again, flipping the sharp blade toward him. His eyes glowed softly in the dim light, a beautiful cyan-blue she couldn't tear herself away from.

"I will win."

His eyes glowed brighter, taunting her.

Without another word Amity charged forward, pushing off the hard ground in a burst of energy. She bent low, darting from side to side. He remained still, leaning into his stance. She thrust the blade forward to the left side of his torso, which he easily dodged.

Rough hands gently pushed her away, deflecting her blow and nearly causing her to fall on her face *again*. This time she caught herself, sliding a bit on the ground before coming to a complete stop.

Luka smiled over his shoulder at her. "I guess you don't want that reward, huh?"

Amity pushed up to her feet with a yell. He turned ready for her charge, his eyes reflecting obvious enjoyment.

She charged for him again, slashing across his torso, which he easily avoided with fluid motions.

"Don't swing it around like that. Be direct." He grabbed her wrist and pushed her back a few steps. "Watch my hands," he instructed.

She spun, quickly regaining her stance, wiped the fresh sweat off her brow, then charged again, her strikes more direct than before.

"Better."

Taking the blade in both hands and she thrust it to his left before quickly changing toward his right side. Her smile widened. She did it! She landed a hit!

Amity's head hit the ground hard. Luka was kneeling over her, one hand holding hers, the one with the knife, to the ground. He flicked her forehead hard.

"And always mind your footwork."

Amity stared at him in a daze. What the hell just happened?!

She replayed it slowly in her mind.

She'd gone for his left, then faked and went to his right.

Her eyes narrowed, trying to remember.

Luka had grabbed one of her arms and pushed her shoulder with the other, twisted his body, tripped her foot, *then* landed on top of her.

Her mouth hung open in shock. He smirked down at her.

"How the hell did you—"

"Practice, kitten, practice and patience."

Brown eyes narrowed on him. That smile faded from his lips along with the bright glow in his eyes.

"It's getting late." He made a motion to stand but Amity was faster. She hooked one of her legs around him and grabbed his arm with her free hand. In one swift motion, she pulled and successfully flipped him onto his back—beneath her.

A wide smile spread across her lips as she hovered over him, panting. Thighs tightly clamped around his sides, securing him in place. Luka looked up at her, wide-eyed as she held the dagger to his throat.

Slowly his hands rose in defeat.

She did it!

Amity leaned forward, pressing the edge of the dagger against the smooth skin of his neck. His Adam's apple worked on a nervous swallow. The cold metal kissed his skin, pressing deep enough to nick it.

"I did it. Now, reward me."

Something twitched against her ass, causing a smirk to curve on her lips and a thrill in her lower belly.

"What? Did I unlock something?"

Cyan eyes glowed a brighter in the dimness.

Amity was right about one thing. They were both covered in sweat.

CHAPTER
TWENTY THREE

Amity stood under the hot water and let out a long sigh of relief. Water was always healing for her—soaking in a hot bath, standing under the shower head. Water was a miracle worker.

"Ow," she groaned, poking at a fresh blooming bruise on her arm.

She was covered in them, most of them coating her ass. Those hurt like a bitch. She moved slightly, letting the water ripple down her body, leaving a trail of heat in its wake. A soft humm escaped her as everything seemed to just drift away, all the small problems of the day that grew into major annoyances that then fused into her muscles creating large knots to work out. Or even just the physical strains of the day. They all melted away with the water that flowed over her and pooled at her feet, warming her toes.

She could stay here forever, but someone was waiting for her. That someone opened the door to the bathroom with his usual fan club trailing behind him, meowing demandingly.

"Five does not equate to twenty. If you don't get out I'm leaving—"

Amity quickly turned off the shower, immediately missing its heat.

"Okay, okay! I'm done!"

Luka laughed from the other side of the curtain.

"That's what I thought. Come out and claim your reward." With a soft *click* he closed the door behind him and Freaya.

Amity bit her lip as something warm churned low in her belly. *He just had to say it in that rough voice!?*

Her cheeks burned brightly as she ran some leave-in conditioner through her soaking hair. She wouldn't have time for her whole routine tonight, not that she wanted to do her entire curl routine and have it turn into a lopsided mass of curls when she took off her bonnet in the morning because she slept on them weirdly. She hated when that happened. It was like her hair was specifically doing that to spite all her hard work. *No. Not tonight, Satan.* Tonight a braid would do just fine.

She flipped her hair over into the bathtub and began brushing, then she took her microfiber towel and wrapped it.

Thoughts about her "reward" consumed her.

What will it be?

Will it be him?

Oh, definitely.

But all of him?

Part of him?

Do I get to choose?

Will he tell me?

Will it just be a kiss?

Would he do that just to spite me? She narrowed her eyes as she pulled an oversized long sleeve over her toweled hair. *Yes, he would definitely do that. When was the last time we kissed anyway?* Her leg tangled in her pants, nearly tripping her. *Wait, when did we last kiss?!*

Wait . . . The memory came back to her. Last night. Last night when she asked him to stay. Last night when he turned her down. She opened the door to her bedroom halfheartedly, disappointed. *I guess I won't find him lying naked on my bed then.*

Quickly, she patted the rest of her hair dry before tying it back into a smooth braid.

Luka was seated on the edge of her bed, her neatly made bed, with one leg bent toward his chest, staring into a lit pumpkin spice candle on her bedside table.

Wait . . . Amity took in her bedroom. Earlier today, her bed was a mass of blankets before she left. Luka was so insistent that she changed as fast as possible and her copious amounts of pillows and fluffy blankets were scattered all over her bed.

Now her bed was neatly made up. Her blankets were folded longways and placed covering the edge of her bed where Luka now sat. The pillows were neatly arranged on the other side of her bed, leaning against the wall in a decorative way like in a mattress store or catalog. Also, the candle hadn't been lit. Her heart swelled.

"You cleaned?"

"You're surprised? You were taking your time in the shower, and I was impatient." He leaned his chin onto his knee and slowly raked his gaze over her.

Amity fiddled with the hem of her oversized shirt, trying to fight off nervous butterflies as he made his way over to her. She felt her body flush as his rough fingers moved her braid over her shoulder.

Luka's fingers brushed the edge her ear with the lightest of touches, sending a thrilling fire burning through her skin and her heart racing. Cyan eyes locked onto her, causing a nervous flinch.

"I can stop."

"No! I mean—" She cut herself off trying to find the right words. Air filled her lungs as he waited patiently for her to continue. "I don't want you to—I . . ." she stammered, avoiding those beautiful eyes. "I mean, you're probably just teasing me, right? It's just going to be a kiss or something small, right?" A nervous laugh bubbled out of her throat.

Luka's eyes stayed locked. His pupils went wide and those cyan irises glowed.

"Do you want me to stop?"

Amity locked eyes with him; his stare was so intense she had to take a slow breath. "I—no. No, I don't"—she gripped her shirt tightly, successfully stopping her fidgeting fingers—"I don't want you to stop."

Rough fingers cupped her cheek as he bent down to her level. Amity swore he could hear her heartbeat; it was so fast and loud. Carefully he traced her nose with his own, drawing in a shaky breath.

"Tell me if you want me to stop."

"But I just—"

"Amity."

Her face flushed deeper. Did he have to growl out her name like that?!

"I promise."

"*Good.*"

Without warning he bent low, picked her up by her thighs then laid her down onto the bed.

A small sound escaped her as her head hit the mattress, a sound that sounded more like a squeak if she was being honest with herself. A low chuckle escaped him as he bent over her. Her body immediately stiffened—*Oh fuck, is he gonna? Are we gonna?!*

Luka kissed her forehead, sweetly. "You did such a good job for me today. It's time to relax."

Amity nodded stiffly. Luka clicked his tongue three times in response, right next to her ear sending a thrilling chill down her spine.

"That's not right, kitten." The bed shifted deeper to her left as he loomed near her ear. He brought his tattooed hand up, gliding it slowly up the side of her neck before resting on her cheek. She leaned into the warmth of his touch. "You want your reward don't you?" he purred, tracing the shell of her ear with the tip of his nose. She shivered at the faint sensation.

Her hands moved on their own, one following the curve of the Midgard Serpent's tail until it found its place above his own, the one currently resting on her pounding pulse on her neck, just holding her, letting her feel the presence of his hand. The weight of it.

She nodded smoothly as her eyes drifted closed. She could practically feel the smirk on his lips.

"Then relax for me, please?"

His thumb swiped up, tilting her face to the side, giving him the perfect view of her neck. Small kisses pressed against her thrumming pulse, feeling it relax under his lips.

"That's it, that's my kitten."

Her other hand found the collar of his shirt and gripped it tightly as he sucked gently at the base of her neck where it met her shoulder. She stifled a moan. Another click from his tongue, followed shortly by his teeth raking over the spot, caused her to gasp.

"That's it. I fucking love that sound."

His satisfied growl vibrated against her skin. Underneath him her thighs pressed together, adjusting to the fresh dampness.

The soft press of his lips kissed her lower, on her collarbone, then over her shirt and down to her chest.

Amity pulled him back up by the collar of his shirt, right to her lips. She had enough of his teasing. She *wanted* his lips on hers. *Needed* them—Right. Fucking. Now.

Luka smiled in their kiss, pleased with her eagerness. Kissing her longingly before she pulled his bottom lip between her teeth, capturing his sweet sounds in another kiss. She barely started to explore his tongue when he pulled away with glowing cyan eyes and swollen lips.

Sharply she tugged his collar in a desperate attempt to bring him down again; it was refused.

"It's time for your reward."

He stared at her lips as if he was about to change his mind, then those cyan eyes traveled down to her chest, which made Amity smile a bit. Despite her insecurity with her breasts, she knew Luka liked them, *especially* how they stretched the fabric of this shirt.

Rough fingers fell from her throat and grasped the collar of her shirt. He looked like he wanted to tear it off her.

"This is staying on, unless it obstructs your view."

Her head tilted to the side, confused, staring at him through half-lidded eyes.

He smiled hungrily at her. "Don't worry, I'll give them extra attention later."

Those fingers unhooked from her collar and ran between her breasts, pressing down on the taut fabric of her shirt and continuing down her stomach, leaving a blazing trail in his wake, before resting his hand just below her navel. She jerked beneath his touch.

He froze, waiting for her to say something. When she stayed silent, he swiped his thumb lower against the waistband of her sweatpants.

Her abdomen tightened under his touch and her stomach rumbled in a silent giggle. She covered her mouth trying to stifle a laugh. His lips curved into a pleased smirk.

"You're ticklish on your stomach?" he asked mischievously.

Her head shook, no. Luka clicked his tongue, and his smirk grew when she squirmed under his fingers again. She failed to stifle her laughter.

"You're so fucking cute."

Amity grabbed one of the neatly placed pillows behind her, a long rectangular white one with an auburn fringe, and chucked it at him. He laughed warmly, catching it before it could hit him in the face.

"Thank you, I needed this."

Confusion was evident on her face, but he didn't elaborate. Instead he leaned forward and kissed her long and sweet, sliding his tongue over her swollen lips before pulling back with his signature smirk. She narrowed her eyes and pouted her lips as he stood.

"Patience. If you're still wearing that pout by the time I'm done with you, I'll give you whatever you want." Luka took the pillow and placed it on the floor.

She regarded him for a moment, wrapping her arms around her torso and keeping a firm grip on her sides. ". . . That wasn't my reward?"

Luka ran his hands up the top of her legs, then her hips, stopping just below her hands. He gripped her tightly then pulled her to the end of the bed so her legs dangled off the edge. Amity's eyes widened.

He bent down and kissed her hands, each of them, as they gripped her stomach tighter. Carefully he tugged the band of her pants down on the left side until he could see the dip of her hip bone. His tongue glided in a small circle before kissing it tenderly. With hungry eyes he looked up at her. Brown eyes widened with understanding, and she took in a shaky breath. Amity knew exactly what her reward would be. That smirk kicked back as he saw her realize it. He hooked her waistband in his hands and tugged at them.

"Lift that cute ass up for me." Slowly her hips lifted off the soft mattress. "Good girl." Amity's fingers gripped her sides tighter as the waistband slowly slipped from her navel to her hips, to her thighs, to her ankles and then finally was discarded onto the floor.

Luka was breathing heavily as he raked his gaze over her half-naked body, silent, like he was carving up every detail, every curve, every freckle of her lower body.

"You're not wearing any panties," he said, his voice a low rumble. Amity instinctively pressed her thighs together and turned her hips slightly.

"I forgot to grab them."

"Really." He definitely did *not* believe her.

Cyan eyes glowed slightly brighter as Luka's face flushed. Amity pulled the hem of her shirt down as far as she could, successfully hiding her center from his view. His eyes were fixated on the spot.

"I did! I swear—"

"Don't do that. Don't hide from me."

He sank to his knees, landing hard on the pillow he placed there. With strong hands he pried her legs apart, nestling in between them. She was open to him now. Completely exposed. Her thighs tensed in his grip as he stared in awe. Amity propped herself up onto her elbows.

"Hey! Don't just stare like that! You don't have to do this if you don't . . ."

Rough fingertips traced up the back of her thigh, turning her rambles into a sweet, breathy moan.

"Believe me, I want to do this as much as you want me to do this. Probably even more." He hooked her leg over his shoulder and kissed just inside her thigh, never taking his eyes off her center. "Definitely more."

"More?!" Amity fell back on the bed with a beet-red face as Luka continued to kiss down her thigh—no, he wasn't just kissing. He was licking. Sucking. Nipping her skin. Using his breath to make her legs *shake*.

Amity covered her mouth, trying to suppress the noises she made, a wave of embarrassment rushing through her as her legs twitched in his grasp. She covered her face.

Why?! Why am I getting embarrassed now!? This is what I wanted and he's finally—fuck that feels good. She took a deep breath. *Why can't I just calm down? Why am I—*

She bit her lip to bite back another moan and from sending herself into a crying fit. There was no reason to be embarrassed. No reason to be nervous. No reason to feel insecure. Because she was feeling all of this, at this particular moment, made her so fucking angry.

Just calm down! He's here. With You. He's not going to judge you. A tear slid down her cheek as Luka hovered just in front of her entrance. Her palms pressed into her eyes.

She felt him retreat, immediately missing his warmth. He studied her for a moment before speaking in a soft voice. "Do you want me to stop?"

Amity let out a shaky breath and shook her head, no.

Luka's voice became stern. "Amity—"

"No!"

She heard the floor creak as he sat back onto his ankles, straightening her legs out in the process.

"Are you not enjoying this?"

"No—I mean yes! I am . . . a lot."

"Then why are you covering your face?"

Amity peeked down at him through her fingers.

Fuck. That's it. I've ruined it.

"No! I just—I-I think I look weird." *And I'm extremely self-conscious and insecure.* She quickly covered her face again. "I'm just very in my head. I'm sorry. I am enjoying this."

"Amity, look at me." He waited patiently, longer than she expected him to. Longer than she would have, but something in his voice calmed her. Amity pried her hands away from her face.

"I love all your faces. When you're embarrassed. When you're angry. When you look like you can't decide whether or not to punch me or tear off my clothes." A small giggle escaped her, and he smiled into her thigh. "I love them all. I want to see them all. Let me."

Luka snaked his hands up toward her, which she took. He entwined their fingers and brought one of her hands to rest on her thigh. The other he ran over his hair, which had slightly fallen out of his braid.

"I want you to hold my hair and guide me; whatever you want me to do, you just need to say. You want my fingers? I can't wait to feel inside of you. You want my tongue to fuck you until you cum? Even better. You want me to stay here until you can't cum anymore? Gladly. I would live between your thighs if I could."

Her fingers gripped his hair lightly while her other hand squeezed his. Through half-lidded eyes she stared down at him. The thought of him burying himself between her thighs made her tighten and glisten. He smiled hungrily up at her, watching her lips swell from excitement. With her determined nod of approval, he buried his face deep between her thighs, getting his first taste of her. Then he *ate.*

CHAPTER TWENTY FOUR

Luka's tongue was warm and smooth against her swollen lips, gliding from their base all the way up to her clit in long languid strokes before circling around her outer lips, then plunging inside of her. In and out. Slowly at first, then faster and faster.

He started by tasting her, taking in her wetness slowly as if he was grateful for just a sip. Now he was feasting, not wanting to waste any of it, any of her arousal. Savoring every last drop.

Her grip on his hair tightened as his nose brushed against her clit. He was moaning into her, sending her legs shaking and vibrating around his tongue. He watched her hips buck into him.

"That's right, Amity, fuck my face." His voice rumbled inside her, sending a wave of heat through her body.

Her body was on fire! With unsteady fingers, she scrambled for her shirt, reluctantly letting go of his hand and hair. Quickly she ripped it off, found his hair again, and shoved him back down.

He laughed against her, causing her hips to jerk.

"That's my greedy girl." His tongue retreated then made a tantalizing slow, long stroke up the seam of her lips. "Does my kitten want my fingers?"

Half-lidded eyes met him, followed by a hard swallow. She was panting, sweating—an absolute mess. And she wanted *more*.

Cyan stared up at her through her legs, waiting patiently with swollen lips. Amity nodded eagerly and that mischievous smirk made its appearance. He licked his lips hungrily, his swollen lips that were already soaked with her.

"You're so fucking sweet."

He leaned up and sent a warm breath over her swollen clit, sending her back into the mattress with a moaned gasp.

He uncurled a finger against her seam, watching her with flushed cheeks and glowing eyes, as it gently split her lips.

"Luka!"

"Yes, keep saying my name. Just like that." He ran his tongue over her clit, and that teasing finger slipped inside.

"Fuck, you're so warm. So wet. All for me—" He flicked his tongue over her, cutting off his words before she could even think of them.

Amity couldn't tell if that was a question or not, and she couldn't care less. She couldn't think straight, let alone try to form sentences. Words. Thoughts. It was all gone. The only thing she felt was pleasure. Luka. There was only Luka.

That finger started curling inside her, pressing against the spot just below where his tongue currently was. Amity let out a sweet sound in response. She could feel him smirk against her skin.

"I can feel you getting tighter." He curled his finger, in slow, long curls, before pulling it out completely. Amity rocked her hips, trying to push him inside her again. A low chuckle vibrated against her pelvis.

"Another? Can I?" he asked against her flush skin. "I want to stretch you. I want to feel you clench around my fing—" He didn't even finish his sentence. Amity was already agreeing.

"Yes, more!"

That made him smile wide.

He pressed the tips of his fingers at her entrance and waited until she bucked her hips impatiently before slipping them inside. Luka explored for a moment, feeling her inner walls and stretching them. Then he began to pulse, slowly at first, slipping his fingers where just the tips were still inside her before plunging back in.

The pulses grew faster as her moans got louder. He watched for a few mesmerizing minutes before returning to her clit. A rough hand put her hand back into his hair. She moved him slightly to the left. That made her buck. He moaned into her, understanding. That was the spot. That was where she wanted him. That was how *close* she was.

Amity felt her legs shaking in his grip. Her breaths were faster. Smaller. Her body became taut. She gripped his hand tightly and he squeezed it in return. She clenched around his fingers as they continued to pulse in and out of her.

"Yes. That's it, Amity. Just fucking cum for me. That's my kitten."

The tension that had been building inside her, twisting like an iron spring, snapped.

She clenched around his fingers and rocked against his mouth. He continued thrusting inside her, gently, as she rode out the pulsing waves of her orgasm.

"Good girl." Wet lips kissed the inside of her thigh, "That's beautiful."

He watched her slowly descend back down with a satisfied smile on his face. Swollen lips kissed the inside of her thigh, sending it twitching before he finally removed his glistening fingers. Amity watched him silently through barely open eyes as he brought them to his talented mouth and sucked them clean of her. He didn't waste a single drop.

Amity leaned back into the mattress. Her breathing slowly grew deeper and heavier. She felt Luka crawl up the mattress and nestle beside her. Instinctively she turned into him, snuggling her face against his chest. He hummed sweetly, kissed her, draped a blanket over her, and wrapped her in his arms. A sense of serenity overcame her, and in no time her body relaxed into him.

With a satisfied sigh she snuggled in closer, lodging her knee between his legs. Luka let out a low moan as she pressed against something large and throbbing.

"I'm guessing you liked your reward."

She did. She really fucking loved her reward. The sweet smell of sandalwood and seasalt filled her, his smell, as her thoughts turned from random blurbs to fully structured.

When was the last time she felt this way with someone? *It was definitely a while.* Who was the last person she even slept with? *Doesn't matter anymore.* Luka's hand was rubbing her back sweetly. Can she just sleep with him from now on? Can he be her only partner? *That would be amazing. And his consent checks—fuck! Where did this man come from?!* No one had ever given consent checks before. In her past experience they would just forge forward, and if she didn't like something, she would say so . . . most of the time. She inhaled deeply, refocusing on the man beside her. He was like a personal fire, wrapping her in his body heat and sweet scent. Amity licked her lips, tasting herself.

I bet he tastes just as sweet.

She hummed softly and nuzzled against his chest, causing him to laugh. Her knee pressed against his erection again, sending a sweet sound through him.

"Don't get greedy now." Luka definitely meant that as a warning, but his voice faltered.

"You like it when I'm greedy." Whatever peaceful afterglow that overcame her before was now gone. She pressed her thighs together in anticipation. He was ready, and now she was too. She slipped her hand down his chest and toward the waist of his pants. He grabbed it before it reached.

"Amity," he growled.

"But I want to, and I want to make you feel good too."

"I'm fine. It's getting late," he bit out and carefully untangled himself from her.

Amity rose from the bed, wrapping the blanket around her naked body.

"But—!"

"No." He picked up her discarded clothes and laid them neatly on the bed in front of her. She stared at them in half disbelief, extremely impressed by how considerate he was and extremely frustrated because it was like he was using it as a distraction from their conversation.

He was doing it again, just like the last time. He was leaving again.

Luka walked to the side of the bed closest to her, placing the pillow he was kneeling on with the rest of them.

"I don't believe you"

"What?"

Brown eyes met cyan.

"I don't believe you don't want to have sex with me."

His eyes narrowed on her, and his voice had more than a bite to it.

"Amity, I said *no*."

Her eyes widened. That came out *wrong*. Like, in the worst kind of wrong possible. She held the blanket tighter around herself, head hanging low, avoiding his gaze.

"That's-that's *not* what I mean! You say all these things, *do* all these things. You act all flirty and you kiss me like you want to, you *touch me* like you want to, so-so why don't you?! Do you not want to? At all? Ev-. . . ever?"

The silence between them seemed to stretch on forever as cyan eyes watched her with a heavy gaze.

"You think I don't want to?"

"I don't know!"

Rough fingers wrapped around the back of her head. After a moment she finally looked up at him.

"I want to."

"You do? Really?"

Something changed in his eyes. He straightened and scratched at his nose piercing.

"It's complicated."

"So you don't want to," she said flatly.

His eyes narrowed on her again.

"That's *not* what I said."

Amity turned abruptly away from him, threw off the blanket, and began dressing in frustration. "Then start making sense!" *It's like you're jerking my chain!* But she didn't say that part out loud.

"I can't."

"You can't make it make sense?" she asked, somehow managing to put her shirt on inside out, making her frustration rise. She tore it off again.

"I won't."

"*Can't* or *won't?*" she demanded, pulling her head through the neckhole of her shirt.

"No. I can't have sex with you!"

Amity fell back onto the bed with her legs crossed. Her eyes were wide, focusing on a random spot of dirt on his shirt.

That. That felt like a stab in the gut.

Great fucking job, dumbass.

"Fuck, Amity, that's not . . . I didn't . . ." His voice was softer now. The bed bowed under his weight, but she couldn't lift her face to see.

"Look at me." He took her hand in his and brought them to his chest. She ripped it out of his light grasp.

Luka drew in a long breath.

"That came out all wrong."

Then start making sense.

"I want to, I want to so fucking badly."

Her gaze met his.

Then why . . . why won't you?

Something else was wrong. Something he wasn't telling her. He had that look in his eyes again, that guilt- and pain-stricken look she couldn't quite place.

"But . . . ?" she probed.

"I won't. Not yet. Not until I fix . . ." He trailed off, avoiding her gaze this time. She waited for him to finish his sentence fully, knowing exactly what he was going to say. They went over this already. She told him so. But that's not how deep-seated guilt worked. She took his hand in hers, entwining her fingers in his.

"My memories being stolen wasn't your fault."

He didn't speak. He didn't move. The only thing that told her he was still alive was his breathing, which was hard, like he was trying to calm himself down before he spiraled.

Guiding him back onto the bed Amity positioning him so they were eye level, even though his eyes were closed. She held his hand between them and in response his clasped around hers squeezing them tightly. Amity pressed her forehead to his.

"Luka. I *saw* what happened. You thought it was a lesser demon, you didn't know it was Dramaur." He tensed at the demon's name. "What happened that night wasn't your fault. I was just at the wrong place at the wrong time."

"*In* the wrong place at the wrong time," he corrected gently.

Those cyan eyes finally opened. He blinked back a few tears before nodding against her.

He shifted down, moving her onto her back, lifted her shirt just a bit, and laid his cheek on her lower stomach. Breathing steadily, it took Amity everything in her to keep from giggling.

She rested one hand on his back and stroked the other through his hair. After a moment she felt comfortable enough to speak.

"Did you think I wasn't going to like you after I regained my memories? I think I've been pretty obvious about how much I've been trying to fuck you," she teased.

Strong arms tightened around her.

She sighed away a nervous laugh. "Right, not the time for jokes." Her hands settled at the base of his neck. "From what I saw in your memories, I've been waiting for you for a while. I can wait a little bit longer." She felt him press into her.

". . . I'm sorry."

"Don't do that. Don't apologize. Just promise to make up for lost time." She felt him smile against her skin. *If we get the chance.* Amity killed that thought before it could take root. The possibility of death could wait. She would definitely freak out about it later. His voice brought her back before she could start spiraling.

"Whatever my kitten wants."

Luka kissed her navel tenderly, making the spot where his lips touched blaze with heat. She opened her mouth to say something, but the words tangled on her tongue. She swallowed them back and held him closer.

A sweet low humm vibrated through him and then through her as she delicately ran her fingers through his undone hair again.

CHAPTER TWENTY FIVE

Amity lounged happily on the park bench under the warmth of the sun.

"You look comfy. How long has it been since you had a day off like this?"

Amity thought for a moment. A long moment. She hadn't been able to have a day off like this all month, at least one that wasn't filled with chores, errands, or catching up on sleep. After her mother's car accident, there really wasn't much of a choice. Luckily Sammy came back from her mini vacation and was manning Halley's with Amity's father. Apparently, according to her mother, they were spending "too much" time together.

"Too long." She sighed, lightly rubbing a bruise on her shoulder. Luka did not let up during their training sessions—*despite* her reward a few days ago.

When she was knocked on her ass for the third time last night and ready to give up, he said she was overcompensated for her last reward, so she couldn't afford to complain. Bastard.

Pretty bastard.

Alex heaved a heavy sigh and sat beside her with two fresh coffees in his hands. "I keep telling Dad that he shouldn't have made you work that much."

She went to take hers from his hands. "I said I would."

He pulled the cup out of her reach just in time. "So you keep saying."

Brown eyes narrowed on her as he turned his wrist, stirring the contents of her coffee. "You should have more energy on your days off than just lounging around."

His eyes softened and he handed her the caramel macchiato.

She held it gently in her hands; it was too hot for her to drink, but it was just perfect to warm her up in the chilly weather. She leaned against her brother's shoulder and grunted in agreement.

The day was significantly warmer than it had been the past week. There was no brutal wind chill, no freezing rain, and no frost. Despite that, it was still a bit chilly out, which, considering it was the end of October, was as warm as it was going to get.

Alex leaned his cheek upon the top of her head after taking a long sip from his coffee.

Together they watched the people pass by, some on bikes, others with rollerblades, most walking. The sun was set high in the sky, creating a delicious, warm glow over them and the river.

Alex kissed her head sweetly, then cleared his throat, the only remaining indicator of his almost completely healed cold.

"You don't act any different from before."

She looked up at him curiously wondering how his mind had drifted there. *She* had thought about it several times.

Was she a different person before?

Did she act differently?

How much of an impact did Luka have on her life? Her personality? Her goals?

"I didn't say I—"

"You don't have to. I'd be thinking the same thing." Amity huffed and took a long sip of her latte.

"Thanks. For the coffee and for . . ."

He nodded curtly, then took another sip of his coffee.

"Anyways I . . ." He took in a sharp breath, drawing her attention. "I'm glad you and that pretty bastard are together or whatever."

Amity laughed, almost spitting out her coffee. "Pretty bastard?"

"According to him, a *very* pretty bastard."

She laughed harder, needing to set down her coffee before she spilled it everywhere. Alex laughed loudly beside her, drawing a few stares in their direction.

Roughly, he clasped her around the shoulders, trying to steady her. He must've set his coffee down too because his other hand was on her knee. About to fall over from how hard he was laughing.

Damn, when was the last time she laughed this hard? What he said wasn't even that funny, but as soon as she started laughing, Amity just couldn't stop. She wiped a few tears from her eyes, smudging her makeup. This made Alex laugh even harder.

He heaved, trying to calm himself enough to speak, "Maybe he can help you be a better aunty, but I doubt it."

"Maybe!" Amity laughed. "I—wait . . ." She looked up at her brother. He had a smile quickly spreading wider on his face. Amity's eyes grew wide. "What did you say?"

Alex rubbed the top of her head with tears pricking the corners of his eyes. His smile was the biggest Amity had ever seen him wear. He took a deep breath.

"I said you're going to be an aunty."

"An . . . aunty?" Amity blinked a few times trying to register the words.

Aunty.

Aun-ty.

AUNTY?!

She grabbed Alex by the shoulders. "Aunty?!"

Alex's eyes seemed to glow in the afternoon sun. He was beaming, shining with happiness.

"I'm going to be an aunty? And you're . . . .and Krystal?! Daddy?!"

Alex burst into laughter, gripping her shoulder tightly so he wouldn't fall over.

"That's right. We're having a baby!"

He caught his sister in a tight hug.

"For real?! That's amazing! Congratulations!" Amity smiled widely and kissed his cheek.

"Alright enough, off!" he laughed, pushing her back onto the bench, then scooped up their coffee.

"So she wasn't actually sick that night we went out?"

"No, she was, we just thought it was a stomach bug. Then she caught an actual cold. Then I caught it."

Amity's mouth dropped open.

"You're saying that like it's the most normal thing in the world?! What happens to the baby when the mother is sick? Does it affect the fetus? Embryo? Baby thingy?"

"It's fine, Amity! Mom was drinking when she had both of us. I'm sure it's fine."

She narrowed her eyes on him.

"The *doctor* said it's *fine*."

Amity swiped back her coffee and took a long sip. A small wind blew past them. Silently she watched the leaves curl into a circle then fly away in a myriad of her favorite colors. She smiled.

"You're going to be a father."

He nodded, letting a tear escape his eye.

"I'm going to be a father," he repeated warmly, then folded over and hid his face in his hands.

She pulled the hood of his jacket over his face and rubbed his back quietly as he cried.

"Krystal is having a baby. She's having *my* baby. We're . . . We're—" He choked, his sobs turning into a small laugh.

Amity smiled down at him and wrapped him in a tight embrace. "She is."

Alex stood abruptly and wiped his face clean of any tears.

"Enough! Fuck, you're so sappy," he said, trying to force a frown.

Amity laughed next to him, then finished off the last of her coffee.

"Where are you meeting your metalhead? I'll drop you off."

"So," Rex probed, elongating the word well beyond what someone would normally do, like it was one of those stretchy jelly hands they used to play with as kids. "When are you going rock climbing?"

Amity stared at her drink before she remembered what "rock climbing" meant, which made her a little agitated because she invented the code word.

"This Saturday, after my morning shift," she said, sipping her pumpkin spice vodka martini.

It wasn't a *complete* lie. She *was* going to go see him on Saturday. He said he would pick her up after her shift and bring her home to get supplies. So, no, not *technically* "rock climbing," a.k.a. "demon hunting," but it was pretty close. It was *prepping* for demon hunting.

Amity smiled to herself, proud that she thought of a code word at all. With the looming demon hunt-meeting that could turn into a very bad situation very fast, the threat was starting to become fully realized. Rex didn't need to be dragged into it. The last thing Amity wanted was for Rex to get hurt or kidnapped or something worse like in one of her dark romance books.

Better to leave them out of it. Though, Amity knew Rex would undoubtedly believe her if she told them.

"You mean no more twelve-hour shifts?" Rex beamed.

"That's right!" She smiled. "Mom's back on her feet and *officially* throwing Dad back to work."

"That's awesome, dude, good for you."

"I know. I'll finally have more time to do stuff. I'll have my weekends back." Amity let out a satisfied breath after taking another sip of her drink. "Fuck, this is good."

"Well I'm happy for you, you haven't exactly been yourself lately. You should do a cleansing ritual to get some of your energy back. You used to take lavender-and-seasalt baths, right?"

Amity stopped her glass just before it touched her lips.

"That's . . ." Something about that seemed so familiar to her. Her cheeks flushed, remembering why. "Yeah, I'll do that."

Rex watched from their seat across the booth with an amused humm. They had taken her to a casual, rustic restaurant, one they used to frequent often when they went to Art School.

"Maybe I'm not the only one who's excited to have more of your free time." They plucked a cheese fry from Amity's fingers with black clawed nails.

"Hey!"

"I bet Luka is just dying to help you 'relax.' "

Amity's face turned scarlet, which sent Rex into a laughing fit.

"Shut up!"

Rex wiped a tear from their eye, impressively not messing up their dramatic winged liner, a style Amity tried to do one day but after an hour got so frustrated she threw her liner across the room. Seriously, how does Rex do it!?

"I'm sorry, I'm sorry, I know you're taking it slow, right?"

Amity took a few cheesy fries from their appetizer plate and shoved them into her mouth. Rex waited for a response. And waited. ". . . Right?"

"Yes!" She took a sip from her drink, then licked the whipped cream off her lips. "And I'm very proud of myself for taking things slow, but . . . I just."

Rex peered curiously back at her over the rim of their glass.

"I just want to do more."

"Does he have like a physical thing or—"

"No! Absolutely not. There is nothing wrong with his dick."

Rex laughed again as the waiter appeared with their burgers. By the look of her face, she definitely caught that last word . . . Amity may have also said it a little too loudly.

After putting her fries directly under the bun of her burger, Amity took a giant bite. She worked hard this week; she deserved these fries. Beautiful, crispy, salty fries. Because fries are po-ta-toes. And potatoes are the best things in the world, according to her.

She cut her creation in half and then took a savage bite, swallowing hard.

". . . We talked about it. And we resolved it. He just wants to take his time, but . . . I just—"

"Want to fuck his brains out, I get it," Rex said, as if it was the most natural thing in the world. They plucked the pickle off of Amity's plate and munched on it loudly. A sly smile spread across their face as they munched on the gross vinegar vegetable.

"Throw him down, ride him until he dies, bite his pickle off, dip his wick, eat ass—"

"Don't talk about eating ass at a restaurant," Amity laughed.

Rex took an exaggerated bite of their own pickle and chomped delightfully.

"Speaking of delightfully delicious pickles," they said. Amity almost choked on her next bite. "I've had the pleasure of sampling a particularly delicious one the other night."

Amity swallowed her next bite quickly.

"Who?!"

A faint blush spread across Rex's cheeks. They scratched at their eyebrow piercing and bit into their pickle again. Amity's eyes grew wide.

"Oh fuck."

A smile spread across Rex's face; they quickly chewed and swallowed before they choked. Amity had never seen Rex so flushed before.

"Oh fuck!"

"Amity!"

"Who is he—they? Who are they? *Were* they? Tell me *everything!*" She stared with a mischievous smile at her friend as the blush spread across their face.

The waiter came 'round again with an amused smile, no doubt eavesdropping on their conversation.

"Can I get you ladies another round of—"

"Yes," Amity finished for him, but then quickly added, "please."

When they finally left, Amity gave Rex a hard look.

"Spill."

Rex took a sip of water, then looked at it like it was some amusing new bug.

"Remember that new club I said I was going to try—"

"You're super-sexy secret sex club?"

Rex nodded with a sly smile.

"And?!"

"And . . ." Rex elongated the word like it was more interesting than her water cup. "I may have met someone."

Amity eagerly shoved a fry into her mouth, desperate for her friend to continue.

"Well . . . sort of? I told you we were all are masked right?"

Amity nodded eagerly, eating another fry as if she were eating popcorn at the movies.

"I've seen him a few times before. Always a very *active* participant." Rex smiled at that. "He would always watch first, standing off in the shadows like some vampire or something. But after a while of watching, he became the center of attention."

Amity tried to imagine it. The dark ambience with the soft blue-and-red glow. The soft satin sheets. The plush couches. The *furry* couches. She'd be a fucking liar if she said it didn't excite her. The voyeurism on the other hand . . . not so much. Maybe if she was really drunk or high she wouldn't feel so insecure or nervous about people watching her and Luka.

Amity's face turned scarlet at how her brain casually assumed he would be with her.

Like he would ever go to one of those places! And how did he even pop into my head anyway?

Maybe he would go to those places . . .

Maybe he already has . . .

"You doing okay over there?" Rex asked, leaning their chin in their palm. Their eyebrow piercing cracked up with their smile. "They do have other rooms, *private* sections. They're behind large glass windows, but they have privacy curtains too."

Amity took a nervous bite of her burger. "I wasn't thinking about going."

"Uh-huh. Sure." Rex smiled, taking another large bite.

Maybe he has been to places like that before? He defi-nitely has a few kinks. Choking for one, and maybe a . . . dom?

Amity's cheeks burned as she remembered their en-counters. He called her kitten, called her a good girl, gave her a "reward." *Definitely a dom.*

She bit into her burger, not stopping until it was gone, thinking about what other things they could explore together.

"He was just . . ." Rex's eyes glittered as they spoke. "He had this bright hair and green eyes. I swear I think they glowed a little. He was *just*—and his *hands*, and his *tongue*." They covered their eyes. "Amity, it was the best sex I've had in a *while*."

"Here you are, ladies—"

"I am so happy for you!" Amity practically shouted, not even noticing the waiter approach or even speak.

"I'll just leave these here then."

"Thank you! It was just—*fuck*, he was—ah shit. Like—*how*?!"

"Will you see him again? Did you get his name? Are you allowed to give names???"

Rex laughed, almost spitting up their drink. "Not here you're not. You have to sign an NDA and all that crap beforehand . . . You can do whatever you want once you leave."

"And did you?"

"Unfortunately, no," Rex sighed. "But he *did* ask to see me again. He said he's there often and he's been dying to taste me ever since the club popped up earlier this month."

"Earlier this month? So this place is *new*-new then?"

"Yeah, apparently it moves around a lot. So it's never in the same place for longer than a few months. Actually, popped up around the time you met Luka now that I think about it."

Amity hummed while biting the last of her burger. *That's a little weird.*

Amity arrived at her house late; well, maybe not as late as she has stayed out the past week. It was only 8:00 p.m.

As per usual, Freaya whined and whined even though she had been fed hours before but because she was so adorable Amity gave her a few treats, which the void greedily accepted.

Amity shucked off her shoes, then carelessly made her way toward the bedroom. She may have accidentally hit the wall on her way there, but that was a problem for tomorrow's Amity, not now's.

With a gleeful noise, she fell face first onto her bed, clutching the soft comforter to try and ground herself.

Everything was still spinning a bit, or maybe because she actually spun down the hall earlier. Didn't matter.

Rex said that guy was super handsome. Redhead with a slender, muscular frame. Freckles across his chest. Green glowing eyes, though that was probably because of the lighting. No one's eyes actually glow. Except Luka's.

She inhaled deeply. Seasalt. Sandalwood.

"His eyes glow when he's mad. Excited. The brightest when he's aroused." She mumbled into her bedsheets.

Clumsily she shuffled off her pants, then her socks, before heaving herself up to take off her shirt.

Amity lay on her back and hummed a sweet sigh, taking in his scent again. Quickly she scrambled for her phone, which was still in her pants pocket, which were now somewhere on the floor.

Once it was recovered, she tossed it onto one of the many pillows before she crawled back upon the bed.

With a satisfied smile, she reached for the box on her nightstand and took out her favorite toy. It was hot-pink silicone and shaped in a soft curve. Amity smiled wide and threw herself back among the mass of pillows.

She licked her lips and scrolled through her messages on her phone until she found who she was looking for.

Fuck just imagining it.

The dark rooms. The red and blue lights. The soft pink couches. Luka standing above her with his face buried between her legs.

Holding her up against the wall as he thrust deep inside her over and over again. His sweet moans. The sounds of their bodies slamming together.

She dialed his number. Voicemail. *Perfect.*

"Hi, you're probably busy or doing something . . . or maybe you're just lying there trying to sleep . . . I thought this could be a fun idea, and please if you're not into it and don't think it's fun or whatever, then please feel free to never speak to me again. Sorry I'm rambling . . . Anyway. I was thinking—and I'm actually really glad you didn't pick up because I would've been too embarrassed to do this. You just—you make me nervous. And I miss you. You have no idea what kind of suffering you've put me through. Leaving your scent everywhere in my home. On my couch. In my clothes. In my bed. It's *tormenting*. It's just—I just can't take it anymore."

Amity took the curved part of her toy and lazily put it in her mouth, letting her tongue lazily roll over it until it was soaking wet.

"This is the part where you can stop listening, but I don't think you will. I think you'll listen. I think you'll save this audio message. And I think that when I'm done, you'll listen to it over and over again until you are completely drained dry."

Amity made sure he could hear her breath hitch as she slipped it inside herself. It glided right in with no resistance. That part would vibrate inside her.

Her toy had eleven different patterns to choose from, and tonight she would use them *all*.

She adjusted it so the top part, the suction, was positioned right over her clit. There were seven suction levels on that part. Tonight she would turn it to *full blast*. She breathed him in again, letting him leave her on a sweet humm. Letting it fill her. Imagining he was filling her.

Then she turned it on.

CHAPTER TWENTY SIX

THREE DAYS UNTIL HALLOWEEN

Amity turned the volume up slightly on her phone, which turned up the music around the shop simultaneously. She bobbed her head in time with the soft music, a nice bluegrass mix—Tom Petty, Fleetwood Mac, Simon & Garfunkel, Indigo Girls, and a bunch of others.

Maybe it's more "mountain music" than bluegrass?

She was refilling the napkins at the pickup counter, then, as she was about to refill the pastry display, someone tall brought her out of her thoughts.

"You're all alone today, Amity?"

"Rune!" she said a little too loudly.

"You remember me." The corner of his mouth kicked up in a small smile.

He didn't look fazed at all that she practically yelled in his face. Amity glanced away, embarrassed.

"Ah, sorry. Not for long, Sammy will be here soon. How are you?"

"Oh, *tired*," he sighed, placing his briefcase down on the stool beside him and taking a seat. "I can only stare at so many papers for so long."

"Papers?" Amity looked him over; he looked nice as usual. His hair was perfectly curled on the top of his head and swept back in a neat wave. Amity wished her hair would behave so obediently. Rune was dressed in a white button-up with a maroon vest, so dark it was almost black, and his usual black coat, which he neatly folded in his arms and placed on top of his briefcase, which actually looked more like a fancy laptop case.

"Ah, yes, unfortunately."

"Are you a lawyer?" she asked, picking up her cinnamon tea from the other side of the counter and making her way back to him. Tea, miraculously, had less caffeine than coffee and was more anxiety reducing, so in light of the current unnatural and horrifying events vast approaching, she had made the active switch.

"Gods, no," he laughed warmly. "No, I don't have the patience for it. I'm just a teacher."

"You don't have the patience for law but you have the patience to teach?" she asked, and then immediately covered her mouth. *There she goes again. Speaking too fast for her own mind.* "Sorry! I didn't mean to offend you. What do you teach?"

He laughed warmly, "No offense taken. I teach herbology. *Herbalism.*"

Amity took another sip from her cup with a quizzical look on her face.

Rune's eyes were sparkling at her with anticipation.

"What is it?"

"It's just . . ." She thought her sentence out before she spoke. "I would've never guessed."

"I don't look the part?" He smiled and began to undo the top few buttons of his shirt. "I know, I've gotten that a few times." He glanced back up at her, catching her stare.

Amity looked away, hiding a blush of embarrassment. *Yeah, no one would suspect a hot redhead to be teaching herbology.*

A smirk kicked up on his lips as he scanned the display case. It was filled with the usual pumpkin tarts, now decorated to look like jacko'lanterns, lemon cakes, and some mini apple pies.

"What do you recommend for me today?"

Amity looked over the display case. "Well, you do like your lemon cakes, but the mini pies and tarts are really good. I haven't tried them yet though."

He looked her over for a moment. "How about all of them, then?"

"You got it."

With a smile she loaded everything onto two plates and put the small pie into the microwave. When it was done she brought everything over to him.

"Thank you, you didn't have to do that."

"It's no problem." She smiled. "Would you like some whipped cream?"

"Always," he hummed.

He watched her quietly as she made three small swirls of coconut whipped cream onto each treat. When Amity caught his stare, she realized his eyes were on her the whole time.

"Thank you, Amity."

Rune never broke eye contact. Gingerly he pushed the warm apple pie toward her. "For you."

"Oh no, I couldn't—"

"Come now, how are you expected to sell them if you don't try them first?"

Amity glanced down at the plate hesitantly. After a moment she dragged the plate toward her. *It's free food and it's not like he's the one that made it or anything. Also, free food—why shouldn't I take it?*

"Thank you."

He lifted his tart sweetly and held it out to her. "You're most welcome. Cheers, to the end of a workday."

She lightly tapped the crust of the pie to his tart. "To the end of a workday."

Amity took a small bite out of her small pie, then immediately took another. It was delicious!

"So how is your . . . boyfriend?"

"Oh, he's good. He's great." Amity tucked a loose curl from her braid behind her ear.

Compared to Rune, she felt very underdressed. However, she was at work; if she did dress like that, she would only feel stuffy and spill coffee on everything.

Amity looked up at him suspiciously, "Why do you ask?"

"Ah, apologies. I didn't mean to pry. I swear I don't have any ulterior motives," he exclaimed, crossing his finger over his chest. "I was actually going to ask you about the books you've been reading, you always seem to be reading a new one every time I see you. I thought maybe we could—"

"Sorry I'm late, Amity!" Sammy yelled from the other side of the cafe, barreling through the door in a heavy winter coat. Sammy *hated* the cold. She quickly turned to the other patrons who were now shivering from the chill breeze.

"Sorry, everyone!"

Amity laughed quietly as Sammy rushed past and into the back room.

"Sorry, Rune, what was that . . . ?" Her attention snagged on a tall figure dressed in black outside the door. Luka waved at her with a smile. She smiled wide. "—Actually I have to go, but I'll talk to you later. I'm here on Monday."

Rune blinked as she quickly removed her apron and re-placed it on the back hook where her jacket was, throwing it on just as Sammy rushed out of the back room nearly slamming the door in her face.

"Boy do I have a story to tell you—"

"Monday, Sammy, I promise. I have to go." She patted down her pockets quickly, making sure she had everything. *Keys. Wallet. Phone. Check!*

Amity turned to the mirror and touched up her hair as Sammy set up her phone at the other end of the counter.

"I already sanitized everything, things have been a little slow, but everything should be fine," she explained, snatching up the remainder of her pie and swallowing it almost too fast.

"Geez, Amity, relax, you don't want to choke before your date." Amity swallowed the last of her tea and put the cup at the end of the counter, completely ignoring Sammy and her vivid pink hair reflecting the tint of her cheeks.

"This is Rune, he just needs to pay and then he'll be all set. He likes to take sweets home."

Rune's eyes sparkled at that. "Amity—"

"Monday. We'll talk then, I promise." She turned toward the door with a wide smile. "Bye!"

Luka held the door open for her with a warm smile. He kissed her forehead sweetly as she passed through the frame.

"Someone's excited."

"I am! You won't tell me anything about today's training, so it must be something cool. Are we going to *work* or—" She stopped herself short. Luka's attention was fixed back inside Halley's.

Cyan eyes glowed faintly. She glanced down at his cornicello. It also had a faint glow to it. A pulsing blue light. Not the constant glow when he was fighting the fox demon or the shapeshifter. A chill ran through her at the memory of *that* demon.

"What's wrong?" she asked, trying to hide the worry in her voice.

Luka looked her over for a moment. He inhaled slowly, then on the exhale ran his hands down from the top of her head down to her fingertips.

Amity stood silent and still, watching him carefully. Was he cleansing her? Rough fingers entwined with her own.

"Nothing."

He pecked her lips quickly, too quickly, causing a pout to form. Those addictive lips smirked down at her, which, of course, only irritated her . . . and maybe slightly aroused her? Not like she could blame herself with that fucking smirk—damn the things she would do if they were back at her place.

She gripped him by the collar of his jacket and pulled him closer, kissing him hard. *If he's going to kiss me, then it's going to be a proper kiss.* Her tongue licked his bottom lip teasingly, managing a brief surprise.

He held her closer, rolling his tongue against hers in one smooth motion. *That's better.* Just when she opened her mouth wider for him, the bastard pulled away.

"We will have plenty of time for this *later*, kitten."

He glared back into the shop for a moment as she wiped some saliva off the corner of her lips.

"Fine," she muttered into her sleeve.

"Don't be too disappointed now. If you're good tonight, maybe I'll give you another reward."

Amity felt her cheeks flush, along with the rest of her body. Luka laughed, placed a warm hand against her back, then began leading her down the street toward his car.

"You know, sometimes I can't tell if you're more of the dominant type or the submissive type," she said.

She felt his hand fist the fabric of her jacket, then spread wide.

"It's a little bit of both I think. A switch."

"A *switch*?" Amity thought about that for a moment.

A switch was someone who liked to be both submissive and dominant during sex. Sometimes it just depends on the mood or their partner or honestly anything at all. She was reading this one scene where the God of Mischief himself started as the dominant one but then ended up on the submissive side by the end of the scene.

"*Why*? What's on your mind?"

She looked away trying to hide her flushed face. "Nothing! I was just curious, that's all."

"Well"—he drew out the word—"I suppose I like both the same, but it's not like I plan ahead to be one or the other."

Amity nodded, still keeping her red face turned away. With his car finally in sight, he guided her over to the passenger side. With the soft *click*, he opened the door for her, and just as she was about to step inside, he slammed it shut.

Amity fell back against the side of the car, catching herself from falling.

"What was that for?" she yelled, turning toward him.

Luka leaned in close. He placed one arm above her, leaning into it. The other remained on the passenger door. She was caged in.

Glowing cyan eyes stared down at her. "How would you like me?"

"Wait, what?"

He leaned closer to her, bending down to speak in her ear.

"How. Would. You. Like me?" he repeated.

"I . . ." Amity tried to focus but her thoughts were too frazzled. That flush ran through her body again as she recalled her *reward* a few nights ago. How his skin felt like fire against her. What his tongue felt like . . . "However you want . . . I guess."

Luka slowly clicked his tongue three times, sending new thrilling chills down her spine with each.

"Would you like me to beg?" His voice grew softer, a sweet whimper. "Please. Please, Amity, let me taste you again. Just one more kiss?"

He nudged the side of her head with his before sweetly kissing her cheek. Amity finally glanced at him through half-lidded eyes.

"Please, kitten? I've missed you so much."

She wanted to kiss him, wanted to hold him close, wanted to feel his tongue on hers. Her mouth opened slightly, taking in a deep breath. She was about to turn toward him, give him exactly what he asked for.

Luka jerked his head back out of her reach. His cheeks were rosy, but that didn't stop that fucking smirk from spreading across his lips. Amity's mouth hung open as her brain fought desperately to keep up and process what just happened.

"*Or*"—he drew out the word mockingly. His voice grew darker, primal even, like a low growl—"would you like me to be more demanding?" He slid his hand up her shoulder and across her collarbone before gently nestling it around her throat. "Would my kitten like that? If I held you just like this"—he tightened his grip slightly, sending a new sensation through her—"would you cum like this?

My hand around your throat. My fingers buried inside you. My mouth on your swollen clit. So fucking hot and sweet. I'm drooling just thinking about it." He kissed her neck hungrily.

Amity's body was growing hot before, but now it felt like she was on fire. If he didn't move first, she would pounce on him!

"Hmmm? Would my *pretty girl* like that?"

Amity reached for his collar again, ready to slam his lips against hers. That fucking bastard pulled back just in time.

Amity drew in a sharp breath as realization dawned on her. He was playing with her.

He laughed low as she flipped, pressing her front against his car, and banged on the door.

"You're—!" She took a deep breath, regaining a bit of her composure, then turned to him with burning cheeks and a wide smile.

"You are such a fucking tease."

"I love it when you swear. Scold me again."

CHAPTER TWENTY SEVEN
THREE DAYS UNTIL HALLOWEEN

Amity shifted nervously in her seat.

"This isn't the way to the park."

Luka shook his head, scrolling through to the next song in his car. Amity narrowed her eyes on him. He glanced at her quickly before focusing back on the road.

"What?"

What . . . WHAT?!

"Are you serious?"

"What's wrong—"

"You do realize that if I was with anyone else this would be on a true crime podcast. Girl goes with her boy on a date, then is never seen again."

Luka laughed as he exited off the highway ramp into Waterbury.

"You have it all planned out, don't you?" He smirked.

Amity narrowed her eyes on him. She didn't actually think any of that *would* happen, but the least he could do was tell her where he was taking her. Not to mention she was pissed as hell. How dare he mess with her like that?! Leaving her all hot and bothered. Her thighs pressed tightly together uncomfortably. She was going to get him back for that. *Definitely.* She sighed, calming herself down just enough to refocus and distract herself from secretly enjoying him messing with her.

"Luka. You still haven't—"

"It's a surprise."

"I don't think I can handle any more 'surprises' in this lifetime." She sighed again, leaning back into her seat. Brown eyes turned their attention toward the window as the sun started to set, and despite the beautiful scenery, she still felt nervous. What kind of training did he have planned for her? Was it even worth all this stress and nerves? Maybe he was just taking her on a date?

She watched the various colors of trees pass by. Vibrant yellow, orange, red, and even gold mixed together in a wonderful kaleidoscope of colors. Connecticut was beautiful in the fall.

Luka rested a hand on her knee, drawing her attention. Even through her jeans his touch was warm, sending a fluttering sensation through her that forced her abdomen to tighten.

"We're going to do a ceremony, a way to protect you. Just in case." He opened her thighs apart with his fingers, then spread them down the inside of her thigh. Massaging the flesh there for a moment before his hand stilled. Those rough fingers held the curve of her just a little tighter. ". . . Just in case."

He had that look in his eyes again. The one she had unknowingly become all too familiar with. Was he thinking about what she had been so desperate to keep out of her mind? The very real danger that she wouldn't make it past Halloween? Or even worse, that *they* wouldn't make it past Halloween?

She hooked her arm through his and kissed his bicep. "Okay."

Amity stepped out of the car with shaky legs, her mouth hanging slack.

"It's going to be fine, Amity—"

"Fine?! You can't just introduce me to your mom without asking and then say it's fine!"

Whatever nerves she had about this "ceremony" immediately left her brain. Not only did Luka drive her to the middle of the woods in Woodbury, but he was actually introducing her to his *mother*!

"Re-introduce," he corrected with a smirk.

"*Re-introduce*, whatever. That's even worse!"

He tapped her mouth closed with a chuckle. then wrapped an arm around her and guided her toward the house.

"Relax, kitten, it's going to be fine. Oh! Whatever you do, don't refuse food."

"Food?"

"Luka!"

Amity watched his mother approach him with arms wide. She was tall, almost as tall as him, with long dark hair, almost black.

He embraced her warmly and kissed her cheek. She glanced quickly down at Amity before narrowing her eyes on her son, clearly communicating something Amity didn't understand.

"Hello, it's nice to meet you—I mean *re*-meet you." Amity held her hand out nervously.

Amity was pulled into a tight embrace and before she could register anything, Luka's mother pulled back and kissed her forehead sweetly. Blue eyes watched her carefully as if she were fighting back words that could make Amity shatter like glass.

"It's lovely to meet you Amity," she finally said. "Come inside, you must be hungry."

She took Amity by the hand and led them to the large New England–style home. It was gorgeous! The kind of house that looks like it came out of *Practical Magic* or something. It was white with black shutters and a domed greenhouse extending off the side of the house. There were windows through the kitchen where you could see into it.

Amity stopped by the front door to take off her shoes, finally stopping to get a good look at everything. The kitchen was enormous! An open-concept style with a plethora of counter space, complete with an island, which was already filled with all kinds of food. Luka sneaked up behind her and closed the door.

"I thought you might like it."

Amity admired the drying herbs hanging over the sink, the subway-tile backsplash, and the large wooden dining room table that looked like it was sliced from a large tree. All she could manage was a nod.

"Amity, sit down, relax. Luka, come help me!"

Luka kissed her temple sweetly before making his way over to the kitchen and placing a large container of salt on the countertop. Amity was so distracted by the beauty of the house that she didn't even see him take it out of the car.

She watched Luka maneuver around the kitchen. He wrapped an apron around himself before taking some boiling pasta off the stove.

"You don't look well. Are you sleeping?" his mother asked—well, more scolded than asked. She was putting the finishing touches on some caprese on the island.

"I am," he said, draining the water into the large sink.

His mother gave him a very long look, clearly not believing him. She turned back to slicing the large loaf of bread, no doubt a product from his nana. He did say on their first date that she loved baking bread.

Amity's eyes widened for a moment. *Wait . . . what did I just—*

"You're lucky your nana isn't here to catch you lying like that," his mother scolded, placing the slices of bread onto the serving platter next to the caprese.

Amity went to the counter, her fingers gripping the granite.

"I can help—"

"Oh, no dear, I'm almost done. Luka, set the table please."

"You shouldn't have made this much food, Mom," he mumbled.

Luka finished turning the pasta in its vodka scampi sauce before making it over to Amity's side of the kitchen where he grabbed the plates. She watched him effortlessly maneuver around the large kitchen, placing the plates in front of her before taking out the water glasses and placing those in front of her too. He went to the wine rack and pulled a bottle of red, took three glasses from the cabinet above, then made his way back over to her.

He popped the corked with ease and waited a moment before pouring her a small glass, then one for his mother, and finally one for himself.

Luka was so focused yet so comfortable, like this was the most natural thing in the world.

"Thank you," she smiled.

He smiled back and lightly tapped his glass to hers. Those cyan eyes watched her as he took a deep sip.

"I don't want you eating too much, just a snack. We can take the rest home."

Amity quirked her head slightly to the side. "But you said—"

"What kind of nonsense is that? She's hungry. She'll eat," his mother stated on her way back from setting the appetizers on the table.

Luka pursed his lips and looked away. Amity failed to stifle her laugh. *He's acting like a little kid with that reaction. So cute!*

"Her stomach didn't handle her other-realm 'encounters' well. I don't want her to get sick."

Something moved inside her empty stomach. It fluttered around wildly and her cheeks grew warm.

Silently Amity watched him as he casually set the table. The way he set the glasses down without making any sound. The placement of the forks. The way he filled the water glasses. A laugh beside her shook her out of her thoughts.

"He's such a handsome boy isn't he, Amity?"

Amity's face flushed deeper. She quickly turned and sipped her wine. "Yes, ma'am!"

"Ma'am?" She laughed, "That's my mother. It's Lucia for you."

She nodded, then together they made their way over to the table. Lucia sat at the head and let out a long sigh slip past her lips.

She did make a lot of food for them.

Amity took a sip of her wine, feeling some of the tension ease off her shoulders. The energy around them was warm and welcoming, no doubt due to Lucia. Luka on the other hand held tension in his stare.

Before Amity could even begin to fill her plate, he'd already picked it up and began serving her, filling it with light appetizers, the roasted peppers, caprese, and three slices of bread. Then he filled his and his mother's plate with the same, only larger portions, as well as the scampi. That mouthwatering, delicious-looking scampi.

Lucia spoke with her son, but considering he wasn't very responsive, it was more like she was speaking *to* him.

Amity tuned out their conversation, too focused on the food on her plate. It was so good! Even if this was just appetizers. She imagined Luka making food for her; he was a good cook. *He's probably amazing.* Amity imagined all the wonderful things he would cook for her as she happily continued to eat.

Luka continued to watch her. He would nod his head lightly and give short answers to his mother's questions, making her more annoyed, until finally her temper got the better of her. She slammed her hand down on the table in front of him, shaking him out of his stare and some dishes on the table.

"For Christ's sake, Luka, let the girl eat!"

"I am!"

"Stop glaring at her then!"

"I'm not *glaring.*"

Lucia turned away from her son and toward Amity.

"Amity, eat as much as you want."

Luka "glared" at his mother, then heaved a sigh.

"We'll take some home for you later."

"Amity. Eat."

"I'll just have a few more. Your food is delicious and I don't want to waste it." *I don't want to throw it up—fuck, even thinking that makes me a little woozy.*

She placed just a little scampi onto her plate, along with some more roasted peppers and a slice of bread. *That should be a sufficient compromise.* The last thing she wanted was to get between Luka and his mom. If it came to it, his mother would win. End of discussion.

The first bite was a burst of flavor exploding across her taste buds. Not too buttery or oily or even garlicky. It was just perfect. There was even shrimp! She didn't see Luka add the shrimp. She glanced up at him quickly.

Luka rested his chin in his palm, watching her eyes sparkle. A small smile tilted up the corner of his mouth. It was gone before she could really savor it thanks to Lucia poking his cheek with a giggle.

Something about this felt so nostalgic. Maybe she had been here before. Practiced spells with Lucia. Baked bread with his nana even. She swallowed another bite of scampi, hoping she did learn spells. Luka did say he was teaching her. That excited her. What kind of wonderful things had she been learning? Amity glanced at Luka just as Lucia tucked a long piece of hair that fell out of his ponytail back behind his ear. *Maybe he'll teach me again when all this is over?*

She took a sip of her wine, a mix of emotions swirling inside of her—nostalgia, yes, but sadness too. Happiness. Frustration for not remembering the magic lessons, but more importantly, these small moments. It swirled inside her like a thick bog, churning and turning over and over again.

How many times did she see this side of him? This shy, slightly embarrassed smile. The way his shoulders relaxed as he ate his mother's cooking. Did she even notice these sides of him?

Did she even realize how much she—

"Amity?"

Her eyes widened as she was pulled back out of her thoughts. Someone was holding her hand. Their ringed fingers squeezed hers lightly. Lucia.

"I know it's hard. Gods know I don't understand what you're going through, but I can only try to imagine it."

Something hot and wet slid down her face. Tears. She was crying? When did she start?

Furious fingers wiped them away. Judging from how wet her cheeks were, she was crying for a while. *Great. Cry in front of his mother, that's just fucking great.*

"You will have your memories back. All of them. I promise," Luka said softly, brushing a stubborn curl behind her ear.

"Luka, get the bath ready. It's time."

CHAPTER TWENTY EIGHT
THREE DAYS UNTIL HALLOWEEN

Luka led her through the greenhouse and around the back where a deep tub sat atop of some broken cobblestones. The white porcelain seemed to glow in the moonlight.

"Shouldn't we wait for Nana?" Luka asked hesitantly.

"No, Nana will be out all night with her new man."

If Amity's nerves weren't frying, she would've laughed. *I definitely want to meet that woman later.*

Lucia made her way over to the other side of the tub and ran her fingers along its edge. "Besides, I can do this alone."

Luka's grip tightened around her shoulder. His eyes began to glow a little brighter.

"I can help—"

"You've only seen it when I performed it on you after your . . . 'incident,' " Lucia snapped. Her eyes were glowing brightly in the dim light. Amity glanced toward the full moon curiously. *Was it because of the moon?*

She felt her ears perk up at the word incident, practically burning to learn more. If she wasn't so fucking nervous, she would've asked about it.

"But it will take longer without her." His eyes were wide. Was he nervous? Amity felt her stomach turn, thankful she didn't eat her fill earlier. If Luka was nervous, then it only made her own unease spike.

A cold wind blew past, causing a shiver to run down her spine. Lucia had her change into one of her old nightdresses, one that had faded with years of age and was extremely thin, providing no comfort on the chilly October night.

Amity glanced down at the tub; it was full and steaming, but even without touching the water, she knew it wasn't nearly half as warm as it ought to be for an outdoor bath. No matter how many large pots of boiling water Luka brought out while she changed, she would still freeze.

He dipped his hand into the thick water.

"It's not as warm as you like it—"

"You mean scalding?" Amity smiled at him nervously. He gave her a hard look, though he couldn't fully hide the upward tilt of his mouth. She tried avoiding his gaze, focusing instead on his cornicello as it swung back and forth. It was glowing too, a steady soft glow as were his eyes.

Didn't he say something about blessing it every full moon?

Rough fingers tilted her chin up to meet his eyes.

"It's going to be okay."

He kissed her forehead lightly. She nodded silently, and he helped her into the tub.

The moment her bare foot hit the water's surface, she knew it wasn't just water in the tub. It was salt. Lots and lots of salt.

Amity stood still for a moment, feeling the sharp crunch between her toes. The hard brush against her calves and the tingle just below her kneecaps.

"You have to sit, Amity," Lucia instructed.

She nodded curtly. Lucia explained everything to her as she changed. The only thing allowed out of the water was her head. She was about to sit when Luka held her arm lightly, stopping her.

"Wait."

He pulled the hair tie out of his hair, letting his fall loosely. Carefully he pulled her hair back out of her face, brushing the tips of his fingers lightly against her neck as they worked, giving her the reassurance of his touch. Amity felt something pool low in her abdomen. He tied her hair into a tight, high bun before helping her sink into the tub.

The salt scraped against her skin the deeper she sank, and the chill of the water sent shivers crawling up her spine. She hugged herself tightly under the surface and pressed her forehead to her knees, trying to bear it.

"I won't bullshit you, this isn't going to be the most pleasant experience. But once the initial blood-blessing ritual is complete, you just need to make sure you ingest salt water that has been blessed under a full moon every new cycle."

Amity nodded, trying very hard to stay focused. Her shoulders were beginning to shiver.

Lucia placed a warm hand on her freezing back. Amity focused on the heat. It wasn't much but at least it was something.

Lucia spread her fingers wide along her back, then skimmed her other hand along the surface of the water. She tsked and turned her glowing eyes to the full moon above their heads. Her cornicello shone brighter.

"This salt was blessed under a supermoon, with it I will infuse it through your skin, into your blood and finally your bones. This won't be like a regular salt bath. We are rearranging the way your bone marrow creates blood cells, making sure that the fresh blood will contain the blessing of this salt. When a creature of the other realm comes into contact with it, it will burn their flesh like acid, eroding it down until it burns through."

Amity nodded once again, trying to process everything Lucia said. Her jaw tensed as her teeth started to chatter.

Lucia's hand slipped off her back. She gently guided Amity deeper into the tub until just her face was left above the surface.

She jerked silently as the ripples stung against her cheeks like knives. Her arms wrapped tighter around her torso.

Cold. That was all she felt. The sound of her own teeth chattering behind her lips was the only thing she could hear. She hadn't even noticed Lucia had started to speak.

Lucia lifted her slightly out of the tub, letting her rest the back of her head on the rim. She jolted at the contact.

"*Luka*," his mother warned.

Amity glanced at him; his hand was frozen midair, like he was reaching out to cup her cheek.

"I *know*. I'm not the caster. I can't touch her once the spell has begun." He moved his hand back to the rim of the tub and took in the sight of her with a cheeky smirk. "Not yet anyway."

A smile spread on Amity's lips, and she couldn't help but giggle, feeling herself relax a bit in the strange water. A slightly rosy tint dusted her cheeks. This dress was already thin and faded, but when she stepped into the bath, it became completely translucent. If she was wearing underwear, it would stand out starkly. But she wasn't wearing underwear or even a bra. In her current state, there was nothing to leave to the imagination. Completely naked.

"Honestly," his mother scoffed from the other side of the tub.

She placed a wet palm on Amity's forehead and spoke again. Her voice was thicker this time, commanding and powerful. Even if Amity couldn't understand what was being said, the intention was clear. She felt it.

The center of her forehead began to tingle. The feeling spread slowly down and across her face, like she could feel the blood pumping in her veins.

Amity watched the Hunter's Moon shine brightly down on them as the sensation spread down her neck and chest. She twitched slightly beneath the water as the sensation peaked at her taut nipples, then down her arms to her fingertips. They fidgeted beneath the water's edge. She let out a shaky breath as the feeling spread down her navel. That warm, familiar feeling swirled low inside of her. *Feeling a little turned on at a time like this might be a little fucked up,* she thought, conflicted.

The feeling continued to spread down her legs, prickling as it went, all the way down to her toes. Her skin felt a little warmer in the water now. Even warmer as Luka's gaze followed the sensation down her body, tracking it as if he could see it moving beneath her skin.

Brown eyes flicked back to the water as it began to glow a faint blue. Amity thought she knew how much salt was in the water before, but now that it was visible, she realized it was much more than she originally thought. It was thick and murky. She shifted her heavy legs along the bottom's edge.

Wait . . . heavy?

She shifted her legs again, fully realizing just how heavy they felt. Like she was strapped down with weights.

Lucia removed her hand and skimmed the surface of the water. Amity watched it silently make smooth passes along the surface, creating as few ripples as possible. That warm feeling that filled her grew slightly warmer.

Is Lucia warming the water? Thank God, I thought I was going to freeze to death for a second there.

Amity's fingers twitched, scratching at the salty water as the heat spread through her hands.

Then up her arms . . .

Lucia watched her closely.

Then her chest . . .

Luka was also watching her closely—expectantly.

Then up from her toes and her legs . . .

Her skin grew warmer like she was under a sweet summer sun.

Luka's grip tightened on the rim of the tub.

The heat continued to spread, continued to grow hotter.

Damn, Lucia, I think it's warm enough now . . .

"Umm, Lucia—" Something dripped down from her forehead cutting her sentence short. Her skin grew hotter still. Amity's eyes grew wide with panic as she realized three things at the same time: (1) Lucia wasn't heating the water at all, (2) Amity's skin was *burning*, and (3) Luka knew this would happen—and he didn't tell her.

Her skin began to burn and itch. She lifted her heavy hands to grip the sides of the tub, ready to hoist herself out of the water.

Lucia was faster. She grabbed Amity's hands and ripped them off the tub, forcing her back into the water.

Amity screamed. It took a lot of strength just to keep her head from hitting the back of the tub.

"Hold her down!"

"But you said . . ." Luka's eyes were wide with panic as Amity writhed and yelled.

She started sweating harder. Her skin was like fire. She tried desperately to get out of the water, away from the salt—to scrape it off her skin.

"The spell is cast—"

Before his mother finished speaking, Luka grabbed Amity's other arm and pressed down onto her chest.

"Don't let her out of the water!" Lucia yelled, holding on tighter, trying to force her down.

"I'll do it! You're hurting her!" He pushed her off and gripped both of Amity's arms tighter crossing them over her chest, and forcing her back into the water. His eyes glowed brighter.

"Amity, please, you have to stop. Amity! *Stop!*" His eyes kept flickering brighter. *Is he trying to use a spell on me?* It was no good. She couldn't think clearly. There was only one thing clouding her mind, consuming her every cell.

Pain.

"Shit!" He tried holding her down with one hand as his other went to his belt. In one swift pull he removed it and tied it in a loop with his teeth. Amity thrashed beneath him, clawing at his strong arm.

He jumped into the tub. Leaning over her. Trying to press his weight on top of her, but it was no use, he only had one free hand.

"Amity, you have to stop!"

She screamed and whimpered beneath him, clawing at him. She was like an animal now. Luka grabbed her by the jaw, pried open her mouth, then shoved his belt between her teeth.

"Bite!"

She bit down hard, screaming through gritted teeth.

The hair that had fallen out of her bun was now sticking to her face with salt water and sweat. Tears fell rapidly from her eyes as she heaved with every breath. Luka took her arms in his, crossing them once again across her chest, then closed her legs with his own, straddling her until she could only jerk beneath him.

Luka pressed his forehead to hers as her screams morphed into cries and whimpers.

He began breathing deeply and audibly. Eventually hers became the same. As Amity's breathing got deeper, slowly the pain became slightly tolerable.

"That's it. Good girl. Slow, long breaths. In and out," he cooed.

More tears slid down her cheeks, stinging them. She muffled an inaudible whimper.

"I know. I know it hurts. Fuck I do. It'll be over soon. I promise. Just keep breathing."

She continued to breathe with him. Slow breaths. In and out. Until the searing need to scratch her skin off was gone. Her skin was still burning though, like she'd been baking under the hot sun for hours. His grip loosened around her wrists.

A muffled sound bubbled out of her scratchy throat. It was so distorted by her whimpers that if she was in a calm state of mind she would've been shocked he understood what she said. The corner of his mouth kicked up. She'd called him a liar.

"Yeah, yeah, I know. I'm a lying fucking bastard." Brown eyes narrowed on him, butting her forehead against his with a loud *thud.* He didn't flinch.

"Don't be angry with him, Amity, I asked him not to tell you."

Amity glanced to the side of the tub where Lucia stood with towels in hand. *I didn't even realize she left to fetch them.*

She glanced back at Luka who had a suspiciously happy glint in his eyes. Amity looked away embarrassed. He bent down to her ear.

"Hit me harder next time, kitten."

Her nostrils flared. She went to hit him again, but he easily dodged, laughing as he did so.

"Honestly, Luka," his mother grumbled. She dipped her finger beneath the water and touched Amity's ankle. "How are you feeling, Amity? Does it still burn?"

Amity thought for a moment. No. She didn't burn anymore. Luka removed the belt from her aching jaw so she could answer. *When did it stop? I didn't even notice.*

"No, it doesn't burn."

They both sighed in relief.

"That's great. Luka's took over an hour. He was so riled, we just knocked him unconscious—"

"Mom!"

"What? It's true—"

"I was just a kid!"

A laugh burst from Amity. Seeing Luka like this, this cute little kid in front of his mom, was so, well, *cute.* His cheeks were bright red with embarrassment and his mouth was hung open in surprise. This was a rare treat.

Lucia smiled and shook out the towels.

As if on cue, Luka rose out of the tub, water dripping off his hair and clothes. He refastened his belt, never taking his glowing eyes off of Amity. Whatever cuteness she thought he was a moment ago evaporated. Perfectly silhouetted in the moonlight, he pushed his dripping hair back and smiled down at her. *Fuck.*

Amity let him pull her out of the tub. When she stepped onto the grass, a wave of exhaustion flooded her senses and she fell into his strong arms.

"Exhaustion is normal, don't worry," he reassured, wrapping her inside a warm towel. Was it warm or was she just freezing now?

Amity leaned her head onto the headrest. After the ceremony was a giant blur. *Did I pass out?* Something irked her about that if it were true. Crying, screaming, and passing out in front of his mother after just meeting her? *Great job, Amity.*

She glanced down at her clothes; somehow she was changed back into the ones she came in. She tugged at the sleeves of her henley lightly. Luka and his mother appeared, carrying grocery bags, one in each hand. They loaded them into the back seat while in the middle of some argument—discussion?

"I want you to take it."

"For the last time I don't need it!"

"Luka!"

Argument.

"Amity, we have enough food to last us a month."

She turned her head back to them, peeking into one of the bags. It was full of Tupperware of what looked like heaven.

"Thank you, Lucia."

"All I'm saying is!—you're welcome dear—I want you to be prepared for anything—"

"And all *I'm* saying is I don't need it!"

Lucia straightened and heaved a heavy sigh, no doubt trying to rein in her short temper. Luka opened the passenger door and felt Amity's head, though she wished he didn't. She felt gross.

"When is your meeting?" Lucia asked.

Luka brushed an unruly curl behind Amity's ear.

"We have time—"

"Halloween," Amity yawned.

"Halloween?!"

Luka narrowed his eyes on her and flicked her nose playfully. She giggled, which made him smile a short-lived smile. He sighed before straightening and turning to his mother. "Halloween."

Amity looked up at him as he pushed his damp hair back out of his face. She smiled tiredly.

"Why is it every time we see each other—*Every. Time*—one of us is about to pass out and leak some kind of bodily fluid?"

Luka bent down to her again with a smirk.

" 'Bodily fluids,' huh?" he teased, running his finger on top of her thigh.

"Blood—fucking blood, Luka," she said, gesturing to the scratches she made on his arm.

"You're so cute when you're exhausted and sweaty in my arms."

"I'm too tired. The one time you want to have sex and I'm too tired."

Cyan eyes widened, "The one time? What are you—"

"That's *enough*, Luka, let her rest! Load the salt into the car," his mother scolded.

Rough fingers squeezed her thigh lightly before doing as his mother said.

With her arms folded over her chest, Lucia watched her son go. When he was finally out of sight, she rushed over to Amity's side. She spoke in a rushed, hushed tone and her blue eyes locked on her.

"Amity, I know you're tired but I need you to listen to me. I want you to take this just in case." She thrust something into her lap, a small bag with some bread in it. Amity lazily brushed the bread aside. Underneath it was something large and jagged in shape. She unwrapped it revealing a large and a strange star-shaped object with geometric patterns carved on it.

"Promise me you'll keep this safe. Promise me you'll take it with you when you see Dramaur." Lucia wrapped it back in its cloth and quickly shoved it back in the bag. "*Promise* me."

Amity nodded. And just as Luka stepped out of the house, Lucia took the small bag and put it with the others in the back seat.

Luka glanced at her suspiciously as he put the salt in the trunk.

"What did she tell you?"

"I didn't tell her anything!" Lucia laughed.

The corner of his mouth kicked up into a small smile, and he opened his arms to hug her goodbye.

His mother hugged him tightly and kissed his cheek. "Call me if you need me."

"I will."

"Good." She glanced back to Amity in the car, "Take care of my son, Amity!"

CHAPTER TWENTY NINE
THREE DAYS UNTIL HALLOWEEN

It took everything Amity had in her to wash the sweat off her body.

What she wanted was to stay under the running water for a while, but if she waited any longer, Luka would burst in and drag her out; and she was too tired to fight him.

With a sigh Amity turned off the water and stepped tentatively out of the tub. Her foot slid forward on the wet tile, sending her tumbling onto the floor. She cried out faintly, too tired to fully scream, even though the pain was searing. She would have a large bruise on her thigh, No doubt about it.

"Are you alright?!" Luka yelled, bursting through the door.

Amity scrambled to cover herself, but Luka was already wrapping a towel around her. Embarrassment consumed her.

"Don't look!"

"Enough already. I'm not looking." He scooped her into his arms and brought her into the bedroom. "Can you stand?"

Amity shook her head clumsily. Luka huffed out a frustrated breath and laid another towel down on the bed before setting her on top of it. *Where did he get the other towel? Whatever. Too tired to think . . .*

Amity pulled the towel tighter around her.

"I'll dry you off."

She shook her head.

"Amity."

Again, she shook her head, "I can do it—"

"I'm not going to judge you."

Her sore fingers clutched it just a little tighter around herself. *I don't want him to see me like this. Helpless.*

"I know . . ." she mumbled, biting into her bottom lip.

Luka watched her quietly, letting the silence fill the room. The warm smell of seasalt and sandalwood filled her as she took in one deep breath after another, almost lulling her to sleep. Luka placed one hand on either side of her thighs. Her thighs were barely covered by the towel. He leaned in close, locking his gaze with hers. Amity leaned back until she was forced onto her elbows.

"Do you?" His lips were so close to hers. If he leaned in just a little bit more they would touch. Would she ever stop anticipating that? The sweetness of his lips on hers? The feel of his tongue sliding along the seam of her lips begging for entrance? The nip and pull of him taking her bottom lip in between his teeth?

No. No, I don't think I ever could.

"What?" Her face flushed, and the close proximity jolted her remaining senses awake. Luka pressed his forehead to hers and nuzzled in softly.

"Do you know? Do you even realize how much I—"

Something crashed from the kitchen, something that sounded *very* breakable. Luka pulled back as if he was on high alert.

"Freaya," Amity groaned.

He immediately relaxed, and Amity finally got a good look at what he was wearing. It was her old Breckenridge shirt and an old baggy pair of sweats.

"Are you just collecting my clothes?" she asked through a yawn.

A proud smirk crept on his lips.

"I want you dressed and ready for bed, kitten."

"That wasn't what I asked," she said through another yawn, slightly irritated.

He winked at her, then as he left the room he said, "I know."

She wasn't sure if she found that wink annoyingly cheesy or super sexy. Either way she was way too tired to decide. Like way too tired.

"And I would've done that ceremony even if you told me. I want my memories back. I'll do whatever it takes!" she halfheartedly shouted, hoping her message was well received on the other side of her apartment despite the exhaustion in her voice.

She struggled to dry herself with the towel, grateful that Luka tied her hair back before the ceremony. *That would've been such a bitch to go to bed with a wet head of hair. Not to mention washing all that salt out.*

Luka had laid out a loose long-sleeve shirt for her and her comfiest pair of pajama pants, another thing she was grateful for. Struggling to keep her eyes open, she rubbed the tops of her thighs, letting the fresh warmth of her clothes fill her. With a smile she slowly crawled into bed. As soon as her head touched that pillow it was all over. She was fast asleep.

Freaya had knocked over a small container of cinnamon from the counter, no doubt long forgotten after Amity had made her coffee that morning. Now it was shattered into a thousand tiny pieces.

Luka eyed her with simmering aggravation.

"You're lucky you're not with me anymore, otherwise I'd take away all your toys," he warned.

Freaya watched him silently from the kitchen's entrance, licked her paw then brushed her ear with it, unimpressed by his threat.

Luka stifled a laugh and got to work cleaning up the mess. The least she could do was appreciate all he's done for her. *But I guess that's just how cats are . . .*

By the time he returned with Freaya at his heels, acting as if she committed no crimes, Amity had already nestled under the covers, burrowed underneath her many blankets like she was going into hibernation. Luka had fully heard what she yelled earlier in her tired voice. He knew she would do whatever it took to get her memories back. She was always this headstrong about what she wanted, and had proven to be that person still when she stood her ground the first night she found him bleeding in the alleyway. Despite that being her first interaction with demons and his orders to stay put, she pursued him anyway. She made it clear she wanted to help get her memories back and didn't back down despite the risk, despite the harsh training he put her through. He watched her for a few beats with a smile, grateful to watch her fall asleep, relishing these small moments.

How long has he been wishing for just that? To come home from a late-night job to find her curled up in bed like this?

Too long, he decided.

Dramaur was a looming threat, and had always been one. Now it wasn't just Luka risking his life, Amity was risking hers as well.

Luka flicked off the lights and made his way over with silent footsteps, carefully untangling the cocoon she had burrowed herself in. He stifled another laugh as she stirred awake mumbling something inaudible. He gently wrapped her in his embrace and curled his body around hers, fighting the horrible possibilities that crept into his mind.

"It's alright, I have you," he cooed, kissing the back of her head sweetly.

Everything is going to be alright. We're going to make it past Halloween. Both of us.

"Hi."

Luka laughed lightly into her hair at her barely audible voice.

"Hi, kitten."

She sluggishly rolled into him; he hummed in amusement watching her struggle with her eyes closed. *Because why would you stay where I put you?*

He re-adjusted her, placing her head in her favorite place. Humming weakly, she wrapped herself around him, like a koala bear on a tree branch.

". . . Mine," she mumbled into his chest.

"Yes, Amity, *yours*." Her leg hooked itself tighter around his thigh, brushing against his groin. A shaky moan escaped him. *You're lucky you're so tired and so cute.* He kissed her forehead sweetly. "Always, yours."

She nuzzled warmly against his chest with a sweet humm.

Rough fingers stroked her hair for a while; the feeling brought those racing thoughts to a screeching halt. It was still an early night for him, almost 10:00 p.m., but after everything that happened today and now watching the way she nuzzled against him, sleep could easily take him.

He stretched out his free leg under the covers, feeling a bit of tension release with a small *crack*, then pulled the blankets up higher around them both.

Luka had been wound tight all day, unable to tell Amity the details of the ritual, the anticipation of Halloween, admitting to his mother exactly how short he was on time. He cursed himself for not taking the configuration with him, then immediately shook his head.

No, we don't need it. We have my blessed knives. That's enough. It's going to be fine.

He closed his eyes in irritation. There was one more thing that had him on edge. When he picked up Amity that day, he sensed someone, someone he hadn't sensed in a *very* long time. That unease burrowed deep inside of him, reminding him of past mistakes. Past failures . . .

He swept his gaze over Amity and kissed her forehead once again. Just to make sure she was really here. In his arms. *Safe.*

"Amity I . . ." He paused, realizing she was fast asleep on his chest. A small laugh rumbled through him before turning into a rare smile. "I'll be here when you wake up."

Amity fluffed up her hair before turning back to her scrap piece of receipt paper on the countertop.

She opened with Sammy this morning, something that she was beyond grateful about. *Because this morning was a disaster!* she thought bitterly.

So many coffee orders, so many *messed-up* coffee orders—yogis on their way to class, and businesspeople who didn't know what they were ordering because they were too busy being on the phone doing "business things" or whatever that means. A few teens also showed up and acted like entitled pricks. Sammy threatened to throw them out when they bad-mouthed her, or at least *tried* to.

Amity smiled thinking about it. Sammy made one of them cry. *She doesn't take shit from anyone, especially not some snot-nosed, pimple-infested teenager.*

Amity idly drew another circle on the scrap piece of receipt paper. The rush of the morning was over, but now . . . she glanced around the shop.

Sammy was gathering the small vases with singular flowers and then some of the larger bundles. She brought them over to the sink to wash out the vases and tossed the dead and wilting flowers away.

There were a few customers in the shop now, couples actually, from the looks of it. There was one sitting on either side of the door, stealing glances and small touches. Then another at the opposite end of the store where it was a bit more secluded. They were doing a little more than stealing glances. If they went any further than kissing, Amity would have to break them up. Luckily they would stop every so often to breathe and remember they were in public.

She leaned against the counter, letting her mind wander. *Yeah, exhibitionism isn't my thing* . . . Not that that was what the couple was remotely close to doing, but it was bordering too far for PDA.

Luka.

Luka was her thing.

Always Luka.

If she was single, right about now Amity would want to smack herself for being so pathetically in the honeymoon stage.

Despite that, she smiled to herself; it was like she could feel him wrapped around her again.

Last night was slow and sweet. His kisses were long and even sweeter.

She suspected he was being extra careful because of the exhaustion, but after she'd flipped him onto his back, he relaxed a bit. She smirked, *Well, more than "a bit."*

Once she was on top of him, his shirt was the first thing to go. She lifted the hem of it as he kissed her neck, and through a low moan, she asked if she could take it off. Surprised by how quickly he agreed, he almost removed it *himself*. Or tore it off? The memories were a little fuzzy . . . Regardless, her shirt quickly came off next, something Luka was very pleased about. *Very, very pleased about.* She blushed.

Her pelvis ground against the proof of it as his fingers explored her torso, making sure he knew every curve of her upper body before he easily removed her bra. Her breasts burst free, and Luka sprung on her, flipping her onto her back and discarding her bra somewhere in her room.

Luka hovered over her with a hungry smile that sent a prickly shiver through her. Rough fingertips grazed up her sides, stopping just at the crease of her underbust. Slowly he brought his mouth down, licking up her torso, starting just below her navel and running it up her abdomen, between her breasts, and up her neck until finally kissing her long and hard on her eager lips. *That. That was so fucking hot.* She remembered her hips bucking in response, desperate to feel more of him. As much of him as possible.

He smirked against her.

"Does my kitten want to grind on me?"

A moan passed through her lips and into his mouth as he palmed each breast, massaging them with skilled fingers.

"Hang on."

Her arms wrapped around his neck so quickly that she barely registered being pulled into his lap. His talented tongue pulled her bottom lip into his mouth just as he sat her back down on top of him. Even through his pants and her underwear, she immediately molded to his shape.

That slick tongue left hers and moved down to her breast, sucking and licking at her one tight nipple as his other hand massaged the other. Leaving neither without constant attention.

He moaned over her tight nipple as she ground against him, sliding up and down the length of him. *And what a length!* His free hand went to her lower back, urging her on.

She fell apart for him.

She sighed happily remembering how happy he was.

Luka peeked up at her from in between her breasts, sighing happily as they held his head in a comforting embrace.

"Again." Wet lips pressed a sweet kiss into her sternum. "Cum for me again, kitten."

Amity almost tripped remembering that. She could still hear the growl of his voice rumbling through her body.

She wished they could've stayed like that forever.

Her gaze shifted out the windows of the shop, the windows she had cleaned earlier that day. *Couldn't we?*

He didn't stay over that night, which was fine, he wasn't exactly in a "hurry" to leave either. Amity's blush burned her cheeks as she remembered his head buried between her legs.

How she came all over his face.

How he held her afterward. *Fuck, the Aftercare—amazing!* Cuddling in his arms, talking about nothing and everything. His whispers like sweet honey in her ears.

How many more moments would they have like that?

Amity glanced back out the windows at the passing couples with a smile, a smile that faded all too quickly. She could feel the cogs spinning inside her skull as her thoughts began to spiral into a panicked crescendo effectively killing any happiness she felt.

It all happens tomorrow.

What if it all ends tomorrow?

Was last night the last chance they would have together?

What if they don't make it past tomorrow . . . ?

Panic swiftly took hold. Wrapping and constricting her. Suffocating her the way a serpent feeds. What if she didn't make it past tomorrow?

Her arms began to shake. The pen scraped hard on the paper, ripping it and marking the counter. Amity felt herself sink. She was on the floor, her body curling in on itself. Her breaths were short and fast. Heat flushed her cheeks. Her throat began to close.

Breathe.

Desperately she tried.

Everything is going to be fine! she internally screamed, a frantic attempt to calm herself down.

A small cry left her, barely audible. She wouldn't want to disturb the patrons. Her nails dug into the flesh of her arms.

Everything is going to be fine! Lucia gave us something. Something Luka wouldn't take. That has to be helpful! A backup plan maybe?

Short breaths began to slow, allowing more air to fill her.

Breathe.

A warm hand pressed into her back, a steady heat guiding her back out of her frenzy.

"Kid, you okay?" Sammy asked, crouching beside her.

Amity didn't look, not with tears pricking her eyes. She hastily nodded.

"I'm fine. I-I just dropped something. That's all," she lied.

Sammy nodded, understanding. Slowly and silently rising to her feet, her vibrant pink hair shifted when she bent down to see the scribble Amity made earlier.

"If you're that bored, why don't you rizz up some of the customers?"

"Rizz?" Amity asked, confused, rising from her place on the floor. Her panic attack had been subdued . . . for now.

"Yeah, apparently all the kids are saying that nowadays."

Amity laughed, thankful that Sammy was able to pull her out of her spiral with something so mundane.

"I don't think that means what you think it means, Sammy," she laughed.

Sammy, "I'll ask those kids in the corner after they stop sucking face."

Amity laughed again, hard this time. Sammy's abrasiveness would always cheer her up.

"Oh! Mind running to the flower shop down the street before you leave? I threw out all the dead flowers."

"Yeah, I need to move around a bit."

"And I need to sit."

"So that's why I'm really going?"

Sammy smiled, making her way over to Amity and pulling a small stool out from behind the counter cupboard.

"No comment."

CHAPTER THIRTY

ONE DAY UNTIL HALLOWEEN

"Welcome in!"

Amity waved politely at the florist, then immediately rubbed her arms. She, like many other times coming to this small shop, did *not* bring her coat. But to be fair, today was strangely warm, especially walking the few short blocks under the midday sun.

Today she had dressed just a bit fancy, at least for her standards. High-waisted dark jeans, a black turtleneck that she refused to throw out because of how it seemed to mold to her body, and some gold accent jewelry.

Silently she admired one of the golden mums in its bouquet with a small smile on her lips.

She really did look good today, despite her unfortunate *mishap* earlier. Hair was perfect, for once, makeup was super cute too—just a soft brown smoky eye with some highlighter.

Today would've been a good day for someone to magically stop by the shop. She sighed, *I'll see him tomorrow.*

Tomorrow.

That word felt like a punch in the gut. It grew heavier with each breath and started to harden.

She wouldn't get any sleep tonight.

Even with Rex coming over for a movie night, something Amity strategically planned so she *would* be tired and fall sound asleep, her anxiety-ridden brain would keep her awake. It would pick and peck. Scratch and claw until it felt like her eyes would bleed.

A horrible image slithered into her mind. That wolfish smile with Luka's face. The sharpened teeth. The ghoulish green glow. Her heart raced.

Amity closed her eyes tight. *No. Not again!*

"It's alright, *breathe.*"

As if on command she felt a rush of cool air enter her lungs. How long was she holding her breath? When did she start?

"Again."

She took in another deep breath, letting it fill her, then released it.

"Good."

He did show up! Amity felt a smile creep on her lips. *Of course he did. He Always does.*

"Thank you, Luka—" Amity first noticed his hand on her shoulder. A hand that did *not* belong to Luka. She turned toward the man slowly.

". . . Rune?"

His green eyes lit up as he gazed down at her, reminding her of his height. A loose curl hung out of place, bobbing as he nodded and smiled. He removed his hand from her shoulder and tucked it back into place.

When did he touch me?

Amity took a small step back.

"I called your name a few times but you . . . Are you alright?"

Something about him felt a little different but she couldn't place it. His voice did sound a little deeper than usual.

Does he feel . . . older? No, that doesn't make sense. Someone can't feel older to you, she reasoned with herself. *Wait, how old is he?*

"Amity?"

"Ah! Sorry, yes. I was just a little . . ." She tucked a curl behind her ear nervously as her sentence died off.

"Lost?"

Her eyes met his and right away she knew it was a mistake. Those eyes were like two shimmery jade pools.

Not. Good. Bad, Amity!

"Yeah." A blush of embarrassment burned her cheeks.

He studied her for a long moment, like he could see through her, before speaking again.

"Fear cuts deep, sweetling. Don't let it overtake you."

All she could manage was a nod. *Wait . . . did he just—*

"Regardless, I'm glad we ran into each other." His smile widened, making the small freckles across his cheeks stand out more.

"Me too." She smiled back before turning back to the chrysanthemums and picking a few yellow bundles, feeling those green eyes track her every move. Patiently waiting.

"Tell you what, you helped me last time, how about I help you?"

"Oh right! You're a plant teacher."

A small laugh escaped him. "Yes, a herbalist. But I also have a passion for floral arrangements."

"Right." She turned, looking at the rows of chrysanthemums. "That's okay though, I'm just buying some flowers for the shop."

"Ah, yes. Yours were looking a little grim. Chrysanthemums are a nice choice. They'll last a long time."

She was well aware of that. One time she made her yellow chrysanthemums last a month in their vase; things are fucking unkillable.

"Yeah, they were definitely on their last limb." She picked up another bundle from the next bucket. More chrysanthemums in a rusty-red color.

These will look nice.

Amity glanced around the shop. She had been here dozens of times; the familiar sweet scent was relaxing and welcoming. Even their selection, bright, colorful, and vast—especially given the shop's small size. The walls were lined with bouquets, and then there was a middle aisle filled with the flowers of the season. The one she was currently stuck in front of.

Let's see, if there are twelve in a bouquet, then I should be fine, but maybe I should buy another one just in case.

She glanced over toward the white roses, one of her favorites.

A greenery maybe? Oh! Those roses look so beautiful, I want roses . . .

"If I may." Rune's voice guided her back out of her thoughts. He gestured toward the bouquets in her arms.

She nodded.

Amity watched him as he glided around the shop like he owned the space, carefully scanning the flowers like he was selecting them for a competition.

He, as usual, was dressed professionally—button-up shirt, long black peacoat, dark slacks, and nice shoes.

Rune went over to the roses, carefully selecting a white bouquet before turning to the eucalyptus bundles. He selected two.

"I think these would pair nicely together. If I'm remembering it correctly, your vases are more of a mason jar style, so you can have a freer range of decorating with smaller pairs."

"Thank you, Rune."

His eyes seemed to glint again. Did they do that every time she said his name? Amity couldn't tell.

He gently placed them onto the counter, politely waited for her to pay, then held the door open for her to exit, his manners as refined as his clothes.

"Can I accompany you back to Halley's?" he asked, after politely closing the door behind her.

"Yes! Actually, would you mind holding one of these?" Amity asked quickly, trying to catch one of the chrysanthemums before it crashed onto the cobblestones.

Rune smiled sweetly, catching it just as her hand clutched around the stems.

"It would be my pleasure."

Amity smiled and handed him two of the five bouquets. That sweet smile of his grew, and he took two more.

He definitely seemed older. Maybe it was the way he talked? *Definitely.* She glanced up at him as they walked down the street. *Definitely. That and his style. Very dark-academia hot-teacher vibe. Not that he's hot or anything!*

She glanced up at him . . . *Okay maybe his profile is very handsome.*

He caught her staring, and she quickly turned away. A small smirk kicked up in the corner of his mouth.

"Can I ask you something?"

"You can ask me anything."

Damnit. That was smooth. Like something the male love interest would say in her romance novels!

They rounded the corner to Halley's.

"How old are you?"

That glint returned to his eyes.

"You wouldn't believe me if I told you."

"No, she *wouldn't.*"

Amity's eyes widened in surprise at the sight of the tall leather-jacket-clad bad boy in front of the cafe.

"Luka! What are you doing here?"

"Came for some sweets." He kissed her forehead sincerely, lingering just a bit too long before turning to Rune. "I'll carry those."

"He was just helping—"

"I'm sure he was." Luka's eyes narrowed on him, pulsing with a blue glow.

Something shifted between them. The air seemed to get a little chillier. Rune studied Luka, watching him as he did with Amity in the shop, but something was off . . .

Rune held out the bouquets he was carrying with a smile. Luka took them from him with gritted teeth. Amity finally noticed their height similarity and how Rune was only an inch or two taller. She noticed Luka's shoulders tense beneath his jacket.

"Hey, what's—"

"Oh, Amity, thank you for today," Rune said sweetly, reaching into his coat pocket.

"Oh, no, I didn't do anything. You're the one who helped me—Is that a mini cinnamon broom?!"

Her eyes grew wide with excitement as Rune placed the small broom, no bigger than her hand, into her palm.

"This will help you keep from getting lost again, considering it's Mischief Night. And *especially* on All Hallows' Eve."

"Thank you so much, Rune!" She beamed.

Those green eyes glittered down at her.

Amity felt something *dark* rise behind her, like how that massive fox demon loomed in the alleyway. The temperature dropped, and without looking she imagined the fox demon behind her—eyes blazing, jaws gaping, and ready to snap Rune in two. That's when she remembered Luka was there. *Her* Luka. And that murderous intent wasn't from a fox demon, it was from *him*.

She looked over her shoulder apprehensively, noticing the darkness in his eyes. The pure bright cyan glowering at Rune. He looked like he was going to make the flowers wilt with the hostility coming off of him.

Yes, something was definitely off.

"Until next time, Amity." Rune waved. For a moment she expected him to kiss her hand. *And as much of a romantic gesture that would be, thinking about that is definitely Not a good idea.*

Amity glanced hesitantly at Luka, then waved goodbye as best she could with the bouquets and broom in her hands. Luka watched him go with a glare that caused Amity's nerves to rise until Rune rounded the corner and was completely out of sight.

"Umm, Luka?"

"I can't stay long. I just wanted to see you before . . . before tomorrow."

She nodded stiffly, then tentatively walked through the door he held open for her.

They brought the flowers in and placed them on the counter, coming face-to-face with a very amused Sammy.

"Send her out for some flowers and she brings back a man. I should've asked you to bring one for me," she teased, her reading glasses tilted so far down they were about to fall off her nose.

Amity's cheeks flushed, but out of the corner of her eye she caught Luka's body ease up.

"Hello, Sammy." His smile was small but practiced.

"Have you come to take her home, handsome?"

"Sammy!"

"Is your shift over?"

"I still have to—"

"It is now." Sammy smiled, leaning her chin in her palm

"Sammy!"

Luka nudged her lightly with his elbow. "Go get your things, I'll wait for you here."

"But—" She cut herself off when their eyes met. She didn't imagine it before; there *was* a hostility in his eyes, but it wasn't just directed at Rune, now it was directed at *her.* "Okay . . ."

By the time she gathered her things and clocked out, Luka was waiting patiently for her, idly chatting with Sammy and holding a small paper bag in his hand.

"Do you want to go back to my place?" she asked carefully as he led her out the door. That murderous rage she felt before was gone, but the glare in his eyes lingered.

"No. There's not enough time," he said, closing the door behind him.

"But—"

"I have to make sure everything is ready for tomorrow."

"I know but it's only four and I can help—"

"Not this time. We have our plan. Trust it. Trust me," he said curtly.

"I . . . I do trust you."

What's up with him? Is he mad about Rune?

Luka guided her away from the door toward the window as another couple approached.

"How long has he been coming into the shop?"

"Hm?"

"*Rune.*"

Bullseye.

"Oh, he's a regular. He saw me in the flower shop and offered to help bring everything back. Why?"

"Hmm."

"Is something wrong?"

A hard exhale left him, like he was trying to steady himself. It was a while before he answered her. Luka paced a tense hand on the small of her back and gently guided her down the street toward her apartment.

"No. No, I guess there isn't."

Brown eyes watched him silently as they walked. He looked like he was lost in his own thoughts. Not even a glance in her direction, not one. Silently, he walked with his bottom lip in a slight pout.

Wait . . . is he sulking?!

Amity's eyes sparkled. She never saw him sulk before. It was adorable. A playful smirk grew on her lips.

"You know," she began, elongating the word in a teasing way, "it's okay to be jealous. It's cute on you."

He stopped walking and shot a confusing glance her way, but when he saw her mischievous smile grow wider, a small laugh escaped him. His frown turned upside down.

"Amity, be careful," he growled.

"Why?" She primped his jacket with a bratty glint in her eyes.

Gently, Luka nudged her backward until she was flush against a brick wall. He leaned down sweetly. Thinking that she was going to be kissed, she leaned in to meet him only to be denied.

Luka's lips pressed against her forehead in a taunting kiss. "*Because . . .*" he mused.

Amity reached up to kiss him again, only to be once again *denied*. She grabbed the collar of his jacket roughly.

Luka clicked his tongue three times, each accompanied by a small shake of his head. He grabbed her wrists and pinned them against the wall above her. She twitched when the cold brick touched her skin. He hummed sweetly as she tried to squirm in his grip. Amity tried to pull away playfully but quickly realized how outmatched she was when it came to brute strength.

Luka's smile widened as he saw that realization dawn on her. He stepped closer, letting his body warm hers.

Amity pulled her bottom lip between her teeth in anticipation, something that he was definitely enjoying. She swore she could hear her heartbeat thrumming in her chest, counting each silent second that passed by. What was he going to do?

Luka carefully traced the length of her nose with his own. Again, she leaned in to kiss him, and again, he pulled away. The faint brush of his nose traced her jawline all the way to her ear, dancing across her skin, an action that sent thrills through her. She leaned into his touch.

"Because when I get jealous, I'll make sure no man will ever lay eyes on you again without knowing *exactly* who you belong to," he purred. Freshly wet lips kissed just below her earlobe, making her jump in surprise. "I'll make sure they know *exactly* who claimed you, whose teeth marks these are." Teeth took a mouthful of her neck. Amity pressed her lips together tightly, trying to suppress the small squeak of surprise. "Whose fingerprints these are." He released her wrists, placing them down by her sides before firmly grasping her hips. Her pelvis moved on its own, tilting toward his warmth . . .

. . . taunting lips hovered over her own.

"Would my kitten like that?"

". . . Yes."

CHAPTER THIRTY ONE

ONE DAY UNTIL HALLOWEEN

"I forgot how much I loved this man."

"I never forgot. The Goblin King will always have my love."

"Especially in those pants."

Amity reached over from her side of the couch and clinked her wine glass with Rex's. Those were some very amazingly tight pants.

They watched the Goblin King, the perfect representation of an American 80s fantasy villain—tall stature, vibrant costume, and excessive hair and makeup, dancing around his throne room with the puppet goblins singing along with broad smiles.

Amity glanced out the window, noting the time. Luka didn't come back to her place earlier. Tonight he'd packed his schedule, preparing all kinds of things, mostly packs of salt for Amity to throw like bombs if anything got too dicey. A smirk appeared on her lips; despite how "busy" he was, he still managed to make out with her in the back seat of his car before she walked back with him. She licked her lips remembering the taste.

I'll text him before I go to bed. Just to make sure he actually gets some sleep.

Rex reached for the bowl of popcorn in between them and sighed.

"Ugh, empty again," they groaned.

Amity snickered from her place on the couch. It was their turn to get the next batch. Rex got up apprehensively to get more.

"Want me to pause it?"

"Nah, I've seen it a dozen times already."

Amity paused it anyway as she heard Rex dish out some more popcorn kernels into the pot they used specifically for this purpose on the stove. She smiled hearing them curse at opening the wrong cabinet by accident.

Mindlessly she flipped through her phone while she waited. The last thing she searched blared to life in the dim light: "demon boxes" and "demon stars".

After their steamy make-out session, she had been searching for answers to this strange star thing Lucia had given her.

What exactly was it? Why didn't Luka want it? And how was it supposed to help them fight Dramaur?

"So have you gone rock climbing again?" Rex called from the kitchen, pulling Amity from her phone and her thought progression.

Amity took a moment to remember what "rock climbing" was.

"Nah, not really my thing in the end." A small lie. Now wasn't exactly the best time to talk about demon hunting. A sigh forced out of her. Even if she compared the possible fatality of demon hunting to falling off the side of a mountain, she knew it would result in another panic attack. Something Rex had certainly seen, given their friendship since college, but something Amity definitely did not want to experience right now or have them bear witness to.

I just want to have a normal night tonight. Considering it might be my last—nope! We're not thinking about that! Amity mentally yelled, trying to force her quickly rising pulse back to its normal tempo.

She pulled Freaya, who had been watching the frozen king on the screen from the back edge of the couch, into her lap.

"Yeah I figured. Apparently it's called bouldering."

"Bouldering?"

The stove clicked on, and Amity kissed Freaya until she was visibly annoyed. The void squirmed in her arms, and her mother smiled turning back to her phone out of habit and coming face-to-face with her last search.

Her eyes widened on the screen. Boxes were used to seal demons! She searched a few more articles, discovering all kinds were used for this purpose. Some were just plain boxes sealed with silver. Some had intricate designs on them—Celtic knots, runes, or talismans.

Amity closed her eyes trying to search her own mind, attempting to find anything else on the subject. Maybe she learned about this before on her own? Unfortunately, like before when she tried seeing the high school version of Luka, she was met with black sludge and a developing migraine.

What about TV shows?

She had definitely seen a lot of them, unfortunately not the really popular one about the demon-hunting brothers. Why did she never watch that? She cursed herself knowing that definitely would've been useful. At least it would be if what was said in that show were true about demons.

She remembered that some religions believed a person's soul could be trapped in mirrors. That's why after a funeral they were covered with veils so their spirit wouldn't get stuck.

But that strange star is neither a mirror or a box. It's more like some weird puzzle.

She typed a new search, a broader one this time: "things to trap demons with".

"Hey, Amity."

"Yeah?"

She looked back over the couch and into the kitchen as her phone continued to load. Her smile dropped.

"What's this?" Rex asked, holding the configuration Luka's mother had given Amity.

"That's—um," she stuttered.

What was it? She didn't even know. She'd been trying to figure it out this whole time and nothing. Her phone screen loaded, coming up with the same answers as before, boxes, salt, etc. *Stupid search engines. That's literally your job! You're only job!*

Rex made their way over, their fluffy slippers shuffling as they did. Amity reached for it as casually as possible, the slightest movement giving Freaya the perfect excuse to escape.

The star thing was large, about the size of her head, it was a miracle she hid it from Luka at all when he was nursing her the other day.

The wood was cool in her hand, and judging by the stain and weathering, this *thing* was old, *very* old.

"I don't know. Someone gave it to me," she mumbled, entranced by the small carvings in the wood.

Amity barely got more than a glance at it when Lucia had given it to her and was so focused on keeping Luka from finding it that this was the first good look she got.

Small shapes were carved all around it then painted a blueish green. What were these called again? Runes?

Amity marveled at them as they circled the star's sharp edges, even delving inside the crevices. They were fascinating to look at even though she didn't know what any of them meant. Without thinking, she twisted one of the points, feeling it jiggle. She stopped, scared she broke it. *Old and delicate.*

"Wait, do that again," Rex urged.

Amity hesitantly tried moving that piece again, this time more deliberately. A soft *click* sounded inside of it, and the piece moved freely without resistance, bending in the directions she put it.

"Woah!" they both gasped.

Amity tried another point of the star, like before, it clicked softly and turned at her will.

"It's a puzzle box!" Rex cheered. "That's so cool!"

"A puzzle box . . ." Amity let the weight of those words sink in. The runes covering it—

A burning smell wafted in from the kitchen.

"Shit!"

Rex ran back into the kitchen and ripped the pot off the stove, quickly pouring some of the popcorn into the bowl before setting it back to pop the rest. Normally Amity would laugh from her place on the couch, but this was too important. Quickly she went back to her phone and typed "demon puzzle box" in the search bar.

A few articles appeared, just like before. They showed depictions of boxes with the same symbols as hers. Other cultures used their own symbols or talismans or wax seals. Some were even carved into the wood like hers. She dug deeper past the examples of boxes. There!

Her face lit up. It wasn't just boxes that were used to seal demons, people used all kinds of things! Jars, bottles sealed with wax, jewelry! Amity went back to the article about Celtic knots carved into the boxes. Apparently these "puzzles" were used as an extra precaution so if the spell broke, the demon would also have to escape the puzzle of the knot!

Her fingers clutched the cool wood excitedly. That's what this was! Instead of carving a puzzle onto a box, this entire thing *was* the puzzle!

"I want you to take this just in case," Amity mumbled, repeating what Lucia had said to her.

This is it! This is the backup plan!

She paused, briefly remembering how Luka was adamant in not taking it.

Why would he—Doesn't matter now. No, definitely matters, but there's no time to think about it now. Later. Later—

"So what are you going to put in it?" Rex called from the kitchen.

A wide, proud smile spread across Amity's face. *I'm not going to put anything in it, but I know a certain demon hunter who can.*

"A demon."

Luka finished tying off the last of the balloons and placed it beside the others on his desk. He also filled a chalk bag, typically used for rock climbing but repurposed for him, with salt earlier that night.

"Maybe I overdid it," he mumbled, tapping one of his knives in its harness and counting them all again . . . Still seven of them, like he counted yesterday, and again when he returned from Amity, and again after he ate.

"I need to calm down."

He looked around his apartment again, searching for something out of place that didn't exist. Cleaning helped him lose track of time. Helped clear his mind.

Well . . . cleaning and cooking . . . and baking. He sighed, *No,* no baking. No cooking.

"Now that Freaya's not here, it is a lot cleaner."

A small tap opened his phone again, an attempt to distract his thoughts. No messages.

"She did say she was busy with Rex tonight," he mumbled.

His head fell back with a loud groan.

I should've stayed with her tonight. We could've relieved our . . . tension.

Luka groaned louder.

"Not yet. *Down,* boy."

Rough fingertips tapped his phone open again, and as if on cue, the screen lit up with a text from her.

Oct. 30, 10:30 pm

Please get some sleep tonight.

He smiled at that; she always turned in earlier than he did. *Always.*

Fingers were already typing when his phone dinged again.

Oct. 30, 10:30 pm

Try not to think of me too much.

He laughed, "As if that's an option."

Luka replied immediately.

Oct. 30, 10:31 pm

I think about you every night.

He rubbed his chin with a satisfied smile, imagining her flushed face. Amity probably slammed the phone down on her nightstand and hid under the covers.

"So cute."

He drew in a sharp breath as he felt himself twitch. Another loud groan rumbled through his chest. With one final glance at his hard work of the night, he let out a sweet sigh.

"I guess a little self-care would release my . . . tension."

Without hesitation he went into his saved files on his phone. Scrolling through folders until he found exactly what he was looking for, a folder titled Amity.

It was filled with photos of her, some taken by herself when she swiped his phone while he wasn't looking. Others he took while she was lost in her own little world—creating new coffee recipes, that time when she tried to eat a burger way bigger than her mouth, of when they went snowboarding a few years ago and she fell pretty hard in a mound of powder.

At the very top of the folder was an audio. Its title: Oct. 26th 8:22 p.m.

Luka turned the volume up to max, then with a wide smile hit play. Amity's lucid voice warmed his ears.

"Hi."

Fuck, just hearing her like that made his cock twitch. Luka made his way back to his room, removing every single article of clothing as she continued to speak in that dreamy voice.

"*You're probably busy or doing something . . . or maybe you're just lying there trying to sleep . . . I thought this could* be a fun idea, and please if you're not into it and don't think it's fun or whatever, then please feel free to never speak to me again. Sorry I'm rambling . . ."

"As if I could do that." He laughed. "She's got me on a fucking leash, and she doesn't even know it." He rubbed his chin, making his way over to the bed as she continued.

"Anyway. I was thinking—and I'm actually really glad you didn't pick up because I would've been too embarrassed to do this. You just—you make me nervous. And I miss you."

Luka pulled his bottom lip between his teeth as he unscrewed the small jar on his bedside table.

"You have no idea what kind of suffering you've put me through. Leaving your scent everywhere in my home. On my couch. In my clothes. In my bed. It's Tormenting."

"Scold me more." He smirked, nestling on top of his covers.

"It's just—I just can't take it anymore."

Eager fingers dipped inside the cool jar, scooping out a reasonable sum of coconut oil with his fingers. He rubbed the small mounds in his hands until they became slick.

"This is the part where you can stop listening, but I don't think you will."

Luka wrapped his dripping hands up the length of his hard cock, making sure he was covered from base to tip. A small moan left his lips as his thumb pressed into the soft skin there. He was already so sensitive.

"I think you'll listen. I think you'll save this audio message. And I think that when I'm done, you'll listen to it over and over again until you are completely drained dry."

"She has no idea how right she is—ah!" Luka held the base of his cock in a firm grip.

Amity's breath hitched loudly in the phone's speaker. He twitched in his hand.

A soft humm came from the phone along with a light thrumming.

She'd turned on her toy. Just the thought of that made him harden to his full length.

He began stroking, lovingly, from base to tip, getting in at least a dozen long, slow strokes before circling the tip of his cock with his thumb again, spreading the small bead of pre-cum around, mixing it with the oil, feeling a familiar tingle at the base of his spine as he repeated the motion a few more times.

He shifted the phone under his ear just as her sweet sounds started. Small gasps. Suppressed moans. Panting.

A shiver went through him as he cupped his balls with his free hand, fondling them as he continued to stroke, adding to the building pleasure. He imagined her next to him, playing with her bright-pink toy. The one he curiously meddled with while she showered. How could he not? That lucky fucker got to be inside her, give her everything *he* was supposed to.

Luka pumped faster.

"Getting jealous of a fucking toy . . ." His cock throbbed in his hand.

Damnit, I'm close. I can't cum yet. Those loving pumps were forced to slow down. Long languid strokes would make him last a little longer.

His hand paused for a moment, letting out a long exhale, waiting for his heartbeat to slow down before starting again.

Through half-lidded eyes he watched his hand slide up and down his long length. Soaked, he was soaked. And when he saw her next, she would be too.

"Making me edge myself this much, you better be prepared for the consequences—"

Luka's hand froze. *Did she just?* No way, did he hear that right?

He hadn't heard this all the way through yet, accidentally first listening to it when he was running. He'd almost thrown his phone into the river he was so surprised. Luckily he was wearing his headphones then and ended up saving it right away, meaning to listen to it later, but he—

". . . *Luka* . . ."

His eyes glowed brightly. Lustfully. He did hear it! A sharp breath sucked through his teeth. That hand moved on its own, pumping faster.

Again. Say it again. Please.

Amity panted heavier through the speaker, and as if she could hear him, she said it again. His name. She said *his* name while touching herself!

"Fuck, that's it."

Desperate hips lifted to meet his hand. Another shiver ran through him. He pumped faster, his hand slick, making the sweetest wet sloppy noises.

Not sweet enough.

She was sweet. Fuck, he could still taste her on his tongue. He wasn't lying when he told her he could live in between her thighs. His tongue, his finger, his dick—it didn't fucking matter.

His abdomen tightened. His legs started to shake.

She would be on top of him for the first time. He would make sure she finished first. Then, right before she collapsed in his arms, he would flip her onto her back and rub her clit. She would finish again with him inside of her clenching around him-

A sweet moan came out of his phone followed by a few breathless gasps. She'd finished. He felt that familiar pressure build inside of him. He throbbed harder against his hand and held his balls just a little tighter. His back arched, feeling the pressure build higher and higher. He pumped faster and faster. He was so close.

"*. . . Goodnight, Luka*," her tired voice hummed.

He gasped as he felt his dick tense up, filling to the brink before bursting undone.

The sweet euphoric feeling filled his body completely, leaving him heavy, exhausted, and satisfied. Luka collapsed back into his mattress, panting heavily, basking in the serene afterglow of his climax. When was the last time he came that hard?

When his breaths steadied, he glanced down at the mess he'd made. And he'd made a big mess.

Better shower . . .

Luka let the hot water rush over him, providing his sore muscles relief. He pushed his wet hair out of his face and leaned his forehead on the cool tile.

"I really should've stayed with her tonight," he sighed. "But knowing her she would've kicked my ass out like yesterday." He laughed.

She always did like her own space. His lips turned down for a moment as he reminded himself that he was already beyond testing those boundaries the other day, even if she was too exhausted to move. He was rushing around her apartment, coddling her—drawing her bath, making her food, cleaning her entire apartment! Something she'd said she appreciated but made perfectly clear she could see through his nervous habits.

His torso pressed against the tile, the difference in temperature pulling a sweet humm out of him. The image of her flashed—from a bath, scolding him while only a towel clothed her.

He could go again if he wanted to. A devious smirk crept on his face. *That sounds like a great idea. It's not like I'm gonna make a mess in the shower.* A laugh rumbled through him.

Luka turned and pressed his back into the tiled wall. Soapy hands ran up his thighs, lightly scratching his skin the higher he went. Just before he could hold himself in a tattooed grip, the worst fucking thing popped into his head. A pair of green eyes. A condescending smirk. And that stupid fucking red hair.

Rune.

"That fucking bastard."

Whatever self-pleasuring plans Luka had vanished in an instant and were replaced with the image of how Rune was looking at Amity. *His* Amity.

And the way she was smiling back at him. That cute, crooked smile she wore so often in front of him—now being directed at Rune.

His Amity.

She was looking at him like she was happy to see him. Like she *liked* him—

He gruffly shut off the water and threw back the shower curtain.

"She's with *you*. There's no reason to overthink this. She would never do that. She *chose* you—"

Wait . . .

Luka racked his brain of every interaction he had with her this month, which took a *while*.

Damn, it's only been a month and so much has happened, it's insane. Focus!

"We're not dating . . . *technically*. But she said at the bar—well, she was tipsy when she said it. and it's not like she asked me either."

Luka stared at his reflection with wide eyes.

"Fuck I don't have time for this! We . . ." He inhaled deeply, forcing himself back to center and cutting off his own words. Rough fingers pushed his hair back and pressed his weight into his feet, grounding himself. When his eyes met his reflection again, they were determined and glowing faintly back at him.

"*She* doesn't have time."

CHAPTER THIRTY TWO
HALLOWEEN

"Go for a walk," Alex said, placing the fresh mug of harvest tea in front of her.

Amity didn't hear anything except a distant mumble. She continued to scratch at her nail against the pad of her thumb from the other side of the counter, not even hearing him.

Her mind was spinning, racing into every direction it could before tearing off into the opposite direction. If she didn't calm down, she would spiral again, collapse into the floor and—

"Amity!"

"Hm?!"

"Don't *hm* me, you've been twitchy all afternoon. Go for a walk or I'm putting CBD in your tea."

Amity thought for a moment. "Why didn't I think of that?" she mumbled.

"Because you've been spazzing this whole time," her brother deadpanned.

He pulled the mug back with a sigh.

"He told me about tonight . . . and wasting all this energy on worrying all day will only leave you exhausted when you need it the most." Alex shoved a hand through his hair, discarding the tea and going back behind the counter to prepare something new.

Amity watched him silently, knowing full well he was right, which was annoying. But what was beyond annoying was that she wasted so much energy already.

Her afternoon shift started at 2:00 p.m. and the entire morning she'd been scatterbrained—cleaning up after her movie night with Rex, which was mostly just cleaning up stray kernels; cleaning her bathroom for some reason; re-organizing her pillows for no reason at all; and a mini yoga class from her workout app. She didn't even dress up for her favorite holiday! She was going to be a cute witch, but that idea too was thrown out the window thanks to anxiety.

Already so much energy wasted.

Anxious brown eyes met hers and he abruptly set down whatever he was making, turned, and embraced her so tightly her back cracked.

"Alex?"

"I know how nervous you get. I didn't want to add to the load. Fuck, I spent all night on the phone with that bastard making sure everything is prepped and ready. He said you would stay out of the way as much as possible.

You better not jump into anything crazy! Listen to Luka, and if anything goes south, I want you out of there." Amity wrapped her arms around him as best she could with her back bent the wrong way. "I mean it, Amity. I'm not losing you to some weird fucking demon." Alex pressed a kiss into her hair, but before she could say anything, he released her and went back to whatever he was doing.

Her mouth fell open, unable to say anything. Tears welled in her eyes as they fell back onto her brother who continued to pace around. In the mirror she could see his flushed face and the tears he was trying to hide. Her heart swelled in her chest. Alex was going to be up all night worrying about her. Amity quickly wiped whatever tears had escaped their prison and pushed off the counter, then pulled on her warm coat.

"Thank you." She smiled tiredly.

"Yeah yeah whatever," he said, continuing to make whatever concoction he was making.

Amity walked around the block, taking her time and focusing on her breathing until the itching anxiety stilled. It wasn't until then she realized it was actually a nice day out. The birds were chirping. People were walking their dogs on the cobblestone streets. Some children were even prancing alongside their parents in their Halloween costumes—a bee, a pumpkin, a strange version of a superhero. She giggled silently as they passed by with half their bodies covered in thick coats, completely ruining their costumes. When they were younger her and Alex would make such a racket about that, especially when he wanted to be a scary werewolf. A puffer coat really killed the scare factor. It totally worked for her werewolf-victim costume though.

Soon he and Krystal will be taking their baby out trick-or-treating. A smile appeared on her lips, desperately trying to divert her brain from slipping into the thought that she might not be able to see it.

I will see it. Luka and I will both see it. She took in another deep breath. *It's a good day, and tomorrow's going to be even better,* she thought optimistically, ignoring that small knot in her chest. *Who knows, maybe I'll be a professional demon hunter when all this is over.* A small laugh bubbled out of her at the thought.

Halley's was fuller when she returned. It looked like Alex had stepped in while she was out. He flipped a small towel over his shoulder with a satisfied smile.

Maybe he misses this a little bit? Amity mused, remembering the last company he'd worked for before going under during the pandemic, when they both worked together in the cafe.

"Better?"

"Better," she confirmed, hanging up her coat back on the rack.

He shrugged off her apron and looped it around her neck, then shoved a new cup into her hand.

"Here, I added some CBD. You're gonna need it," he explained, tying the apron at her back.

"Decaf too?" she asked. Alex nodded. "Good. Wait, why would I need it—"

"Amity!"

Amity's eyes widened, her brother returned her surprise with a sly smile. She took a long sip of her decaf iced pumpkin spice latte with CBD, then turned to her mother.

"Hi, Mom!"

"Oh, honey! Thank you so much for watching the store. I know it's been a lot," she commended, pulling Amity into a tight embrace. Their mother had the same dark curls as her children and was only slightly taller than Amity. "You should take a vacation soon, where would you like to go?"

"Mom, let her breathe." Alex laughed.

"And my sweet boy," she said, hobbling over and pulling him into a tight hug. "Helping your sister even though you have your own job." Her lips pressed his cheek, leaving a small red imprint from her lipstick.

Amity's gaze shifted to her mother's knee, which was a heavy-duty brace. That would explain why her steps were stiff, but still . . . Amity took another sip of her latte, feeling the effects of the CBD slip past her anxiety that this surprise gave her.

"Mom, I thought you weren't supposed to be on your feet until the end of the month?"

Her mother let go of Alex and leaned back onto the counter.

"Well, it's close enough, besides the doctor said if I use my cane, I'll be fine."

"So where's your cane?"

"Oh, there he is," she said, pointing to their father who walked through the door.

"Hey, kids." He kissed his wife on the forehead before handing her the cane in his hand.

"See, right on time."

"I aim to please, my love." He smiled, causing one of his dimples to appear in his cheek.

"I thought we could all get dinner tonight. You aren't doing anything tonight, right?"

If Amity weren't so calm, she might've taken that stab to heart, but it only felt like a little prick to the chest.

"She's free," Alex answered for her. Amity gave a lazy look, one he knew that said she was more pissed off than she appeared to be. *Probably also why he said I would need CBD. Don't think my poor nerves can handle my mother right now without it . . . haha.* "Poor nerves."

"You always have plans on Halloween though." Her father said, scratching the back of his neck.

"Later she does—"

"Alex!"

"Oh!" Her mother beamed.

"Plans later then?" her father asked.

Amity bit her lip but couldn't hide her smile. She nodded.

"Oh, well at least tell Luka we said hi." Her father smiled smugly.

Amity took another long sip of her latte, trying to hide behind the enormous mug.

Oh if I didn't have this latte right now!

"You're dating Luka? *Your* Luka?!" their mother asked, looking between her and Alex with astonishment.

"Don't call him *my Luka*, Mom." He grimaced, something his mother didn't notice.

"You should bring him. Alex, bring Krystal too."

"She's out with friends now, I'm meeting her tonight. Horror movie night."

Amity snickered at that; Alex *hated* horror movies.

"Honey, I told you it was him—"

"Yes but you said it so fast that I thought you were joking."

"The store, Mom, what about the store?" Amity asked, glancing around. There was only one couple left. They were deep in conversation over a few books in the corner by the window. *Cute.* The rest had filed out when their mother came in, taking their to-go coffees and treats with them, no doubt going to enjoy the festive activities the city provided tonight. Another thing Amity was looking forward to that she wouldn't get to enjoy.

"Oh, Sammy's coming."

"Isn't she going trick-or-treating with her boys?" Amity asked, scanning over the tiny bouquets that were arranged around the shop, the pops of gold, rust, and white making a lovely contrast. There were even a few that just had the roses and greens. *I should save those once they are dried out,* Amity thought.

"No, they're trick-or-treating with their other mom right now."

Amity glanced at her phone to check the time, 4:35 p.m., so not too-too early of a dinner.

There's plenty of time for everything.

Her phone lit up with a call, and a smile quickly spread across her lips as she answered turning toward the back counter, away from her family.

"Luka," she hummed into the phone, her voice dragging out his name a little too long.

"Hello, are you alright?"

"Yeah, just had a CBD latte. You?"

A chuckle came from the end of the phone.

"I just finished working a shift at Mom's shop. I thought we could relax before . . . before tonight."

"I'd like that."

Amity glanced up at the back mirror catching her family's stares. Her tone immediately changed.

"Actually, my parents are in town today—they actually asked if—well."

Alex swiped the phone from her hand. "Come to dinner with us."

Their mother swiped the phone next. "Please, honey, I haven't seen you in so long."

"Hello, ma'am."

Amity giggled hearing his polite voice over the phone.

Her father took the phone. "Hello, Luka."

"Hello, sir."

"What are your intentions with my daughter?"

"Dad, I'm twenty-eight!"

He went over to his wife and bent low so the phone was between their ears.

"Well?" his mother pried.

Amity strained to hear the conversation.

"To make sure she is the happiest woman on earth."

Her parents looked at each other and then to Amity's flushed face.

"Fuck that's so corny."

"Nobody asked you, Alex!"

CHAPTER THIRTY THREE
HALLOWEEN

Luka tucked a stray curl back into place, causing her to lightly stir on his chest. He leaned forward to kiss the top of her head.

Amity was mad he didn't come to dinner; although she didn't directly say it, he could tell. It wasn't like he didn't have a good reason though. Being interrogated by her mother about their relationship wasn't a conversation he was "dying" to have. Especially not *today*. And besides, he was busy making preparations for tonight.

He had spent hours going over the park's layout, which, being an avid jogger there, made it somewhat manageable; he ended up narrowing down the possible meet-up spots to a few.

Who am I kidding? Narrowed it down to a few spots? Yeah right. He spent hours walking around under a cloaking spell, so he wouldn't draw unwanted attention, and setting spell traps. His gaze fell back to Amity who was still nuzzled in his chest. Last year she would've been able to help with those but not now. She didn't remember the runes, and there wasn't enough time to reteach them to her.

Amity nuzzled against his chest again when a loud noise came through her TV. They were watching some show, which of course had dragons. House of . . . ? Game of Prequel? or *something*. Last year they were excited to watch it together. A small smile claimed his lips. He knew full well she'd seen it a dozen times already. His thumb worked on its own, making small circles on her hip.

I'll have to wake her up soon.

He smiled down at her, then up to where Freaya rested on her back. The void yawned silently, making a cute squeaky sound before curling back into herself.

Luka continued to watch them silently. He was going to tell her when she came home. When he was waiting by her front door. Something that *delighted* her mother. He was going to tell her when they settled into the couch. He *should* tell her now.

"Amity," Luka cooed, gently shaking her until she scrunched her eyes tightly.

A chuckle ran through him, causing his chest to rumble. She glared up at him through half-lidded eyes. Then her eyes went wide, and she shot up, using his chest for support. Freaya jumped off her napping place with a start.

"Is it time?!"

He laughed again at her urgency, but if he was being honest, he was just as on edge as she was. No, that's not true. He was *more* nervous.

"Not yet, kitten, settle back in with me." He saw her body immediately relax. She reached for the remote on the coffee table and paused whatever was on screen and laid her head back on his chest, hugging him tightly, silently breathing him in as his hand ran up and down her back, the action soothing them both.

If he could just stop time for another hour, just to watch her sleep, to know she's here, that she's safe, then—

"Luka?"

"Hm?"

Amity tilted her face up to him, resting her chin on his chest before deciding that that wasn't as comfortable as she thought it would be and propped herself up onto her elbows.

"I—" She cut herself off. He waited patiently for her, silently watching the wheels turn in her head. "I—" She bit her lip in frustration.

"Amity."

She hid her face in his chest and took a few deep breaths before finally looking back at him.

"Ev-. . . everything is going to be fine," she said with a shaky voice. Luka watched her for a moment before the corner of his mouth turned up into a small smile. *Was she going to say something else?*

"Everything will be alright," he confirmed.

That's what he said, but now . . . He glanced over at Amity in the passenger seat. She was clutching her backpack that she had put the salt balloons in, or "bombs" as she jokingly called them, like it were a lifeline.

I can't tell her now.

After smoothly parking the car, he sat there quietly drumming his fingers on the steering wheel. Tension pooled around him like a bog, suffocating him. He inhaled deeply and then again, in and out, steadying his breathing until he was calm.

I am ready. I am prepared. She is safe with me. I have to be the strong one. He glanced back at Amity. Brown eyes were focused straight ahead, barely blinking.

Luka abruptly opened his car door, making her almost jump out of her skin. He went to the trunk where his holster was and strapped it across his chest. Next he strapped the chalk bag, which was filled with salt, across his hips. He breathed out another sigh, trying to calm himself. It left his lungs in a breath of smoke. On top of everything else, tonight was freezing.

Amity peered around the back of the car with timid steps; she was pale, too pale. The corners of her mouth tilted into a brief, tight smile.

Without a word, he lifted her by her shoulders and sat her down in the trunk of the car. The heavy backpack fell to the ground. She was as stiff as a board and stared up at him with wide eyes. Luka leaned over her, one arm on either side of her body, then embraced her tightly. Rough fingers ran up and down her spine where her tattoo was hidden under thick clothes until she finally relaxed against him.

If he could lock her up in here for the night, he would.

She wrapped her arms tightly around him, inhaling deeply, letting her stiff body melt against him for a while.

Luka pulled back and kissed her forehead sweetly.

"If things go south"—nervous brown eyes met his. He pressed his forehead to hers gently—"remember, it's a dream demon. It feeds off your thoughts, the good and the bad, *especially* your nightmares. I need you to stay focused. I need you to stay silent. And I need you to do *exactly* as I say."

He ran his hands up her arms, squeezing them lightly. As usual, she did not bring a jacket and, as usual, she was now freezing.

Her chin tilted in a small nod.

"Use your words, kitten."

A small laugh left her followed by an overly elongated "sure."

Luka smirked at her sass.

"Why do I have to stay silent?"

"Just in case."

Brown eyes narrowed on him. For a moment he was silent, shrugging off his jacket and wrapping it around her.

"This one likes to toy with people," he growled.

Luka forced a sigh, trying to calm himself once again. Amity waited patiently, taking his cornicello and playing with it between her fingers.

He watched its light glow faintly against her skin. They should leave soon. He knew they should.

Luka rubbed her arms again, trying to give her as much warmth as he could, then straightened the collar. He stared at her beautiful brown eyes until they met him. A feeling swelled inside of him, warm and sweet, like cinnamon apples and cream.

Despite the cold, Luka felt his cheeks lightly flush.

"Can I?" he asked, leaning in closer to her. Amity's cheeks burned brightly in response. *So cute.*

"You don't have to ask. You never have to ask."

Their foreheads pressed together tenderly. She was wearing that sweet perfume again. The one that smelled like flowers. His mouth tilted into a small smile.

"Yes, I do." Without another word, his lips met hers.

How long had he been waiting to kiss her? Too long. Since he saw her at that summer college party? Alex almost kicked the shit out of someone that day. Who was it?

Doesn't fucking matter. She's here. That's all that matters.

He kissed her deeper, running his hands up his jacket before settling her in a delicate hold. He kissed her until she gripped the front of his shirt pulling him closer, earning a sound of approval from him.

That nervousness inside him finally stilled, replaced by a sweeping serenity. For a moment, as her body warmed him, as he pulled her closer, let her hand run through his hair while the other traced his waist, as her legs pressed tighter around him . . . Just for a moment, he forgot why they were there. And in that moment he didn't fucking care. Because, right now, for some unknown reason, a strange feeling crept up Luka's spine. A feeling that said this would be their last kiss.

Luka kept kissing her soft lips until he was forced away and she was a panting mess with swollen lips. Lips that he playfully nipped before tracing the shape of her nose with his own.

"Now, let's kick some demon ass."

CHAPTER THIRTY FOUR

HALLOWEEN

"Do you know where you're going?"

"No."

"No?!"

"They'll find us."

"How do you know?"

"I *always* know." He smirked, grasping her hand in his. Amity smiled briefly.

Cheeky bastard.

Amity held his hand tightly as they made their way farther down the concrete path, past the small playground—where no doubt in a few short years Alex and Krystal would find themselves—and then circling back past the boathouse. They began walking along the path that led through the woods.

Great, just out walking in the woods. At night. On All Hallows' Eve. Hunting a Demon. No pressure.

Amity nearly jumped out of her skin as something rustled in the trees above them.

"You're alright. I've got you," Luka said, steadying her back to her feet instead of on top of him.

She relaxed her death grip on his hand a tiny bit.

"It's too quiet. I don't like it." A chill wind blew past, sending another shiver up her spine. "And it's *cold.*"

Luka chuckled beside her, earning a glare. Silently he rolled his shoulders as they walked. Amity was in the process of unzipping her jacket, technically *his* jacket, when Luka took her hand back in his.

"Keep it."

"But you—"

Luka placed a finger to his lips, silently telling her to stay quiet. Brown eyes narrowed in brief annoyance before scanning the area.

They had come to an opening in the trees. A small clear area with a large formation in the center. Two large boulders, both flat, one rectangular leaning up against a smaller square-shaped one. Another chill breeze blew past taking with it some leaves, dirt, and a soft humm. It carried over the gales in a sweet lullaby, one like her mother used to sing to her when she was little.

Amity glanced at Luka nervously. The lampposts were still lit; they weren't flickering at all but brightly shining as they had been the whole way.

That should be a good sign. A sign that it's not a demon.

The soft humming continued. It sounded melancholic but had a happy tone. *Very weird.*

Luka let go of her hand and moved a step in front of her, covering her from whoever was there.

Amity gripped the straps of her backpack tightly.

It's just a random jogger, she reasoned, *walking in the park at midnight. On Halloween.*

Brown eyes glanced up at Luka's tense shoulders.

Yeahhhh, not likely.

Her pulse spiked as they cautiously approached the rock formation, as the humming persisted. There was a shadow on the tallest boulder. As they got closer, Amity realized it was actually a person. They were sitting tall and had a slender form, one leg swinging off the edge carelessly, like falling wasn't even a thought.

Their silhouette stood out starkly in the bright moon-light. Dressed in a jester costume with an overexaggerated hat that, from a distance, looked like horns. Through the dimmed lampposts, Amity could see the vibrant colors of the outfit. Pink, lime green, teal blue, purple, and black. So many vibrant colors that had no business looking so well together, but they did. They came together in stripes and ruffles and cuffs and pom-poms—

Something flicked against the rock, causing Amity's eyes to go wide. A tail. It was a *tail!*

Luka stopped and looked over his shoulder at her, eyes glowing that familiar cyan. She gripped the backpack's straps tighter, knowing exactly who that was, *what* that was.

"Remember what I told you."

She nodded stiffly. His eyes turned back to the thing lounging on the boulder. The tail flicked again, slapping against the rock.

"Promise me."

Amity wanted to turn him around and kiss him until the sun came up. Her hands started to move on their own, letting go of the backpack's straps and gripping firmly around his waist. She felt a shiver of surprise run through him, but he didn't turn. Luka remained focused, eyes fixed on the creature.

She pressed a kiss into the center of his back.

"I promise."

His muscles relaxed against her touch, and then she felt him take a deep breath before stepping forward, breaking the small contact.

Cold air filled her lungs fully before she followed. The humming stopped. Dramaur spoke in a strange reverberating voice.

"I was starting to think you would never come, witchlings." The tail thrashed against the boulder once more. It kept its face turned up to the moon, looking at it as if it were an old friend. Amity shifted slightly to get a better look. "Another minute and I would've left and never looked back."

Luka's shoulders stiffened.

It finally turned away from the moon and fixed its large slitted eye on Amity. The pupil dilated and a wide sharp smile, too wide, spread across its face. This wasn't the form she had seen in the memory spell. This time it was different, appearing almost human. *Well, besides the tail, sharp teeth, one eye, and midnight skin.*

"There she is," It sang.

Luka stepped in front of her, blocking her from the demon's view.

"Amity, last time I saw you there were two of you. When you stabbed me." Its eye glowed angrily at her, a horrid bright green.

"I've played your game, Dramaur. Now give her back her memories, she has never had anything to do with this."

The demon ignored him.

Wait, two of her? She peeked at it in confusion. *The memory projection spell—*

"You saw me?!"

"Yes!" It clapped its hands joyously. "Memory projection is so much fun, honestly, I'm surprised the youngling could do it. Those spells go wrong so easily." It smiled wide again, revealing those sharp teeth.

Luka tsked and moved his arm in front of her, pushing her back behind him. A forked tongue licked the demon's lips and its eye glowed.

"As clearly as I see you now."

Then that means it could see me through the whole memory spell. Oh fuck. She felt like she was going to be sick again.

"Dramaur."

"Yeah, yeah, yeah. Gods! You're so serious, little one. Always have been."

With a gloved hand it pulled out a necklace from beneath the large ruffle around its neck. Amity recognized it immediately. It was her cornicello. The object that held her memories. The thing she had been searching for, preparing for, working for. And though it should be the main focus of her attention right now, it wasn't.

Always? ALWAYS?!

Dramaur's eye locked onto her and widened, too big for its own face, at her expression even though she tried to keep her surprise under control.

It pushed off the rock and floated down to the ground.

"Now. Isn't. This. *Interesting*."

Amity shifted nervously on her feet, which did *not* go unnoticed.

"You haven't told her about *us*. You wound me, *witchling*."

It was taller than Luka in this form, and with a snap of its fingers, the jester outfit vanished. The bright clashing colors faded, leaving behind midnight skin, high Triassic legs, and a thick spiked tail. The hat revealed two large horns on either side of the demon's head and a smaller spiked trail running down the center of its spine.

Amity's shoulders started to shake.

"Luka—"

"Her memories, Dramaur. Give them back."

"Luka—"

"*Later*." His voice was final.

It toyed with the necklace between its claws. The obsidian glowed brightly, reflecting against its glittering beautiful skin.

"Why not tell her? We have all night."

She should focus. She *knew* she should. She was here for her memories. The sooner they got them back, the sooner she could get home and deal with whatever bullshit reason Luka had for keeping secrets. For *lying*.

Amity opened her mouth to speak, but something popped into her head.

This is what they want. Amity gritted her teeth. *It's playing with me.*

She straightened her shoulders and widened her stance, forcing a deep breath to calm and center herself.

"Quit playing games. He played your scavenger hunt, now return my memories," she demanded.

Luka sneaked a proud peek over his shoulder. She did not meet his eyes.

Another chill wind blew by carrying more crinkled dead leaves, twigs, and the demon's mood. Its claws halted. The cornicello fell around the bare skin of its chest, still glowing brightly against its dark skin, but there were no more glittering stars. The color seemed to churn under its skin; the glittering particles dimmed until they were all snuffed out.

"Careful, witchling. I enjoy you, but be careful."

Luka stepped to block her completely from view, shielding her from another cold breeze. His skin visibly shivered.

"She is right. We've *both* played your game. Give back what you promised and we'll leave you to the rest of your night."

It tilted its head to the side. Slowly its pupil shrank until it was only a slit. For the first time since they arrived, it looked at Luka fully, studying him carefully.

The lampposts started to flicker. The temperature dropped noticeably. A cold chill slithered up Amity's spine;

it wrapped around her throat, chocking her air supply. She unintentionally scratched at it. It didn't go unnoticed.

Dramaur's eye was on her in an instant. Its lips peeled back into another sharp smile.

"I have a better solution. Let's play a *new* game."

"Shit." Luka pushed her back quickly and caught the demon's clawed hands in his own.

Amity quickly caught herself. This was it. They would put their plan into action.

We're going to trap you, demon.

She unzipped her backpack as fast as she could and pulled out two of the salt grenades. She tore open the top and ran, circling them both, avoiding the thrashing tail. Luka was forced down onto one knee, her cornicello swinging tauntingly close to his face. Amity tore open the second balloon, accidentally spilling some salt in the process. She was thrust back by the thrashing tail.

"What do you think you're doing, witchling?" It spit.

Amity quickly got up; luckily no more of the salt had spilled. She went back to her salt line to complete the circle.

"This game of yours is just what I would expect from you," Luka smirked.

"You should know me better, little one," it hissed.

It dug its claws into Luka's hands, earning a scream from him, not caring that it drew blood, blood that was burning into its claws like acid, making them jagged at the tips. With a sharp cry, Luka was forced back down onto his other knee.

Amity circled back around them.

"It's done!"

Luka smiled proudly.

"*Let go!*" he commanded, his voice echoing as he did. Dramaur's mouth twitched in annoyance. For a moment its snakelike pupil dilated. It unwillingly and very briefly let go.

It was enough. Luka jumped back and out of the circle. His eyes stayed fixed on the demon as he rubbed his throat.

"Good work."

Amity was panting. Adrenaline, stress, it was all pumping through her at once. But she was mostly panting because running was obviously not her strong suit, something that would've been nice to have corrected prior to being in a life-or-death situation!

The salt circle began to glow brightly. Amity's face lit up. She did it! She fucking did it!

Luka wasn't smiling. His eyes were fixed on Dramaur whose tail was thrashing. Its teeth ground together, creating a horrible scratching sound.

"Did you just use speaker magic on me?" it asked, impressed.

Luka cleared his throat, drawing a curious glance from Amity. *Did using that kind of magic hurt his voice? He didn't seem to be in pain when he used it on me or the other demon. Is it because Dramaur is more powerful?* She shook her head. Now wasn't the time to think about that. *Stay focused,* she reminded herself.

Luka scratched his throat and swallowed hard.

It drew in a sharp breath. When it spoke next, its voice came out in a horrid growl. "Don't ever use speaker magic on me!"

The air around Dramaur seemed to pulse. It beat against the confines of the salt circle, causing a soft humm.

Amity took a step back, and pulled out two more balloons from her backpack.

"Luka?"

Luka took one of the balloons from her hand. He sliced a clean cut across the center and, without a word, started tracing the salt line, placing fresh salt in the weakest spots. The ring glowed brighter. Amity noticed just how brightly his cornicello was glowing, mirroring her own around the demon's neck, almost blinding to look at. Dramaur's eye tracked him, turning with him.

A large rustling in the trees drew her attention upward. She expected a murder of crows to fly out of the tree, but there was nothing, just loud rustling. That meant—

Amity's eyes went wide. Before she could call out to warn him, it was too late. A large gust of wind blew past them, sending her jacket flying open and her hair whipping in its ponytail.

Amity threw her arms up to block her hair from thrashing against her eyes, but that didn't stop the wind. It hit her hard and fast, stinging her eyes and causing them to water.

It's alright. This won't be enough to damage the circle.

Cold tears stung her face as she traveled. She couldn't see Luka behind Dramaur.

Right?

The demon tilted its head down. Its shoulders rose and fell with a deep reverberating laugh, one that scattered through her skin like scurrying spiders.

Right?!

"You didn't think it would be that easy, did you?"

Amity's legs began to shake. *It didn't work. It didn't fucking work!* Without another thought, she pitched a balloon toward the back of the demon's head. But just before it could make contact, it was swatted away with a flick of its spiked tail like it was no more than a gnat. No more than a nuisance.

"You're starting to get on my nerves. Take five, witchling!"

With a swipe of its hand, Amity was forced back into the air. Something heavy pressed against her chest, then spread through her as if crawling through her veins. It sank into her throat, trapping a dying scream, traveling up her neck and through the veins in her face until it reached her eyes. She tried screaming, tried crying out. It was no use. Her vision started to fade. The last thing she heard was that reverberating voice, then everything went black.

"Now where were we?"

CHAPTER THIRTY FIVE

HALLOWEEN

That was the last thing Amity heard before everything went black. That strange reverberating voice echoed in her head like a plague.

Images began to flow through her as she felt her consciousness drifting. Was she awake? Was she dead? Did they win? Did it matter? *This place is warm.*

She saw an old white house and a small boy with dark brown hair playing with a dog. He ran from one end of the yard to the other, crunching the fresh autumn leaves under his feet. Happily he threw the stick he was carrying across the yard and like a rocket the dog went after it, barking with joy. An old woman sat on the front porch beside a younger woman. They were tall with dark hair. They all had blue eyes—not just any color blue—they were *cyan.*

Everything was wiped away as if it were dust on an old painting, revealing another image underneath.

The boy was restless, thrashing his covers off as he slept. The sweet labradore at the end of the bed almost got kicked in the face. Then he awoke with a start. Poor boy was sweating and panting. He must've had a nightmare.

Immediately he went to his small desk in the corner of the room, turned on the lamp, grabbed a pencil, an old composition journal, and began scribbling. As he flipped through the pages, it became obvious this wasn't the first time he'd done this. There were so many strange symbols. So many notes. *Detailed* notes. What was he doing?

Once again the image was wiped away and she saw him again. The leaves were still on the ground, crusty and rotting. But something was different. With a look of determination, the boy left the house and walked behind an old barn in the backyard. In one hand he held a large stick of chalk, in the other his journal. He was taller than when she last saw him.

With a triumphant huff he began drawing those same sigils he had recorded in his journal on the ground. He drew them encased in a large circle, then inside of that a smaller circle to separate them. In the center was a large eye.

"Here we go!" The boy smiled.

He inhaled deeply, and on the exhale his eyes began to glow brightly. He spoke in a strange tongue, almost like his words were reversed.

The sky grew dark and the wind started to howl, no doubt a warning for the danger that was quickly approaching. The boy didn't notice. With a wide smile, he continued to chant.

Lightning struck fast and loud in the sky. Clouds of thunder began to rumble.

The two women ran out of the back door, shouting for him. But the boy didn't stop. He continued to chant as if the sky weren't dark and the lightning didn't strike with hostility.

One of the women, the younger of the two, ran to him. She shook him until his eyes returned to their normal cyan and he went quiet. She gathered him in her arms as he cried, terrified of what he had done.

The women joined hands and started chanting a new spell. They were too late.

A bolt of lightning struck the sky and with it the summoning circle glowed brightly. The eye that was drawn in the dirt blinked once and then twice. Its pupil, a thin slit, enlarged and the eye itself rose from the ground. It hovered above them in one large mass of black glittering miasma. A strange otherworldly sound came from it and formed a twisted laugh.

"You tricked me!" the boy screamed.

"I'll see you soon, witchling!" it promised.

Everything went black again.

Amity opened her eyes in a panic as she felt her body fall. She only had enough time to glance at the ground. She was high in the air, like *really* high. Before she came crashing down onto the hard ground, strong arms caught her. Luka's arms.

She clung to him as her brain caught up with what was happening. A battle! That's right, they were fighting a demon. Dramaur. Her memories—Luka. *That was him I saw, wasn't it?*

Brown, panicked eyes glanced up at him; he was sweating and panting like he had been running for a while. How long was she out? What happened to her?

Luka smiled down at her, causing some loose strands to fall out of his top bun and brush her face.

"I thought I lost you there," he said, touching his forehead to hers. There was a small cut on his cheek. The blood was warm when it touched her.

Just as he placed her on the ground, his body lurched forward and a sharp cry escaped him.

"Don't turn your back on me, witchling!" The demon seethed. It glanced at its tail and clicked its pointed tongue as the spikes sizzled.

With Amity's help, Luka rose unsteadily to his feet. She quickly glanced at his back. Despite the demon swiping it with its tail, the cuts weren't deep.

Luka straightened and squared his stance. He pulled one of his knives from its holster and handed it to her, handle first.

"Stay here. Throw whatever salt balloons we have left but be careful. Make a salt ring for yourself. Its attacks won't get through."

She took the knife and looked at him with shocked eyes. "What?"

Amity continued to gape at him, and he couldn't help but chuckle. He smirked and closed her mouth with the tip of his finger, then darted off.

Amity blinked herself out of her confusion and ran to find her backpack. Luckily it was close by.

"What? What?! You summoned a demon when you were like ten!" She pulled out one of the balloons, cut it open, then quickly encircled herself.

"How do you even know about that? Was that what you saw just now?"

"Yes!"

Luka's knives were hovering over him, glowing brightly. He snatched one out of the air and with a quick word it grew to the size of a sword. A smirk grew on his face too, like the adrenaline pumping through his skin made this seem fun for him as he charged.

"I was a kid and I was unsupervised, what was I supposed to do? And I was tricked!" he yelled back, slashing at the demon and narrowly missing a swipe of its claws. He cut its side; the demon screamed and pushed him back with his tail. It hissed again as its spikes sizzled.

"I don't know, climb a tree or set something on fire like a normal kid," Amity muttered, digging through her backpack. She threw one of the balloons high into the air above Dramaur's head.

"Wha—" Luka thought for a moment, noticing the balloon. Quickly he sent one of the floating blades after it. It sliced the bag wide open, raining salt down on the demon. It screeched and shielded its eye. The salt burned its skin at contact, making it sizzle like acid, the same reaction when Luka's blood came into contact with it.

"Yeah, no, that tracks for you. You were a weird fucking kid."

"Shut up!" she yelled back, but he was right, she was a weird kid. Not like he was any better.

Luka charged forward again, slashing the back of the demon's leg, turned, then slashed at the other.

"Both of you shut up! Gods you're like an old married couple. Just keel over and die!"

The demon threw Luka back with its tail, sending some of the spikes into his side. Dramaur lifted a hand and shot something toward Amity, too fast for her to see anything other than a black mass. She braced for it, but when it hit the barrier of the salt ring, it fizzled. That horrid green eye narrowed on her. A surprised smile of relief spread across her face.

"You're really starting to get on my nerves, witchling—" Two blades whizzed past it, slicing each arm. A growl erupted from deep inside the demon. Its skin churned as blood oozed from the wounds; it swirled until the color became a dark green. In a blink of its snakelike eye, its wooden mask appeared. Sharp teeth bared in a snarl.

Amity took a hesitant step back. She thought for a moment they had the advantage, but now she was afraid it was only toying with them this whole time. Another strong gust of wind blew past, and Amity braced herself. She glanced down at the thin line of salt, praying it would stay in place. A proud feeling surged inside of her when it was still intact. Luka charged again. He ducked under its arm, jumped over the tail, and sliced its back.

Amity threw another salt balloon into the air.

"Luka!" she screamed.

The adrenaline was pumping fast and hard through her veins. Whatever doubt she was feeling before quickly vanished. *We can do this*, she thought proudly. *We can win!*

Luka saw the balloon high in the air. He sent one of his knives after it. The salt rained down on both of them and the demon shielded its eye. That's when he charged again. He took a handful of salt and rubbed it into the slash in its back. It howled in pain, sending another thrill of excitement through Amity.

We can do this!

Luka went to make another pass with a smile on his lips. Before he could blink, he was sent slamming into the ground; the tail had snaked around his ankle. The demon thrashed him about like a rag doll. He was becoming a bleeding mess. That pride and determination inside her chipped away each time his body hit the ground with a loud *thud!*

Amity glanced down at her last salt balloon in a panic. It was her last one.

Please please please hit that fucker in the face!

With a deep breath, she reared back and threw it as hard as she could at the demon. It turned to her.

The salt balloon exploded on impact with its eye. It sizzled and burned as the demon wailed and screeched. But it didn't stop thrashing Luka around. It slammed him into the ground a few more times before finally tossing him away.

Amity stared at it, watching the smoke billow from its bloodshot and molten eye. Very Slowly it began to regenerate. Blood pooled together in large clots, reforming veins, muscles, and then an eyeball. It glowered at her.

"You!" it roared.

Amity's body jerked back. The demon's claws were around her throat.

Amity glanced down, terrified, and tried to pry the claws off her neck.

The salt circle was broken by her footprint. She must've overstepped when she threw the balloon. Didn't matter now. Now she couldn't breathe.

She kicked against its rigid body desperately, but it was no use. It only made its jagged smile widen.

"Your neck is so tiny—one little squeeze and *snap!*"

With Luka's knife she stabbed at the arm holding her. The demon merely twitched before nonchalantly ripping it out of her grip and its arm before tossing it away.

Amity's body started to shake. Her legs grew heavy and limp. She was choking. Frantic, she bit her cheek hard as the demon watched her consciousness start to slip. Blood pooled in her mouth. Brown eyes narrowed on the demon and sucked the warm liquid into the center of her mouth. She inhaled deeply and spit it into the demon's snake eye.

It released her, stumbling backward, clutching its eye as it burned.

"You blessed her blood too?!" it yelled, turning toward where Luka was thrown.

Amity fell hard on her knees, descending into a coughing fit.

"Touching her will be the last grace you are given on this earth." Luka plunged his sword into the demon's torso, twisting it.

Time seemed to slow down as the half-regenerated eye stared down at him. Luka sent the rest of his knives into its neck. Amity's cornicello fell to the ground.

Amity ran over to him, jumping over the demon's thrashing tail. Luka jumped back, narrowly avoiding the sharp claws slashing at his face.

The demon growled and prepared to launch itself at him. Luka mumbled a spell under his panting breath.

The blades grew in length. Dramaur keeled over clutching its neck with gurgling, wet screams.

Amity grabbed the chalk bag from around Luka's hips and dove her hands inside, filling them with salt. Under normal circumstances, watching Luka fight a demon to protect her would be incredibly cool and arousing, but these weren't "normal" circumstances.

She briefly glanced up at him. He was a panting mess. Bleeding in multiple places. His shirt slashed and torn—something else that would be nice under completely different circumstances. Cyan eyes remained focused on the demon.

Without a word, they quickly circled it, pouring salt on the ground as they did. This was the last of it. They had to make it count. When they reunited at the revolution of the circle, they watched as it glowed.

It will hold, she thought. *It has to.*

When Luka spoke again, the knives slid from its neck and rose high into the air.

It glanced around in a panic. Its eye glowed a furious green. Its tail, or what remained of it, was slashed and torn, thrashing wildly. It grabbed at its neck desperately. It choked on its own blood, willing the words out.

"You godsdamn brats!" it spewed, blood pouring from its sharp teeth and onto the grass.

Amity thought it might charge at them. Luka took a deep breath and—

"Shut up and lie down!" Luka roared.

The demon's eye went wide as its mouth aggressively sealed itself shut. Its face twitched into a snarl as it fought back the command. If that made it angry before, it was furious now. Its body shook as it slowly sank down to one knee and then the other. Luka never took his eyes off of it. They were locked, focused. Even when he started to bleed from the nose and mouth, he didn't stop looking until the demon was on the ground, on its back, its arms, legs and tail spread.

Luka gripped his throat and fell to one knee. His body slouched as he desperately gasped for fresh air. He heaved and heaved until his breath evened. Amity knelt down to steady him. Bloody finger gripped her hand tightly where it rested on his shoulder.

Luka wiped the blood away with the back of his hand.

He spoke quietly, and the blades came soaring downward, one landing in each of Dramaur's limbs and then another slicing into its abdomen and the other into its tail. Then, the seventh and final one, the one Amity had stabbed it with, went straight into the slit of its eye. The demon writhed.

Using her shoulder for support, Luka hoisted himself back on his feet.

"I'm going to watch you burn with the sunrise for what you've done to us, Dramaur. And I'll enjoy every second of it." His voice was scratchy, but it was powerful.

Amity wiped some blood from the corner of his mouth, not stopping to revel in the revelation that demons could be killed with sunlight. It wouldn't take long. The sun would be up soon. The salt circle would hold.

Luka turned to her with wide eyes. He held his closed blood- and dirt-stained hand out to her. His fingers were clutching something. Slowly he opened his hand, as if he didn't believe what he thought. Something was glowing between his fingers. Something blue.

Brown eyes went wide. A laugh bubbled out of her throat. It contagiously spread to him. He smiled widely down at her, the widest most beautiful smile she had ever seen. Tears escaped their eyes. She jumped into his arms.

"You did it! You did it, Luka!"

"We did it," he corrected, kissing her temple. He embraced her tightly. "We did it."

Amity took his face in her hands and pulled him into a sweet kiss, one that tasted like iron and victory and love. Luka wiped the tears from his eyes.

"Are you ready?" he asked with a scratchy voice.

She nodded eagerly.

We did it! she thought proudly.

We really did it!

Luka smiled warmly at her and reached the two broken strands around her neck.

She could jump into the air again she felt so giddy. So excited. So free.

He tied the strands and let the necklace fall to her chest. It glowed brightly against her skin.

We did it! she shouted in her mind again. *We finally did it!*

She took deeper breaths, trying to steady them. Her smile faltered.

Wait . . .

Amity felt herself swaying.

We finally did it . . . didn't we?

Then everything went black.

CHAPTER THIRTY SIX

HALLOWEEN

"Amity? Amity! Wake up!"

Who is that?

"Amity, please!"

She scrunched her eyes tightly. She knew that voice.

"Open your eyes!"

Groggily she obeyed. It took a while for her eyes to adjust in the dim light. Shapes and colors slowly became clearer. She blinked a few times until she was met with a beautiful pair of cyan eyes.

Luka was bent over her, holding her tightly in his arms.

"I thought I lost you there, kitty."

"Yeah? Me too." She smiled weakly.

He smiled back, not the full smile he showed her before but a small one. She rubbed her eyes tiredly. How long was she out? She glanced up at Luka again; he hadn't taken his eyes off of her. His skin was pale.

Amity took his face in her hands. His skin was a little chilly too. Her eyes widened.

"Are you alright? Did you use blood manipulation? Where's Dramaur? Did we win?" she asked, her worry causing her words to tumble out of her in a hurry.

A short laugh escaped him, "Yes, we won," he confirmed. "You stabbed it right in the neck. Totally badass."

Amity smiled up at him and pulled him into a kiss. His eyes went wide for a moment; if she blinked, she would have missed it. His lips were hesitant at first, but they quickly melted into hers in a chaste kiss. Long and sweet. Much like their first.

When she pulled back and smiled, his cheeks were dusted with a warm blush. He blinked a few times before speaking.

"That's one hell of a first kiss. Never thought it would happen after a demon battle." He chuckled, helping her to her feet.

Amity laughed along with him.

"Best time for it." She smiled, trying taking a step but quickly fell against him.

"You were out for a while, just lean on me. I'll get you back to the car."

Amity's foot scuffed the concrete floor as she repositioned herself against him.

"Yeah, my legs feel weak . . ."

Her sentence died when she glanced at the ground below her. Concrete. She was standing on concrete. Hesitantly she placed a hand on her heart, feeling it begin to beat faster under her shirt. Shirt . . . she wasn't wearing Luka's jacket anymore. She rubbed her chest, trying to calm the confused panic that was quickly rising.

Her fingers tapped her cornicello, hanging safely against her chest as if it were never taken off. Amity picked it up curiously and it glowed softly between her fingers. Luka did put it on her earlier, but . . . She glanced around, and her eyes widened as she took in her familiar surroundings.

She was in the abandoned warehouse. And not just any warehouse, this was the one she saw in the memory projection spell—she was sure of it. There were remnants of snacks where the teenagers were. There were blood splatters on the floor from Luka's spell.

What the fuck is going on?

"It's alright, just breathe," Luka said calmly. "I won."

"First."

"What?"

"You said first kiss."

"Yeah, that was our first kiss. Honestly I should've known you'd just jump on me, but you were always so reserved I was starting to think you just didn't like me."

"What? Why wouldn't I—" She gripped her head as a wave of nausea came over her, along with a chilly *loud* breeze. "First?"

Luka ran his rough hand carefully over her head, feeling for any bumps or bruises. "You must've hit your head harder than I thought."

She looked up at him with wide eyes.

"First."

"What?"

"You said 'our *first* kiss.' "

What the fuck is going on?

"Look I know this was your first time 'in the field,' but you're acting weird."

He took a step forward and then another, pulling her along with him until they were fully walking.

Amity clutched her cornicello as her heart raced. Her breathing became erratic.

Just calm down . . . Right, like that's gonna help—"Calm down." Ha!

She inhaled deeply and counted.

One. Two. Three. Four. Release . . .

Again.

One. Two. Three. Four. Release . . .

Okay, what was the last thing you remember? She raked her brain trying to find it. Her head hurt more. The wind screamed loudly again. She ignored both.

The last thing I remember is . . . Dramaur was trapped in the salt circle. She scrunched her face trying to remember more.

Amity went quiet as her brain scrambled together multiple possibilities:

(1) This was a trap set up by Dramaur to distract her or take her out of the fight altogether. She can't fight back if she's in some trippy-dream time-loop thingy. *If that's true, then I have to find a way to get out of this mess and fast.* (2) She'd been dreaming this entire time, which meant everything that happened within the past year, according to her memories, was a fucking lie. And if it was, doesn't

that mean her memories were never stolen? (3) When she first saw Dramaur, back in the warehouse last year, she was sent into a weird, trippy dream so she would be taken out of the fight, which would mean that everything—(*a*) losing her memories, (*b*) her sexy time with Luka, (*c*) Rune, (*d*) Alex becoming a father was all . . .*a fucking DREAM?! I swear to Satan if that was all a fucking dream, I'm gonna lose my shit! I'm gonna be so fucking traumatized!!!*

Luka glanced down at her a few times as she hobbled against him.

"You never get this quiet," he said.

Think, Amity, think! How would you figure out if this was a dream or not?

Another loud breeze blew by and her head pounded harder. At least her heartbeat slowed enough to think straight, kind of.

She opened her mouth to speak, but no words came out.

Think! Ask something only he would know.

"I—" she began, but quickly cut herself off. *Damnit! I can't think of anything!*

She gripped his waist tighter in her frustration. He glanced down at her but made no comment.

"What's my favorite holiday?"

Luka looked at her like she was crazy.

"Umm, Halloween. Are you okay?"

Fuck! No shit, stupid. Anyone who glanced at me would know that! She pressed her lips in frustration trying to fight back tears.

When they finally reached the car, Luka leaned her against the side. He bent down to feel her head.

"You don't have a fever," he said with a conflicted expression. His hand was warm on her forehead.

A few tears escaped her and stung her cheeks as they slid down her face.

"Hey, hey, what's wrong?" he asked with a soft voice.

Amity shook her head furiously. It was hurting again, and this loud wind wasn't helping. Was she wrong? *Maybe this is all real.* Maybe everything before—losing her memories, meeting Luka again—maybe it *was* all a lie.

More tears slid down her face.

I can't lose him. Not again.

Somewhere far off, someone screamed.

If this is real, then I will never lose him again. I will never lose myself, she vowed.

Amity lifted her chin stubbornly to him. He waited patiently, like he always does. Cold fingers gently tucked a loose curl behind her ear. He was looking at her with concern in his beautiful cyan eyes.

Her cornicello glowed brightly.

Without a word, she took his face in her hands and pulled him down for a kiss. Luka wiped away her tears before their lips touched. It was long and sweet. Not like the iron from his blood that she tasted in that dream—hallucination? She chased away the thoughts.

She didn't want to think anymore.

Luka cradled her cheeks in his hands. He tilted her face to one side and kissed her deeper.

This felt right.

This felt *real.*

Dreams can be deceiving though. Her head ached again, the pain gnawing at her temples and pulsing through her skull. *I have had dreams where I thought they were real and I felt pain. Like, I remember I actually pinched myself in a dream before—*

Luka slid his tongue across her bottom lip. Whatever she was thinking vanished.

Amity opened her mouth on a soft moan, letting him inside. He tentatively tasted her, or was it a tease? Didn't matter. She gripped the front of his shirt and pulled him in deeper.

Their lips melted and molded together as he explored her mouth for the first time. *That's right. Because this is the first time,* she reminded herself. *It's okay. He's here.* Their kisses became hotter, wetter. He gripped her by the waist tightly, his nails digging into her flesh. Those would leave marks.

Luka pulled back, panting, then cleared his throat. "We should probably head back . . ."

A small laugh escaped her. "Yeah, yeah you're right."

Amity released his shirt and tapped his chest lightly, feeling the chill under his shirt. Her fingers stopped.

Where is his necklace?

She stared at his chest, not believing her fingers. Maybe she just glanced over it?

She didn't. It wasn't there.

Amity looked down at her own cornicello. It was still glowing. Glowing *black.* Not the soft light blue she had seen it glow before.

A loud gust of wind blew by again, carrying another scream. Who was screaming?

She listened carefully as she regained her breathing.

Amity! it screamed.

Fear slithered up her spine leaving a grotesque trail of sweat in its wake. Her heart started beating faster again.

"Luka?"

"Hm?" he asked, tucking that stubborn curl behind her ear. His touch was icy like the air around them.

"Where's your cornicello?"

"My what?"

"Your cornicello necklace. Where is it?"

"Oh, that old thing, I lost that a while ago."

Amity's eyes went wide.

"You . . . lost . . . it?" she said slowly, trying to process his words.

He smiled and kissed her forehead sweetly.

"It's not a big deal, kitty, now let's go home." He opened the passenger door for her.

"Not a big deal? Wait. Did you just call me *kitty*?"

Amity squared her stance. Her head pounded again. He raised an eyebrow at her.

"Uh, yeah, been calling you that for years. Now come on, let's go," he said casually, taking her hand in his.

She pulled back at the frigid touch of his skin.

"What's going on?"

He looked at her sternly.

"Is it your head again? It's okay, let's get you home and—" He reached for her again, but she jumped back out of his reach.

"Who are you?" she demanded.

"Kitty, it's me—" His voice grew dark. Her cornicello glowed fiercely.

"Luka doesn't call me that!" She took a step back.

"Amity," he warned.

"I said what the fuck is going on?"

Luka prowled closer, reaching for her arm again. Her cornicello lifted into the air. It hummed and seethed a black miasma.

"Just get in the car. You're not yourself."

He was getting closer. Amity's pulse raced faster. The wind howled loudly. She heard the scream again. It was louder. *Clearer.*

It screamed her name.

He was screaming her name.

Luka.

Her Luka.

She squared her stance, took in a deep breath, and stared up at him defiantly, a look that made his eyes glow green. The air around her pulsed.

"Don't ever," she began in a commanding voice. "Don't you *ever* tell me what to do!"

Amity grabbed the vibrating cornicello from her neck and ripped it off. The chain broke with a loud *snap!* He lunged for her aggressively, but it was too late. Darkness took them, sending them into a free fall of nothing. Nothing but the blackness of the night.

Someone was holding her tightly. She fell back onto her scratched-up hands and backed away as fast as she could. Luka gaped at her.

"Amity, it's me! It's me."

She recoiled. Fear—that was the only thing she felt now. The only thing pumping through her veins.

"What did you tell me back in my apartment?"

"Amity—"

"Answer me!"

He swallowed hard. "I told you everything would be alright."

Amity inhaled a shaky breath. Her body rocked slightly back and forth. He waited where he was, like he always did. Those cyan eyes were wide with desperation.

"Luka?"

Luka let out a relieved sigh and nodded. Amity scrambled to her feet, slipping on the damp grass and into his arms. He embraced her tightly, kissing her temple multiple times.

"Is it really you? I'm not dreaming or hallucinating or—"

"Yes, kitten, it's me. It's okay now. I have you."

Amity hugged him tighter. Tears streamed down her cheeks. She pulled away quickly clutching her shirt, feeling for her necklace that wasn't there.

"Where is it?" she asked, wiping the blood off his face. More blood had stained the corner of his mouth. She was right earlier, speaker magic did hurt him, and it looked like he used a lot of it while she was gone—wherever she was.

Luka held out his hand. The cornicello was pulsing in his palm, oozing a black miasma, and burning into his skin. Amity snatched it by the cord and threw it toward her backpack.

A crude laugh sang through the air, splitting and fracturing it with pure delight.

Luka's eyes began to glow as she examined his palm, his furious eyes on the demon. It continued to cackle, its bloodied, oozing eye throbbing under the blade.

"What? You thought I was gonna let you win just like that? You're even more pathetic than I thought, witchling!"

Luka's eyes glowed so brightly, they burned.

"What did you do to it?!" he snarled.

The demon continued to laugh. Amity's blood was boiling. She lunged for the mangled creature, but before she could reach the edge of the salt circle, she was dragged back.

"Don't!"

He was right. What was she going to do? *Jumping into the circle and slicing its neck would be a great start,* she thought bitterly. No. Thinking like that doesn't do them any good. It just gives it a chance to escape or worse.

Amity sucked in a deep breath. She was furious, but that would have to wait to be dealt with later. Luka, on the other hand, was seething beside her, the warm air escaping his lungs looking like a dragon's breath.

"Good luck trying to get that curse off!" it cackled with a bloody, sharp smile. One of pure enjoyment. Its tail flicked back and forth beneath the blade that held it down.

Amity's eyes widened in horrific realization. *Wait, if it's speaking, then that means . . .* Her eyes went to Luka. He was a wreck. His shirt was slashed and torn, and he was bleeding all over—his temple, his torso, his arms, his knuckles, his mouth. Not to mention he looked exhausted. The state he was in . . . This was bad. *Very bad.*

She had to hurry; at this rate the spell wouldn't hold.

Painfully she pushed herself up to her knees and then her feet, ignoring the screams of pain her body made every time she moved. Amity had to hurry. As fast as she could, she ran to her backpack, practically limping all the way over.

She wasn't in great shape either. Her body was scraped, bloody, and bruised. Amity was almost positive she broke her foot in that fall earlier, and each step she took felt like a thousand needles stabbing through the nerves of her leg.

Amity crashed on the hard ground beside it, struggling to sit on her knees. Desperately she ripped the bag open, hoping, praying, that it was still there.

Her backup plan.

She breathed a heavy sigh of relief as she pulled out the strange star configuration.

"Thank the fucking gods!"

She turned back to Luka with a wide smile, which vanished immediately.

CHAPTER THIRTY SEVEN
HALLOWEEN

Luka was leaning back on his knees, his eyes glowing bright blue. So bright she could no longer see any indication of his eyes. It was like they were shrouded in a glowing, thick mist.

Blood started to trickle from his body—his mouth, his torso, his hair—lifting into the air in small droplets collecting together and forming one giant mass above his head. Amity recognized this spell.

Not good!

"Luka!" she shouted, painfully scrambling back to her feet. "Stop!" She slipped on the wet grass and fell hard on her hip, making it even harder for her to rise again.

Dramaur continued to laugh maniacally all the while, at her failure, at Luka's loss of control. And that's exactly what had happened. He had lost control. The blood molded above him, reshaping from the blob of crimson until it formed into a giant scythe. Luka rose to his feet.

"You're losing too much blood!" she screamed.

He took the blood scythe in his hands.

"That's it, witchling. *Kill me!*" Dramaur laughed. The blade holding its tail down was thrown away.

Amity finally reached him. She grabbed him by the arms, trying to force him to drop the scythe. He didn't budge. He took a step forward. The ground around him seemed to tremble.

"Enough!"

He didn't hear her.

"That's it, witchling. *Closer.*" it taunted, pulling its head up through the stuck blade until it sliced through its skull completely. Blood and other fluids poured out of the open wound and into its wide pointy smile. It slowly started to regenerate, reforming bone and muscle.

Amity gripped Luka tightly by the torso, dropping the star configuration at his feet. She held onto him as tightly as she could, until it felt like she would squeeze the life out of him. She could see the blue veins bulging in his neck and cheeks, pumping hard beneath his too-pale skin.

He lifted the scythe high above his head. It extended taller as the seconds passed. He didn't feel her holding him, didn't even acknowledge that he was being held. *Can't he feel me? Is he already so far gone?!* His eyes continued to glow in that strange mist. His breath was leaving his mouth in thicker clouds. Skin was paling by the second, becoming stark. He was just about to bring it down when Amity took in a deep breath. Without thinking, she shouted as loud as she could.

"As my *boyfriend* I expect good-morning texts or at least a minimum of one text—No!—two texts a day! None of this silent, stoic bullshit! I'm talking good morning, good night, I want it all! Do you hear me, you pretty bastard!?"

Luka's arms froze midair.

"I want a designated date night at least once—*twice* a month! Three times a month!" She took in another deep breath and forged onward. "I want you to promise me I'll never *ever* find you bleeding in the street again!" Luka's grip on the scythe tightened, briefly. "Promise me that you'll never lie to me, that you will *always* be honest. No matter what!" Luka's head flinched, as if awakening. Like he was regaining consciousness. "That you never blame yourself for something that isn't your fault." His grip loosened on the scythe. It tilted back out of his grip. His head shook violently. He gritted his teeth, releasing another puff of smoke. "That you'll never let me forget you again." She inhaled deeply. Her throat throbbed, begging for her to stop shouting, but she couldn't. She wouldn't. *Never.* "That next time you fall in love with me or want to kiss me, you just do it! Don't think about it. *Just do it!* Because I love you. I loved you before. I loved you when I couldn't remember you. I fell in love with you all over again after we met. And I love you now! I will *always* love you, Luka! You hear me? You're *mine*! Now wake up and promise me!"

Amity's heart was racing, ramming against her rib cage with each second that passed, each second he didn't speak, didn't move.

Did I get through to him?! she thought desperately.

I can't lose him again. Please!

Give him back to me!

She shoved her face into his side, bracing for the worst.

". . . I promise."

The words left in one last thick puff of smoke. Slowly his hands lowered, the blood that had once created the scythe dispersed into one large mass, then into smaller blobs, until finally they became no more than droplets feeding back into his body from whence they came. The smoke seeping from his eyes and mouth slowly started to evaporate until all that was left were his eyes. His beautiful cyan eyes.

Amity released her grip slightly, looking up at him in disbelief.

Brown eyes met cyan.

"I promise," he repeated.

She looked up at him starry-eyed. Tears of joy formed in the corners of her eyes. She smiled brightly.

"Good. Did you remember all that? Because I sure as hell can't."

Luka smirked in that playful way of his.

"Yes, kitten, I remember. Romantic dates, good-morning texts, covering you in bruises and bites."

"I didn't say that part."

"You didn't have to."

Amity smiled wide as a small laugh burst free.

"I hate you," she lied.

"I love you too."

"Good!" She picked up the configuration and placed it in his hands. "Now fucking seal it."

Luka's eyes widened in surprise, recognizing his mother's configuration.

"No!"

Luka approached the demon with quiet steps. It writhed, trying desperately to escape its shackles. The demon screamed.

"Kill me, witchling! Do it! Watch my body burn under the rise of the sun! Do it!"

Luka stopped right before the salt line. He held out the configuration in front of him. He cleared his throat as Dramaur continued to writhe and wriggle and scream.

"Just kill me!" it begged.

There was no place for begging. Not after what it had done. To him. To *her*. There would be no mercy, and Dramaur knew it.

Luka's eyes began to glow. Clear and true, he spoke words Amity couldn't understand. But the configuration knew. It hummed in response. The carved runes glowed a bright blue. Something inside snapped open, like a lock that waited an eternity to burst free. The wood opened for him.

Luka spoke again and a blue mist rose out of the configuration and high into the air. The mist returning over his eyes before rising and mixing with the configuration's. But this time was different. He was conscious. He was safe. He was in control.

Dramaur screamed and screamed to no avail; they did not hear it.

The mist sank over Dramaur, ensnaring and tangling around like vines. Then it was pulled from the ground. Its body twitched and shivered. It tried to scream, but it was no use. Dramaur was engulfed in the mist, consumed by it completely, and then was dragged into the configuration itself.

With a loud snap, the configuration closed. The demon was sealed. Dramaur was gone.

The sun rose over the horizon.

CHAPTER THIRTY EIGHT
DÍA DE LOS MUERTOS

The soft wind chime blowing in the breeze outside was the first thing Luka heard. It leisurely awakened his senses. The scents of fresh cotton and cinnamon surrounded him, bringing with it a sense of comfort. He took in a deep breath and lazily stretched out his legs. His toes gave a few satisfying cracks, but he almost immediately regretted stretching. A low groan escaped him as his legs screamed at him. They felt like they were going to tear off.

His face scrunched in pain, but even that hurt. Luka tried slipping back into an unconscious state. He was exhausted and his bed was warm. The navy blankets were practically lulling him back to sleep. He took in another deep breath, inhaling the sweet smell of bread and oranges.

Luka nuzzled the blanket higher up his face. His stomach growled loudly and he groaned in response. He would have to get up soon or he would starve. How long had it been since he ate? Considering how loud his stomach was growling, it must've been a long time.

Somewhere in the distance he heard some commotion. Someone—no, some*ones* were talking.

So *loud. Just let me sleep*, he thought groggily.

His stomach growled again.

"Shh!" someone hushed from outside. "Did you hear that?"

Luka peeked a heavy eyelid open. He knew that voice. Before he could close his eyes again and try to fall back asleep, his mother rushed into the room.

"Mama! He's awake!" she shouted over her shoulder. There was the sound of plates clinging and frantic scrambling as his mother made her way over to the bedside.

"Hi, figlio," she said in a quiet voice, brushing his hair out of his face. "How did you sleep?"

"Like the dead," he yawned, his voice no higher than a gravely whisper.

Carefully, he sat himself upright, wincing at the horrible pain shooting through him with each muscle movement, no matter how small it was.

His mother adjusted the pillows so he could sit up comfortably.

Luka rubbed his eyes with a groan. When they adjusted to the midday light peeking through the window, he finally got a good look at his surroundings. He was in his old room. Though if anyone were to see it now, they wouldn't know.

The only thing that remained was his old bed. His mother had placed all his old "junk" in an antique trunk at the end of the bed. This room was converted into a "guest room" as soon as he left the nest.

"I'm home?" he asked, confused, leaning his head back on the headboard as gently as he could, but even the light *tap* against his skull made him wince. Loose hair fell in front of his face.

Luka closed his eyes trying to remember exactly how he got here. Was he helping Nana with a spell and had slept over?

His mother nodded.

"Honestly, I can't believe you would do something so reckless," she huffed. "Fighting it alone and in the middle of the night like that—what were you thinking! And then dragging that sweet ragazza into it! If I didn't use a locator spell to track you down, you would've been dead by the time anyone else found you. You almost gave your nana a heart attack, you ungrateful child!"

Lukas eyes went wide; he sat up so quickly some of the pillows went flying. Everything came rushing back to him all at once. His heart raced in a panic. A cut up and bruised hand gripped his side as it throbbed and ached. Obviously, he was far from healed.

"Where is she? Where's Am—!" Luka gripped his throat immediatelyutting off his yell and gripped his throat It felt like sandpaper when he spoke—scratchy, sore, and painful. He keeled over coughing.

Yeah, I'm "far" from healed.

His mother immediately leaned him back against the headboard, shuffling the pillows back into place.

"Sit down!" She took in a breath and spoke in a much calmer voice. "She's fine—"

"Where is she? Why isn't she here with me?" he asked in a panicked whisper.

His mother laughed loudly at his earnest. It was obvious he didn't hear a word she said, especially not when she was chastising him.

"She is sleeping in *my* room. *You* wouldn't stop clinging to her the whole time you were unconscious, so I had to separate you."

Luka's body visibly relaxed. He focused on his breathing until his panic subsided.

His mother smiled at him knowingly. Luka scratched his throat, feeling a sense of guilt rise in him.

"What about the shop?" he asked softly, looking away from his mother.

"You're really asking me why I'm not at work instead of taking care of my mangled and bloody son?" She sighed, annoyed.

His head tilted downward.

"It's closed for Día de los Muertos."

His head perked up.

"We don't celebrate Día de los Muertos."

"No, but Rosa does."

"Ah," Luka hummed. "That's Day of the Dead bread I smell?" His stomach growled again, loudly. His mother laughed so hard she snorted.

"Mom, the configuration," he said groggily.

"It's in the basement, the coven is coming to collect it."

"The coven?!" Luka gripped his throat, the rise in his voice sending it throbbing again.

"They want to thank you personally, *both* of you."

Luka stared at her in disbelief. Was that her reason for pestering him to seal it away? So she could win back favor with the council? Something about this made his stomach turn—along with the way Dramaur begged to be killed instead of sealed.

"Why? What do they want—"

"I told you to lie down, child!" his nana yelled from the hall.

Luka turned his head to the sound. Amity was leaning against the doorframe, hair askew and in an old pair of his pajamas. His nana, the spitting image of his mother only shorter and with silver hair, quickly held Amity before she could fall over.

He moved to go to her, nearly throwing the blankets off the bed when his aching body said otherwise. Luka fell back onto the bed with a hard *thud!*

"Mama, help the poor girl to the bed." His mother smirked from her seat.

Luka's eyes never left Amity. *She's here.* That's all he could think. *She's alright.*

Nana helped her hobble over to the bed; the closer she got, the more scrapes and scratches he could see. But that wasn't where the damage really was. Dramaur, that fucking bastard, did something to her. It messed with her head. He couldn't fix that. But what's even worse is—

Luka bit his lip, trying to fight back the tears, but they still came. Flooding down his cheeks like a waterfall. Seeping into the bandages and cuts he didn't even register were there. Amity looked at him with those beautiful brown eyes of hers.

Luka squeezed his eyes shut.

I failed.

I failed her.

I failed.

I didn't fix anything.

It's still my fault.

My fault.

He felt her hands cradling his face, her bruised fingertips brushing away his tears.

"Amity—" he choked.

She pressed her forehead to his. His body was trembling. He helped her under the covers. Gently she guided his body back down and held him close. At some point his mother and nana had left the room, but he didn't notice. He couldn't focus on much of anything right now.

". . . We won," he said.

She nodded against him.

"We did," she agreed.

He held her tighter, despite his arms screaming at him to ease up.

". . . We won, but I—" His words caught in his throat. He swallowed hard. "We won but I still failed. I failed you." Luka buried his face in the crook of her neck and wept harder. "I'm sorry, Amity. I failed. I'm so sorry!" he repeated over and over, despite how much his throat hurt.

She waited patiently, stroking his hair in long comforting pets until his sobs subsided and his breathing was relatively close to normal.

"Luka."

He flinched in her arms.

"You didn't fail me."

He shook his head, burying it deeper into the crook of her neck.

"Luka. Look at me."

He squeezed her just a little bit tighter. Deep down he knew she didn't feel that way. She was kind and sincere. She was better than he could ever hope to be. Amity waited patiently as he slowly eased his grip on her, but he didn't let go. He couldn't. Not now.

She helped him the rest of the way, lifting his face to hers. Gently brushing his hair out of his eyes. The corners of her lips tilted up into a small smile.

"You did *not* fail me," she said carefully, making sure he heard every syllable, making sure every word sunk in. "You did it. You got my memories back."

He looked away. She took his chin in her fingers and turned his gaze back.

"You did it," she repeated.

"I didn't. They're *cursed*," he said remorsefully.

"Then we'll remove it," she said simply, even though they both knew she didn't know anything about removing curses.

Amity stared into her eyes for a very long time before taking a breath. Her skin was paler than normal scratched and bruised like his. Dark circles hollowed under her eyes.

She must've had a fitful sleep—or worse, none at all. A pang of guilt went through him.

"*You*." He smiled. "You say that so self-assuredly. You really are amazing."

"Damn straight. I'm the best girlfriend in the world."

" 'Girlfriend' . . ." He smiled wider. "Yes, yes you are." He tapped her forehead to his, and she smiled widely.

His girlfriend sighed into the pillow and yawned. She was definitely tired, despite how well she thought she was hiding it. *And there's no way she's sleeping alone from now on,* he thought with a mischievous glint in his eye.

"Luka."

"Hm?" he asked, feeling himself sink back into the pillow beside her. He was still so exhausted, but knowing that she was safe in his arms made him more relaxed.

"It's okay if I don't have my memories back."

Cyan eyes met brown.

Luka waited impatiently for her to continue. He could see the cogs turning in her mind as she sorted her weary thoughts.

"It's okay," she assured, though whether she was assuring herself or him he couldn't tell. "It's okay because I've made so many new memories with you. And even if I don't get the others back, I will have these to look back on to remember you by. And now," she moved closer so the tips of their noses touched. Carefully she traced his with hers, just like he had done so many times before. His heart burned at the gesture. "Now I'll have so many more. And we'll just keep making more and more together." She smiled tiredly.

Luka pressed his lips to hers in a long, sweet kiss.

"Yes," he agreed. "We'll make as many memories as we can. So many you'll never want for more."

A flush dusted her cheeks as he ran a rough hand down her spine. Her soft lips kissed him again.

And again.

And *again*.

His body was aching horribly, but he ignored it. The pain didn't matter.

She was here.

She was safe.

She was in his arms.

She was in *his clothes*.

And she looked so fucking *edible*.

Luka moaned into another kiss remembering just how edible her lips were. The ones that were getting wetter by the second. Hidden under the covers and under his clothes that covered her. The ones that were unfortunately out of sight.

Amity shivered when he firmly palmed her ass.

"I brought you both some food—LUKA!"

Amity hid under the covers in embarrassment, her face as red as a tomato.

So *fucking cute*.

His mother stood aghast in the open doorway, nearly dropping the tray of whatever it was she was carrying. Luka groaned at the intrusion. He was already tasting something better than anything that could possibly be on that tray. In spite of that, his stomach growled loudly. *Damn traitor.*

Amity laughed shyly, burying her face in his chest. Her favorite place.

"You're lucky your nana didn't see you—"

As if on cue, like she was listening through the wall the whole time, his nana yelled from the kitchen.

"There will be no *fornicating* in this house!"

"Mama!" Lucia looked back at him with a glare, "Just make yourself presentable!"

With that, she slammed the door, taking the tray and all with her.

Amity peeked out from under the covers and laughed.

"We should probably go before your nana walks in next."

Luka hummed and tucked a piece of her hair back behind her ear. He lay on his back and tucked her into the crook of his shoulder. She snuggled up warmly, as if she always belonged there, wrapping one arm around his torso and intertwining her leg in between his.

"I want to stay here just a little bit longer."

"But aren't you hungry?"

"Starving." He smirked.

Roughly bruised fingers traced down the curve of her spine a few times before settling on the curve of her ass.

"Then . . ." Her beautiful brown eyes widened when she felt his fingers; they traveled farther and pressed up into the gap of her lips. A moan tangled with a gasp. The sweetest sound. "Luka!"

Cyan eyes glowed mischievously.

"I told you before, I could live between your thighs."

AUTHOR'S NOTE

Hello, fellow readers! I'm so happy to share this book with you. I had so much fun writing about Amity and Luka's adventures, and I can't wait to continue their journey—discovering some demons, maybe learning more about the sexy man in the council, traveling around the world? Wherever it takes me!

In all seriousness though, I can't tell you how much your support means to me, whether you know me personally, have been following my socials, or have read my Duchess and the Thief series.

I would like to give special thanks to my two male beta readers who will remain anonymous. You have both provided excellent feedback as far as plot, character development, and spice (especially how certain *ahem* "parts" work). The best feedback is reading your reactions toward the men I've written, especially when it comes to how they interact with each other. For example, when Alex apologizes without actually apologizing to Luka in the park.

I would also like to give special thanks two my editors, Jennifer Safrey and Michael Jarnebro. Thank you both for taking the time and patience to work with me. I learned so much from both of you and I hope our paths cross again in the future!

Finally, thank you to everyone who listened to me explain the first few chapters of my book whenever they asked, "What's your book about?" Seriously, thank you so much for listening!

I wanted to talk briefly about Amity's anxiety. I struggle a lot with anxiety, to the point it stops me from completely connecting with someone, much like when Amity gets "stuck in her head" when being intimate with Luka. If you ever have these thoughts or feelings around intimacy or even speak badly about yourself (which I understand is a hard pattern to break), please seek help from a professional. Remember, you are *powerful*, you are *beautiful*, and you are *deserving*.

I can't wait to see how you all react to the sequel—I have so many plans. Such plans.

Until then, dear readers.

ABOUT THE AUTHOR

Danielle Kucky (pronounced cookie) is an indie author, actress, award-winning cosplayer, and black cat mother in Denver, Colorado, with a passion for mythology and magic. Echoes in Obsidian is her first officially published book, but it will not be her last.

Her cat's name is Salem. Salem approves of Luka. He may be the only man she approves of besides the countless other fictional men she has heard so much about.

You can find out more about Danielle @Danielle.Kucky